Praise for *The Façade*

The Façade is an intelligent thriller with a fascinating plot. There are a lot of theories and novels out there about aliens and demonic deception. *The Façade* is a breath of fresh air with a responsible and believable yet imaginative take on the issue. The story entertains but also informs with true and interesting theological and paranormal research. Heiser's work has been a major inspiration on my own novel series. I can't wait until his next one comes out!

—Brian Godawa, author, *Chronicles of the Nephilim,*
and screenwriter, *To End All Wars*

Michael Heiser's *The Façade* is the essential primer for those interested in the factual basis and the historical truths of the UFO phenomena. It is also the most accurate presentation of the biblical texts related to this topic I've ever read. This is entirely a revelation-driven read. Along with revealing biblical facts that most of Christianity won't confess to, the novelization of what is likely going on in all those underground bases is probably the closest to "the truth" to ever see print. The research is simply astounding. My only concern is that Heiser is too close to the truth and will become an X-file before publishing the sequel!

—Guy Malone, AlienResistance.org

In this supernatural thriller, a group of complex characters assemble to solve a cleverly designed mystery and to convey answers to complicated issues at the heart of the UFO controversy. While *The Façade* is a thoroughly entertaining work of fiction, it is also a significant investigation and conclusive factual analysis of many "extraterrestrial" elements unlike anything published before.

—Thomas R. Horn, best-selling author,
Defender Publishing Group

One of the most portentous books of the decade, *The Facade* is a theologically astute supernatural suspense thriller. While the jury is still out on the UFO phenomenon, The Facade is not only prescient in its analysis, *it might turn out to be true!* The book falls in the genre of "faction" because it contains as much fact as fiction. In researching my own project on the subject, I read *The Façade* for the third time. Michael Heiser is a mentor to all thinking Christians writing on the subject.

—Cris Putnam, best-selling author and Christian apologist

The Façade is the only work of fiction I use for reference. Dr. Michael S. Heiser presents a compelling examination of a topic most Christian theologians avoid—the UFO phenomenon—and he does it inside the framework of an exciting story. As the plot unfolds, the reader is treated to a primer on the history of UFOs, cattle mutilation, Operation Paperclip, underground bases, black budget projects, and—best of all—a Christian interpretation of the whole phenomenon. At the end of *The Façade* (besides a strong desire for a sequel), Christian readers are left with the understanding that UFOs are no threat to their worldview.

—Derek Gilbert, author, *The Great Inception*;
host, *SkyWatchTV*; co-host, *SciFriday*

Mike Heiser is one of the few genuine theological scholars who are thinking seriously about the UFO phenomenon. This novel shows both his incredible creativity and his brilliant scholarly mind. For a genuine theological analysis of the strange experiences with apparent space aliens, one can do no better than this book. It is insightful, carefully written, and wonderfully entertaining all in one. I highly recommend it.

—Samuel Lamerson, PhD, Knox Seminary

THE FAÇADE

Volume One of *The Façade* Saga

Michael S. Heiser

DEFENDER

CRANE, MO

The Façade
Volume One of *The Façade Saga*
Copyright 2017 Michael S. Heiser

Defender Crane, MO 65633 ©2017
All rights reserved.

To learn more about *The Portent*, volume two in *The Façade Saga*, visit ReadThePortent.com.

First Defender edition. Previous editions of this novel were published by SuperiorBooks.com, Inc. (2001) and Acid Test Press (2007) and Kirkdale Press (2014).

Cover design: Patrick Fore
Typesetting: ProjectLuz.com

ISBN: 978-0-9991894-5-0

"More heroism has been displayed in the household and the closet than on the most memorable battlefields in history."

—*Henry Ward Beecher*

A hero puts aside their own hopes and dreams to help someone else achieve theirs.

To Drenna—my wife and my hero.

Prologue

God has taken his stand in the divine council;
among the gods he passes judgment ...
You are all gods, sons of the Most High, all of you.

—*Psalm 82:1, 6, the Bible*

The Bible is a peculiar, mysterious book. If those who regard it as sacred read it closely, penetrating the camouflage of sanctioned translations, they would be shocked. According to its 82nd Psalm, there are other gods of the supernatural realm besides the God of Israel, and there are other sons of God besides Jesus Christ. These other gods, "sons of the Most High" in Psalm 82, serve the God of Israel in a divine council. According to the 38th chapter of the book of Job, before the world was created and the earth first brought forth life, *they* were there. Genesis 1:26 hints that when humans were first put on the earth, *they* were there. And when God withdrew their inheritance as lords over earth and gave the planet to mortals, *they* were there and were obedient ... for a time.

Demoted to watching the affairs of humankind, they observed the human creature, witnessing the transmission of the divine image from generation to generation, a potentially endless succession of the right to rule. But they also gained knowledge of human weaknesses, proclivities, susceptibilities. And so it was that the Watchers began to crave what they had lost, to seek their own dominion and succession. In the fullness of time they arrived on earth in celestial flesh and mingled their seed with the seed of human women, bringing forth a dynastic line of immortal gods cloaked in mortal flesh. They would take back what was theirs. They would rule the earth as it should have been from the beginning, and humanity would take them as their gods. But the Maker, filled with outrage, betrayed them, exiling them to the Abyss, sentencing their bastard sons to death in the great flood.

Before their extermination the divine half-breeds were known by men as *nephilim*—giants. After the slaughter, their disembodied im-

1

mortal spirits were called *shedim*, demons. But the Maker had played the fool. They were reborn the instant they died, and so they cannot be killed. They had become as their fathers: ageless, free, uncontainable—and angry. The ancient Book tells us that after the flood, more of God's cosmic sons, the members of his council, broke rank, descended to earth, and stole the hearts of men. Humanity worshiped them as teachers, healers, deliverers, and their gods. They raised up other hybrid races known from the ancient biblical text—Anakim, Emim, Rephaim, and Zamzummim. These too were massacred, swelling the ranks of the *shedim*.

Condemned to roam the earth, for millennia, the horde has continued to watch ... and plan ... and wait. Jesus understood, and He warned His listeners. One day the Watchers would return—and in a manner so cunning that even His own followers could be deceived. To a timeless being, time means nothing. But timing is everything.

1

For our struggle is not against flesh and blood,
but against the principalities, against the powers, against
the rulers of darkness, and against the spiritual forces of evil
in the heavenly realms ... Being bold and arrogant,
some men are not afraid to slander the celestial ones;
yet even angels, although they are stronger and more
powerful than men, dare not bring slanderous accusations
against these celestial beings ...

—Ephesians 6:12; 2 Peter 2:11, the Bible

"I'm so eager to hear your explanation," the graying, middle-aged man patronized his burly associate. With a dismissive smirk he scattered a half dozen faxes across the polished, brown table that separated them.

The seated man's pudgy fingers pawed at the documents, gathering the strewn pages, a look of consternation forming on his face. His accuser straightened the vest under his suit coat and strolled slowly across the room's plush carpeting, patting each of the high-backed leather chairs as he passed.

The man sifted carefully through the pages. His rage quickly turned to despair. His mind searched for a new strategy, but the thought of losing what appeared to be the find of a lifetime gnawed at him. "How could they lose the artifacts?" He sank back in his chair with a groan of exasperation.

"I think it's quite understandable that Iraqi Customs wouldn't want their property leaving the country, professor. The real mysteries here are the ineptitude of your associates at hiding the tablets." He shook his head. "I should have taken care of this myself."

"And what difference would that have made?"

"You know the answer to that! I know people who could have helped us get the tablets past customs. We just have to keep digging. The site is a royal building, and they weren't the only tablets found. There's bound to be more."

"Frankly, Dr. Weston, we both know this door is completely closed now. You'll be arrested on sight in Iraq if you return. Well done, if I must say so." The well-dressed man clapped slowly in mock celebration.

"*What?*" The professor cocked his head as if to strain at the words he'd already heard. He squinted in disbelief at his accuser. "Do you seriously think I've acted to undermine our goal, not to mention decades of my own work?"

"You stupid ..." The well-dressed man suddenly stopped pacing and stood still. He glared at the seated man with contempt.

"How dare you address me in such a way!" The professor rose from his seat, his complexion reddened with rage. "Need I remind you who you're speaking to?" Dr. Weston blustered. "How many Dravidian linguists do you know? And how many of them know Elamite and Sumerian? There isn't a linguist alive who's done more work in this area."

"Yes, so we've heard—more than once." The well-dressed man resumed his gait without so much as a glance.

"These things take time!" the scholar protested. "This isn't like checking a book out at a library. Finding tablets, especially one like these, is rare."

"You've been given months and every resource you've requested, and you've failed!"

"Give me more time! We may still be able to get the tablets. Send me to Iraq and let me try. Nineteenth-century linguists would have killed for this."

The professor's accuser now stood next to him. He leaned on one of the high-backed chairs. "An interesting choice of words, professor." He straightened his tie. "You should be happily translating now but for your own presumption. That's why you were brought here to Mount Weather. You've been in and out of Iran a hundred times. Yet somehow, Customs was in the mood to search your team more thoroughly ... I don't believe in Providence."

"This is preposterous! I did nothing to sabotage our work. We mustn't give up! The world must know the truth and believe!"

"Oh, they'll believe, and we won't give up ... but your work here is done."

"No! I've devoted my whole life to this search!"

"Then I guess you have no reason for living."

"Wha—what?" he stuttered. "Are you threatening me?"

Without another word, the well-dressed man turned on his heel and left the room, leaving the dumbfounded scholar alone.

Dr. Weston stewed for a few seconds and then angrily tossed the papers in his hand across the table. He took out a handkerchief and wiped his brow and upper lip, his mind racing. What were his options? He had to act, but how?

He reflected a moment and then grabbed the edge of the table to push himself away. To his astonishment, his chair refused to move, as though it were bolted to the floor.

"What the h—"

His own frightened gasp cut short his expletive. The terror within him built to a silent crescendo. He wanted to scream, but the sound refused to escape from his gaping mouth. He gazed in transfixed horror at his own reflection in the polished veneer of the tabletop, and at that of a hideous figure towering over him from behind. Completely immobilized, Dr. Weston watched the monstrous reflection glide around the edge of the table until the figure to which it belonged stood directly in front of him.

You have failed us for the last time, the entity's thoughts invaded the scholar's mind.

Immediately the helpless man's mouth clamped shut, and his limbs shot outward, leaving him in a grotesque cruciform position. There was no expression on his executioner's face, but the doomed prey could feel the laughter emanating from the powerful creature.

Who ... please.

The faint plea surfaced in the victim's mind only seconds before his face smashed violently and with terrific force forward into the solid oak. The man's head jerked backward, blood streaming from his broken nose. Again and again, an unseen energy slammed the professor's face into the unyielding, stationary surface. Blood and mucus spattered against the walls and the room's lone decoration—a black solar disk with tentacle-like rays that hung directly behind the defenseless victim. Several gratuitous thrusts preceded the release of the lifeless corpse, his face a featureless, unrecognizable mass. The assassin turned dispassionately toward the wall at his back and passed through it.

2

The greatest test of courage on earth
is to bear defeat without losing heart.

—*Robert Green Ingersoll*

The parking lot was completely empty, save for a black Bonneville idling in a remote corner, purposely out of view. All of the businesses in the unpretentious strip-mall had been empty for nearly an hour, the lone exception being the used bookstore that the two men in the front seat of the black sedan watched intently. They sat motionless, exchanging no words, patiently waiting for the man inside to close up shop for the evening. The stifling humidity of another Philadelphia summer night seemed to give them no discomfort, despite the fact that both were dressed in black suits. It was nearly ten, yet from behind their blackened sunglasses, their cold, unsympathetic eyes followed their unsuspecting quarry as he performed his nightly routine. This would be effortless; they'd done it hundreds of times.

The two heads turned slowly, in unison, following the solitary figure as he approached the front door from the inside of the now dimly illumined store. After nearly two weeks of surveillance, his large-framed build was familiar: several inches over six feet, broad-shouldered, slightly overweight. His wavy, dark brown hair was cut short and unimaginatively styled. His round glasses gave him the bookish look he no doubt preferred, but the high forehead and receding chin made him visually unimpressive.

The unwary man turned off the last of the lights, locked the shop door behind him, and headed wearily in the direction of the bus stop, oblivious to the automobile drifting silently toward him, headlights off. The vehicle suddenly accelerated recklessly, screeching to a halt alongside the startled figure. The man whirled toward the car, visibly shocked that he had been unaware of the vehicle up until now. Heart pounding, the man's eye caught the expressionless face of the driver as he shut off the car. The driver's partner cocked the door open silently.

"Dr. Scott," the driver said stoically from the window, "my partner and I need to speak with you."

"Do I know you?" Brian wasn't sure which was more unexpected, the car or being recognized by someone he knew he had never met before.

"No, sir, you most surely do not."

"Who are you, then? How did you know my name?"

"We know a great deal more about you than your name, sir," the driver's companion deadpanned.

"Are you guys cops?"

"No, sir."

"Show me some ID, then."

"We don't carry any," the driver replied. He stood in front of Brian, who had somehow missed his exit from the car.

"Then I guess this conversation is over." Brian tried to mask his fear.

"No, sir, it's not," the man in the passenger side said as he deftly moved to the back of the car, positioning himself behind Brian, blocking any escape.

"No need to be alarmed, sir. We have no intention of harming you—unless you give us no other choice."

Brian hesitated again, unsure of what would happen next. He knew he couldn't take both of them in a fight, and they were most likely armed. "What is it you want?" he asked quietly after a few strained seconds, trying to relax.

The driver's companion answered, "Your country needs you, Dr. Scott. We're here to pick you up and transport you to your destination."

"If you guys really knew anything about me, you'd know how ridiculous that sounds," he protested, his fear now giving way to aggravation. "And who in the government needs *me*? Oh, wait, let me guess—the president, right?"

"Not a bad guess," the driver said in monotone, glancing at his partner.

"Well that's different! It's about time he returned my calls! Really, guys, if you're not going to arrest me or something, I'm going home."

"Please get in the car," the driver's companion said. "We have our assignment, and we're prepared to do our job."

"Give me a break." Brian sighed in annoyed disbelief. "What if I won't go with you?"

"But you will," they both said in eerie unison.

"Sorry."

"We can do this with or without a scuffle, sir," the driver replied in what seemed to Brian an almost robotic way. "Your compliance will be gained, I can assure you. My partner is rather skilled in compliance measures."

Brian looked at the driver's companion, who stood motionless but ready before him. Although he couldn't see the man's eyes, he felt as though they were probing him, searching for any vulnerability. His fear returned.

"Sir—in the car."

Brian hesitated again for a brief moment, and then acquiesced. He had no real choice. As he got into the car, he breathed a prayer.

"We apologize for the inconvenience," the driver offered after they were on their way.

Brian said nothing. He leaned his head back on the seat and sighed.

Now what? he thought to himself. *As if life isn't complicated enough. Just once I wish something would happen to me that's just a little predictable.*

The thought suddenly struck him that these men had to be lying. For all he knew, he was the victim of mistaken identity and might be in terrible danger. But if they meant any harm, they had certainly passed up a perfect opportunity in the parking lot. *They also wouldn't be doing what they're doing now*, he mused, peering through the darkened car window. *Now I know I'm dreaming.*

Brian watched in suspicious incredulity as the car pulled up at a fast-food speaker, and the driver placed an order for three drinks. He could make a break for the restaurant or another building, but what if that only put other people in harm's way? As the car drifted to the pickup window, he glanced at the open lock on his door and took a deep breath. He could feel his heart racing. He clasped the handle and glanced toward the front seat. The driver pulled the drinks through the window, and Brian let go of the handle and wiped his brow nervously.

"We know you always stop for a drink at the 7-Eleven next to the bus stop," the driver notified him. "I don't think I've ever had a more predictable assignment."

"Yeah," his partner added, "you're about as spontaneous as a Swiss watch."

Brian heard the familiar sound of the straw piercing the lid.

"Here," the man offered, handing Brian one of the drinks. "Just to show you we're not all bad."

"Right," Brian replied, taking the soda, "this would convince anyone."

Brian looked away and quietly took a few sips. Neither man in the front touched their drinks. Brian said nothing as the car headed onto the interstate. Ten minutes passed before he broke the silence.

"So how long have you two been watching me?"

There was no answer.

"Are you sure you aren't looking for another Brian Scott—maybe one who deals drugs or owes somebody some money?"

Again there was no reply.

"So which one of you is Dan Aykroyd?" Brian said dryly, trying to draw a reaction.

"What matters to our superiors is who you are," the driver said. "You're Dr. Brian Scott, the bookstore clerk with a PhD and not much else. You don't even have a car."

Brian didn't respond to his captor's stinging reply. He didn't know which he resented more—the tone, or the fact that he actually had been spied on. He didn't feel like getting into an argument or explaining his career disappointments. "I'd like some answers," he finally said, yawning as he changed the subject. "Where are you taking me?"

"We're not authorized to answer that question," the driver answered, glancing at his suddenly drowsy passenger.

Brian barely heard the response. He unexpectedly felt disoriented and could hardly keep his eyes open. The driver's partner glanced over his shoulder into the back of the car just in time to see their passenger collapse on the seat.

"Nighty-night, Dr. Scott."

3

There are a terrible lot of lies going around the world,
and the worst of it is half of them are true.

—*Sir Winston Churchill*

"The makeup of our country's far-right militia groups is not so easily categorized," the young, auburn-haired woman, smartly dressed in a cream-colored mock tunic dress, explained to her audience as the slide projector whirred and clicked, producing the next image. "Militia groups are actually made up of a variety of sub-movements, including apocalyptic Bible-thumping cultists like David Koresh, constitutionalists, tax protesters, and more 'reasonable' Christians enamored with the militias' conspiratorial world view. By some estimates, as many as five million Americans retain membership in a militia group."

At the back of the nearly filled auditorium, a well-dressed couple listened quietly from where they stood. The speaker continued her lecture, which had turned toward a denunciation of mixing politics with religion.

"She's going a little overtime," the man commented as he straightened his tie.

"The crowd doesn't seem to mind," his companion noted, arms folded across her chest. "She certainly doesn't take any prisoners. Check out the slide."

The man shook his head. The screen featured a caricature of Pat Robertson, complete with the insignia of the Third Reich on his upper arm. "I'd give anything to see the good undersecretary face-off with her; she's brutal," the man noted, his lip slightly upturned in a suppressed grin. The woman nodded.

"My own suspicion," the speaker continued, "is that if you eliminated the so-called 'born-again' Christians from these groups, they'd collapse overnight. Their leaders are the ones who give intellectual weight—and I use the term loosely—to a good deal of militia ideology. They cloak hate and white supremacy in respectable garb, and sell it to disgruntled Americans who believe in the myth of a Christian America."

The lecture lasted a few more minutes, the mostly late-teenage audience politely applauding at its conclusion. The couple began to move toward the front of the auditorium against the flow of the sizable crowd. They waited as the she answered a few questions put to her by an audience member, and then approached.

"Good afternoon, Dr. Kelley," the man said extending his hand. The speaker shook it, as well as his partner's.

"You two are with the Bureau, right?" she asked with a plastic grin.

"Well ... we do work for the government," answered the woman. "Are we that transparent?"

"Let's just say I'm getting used to it. I've worked for the FBI on a few assignments, and I always seem to be contacted like this. Never a phone call or a lunch invitation, which is just as well, mind you. Always popping up after lectures or classes. Is that somewhere in the training manual, for dramatic effect maybe?"

"We won't take much of your time, doctor. We're here to present you another assignment."

"You're here to 'present' an assignment? I think it's more polite to say 'offer'."

"You'd be correct if that's what it was," the woman remarked curtly.

Dr. Kelley eyed them suspiciously for a moment. "Well then—no, thank you. Don't get the idea that I'm not grateful, but I really don't need the work."

"Oh?" the man asked in feigned surprise. "How can that be? This is your last summer term lecture, and you've been granted a leave of absence for the fall."

"I'm afraid you're mistaken. I have several more lectures scheduled for July, and they don't give that much time off to someone who hasn't earned tenure yet."

"But the paperwork is in your own briefcase," he answered with a confident smile.

Dr. Kelley looked at him incredulously, then opened her case.

"Inside the upper sleeve," the man coaxed.

She pulled a manila envelope from the case, opened it, and scrutinized the contents, a look of puzzled concern creasing her face.

"The university letterhead is quite attractive," the man's partner noted in feigned admiration, "but the dean really ought to improve his penmanship."

"What's going on here?" she demanded, startled.

"We have a job for you. Your presence on a particular project is a very high priority."

"I don't like being manipulated."

"But you certainly don't mind being sought out."

"Dr. Kelley," the female agent jumped in before the professor could respond, "your reputation has preceded you, and is no doubt well-deserved, but you would be wise to be less hostile. You may even be glad you've been selected."

"Is that so?" Dr. Kelley angrily slammed her briefcase shut. She took a step past them. "You two can just go to hell."

The male agent grabbed her arm tightly. "Apparently we haven't been clear." His partner took another manila envelope from her purse.

"Get your hands off me!" Dr. Kelley snapped, her green eyes ablaze.

"Not until you see this," the woman said, handing her the envelope. The man released his grip.

"I'm not looking at anything. The only thing I'm going to do is walk out of here, and if either one of you touches me again, I'll scream."

"If you're interested in keeping your academic career, you'll want to see the contents of that envelope," the man said, blocking her path. "Personally, if you want to throw away tenure, not to mention any hope of ever securing another appointment, it's your business. Take the envelope, or you might as well go back to your office and start packing."

The young woman flushed once more with anger, and she ripped the envelope from the agent's hand. She opened it and pulled out a small stack of papers and began reading. Her complexion paled as she flipped hurriedly through each sheet.

"None of these accusations are true!"

"Of course not," the man agreed pleasantly, "but you'll never be able to prove otherwise. We've manufactured a paper trail in support of what you're reading. Now, you can either come with us back to your apartment, or we can mail a copy of what you're holding to your department chair. It's your choice."

"This is blackmail!"

"Of course," he agreed again, "but do you honestly think that we'd be so up front about it if there was any chance it wouldn't work? You were right when you pegged us as working for the Feds, but we're considerably higher than the Bureau. You have no idea who or what you're dealing with."

The young lecturer stared at them in disbelief, but recovered quickly. "You know, teaching at Georgetown has some advantages, one of which is getting to know some powerful people."

"Ah, yes," the man answered, "you must be referring to the distinguished senator on the university's board, whom I believe—correct me if I'm wrong—you met at your department's Christmas party last year."

"Well ... yes," she confirmed, "how—"

"How did we know? Oh, come on, professor," the woman said with a smirk. "Do you think our choices for important projects are made in a few days? You've been closely surveiled for months. In fact, the senator's attendance and interest in your career aren't an accident. The senator was paid for his services, as usual. If you don't believe us, call him right now." The woman reached into her purse, drew out a cell phone, and offered it to the stunned scholar.

The three stood in silent confrontation. The young woman inserted the pages back into the envelope with a sigh of resignation. "Let's go," she muttered, pushing by them, swearing under her breath.

4

*Unthinking faith is a curious offering to be
made to the creator of the human mind.*

—*John A. Hutchinson*

"Dr. Bandstra," the secretary's voice echoed over the intercom.

"Yes?" the seated figure answered with a sigh, making no effort to divert his gaze from the window behind his desk.

"The Colonel is here, sir."

"Send him in—and hold the rest of my calls until he leaves."

"Yes, sir."

The office door swung open, and the rugged Air Force officer entered quietly and removed his hat. Though just having entered his sixties, Colonel Vernon Ferguson conveyed the energy and vigor of a man half his age. His sparkling, penetrating blue eyes accentuated the fading blond hair left atop his whitened scalp. The man behind the desk didn't move, his gaze still fixed on the Washington panorama.

"Good morning, Neil," the officer greeted energetically, standing erect in his dress blues, awaiting visual recognition. There was no response.

A few seconds elapsed before Neil Bandstra broke his gaze at the clouds. He hadn't been looking at anything in particular. As he turned to face his highly decorated caller, his drawn face betrayed a tired, distracted owner. The Colonel couldn't manage to completely conceal his surprise.

"When's the last time you had some sleep?" the Colonel asked as he seated himself.

"A day or so ago."

"You really need to get some rest. We have a lot of work to do."

"Yes ... we certainly do."

"Still thinking about the tour, eh? You know, you're not atypical, Neil. I did the same thing. I've seen people who've spent their whole lives spinning lies to cover up something they'd only been told about just crumble when they finally witnessed the truth, just as you did. But I know you're different."

Neil stared uncertainly at the soldier from behind his desk. Compared to the alert and dapper Colonel, he was a wreck—tie and collar undone, his suit coat thrown across the chair next to the officer's. The paperwork on his desk awaiting his attention remained untouched in the same pile from the evening before. He was physically and emotionally fatigued.

"I'm still a little curious why you even wanted to risk exposing me to all this. After all, you and I haven't exactly seen eye-to-eye in the past."

"I not only knew you could take the exposure, but I also need someone within official channels who I can trust," the Colonel responded. "You're one of the few people I know who isn't interested in kissing my rump, or anyone else's. It'll be refreshing—and essential—to have someone on the project who will provide blunt, honest evaluations. As for your current preoccupation, you'll be just fine. The Group never okays anyone if there's even the slightest doubt."

"Thanks," Neil managed with a weak smile. "It's not often your whole view of life changes overnight. I've been doing a lot of thinking."

"No doubt. But when it really sinks in, you'll begin to imagine the incredible possibilities, and—"

"And the threat to the nation's stability—to our whole way of life, really?" he interrupted, leaning back in his chair.

The officer paused awkwardly, and the room fell silent.

"I do have good news for you," the Colonel resumed after a few moments. "Your request has been honored and secured."

"Thanks so much, Vernon," Neil said gratefully with obvious relief, his countenance lightening.

"Glad I could help."

"The Group had no problems with what I wanted?"

"Interestingly enough, no. I've been with them for twenty years, and they usually chaff a bit at adding to a project personnel they haven't hand-picked."

"But in this case?"

"In this case it only took a week or so to get approval. I didn't even get quizzed on the addition. I think they realize, after all this time, that I don't pick people whose judgment can't be relied on. I have to admit, though, I am a bit curious at the choice from your perspective. There's no doubt that someone in this area is absolutely critical, but you could certainly have asked for someone with much more stature."

"Once you hear what he has to say, you'll know why I want him. In my mind he's the best person we could get for this. And he can be trusted. For sure, he won't know what hit him, but he'll adjust."

"He won't have any choice," the Colonel reminded him. "I know you don't like the idea, but we're going to have to dump the truth on them right away."

"We've profiled all of them psychologically; they should be able to handle it," Neil replied. He wasn't so sure about himself much less people he hadn't met yet. "I hope I'm not the best case scenario."

"Like I said, your response is perfectly normal. We profiled you, too, remember? We're confident all of them will be able to handle the truth."

"Right," Neil said softly, tapping his desk with his fingers, "the truth."

The Colonel got up from his seat and took a step toward the door. "The president is holding up his end of the plan. He's scheduled to make even more trips to raise awareness regarding regulation of agriculture, but he doesn't know why he's doing it, yet. The Group hasn't decided on when he'll be informed. You're our highest contact within official government channels. You answer to no one but me."

"Understood."

"I'll let you know when the decision has been made. We can't risk national security—"

"In the hands of the commander-in-chief?"

The Colonel sighed and looked at the floor momentarily. "I know how it sounds, but we work this way all the time, and we both know it's necessary. I know he's a personal friend, and I promise you, Neil, he'll be brought up to speed when it's time. The Group won't ignore him. In fact, they believe his popularity in the polls will work to their advantage. They just need to ensure that they'll retain control after full disclosure. This has to stay in the hands of people who know what they're doing, not people who need to get re-elected. And above all else," the Colonel said in a low voice as he reached for the doorknob, "Central Intelligence and the Joint Chiefs must be kept completely out of the loop. We can't take any chances."

"I know."

5

Brian sat up groggily and waited for his eyes to adjust. For a moment he was startled by his unfamiliar surroundings, but then the memory of his abduction came rushing back. *So where am I?*

There was a nightstand next to the bed, on which lay his glasses, an alarm clock flashing "12:00," and a small lamp, the room's only illumination at the moment. Putting his glasses on, he cautiously left the bedroom, emerging into a fairly spacious, three-room, fully-furnished efficiency apartment, its walls lined with empty bookshelves. There was no telephone.

He looked at his watch in disbelief. *Seven o'clock p.m.* He'd lost nearly a day—but to what? The main living area was choked with a few dozen boxes, each bearing his initials, which had been hurriedly scrawled with a black magic-marker. His filing cabinets had been brought as well. Other than the furnishings and shelves, the only item in the room that wasn't his own was a computer system already set up on a desk. There were doors at either end of the room, each with handles instead of knobs.

Brian noticed immediately that the door closest to the sofa had some type of electronic locking mechanism that resembled a calculator, along with a small red light that flashed at a regular interval. He tried the handle on the door, but it was locked securely. "Not that I have anywhere to go," he muttered to himself. He didn't dare touch the buttons on the keypad.

Staggering slightly, he headed for the second door at the far end of the room and tried the handle. The door opened to a full bathroom. Thinking a shower would help clear his head, Brian relieved himself and, after a few minutes of searching through the boxes, found his toiletry items and undressed.

As the spray hit his face, his thoughts drifted to the recent past. He had to admit that his life was in total disarray. The upheaval that had begun two years ago when he'd lost his parents now seemed to have climaxed. He kept telling himself that God was good, and that he should be thankful for what he had, but the mantra was losing its efficacy. His heart was slipping into the quagmire of doubt.

Other than the senseless violence, what was especially cruel about his parents' deaths was that their lives had been taken on the day he had walked the line for his PhD. The day was supposed to be one of celebration, the triumphant climax to years of study and determination. It had promised to be a day of reconciliation as well.

His parents had never understood his desire for an academic career, much less his field of choice. In fact, they'd never understood *him*. Someone interested in books in a proud blue-collar family just didn't fit in. Working in the family's landscaping business during his high school summers hadn't helped, either. He eventually came to understand that this arrangement had been part of a plan to groom him for the family business; he was the anointed successor. This all made sense to his parents, since Brian was the only child. He just had no desire to spend his life manicuring shrubs and sod.

Brian recalled wistfully the day he had told his parents he planned to attend college to study ancient history. Explanations of his aspirations to become a college professor and to travel through the Mediterranean fell on deaf ears. He was soft and lazy, his father had retorted angrily, and he was abandoning the family. His mother openly lamented that throwing away the opportunity to walk into a profitable business was proof that her son hadn't an ounce of common sense.

Of course, by the time of that conversation, he'd become accustomed to being misunderstood, and even ignored. He'd lacked the good looks and the drive to inebriate himself on a weekly basis, the two prerequisites for acceptance in the right cliques in high school, and he managed to graduate without having gone on a single date. Even the kids who liked him thought he was odd. They were going to be doctors and lawyers; he was bent on wasting his education on something that wouldn't earn him an income worth bragging about. None of this had mattered to him, save for the confrontation with his parents. Deep down, they were the only people whose opinion ever really mattered.

His performance in high school and the obligatory entrance exams earned him acceptance to his first choice among colleges, Johns

Hopkins University. Predictably, the accomplishment elicited no excitement from his parents. In fact, the only thing that generated any response at all during his undergraduate years was the news that he'd decided to stop going to mass and had begun attending a Presbyterian church. His parents were staunch Catholics, and they interpreted his decision as more evidence that he wanted no part of the family heritage. The punishment meted out was apathy toward him.

He drowned his loneliness in study. Were it not for the spiritual and intellectual camaraderie of a professor at the university, his college career would have unfolded in near total emotional isolation. It was the same during his graduate program at the University of Chicago. But after nine years of academic toil, he'd accomplished his goal. A month before he would receive his degree, his parents had surprised him with a phone call to tell him they would be there to see him graduate. He never spoke to them again.

What followed in the subsequent year was nearly as unimaginable. Shortly after burying his parents, he'd been offered an appointment teaching Old Testament and biblical languages at a small denominational college. The money wasn't good, but he hadn't cared. Teaching was all he'd ever wanted to do. Everything was fine until a parent of one of his students—one of the college's trustees—objected to a few comments he'd made in an article. After only a few months of living his dream, he found himself fighting unsuccessfully for his job.

Brian turned off the water and leaned with both hands against the wall of the shower. Watching the steamy mist dissipate and the water drip from his nose, he could still hear the "we have to cut untenured staff" excuse from the dean, calculated to insulate the school from a lawsuit. *Liar.* He still couldn't believe the whole ruckus had happened. He'd assumed that people of faith would want to think about their worldview, that they would enjoy engaging questions that mattered, rather than feel threatened. His miscalculation had cost him his job, and academic jobs in his field were about as common as a selfless politician. *Talk about naïve.*

Lacking any other direction, he'd moved back home to Pennsylvania to enter seminary. It was a far cry from where he'd been. The job at the bookstore was barely sufficient for his needs, but at least it was stimulating. And now here he was, apparently in the middle of nowhere, for no telling how long. The job was history now.

He finished dressing and leaned on the desk in his new living quarters, his eyes filling with tears. *"If you faint in the day of adversity, your strength is small."* The proverb echoed inside his head. There had to be some purpose for all of this.

Suddenly he heard a distinct click behind him. What he had presumed was the front door opened, the red light now extinguished. Brian stood up. A lone figure attired in a gray business suit, nearly as tall as Brian, stood in the doorway, briefcase in hand.

"Good evening, Brian," the man said with a sincere smile.

"Neil!" he exclaimed and strode toward his visitor. The two exchanged a brief but strong embrace. "You're the last person I expected to see in this place—wherever it is we are."

"I have no trouble believing that. How was your, uh, trip?"

"I'm in one piece, but since you asked," he responded, irritation surfacing in his voice, "I don't like being drugged. I must have missed that part of the Patriot Act."

"I know it's disorienting, but I'm afraid it was necessary," Neil said, his expression turning more serious.

"Necessary? What's going on?"

"That's why I'm here." Neil seated himself on the small couch and opened his briefcase. Brian sat on the floor, his back to the wall, listening as he put on a pair of socks. "I can't tell you everything that I'm sure you'll want to know," he continued, "mostly because it's classified. Believe me, I know that'll be frustrating for you, but you'll have to trust me."

"Where are we, the Pentagon?"

"No—their rooms have bars on them," Neil answered with a chuckle.

"Then, where?"

"That's one of the things I can't tell you—at least at this point. Everyone who's been brought here in the last few days as part of this project was brought under the same circumstances as you to maintain the secrecy of this location. You may be allowed to know eventually."

Brian looked at him uneasily.

"Brian," he said with a pause, "you're here at my specific request. I almost want to apologize to you for it, but I need you to be part of this assignment. This will introduce you to some of the details—although painfully few right now."

Neil handed Brian a small folder. Brian took it and looked at the cover. Aside from his embossed name, there were only the words: *"Above Top Secret."*

"Wow, this is cool."

"I doubt if you'll think so in a few days. In fact, you'll probably ask me again what you're doing here, but for different reasons."

"You know that if you need me, I'm here for as long as it's necessary."

"Thanks, Brian. I knew that's what you'd say, but it's still a relief to hear it. You no doubt have noticed that your whole library is here with you."

"Hard to tell in this landfill."

"Sorry again, but things needed to be done quickly. We also took the liberty of backing up your entire hard drive and loading it onto this computer."

"Was all that just for my sanity, or will I actually use the stuff? Bringing it all here tells me I'm not going anywhere for a while. Someone in Homeland Security need some Aramaic verbs parsed?"

"Not exactly," Neil said, putting all five fingertips of each hand together. He was smiling, but Brian remembered his friend's habit. Neil was choosing his words carefully.

"You've been chosen to be part of a team that will be working on a solution to a problem that will irreversibly change life as we know it—not only in the U.S., but all over the world."

Brian couldn't disguise the amused look on his face. "I'm an Old Testament scholar, not a scientist."

"It'll make sense after we get started. You need to realize that you've been given a very high security clearance, one that's necessary to even be admitted to this complex. There are a few items I need to go over with you because of that."

"Such as?"

"For starters, this is officially a military operation, so your access within the Facility—that's what we call it—is restricted to certain areas. The military often recruits outsiders like you for specific tasks, although such recruitment nearly always targets scientists. When the military does this, they like to break people in gradually, and always under an extremely careful watch. It's kind of a studied paranoia, really. Even though I have a fairly high government position, I'm still a civilian, and it's taken some of the people associated with this project a good deal of time to get used to having any civilian participation at all."

"Aren't we all on the same side?" asked Brian.

"Of course, but the military and the government are just like the business or academic worlds. There's a lot of internal competition, even mistrust among colleagues. Rivalries, petty grudges, office politics—they're all part of the picture."

"I see ... anything else?"

Neil looked at Brian pensively. The fingertips again. "Yes. I feel pretty confident saying that your faith will be tested more severely than it has been up to this point ... even with your circumstances." His voice trailed off as he broke eye contact.

"Why is that?" A sense of apprehension crept over Brian. He wondered how his friend could be so sure.

"To be honest," Neil began anew, "you'll hear things ... learn of things that will make you wonder about God's interest in our world ... and about whether God is really who we thought He was."

6

And there will be signs in sun, moon, and stars ...
Then will appear in heaven the sign of the Son of Man, and
then all the tribes of the earth will mourn, and they will
see the Son of Man coming on the clouds of heaven with
power and great glory.

—*Luke 21:25; Matthew 24:30, the Bible*

The solitary priest gazed intently at the computer screen, his face glow-ing eerily, reflecting its soft light. The library at Castel Gandolfo had been closed for hours, dutifully locked down and completely dark, save for the exit lights, as his duties required each night. But, as on many other occasions, the silence and solitude proved irresistible. His days consumed with helping scholars find information, he coveted the time to pursue his own avocation.

Astronomy had been the mistress of his mind for many years, but on this occasion, the rapture that always filled him as he searched the heav-ens, even from his desktop, had slowly and inexorably passed through stages of amused curiosity, unexpected unease, and now a mounting dread. It was human nature to fear the unknown; but now the known had opened the door to terror.

Father Mantello stroked his beard nervously as he watched the sim-ulation again, as he had dozens of times before, still hoping that what he now knew to be true was somehow incorrect. *Perchè se lo siete distur-bato, Benedict!*

He couldn't help questioning the priest who had put him on this trail, but it was half-hearted. He loved Father Benedict, who was more than twenty years his senior, and agreed with his cause, at least as he under-stood it. Who better for Benedict to put his question than his trusted friend, who happened to be the librarian at the Vatican Observatory in Rome? He had access to hundreds of ancient astronomical manu-scripts collected over centuries and knew how to read the heavens.

At first he could not believe his comrade's request was serious. He should have known. Benedict did nothing in jest.

He took the photocopied pages of the Talmudic passages Benedict had sent him, along with the hand-copied facsimiles of the Greek and Latin codices he had discovered in his pursuit of an answer to the question asked of him, and retranslated them at sight, pressing again for some nuance that would help him escape the evidence. He hit the now-memorized keystrokes one more time and watched the time move forward into the future at monthly intervals, the constellations and star clusters performing the dance composed aeons ago by their celestial choreographer. The dénouement was the same, as he knew it would be.

This cannot be real. It was simply impossible that the Christian question of the ages had been literally over his head and at his fingertips since he had begun to serve the Holy See in this place. *The Lord Jesus couldn't have literally meant what he said ... could he?*

He paused, seeking courage and wisdom for a course of action. He would not tell Benedict without independent confirmation. He would ask a colleague to check his work, but who? After a few moments his mind cleared. Though they had only met online, he knew who his guide must be and just how he could be contacted to safeguard such sensitive material. He kissed the small cross dangling from his neck, closed his eyes, and blessed God that he had been allowed to know such secrets and had been given a friend with whom to share them. His head still bowed, he prayed for protection. *Sancte Michael Archangele, defende nos in proelio; contra nequitiam et insidias diaboli esto praesidium. Imperat illi Deus; supplices deprecamur. Amen.*

Father Mantello quickly saved his work, opened the embedding software he and his associate had used before, converted the file, and uploaded it to the observatory's website. He opened his email account and jerked to a stop. He peered over the top of his computer, then scanned the darkened library. He shook off the sense of being watched and typed a terse missive:

Silent One,

Castel Gandolfo is beautiful this time of year. I sent you a good envelope today. Tell me what you think of it.

God be with us all.

Mantello.

The astronomer priest sent his message and closed his programs. He watched the screen as the computer cycled through its shutdown. The screen went black, and in the same instant, the priest let out an audible shout—the last sound that would ever come from his throat. On the blank, black screen, the outline of a triangular, asp-like face was peering over his shoulder.

Father Mantello fought desperately to move and run, but he could not. The creature quietly removed the papers from his hand. The sight of its freakishly long but powerful fingers sent Mantello's diaphragm into spasms. Unable to even scream, he struggled to control his breathing and nearly passed out. But for some inexplicable reason, he could not look away. Out of the corner of his eye he watched it, now standing erect and shockingly tall, as it scanned and shuffled the pages.

The priest suddenly felt himself being lifted out of the chair. His stiffened body rotated slowly toward the terrible form until he and the creature were face to face.

I don't think Michael will be here any time soon, a voice reverberated inside the priest's head.

The priest's face twitched in horror and revulsion. He tried in vain to close his eyes.

You have discovered an important secret, but I ask you, which of the two signs will the faithful believe? You now know how perfect the first will be, and when the first fulfills all prophecy and expectation, will anyone be looking for the second?

The words of the towering, grotesque being pierced through his fear and brought a clarity to his mind that filled him with despair.

Yes ... I can feel your anguish ... what heartbreak.

At the creature's words, Father Mantello's chest was seized with intense, burning pain.

One can only imagine the distress of knowing your brethren will venerate us at our unveiling, how their children will embrace us, the sadistic entity taunted him as he accelerated his victim's heart rate. *We, of course, cannot appear in this form. No, that isn't how they envision the return of the gods of old, their shining saviors.*

The priest's skin turned pallid and sweaty. His gasps quickened, synchronized with each stabbing throb.

We will appear, dare I say it, human. Why, one of us might even look like you, Father.

Mantello retched, his vomit spraying the floor beneath his dangling legs. Suddenly, his head collapsed, his chin slumped on his chest.

Urine dripped to the floor from beneath his pant leg. The creature released its unseen grip, and the warm but lifeless corpse tumbled to the floor.

    Then again, perhaps not.

7

Coincidences are spiritual puns.

—*Gilbert K. Chesterton*

Brian stared for a moment at his mentor's face. His eyes had lost the sparkle of only a few moments ago, dulled by some nagging uncertainty. "Is there something about this project that has created doubts about your faith, Neil?" Brian could hardly believe he was asking the question.

"Well ... no ... I mean, I guess I wouldn't use those terms. I'll confess that I'm feeling some spiritual anxiety right now, but I have a strong inclination to believe that there are answers to my questions. At least, I hope you can help me find them."

"I won't prod, then."

Neil forced a smile. "I know. I wouldn't have gotten to my position if I didn't honor protocol. I'm working on clearing the way for a greater flow of information to all the team members, but for now we'll all have to be patient."

"What makes you so sure you'll be authorized to tell us more?"

"Because I have a great deal of authority over this project. I still have my own superiors to report to, but they've been very pliable. They agreed to recruit you when I asked."

"Yeah, they sure did. What else can you tell me about the team?"

"There are eleven members. Three are scientists, and the others, like yourself, have a variety of areas of expertise. There's an Air Force colonel who's the military project leader, to whom I report, and two other base employees. You'll meet most of them tomorrow morning. The schedule is in the folder."

"I suppose I'll be expected to have read through this by then?" Brian asked, flipping through the pages of his folder.

"Absolutely. It's not Hebrew or hieroglyphs, but try and stay interested," Neil kidded.

27

"You bet."

"I know you probably feel otherwise, but you shouldn't feel like you're a prisoner. You're actually a VIP here."

"Makes me wonder what they do to people who aren't invited."

"Trust me, no one ever gets here uninvited."

"Well, since I'm so esteemed, can you tell me how to get out of the room?"

"Oh yes," Neil answered, reaching into his shirt pocket. "I'm glad you reminded me." He retrieved what had the appearance of a credit card and handed it to Brian. "Just swipe this through the card reader face up, and then punch in your numeric ID on the pad. You'll need to do the same to open doors that lead directly to the conference rooms that team members will be using. To get out of the room or open it for someone else, you'll need to punch in the same number. Yours is the last four digits of your social security number. Don't let anyone else know it. The security system only allows you one attempt at opening a door from either side. If you use the card incorrectly, or punch in the wrong code, the MP's will be alerted to an attempted security violation. Make sure your read the security protocols in your folder."

Brian nodded. "How do I know where the permissible areas are?"

"There aren't that many, but if you want to know now, there's a floor plan in your notebook. It shows a layout of the section of the facility that you're authorized to use. Basically, the map shows only the location and number of other team member rooms, meeting areas, a recreational and exercise facility, and a cafeteria. There's also a laundry room."

"What? No maid service?"

Neil grinned. "No, but we've taken care of you in other ways."

"I'm all ears."

"We've arranged for your mail to be sent to a servicing location. You'll get mail—opened, as you might guess. As far as your bills, you won't have to worry about them anymore."

"What do you mean?"

"We've electronically transferred all your financial resources to a banking facility used by the Defense Department Everything is intact, and, as you'll be briefed tomorrow, the government will compensate you financially for your service. If you don't mind my saying so, I know you could use the money. I made sure it was enough to get you off to a new start."

"No problem," Brian said softly. "Thanks."

"One last thing. While you'll be able to get online to do research, you won't be permitted to email anyone outside the base without filtering permission, and even then it will not be private. Your email program is already set up with the addresses for the other personnel associated with the project, including a steward who can get you any living necessities."

Neil looked at his watch and stood up. "Time to get on with my other visits," he said, snapping his briefcase closed. "Remember, if you need anything, just email the steward. Even at this hour, it's fine; the system is constantly monitored."

"How reassuring," Brian joked. "I have to tell you, Neil, this whole setup makes me a little queasy. I can't help but get the distinct impression that the only people who'll know that I'm still alive will be those connected with this project."

Neil looked at the floor for a moment and then turned his attention back to Brian. "Precisely."

***

It took Brian three hours to get all his things in order. His mind kept wandering back to his conversation with Neil. He'd lost his enthusiasm for a late-night visit to the cafeteria after Neil affirmed the extent of his anonymity, opting instead for a hot cup of tea and some cookie fragments he kept in one of his filing cabinet drawers.

Despite his friend's assurances that all the precautions were necessary, he was troubled at how easily the government could erase any trace of his whereabouts. The truth was, no one except his landlord and boss would ever notice he was gone. And if anyone wanted to find out where he'd gone, there was no one who would have the drive it would surely take. He had every confidence in Neil's judgment and friendship, but it was obvious that there was a great deal about this assignment that he hadn't been told. He didn't like the vulnerability.

The contents of the folder Neil had issued him consisted of little more than schedules, rules, a floor plan, and the names of the other scientists and scholars on the team. The thought dawned on him that, although his folder contained a list of participants and their respective fields of expertise, it contained no information on their academic backgrounds. Brian decided to spend some time searching online in the hope that he could find more information on those who would be his colleagues for the foreseeable future.

The results were predictably unfruitful—not one of the names produced any meaningful hits other than their professional affiliations or email addresses—until he typed *"Mark Chadwick"* into the search engine.

"A bovine biochemist on a secret military project?" Brian shook his head. "Makes about as much sense as inviting me."

Brian glanced disinterestedly at the screen, which was cluttered with articles and research reports whose titles he couldn't understand. Suddenly one article grabbed his attention. He hurriedly clicked on the reference and hastily read the online abstract, his eyes widening more with each paragraph.

After a few moments, he sat back in his chair, his mind racing. "This just has to be a coincidence," he whispered to himself. "But ... what if it isn't?"

8

The harder you work, the harder it is to surrender.

—*Vince Lombardi*

Brian awoke the next morning fully refreshed. Energized by the revelation of the previous evening, he hastily showered and dressed. Neil wanted him here, and he had no reason to let anything adverse happen to him, he told himself. He removed the page in his folder that contained the facility's floor plan, stuffed the rest of the folder and a few other items for note-taking into his backpack, and punched out of his room.

As the door closed behind him, a glance at the floor plan told him that the cafeteria was situated at the far end of the long hallway before him. As he walked, Brian noted a number of other doors dotting the hallway. Those closest to his own room were noted on his map, and he drew the conclusion that these were the accommodations of other team members. The only other rooms marked on the page lay close to the cafeteria itself and were variously marked according to their functions. Along the way, there were dozens of other doorways unmarked on the map, all of which were solid, allowing no visibility as to where they might lead.

As he reached his destination, the wonderful aroma of fresh eggs and bacon captured his senses and reminded him that it had been two days since he'd last eaten. To his delight, breakfast was served buffet style, and he eagerly availed himself of it. He bowed silently over his meal and then surveyed the room as he ate.

The cafeteria was much smaller than he'd expected, only housing a dozen or so tables. It had an antiseptic feel to it. There were five other patrons, four of whom were men. Two of the men, trim and impeccab-ly groomed, sported Air Force and Army officer's dress, while a third, more aged gentleman, who seemed to be somewhat agitated, wore a drab olive suit. The final male member of the assemblage was a tall, lanky black man in a white lab coat, whom Brian guessed to be in his early thirties. The man's high cheekbones held up a pair of dark, horn-rimmed glasses, and his large, smiling mouth, set with perfect white teeth, drew his immediate attention. The man waved his long arms in exaggerated gestures as he talked, but no one at his table appeared very interested. His faded jeans and designer sneakers did nothing to disguise his eccentricity.

The woman, smartly attired in stylish light-gray pleated slacks with a matching jacket, was also African-American, and in the same age range. Her close-cropped hair made her rectangular face appear broader than it actually was, and the faddish, dark glasses through which she peered with amusement at the animated black man gave her what Brian guessed was an intentionally sassy look. None of them paid Brian the slightest attention.

At about the same time that the men across the room arose from their table, leaving the lone woman to finish her breakfast, Brian went back to the buffet. The military brass and the suited man filed out past him silently with nary a glance, but the fourth stopped as soon as he reached the place where Brian stood.

"Well, Dr. Scott," he said, extending his hand eagerly, "glad to see you're finally up and around!"

Brian set his tray down and shook the man's hand firmly. He tried to snatch a glance at the ID badge on the man's white coat. "Glad to meet you, too, Dr., uh ..."

"Malcolm Bradley. No relation to Milton or Omar, of course—wrong color."

"No kidding," Brian remarked with a grin.

"Guess you're wondering how I know who you are," he continued, anticipating the question. "I'll tell you while you finish your breakfast. Go ahead—sit down and finish. I don't intend to make either of us late. Colonel Ferguson is fanatical about punctuality."

Brian obliged.

"I discerned your identity by simple deduction, actually," Malcolm continued cheerfully as Brian put ketchup on his hash browns. "The team got permission from Dr. Bandstra to have a late-night meeting over some snacks two nights ago—boy was that interesting. It's too bad you weren't there."

"So what did I miss?"

"Let's just say some people are less than thrilled to be here. You'll know what I mean when we get together this morning. I don't imagine attitudes have changed over the course of only another day. Anyway, I already know the other scientists in the group. They've been here ten months."

"*Ten months?*"

"It only *seems* like years. I've been here about a month myself."

"Great," Brian sighed, suddenly a bit depressed.

"Of the four non-scientists like yourself," he continued, "two are female in gender. Dee over there seems nice enough, to me anyway. Just met her. The other one is worth a second look, though. Since none of us are going anywhere soon, I hope to get lucky. Brainy babes are the best kind, if you know what I mean."

"I'm sure I don't have the benefit of your experience." Brian salted his eggs.

"Just wait 'til you see her—thick reddish hair bobbed to the chin, not too tall, about 5'5", and everything just perfectly proportioned. Simply scrumptious."

"I'll try my best to stay out of your way."

A perplexed look creased Malcolm's face as Brian took a sip of orange juice. "Oh ... okay, I've got it. I remember your field was religion or something like that, right? I'll bet you're a minister or something. Hope I didn't offend you, man. I'll have to toe the line with two men of the cloth around here."

"Take it easy. I'm not a priest—and what do you mean by two?"

"We've already got a priest on the team, man."

"You're kidding—why is that?"

"Beats me—why do we have you?"

"I give up, why?"

"Aww ..." Malcolm grinned.

"I have no idea why I'm here, if you really want to know. Now I have a question for you."

"Shoot."

"You had breakfast with those men this morning. Are they your friends?"

"An act of desperation on my part, pure and simple. Getting any of those guys to say two peeps is almost impossible. They spend so much time guarding their little secrets that they think everyone outside their cabal is trying to milk them for information. It's pathetic. I guess they just don't want stimulating conversation."

"I find that really hard to believe."

Malcolm smiled understandingly. "I really don't usually just blather on like this."

"Bummer. I was kind of hoping you did. Just keep it clean, and you can chatter all you want."

"Thanks." Malcolm looked at his watch. "You still have a few minutes."

"Right," Brian responded as he hurried to finish his meal.

"Here comes Dee," Malcolm noted dutifully. "She's sharp, but watch out for her temper. She and the Colonel got into it two nights ago, and it wasn't pretty."

No sooner had Malcolm's comment ended than the woman Brian had noted at the table appeared at his side. She was tall for a woman, a few inches under six feet, and was on the chubby side.

"I see you've met Malcolm," she said, grinning.

"Yes, he's been very entertaining."

"Now you know what Jar Jar Binks evolved into," she quipped, glancing over at the butt of her joke. Brian laughed heartily. "Deidre Harper," she said, extending her hand.

"Brian Scott," he answered, shaking her hand.

"The trays go over there," she informed him, looking at her watch.

"Right. I've heard about Colonel ... what was his name?"

"Ferguson—charming man," she said with transparent disdain.

"So, do either of you know what this special project is about?" Brian asked as he stood up and pushed in his chair.

"I don't, and other than the fact that we're somewhere in the southwestern United States," Deidre butted in, "Malcolm doesn't know squat, either, no matter what he tells you."

"To the contrary; I know everything," Malcolm said confidently as they started toward the open doorway of the cafeteria.

"You do?" Brian stopped. He was eager to learn if his suspicion was correct.

"Well, they haven't *officially* told me anything beyond what they've probably told you, but I've got some of it figured out ... I think."

"I doubt if the Group would let them tell anything to anyone," Deidre said.

"The Group?" Brian asked, his curiosity piqued. "What's that?"

"Not what—who," Deidre broke in. "They're the ones who are running this operation. You'll hear about them, but—"

"But don't count on ever meeting any of them," Malcolm finished. "Nobody knows who they are. Like cockroaches—they'd rather stay out of the light."

9

The man who fears no truths
has nothing to fear from lies.

—*Sir Francis Bacon*

The conference area was quite a contrast to the austere atmosphere of the rest of "the Facility," as it had been dubbed by Neil. The walls were undecorated, but pleasantly painted in aptly coordinated colors. There were eleven high-backed, burgundy leather chairs surrounding a large, polished, black marble table. A thick three-ring binder crammed to capacity was placed at all but two of the seats.

Brian looked around the room, taking note of the team's membership. Several of the team members were dispersed about the room, engaged in hushed conversations among themselves. One of Malcolm's foursome, the Air Force officer, whom Brian now inferred was Colonel Ferguson, stood behind a podium situated at the head of the table. Behind him was a large viewing screen suspended from the ceiling.

Malcolm took one of the empty seats; Brian was headed for one of the remaining chairs himself when someone grabbed his arm from behind. He turned abruptly, and his gaze fell on the unfamiliar face of a thin, balding, elderly priest. The old cleric was a good bit shorter than his own six-foot-three stature and conveyed the impression of frailty. His eyes brightened in response to Brian's attention; his ebullient smile seemed to stretch the corners of his mouth beyond the tip of his tapered nose.

"Excuse me," Brian said. "Were you sitting here?"

"Not at all, Dr. Scott," the priest said politely. "I just wanted to meet you before we got started. My name is Andrew—Andrew Benedict."

"It's good to meet you, Father," Brian said pleasantly and shook the priest's hand. To Brian's surprise, the grip was strong and sure.

"Please call me Andrew. I've spent more years in the classroom than days in a parish. The Church and my Order deemed my gifts more appropriate to a life of study than pastoral ministry."

"Is there necessarily a difference?" Brian asked good-naturedly.

The priest smiled and shook his head. "There shouldn't be. How refreshing to find someone with my own viewpoint on scholarship."

"Please call me Brian."

"Very well. You know, Brian, our paths nearly crossed last November at the American Academy of Religion meeting. I went to hear you read your paper, only to discover you'd been scratched from the program. I was quite disappointed."

"So was I ... I couldn't afford the plane fare, so I had to cancel."

"Unfortunate ... but providential."

Brian couldn't hide the hint of surprise on his face at the priest's choice of words.

"Don't look surprised. You Presbyterians aren't the only people who believe in predestination!" the priest exclaimed, chuckling.

"No offense meant."

"None taken. I should tell you," the priest said in a lowered voice as he looked past Brian in the direction of the Colonel, "I've read your dissertation through several times. Some of my own academic training is in the area of Semitics as well. A brilliant piece of work, really."

"Thanks. You're one of the few who's taken an interest. The microform service hasn't exactly had a run on them."

"It's not unusual." The priest shrugged.

"Well, it's to be expected. There isn't much scholarly interest in my perspective. I had no idea anyone was even paying attention."

"Someone is *always* paying attention, Brian," Father Benedict replied with cryptic smile. "You would do well to remember that."

10

The Colonel cleared his throat, and the team members who were not already seated began moving toward the table. "If I could have your attention, now that all the appropriate parties are present, we can get to know each other properly. I'm sure you remember some of your comrades' names from our earlier get-together, but today's program will include more formal introductions. And in case you're wondering about the two vacant seats, the rest of the team will be introduced to you when that becomes necessary."

Neil opened his briefcase and withdrew a stack of manila envelopes. He rose from his seat, glancing at the label on each envelope and handing it to its designee.

"Please wait to open the materials Dr. Bandstra is handing out. We'll be getting to the contents therein momentarily. I want to first introduce myself again briefly for those who were not present at the other meeting, and then bring some preliminary details to your attention. My name is Colonel Vernon Ferguson," the officer continued, "and I'm a thirty-two-year veteran of the United States Air Force, a former combat pilot, and intelligence officer. You've already all met Dr. Bandstra, one of the Defense Department's undersecretaries and the civilian director of this project. He answers only to myself in the chain of command. I trust you will all give him the appropriate respect."

"What about the commander-in-chief, or maybe even that Constitution thing?" Deidre interrupted sarcastically, visibly agitated.

Brian was taken aback by her overt hostility, particularly in light of the contrast to his own introduction to her just a few minutes ago. It didn't take too much imagination to conclude that her interjection marked a continuation of the antagonism to which Malcolm had alluded.

"Ah, yes, Dr. Harper," the Colonel said with a confident air, "I see that you're determined to pick up where you left off. I apologize once again for the painful disruption this project has caused in your life, and I sympathize with your concern for legal protocol. Tell me, doctor, you are familiar with the phrase 'plausible deniability,' are you not?" he asked condescendingly.

The woman responded with only a smirk, arms folded across her chest.

"Well then, for your benefit as well as the rest of your colleagues, I must inform you that your government, at least as you are familiar with it, has no knowledge of this project. Plausible deniability is, in this case, absolutely plausible. Using another term you may have heard, this is a 'black op.' Every dollar spent on this project is undetectable to those who hold the purse strings of congressional budgetary oversight. It is certainly true, Dr. Harper, that the president, as well as most of the elected members of Congress, have no knowledge of what you'll be working on. And, contrary to what you may be thinking, it's all entirely legal. If I deemed it necessary, documentation from both the National Security Decision Directives and United Nations Security Council Resolutions could be produced for your reading pleasure."

"I want to see them!" Deidre demanded defiantly.

"The entire rationale I sketched for you," he continued, "has been in existence since the forties. Then President Truman had the foresight to move certain operations beyond the grasp of his own office, since the duties of that office are often carried out under political duress or expediency, depending on one's perspective, and the outcomes of national elections."

"The public has a right to know … whatever it is you're hiding," Deidre continued, not content to let the Colonel have the last word.

"No it doesn't!" the Colonel suddenly erupted, and he slammed his fist onto the podium, jolting his antagonist in her seat. "We're talking about matters of national security that have always been exempt from public or journalistic scrutiny. No one has a right to know *anything* concerning this project except those of you in this room!"

The room fell completely silent, the team members transfixed upright in their chairs like a bunch of scared Marine recruits on the first day of boot camp. Brian unconsciously held his breath as he watched the Colonel stroll around the table like General Patton inspecting some petrified draftees. Malcolm's description of the tension had been only the tip of the iceberg.

"And if you do your jobs well," the Colonel continued in a calm, assured voice, "if you're worth the confidence your country has in you, if you're really as good as you think you are, the public that you and I care so deeply about will get what it really wants: the security of the status quo. You represent the key to guiding the citizens of this country through an impending crisis of which, at the present, they are blissfully unaware."

The Colonel sauntered back to the podium and straightened his uniform. Brian hadn't appreciated the tongue-lashing any more than anyone else in the room, but he couldn't help admiring the man's commanding presence.

"Now," the Colonel resumed his introduction, "if you'd like to find out why I've bothered to reveal this much to you already, and what exactly you've been selected to work on, I'll thank you ahead of time for withholding any irrelevant comments or questions. Is that understood?"

Brian almost expected someone to salute, but no one at the table moved or spoke.

"Good. Look around you at your academic colleagues. You'll notice something immediately: The seven of you, with the exception of Father Benedict, are in your thirties. Besides something as obvious and superficial as your age, you all possess earned doctorates from some of the most prestigious universities in the world and were regarded by your professors and the Group as the brightest young minds in your respective fields. Each of you is also single and has no children. In addition, your parents, grandparents, aunts, and uncles are deceased. With one exception you have been continuously surveiled for at least two months, and in some cases much longer. The content of your conventional mail, email, internet usage, and phone records all helped us conclude that none of you has any relationship with anyone that could be considered close. You see, we were not only looking for sharp minds, but individuals who would not be readily missed—at least not right away."

"Why did you go through the trouble of placing our financial records under government accounting control?" Brian ventured to ask, eyeing the other team members. "Or is that just something that was done to me?"

The panicked expressions on the faces of several of his associates revealed to Brian immediately that this was a new revelation to the others. Only Father Benedict seemed detached.

"No, Dr. Scott, you are not alone," the Colonel replied, looking Brian in the eye, unperturbed by the inquiry. "The Group has indeed taken the same liberty with each of your records."

"What gives you the right to our privacy?" Deidre exploded again indignantly, only this time, her sentiments were immediately echoed by a majority of the others.

"So glad you asked," the Colonel, unflappable, answered. "The facility in which you are housed is completely equipped with a full hospital and staffed by one of the military's top personal physicians. Consequently, your health insurance has been subsumed by the military. Your regular salaries are being electronically funneled to new personal accounts according to whatever schedule your outside employer has created. Your monthly bills have all been converted to an electronic payment format, each payment being deducted from your account. Lastly, $100,000 has been placed into individual savings accounts as payment for your services on this project. Do you have any objections, Dr. Harper?"

"Yeah, how do we know this isn't just a pile of crap?"

"A private access code to your accounts was sent to your computers via email this morning. You can use it to access those accounts and verify what I've said. Please remember to open the message by this evening, since we will be deleting it from the system at midnight. Dr. Scott, does that satisfy your curiosity as well?"

Brian nodded readily, more than a little overwhelmed by the money.

"I take it that the rest of you are more at ease now?" the Colonel asked, reviewing his audience.

No one uttered a word.

"Now, on to the next line of business. I'm sure you won't be surprised when I tell you that it is mandatory that you take an oath of secrecy before I go any farther. The security oath required for this level of clearance is on the first page of the materials enclosed in the envelopes before you. Please remove only the first page and sign the form. I'll collect them now."

The team members began opening their envelopes.

"What makes you so sure we're going to sign them?" a striking, auburn-haired woman seated next to Deidre asked, her envelope untouched. Dressed in a double-breasted olive business suit, she was unmistakably the object of Malcolm's earlier comments in the cafeteria. Her classic oval face was surrounded by impeccably bobbed hair, styled off her forehead to reveal an understated widow's peak. The speaker's now-pursed lips had a barely discernible pout, and her green eyes were positively mesmerizing. She wore little makeup; she didn't need it. Malcolm hadn't exaggerated.

"I believe you already know the answer to your question, Dr. Kelley. You have no choice."

The Colonel's bold statement caught the attention of everyone. Expressions of anger and annoyance formed again on the faces of the team members.

"He's right," the woman agreed, turning her attention away from the Colonel's gaze to the others seated at the table. "Unless I miss my guess, the rest of the contents of the envelopes in front of you contain some blackmailing scheme similar to the one handed to me when I was, how do you say, 'recruited' for this patriotic venture." Her voiced dripped with sarcasm, but her look told everyone she wasn't kidding.

The others immediately withdrew the contents of their envelopes and began shuffling through the documents.

"This is unconscionable!" a wiry, bearded man with curly red hair exclaimed. "These are absolute fabrications! I've been here almost a year, so why is this necessary now? What are you trying to do, ruin my career?"

"How many years do you suppose you can live on $100,000?" Malcolm spoke up cynically, scanning the contents of his envelope. "If anyone in my profession ever saw this I'd be completely unemployable."

The mood of the team grew more irate, but the Colonel had yet to make any attempt to intervene. Brian looked up from the pages he had drawn from his envelope. He looked directly at Neil, whose attention had been riveted on his friend as soon as he'd reached for the envelope. There was sorrow in the older man's gaze. His expression pleaded for understanding. Brian held his tongue.

The Colonel finally motioned for quiet. Once it was obtained, he began to speak. "You should all know that the Group has no intention of ever making any of these allegations public. You have our word that, as long as you abide by your oath of secrecy, none of what you've read will ever surface. On the other hand, if you refuse to sign the oath, sabotage the project in any way, divulge any information concerning the project at any time as long as you're alive, these records will be made public."

"How long does it take you guys to dream up this bull and produce the paper trail to legitimize these lies?" the red-haired man growled angrily. "And I still want to know why this wasn't necessary when we began our work. We've worked together before, and I've never had to sign anything like this before!"

"You've also never had this high a security clearance, Dr. Chadwick," the Colonel responded. Brian took immediate note of the man's identity while the officer continued. "The material is, of course, completely untrue. But thanks to the magic of electronic information retrieval and storage, it is a painfully easy thing to, say, fatten your bank account and alter the records of your employer to make it appear as though you have a problem with embezzling, or that you cooked the numbers on the research project that won your company a key government contract, or that you plagiarized in your dissertation—the possibilities really are endless," he explained matter-of-factly.

"Why don't you just kill us when we're done?" Malcolm cracked cynically.

The Colonel gazed intently at the lanky scientist, his lips pursed tightly together. After a few awkward seconds, everyone in the room knew that he wasn't searching for answer. The implication was obvious. Brian couldn't tell if the swallow he heard was his own or someone else's.

"Let's just hope that never becomes necessary."

11

Melissa Kelley marched down the corridor toward her room with a brisk, deliberate gait, still fuming after the morning's exchange. As soon as the Colonel had called a fifteen-minute recess to clear the tension in the room, she'd bolted. She knew it was irrational. She wasn't going to find any refuge. If open defiance was all she had, she'd get the most of it.

She swiped her card and punched in the pass code. *Creep.* She stepped inside the dimly lit room and threw her briefcase on the chair opposite the entrance. Suddenly, a man's powerful hand shot forth from behind the door and covered her mouth with a powerful grip. He quickly wrapped his other arm around her waist, and in one motion, swung her off her feet, carried her into her bedroom, and slammed her face down onto the bed. She struggled to move, but her arms were pinned underneath her body. She was completely immobilized.

"Now, listen very carefully, Dr. Kelley," a voice snarled into her ear. "I'm going to let you go in a moment, but you're going to keep your face to the wall. If you make any effort to make visual contact, I'll put a bullet in your skull."

The man jerked Melissa's head backward, and she felt the cold steel of her assailant's gun press behind her ear. Pain shot through her neck from the awkwardness of the position.

"Do we understand each other?"

She managed a slight nod.

"Good. Now that I've contacted you, my life depends on anonymity, and, as important as you are to my own interests, I won't think twice about killing you to tie up any loose ends."

The man slowly removed his hand from Melissa's mouth, but he kept his gun nestled behind her ear. Her heart pounding, she labored to catch her breath. "I'm going to get up now, doctor. Let's hope you're a woman of your word." Melissa felt his weight lifted from her back.

"That's a good girl," he snickered. She could hear the sound of his weapon being re-holstered. She turned her head toward the wall and recovered her breath; otherwise, she didn't move. "I'm so pleased to see that you really are capable of controlling your temper," he added with an air of disdain. "You left the party in such a hurry."

Melissa's mind raced through the events of barely minutes ago, trying to deduce how her attacker had seen her leave. Had she seen anyone else been in the room before the meeting started?

"I can only guess that since your mouth isn't engaged, you must be trying to figure out who I am," her assailant remarked contemptuously. "We can hear everything. It's called audio surveillance, professor."

"Can I move my arms?" Melissa asked in a subdued voice.

"Is there something wrong with your short-term memory?"

"What do you want then?"

"I'm sorry I gave you the wrong impression. I'm here to chat about what I can do for you."

"And what's that?"

"Advise you ... protect you, perhaps."

"Why am I not breathing a sigh of relief?"

"Be glad you're breathing at all. I could do anything I want to you, doctor. I think you know the feeling."

Melissa felt the rage well up inside her but regained control. "What do you want with me? You don't know anything about me."

"I know all there is to know about you, Dr. Kelley—the things not on your transcripts or your resume. Things like where you went to school before Notre Dame," he droned casually, "what happened there, your family's reaction—wonderful man, your father—your ensuing sexual 'escapades,' if that's the right word for what it is you do. Oh, let me assure you, doctor, I know *everything* about you."

Melissa stiffened at the revelation, a blend of fury and panic coursing through her. "So?" she finally said, trying to conceal her anxiety.

"So *shut up*—at least give me the chance to help you before you shoot off your mouth. By the time your little project has run its course, you'll need a friend. You needn't worry about your reputation here, either. I'm not interested in supplementing your biography for your peers."

"Fine."

"That's better. The reason I know what I know," he continued, "is because, as a member of the Group, I've not only gathered the information on you, but I've taken an interest in your career."

"Why is that?"

"It's about debts, doctor. I do something for you now, you do something for me later—perhaps years later, but you will reciprocate. All you need to know for now is that I have my reasons, and that the Group is divided over the wisdom of your team's project."

"But Colonel Ferguson said ..."

"Don't mind what he says; he's only a mouthpiece. To be more precise, there was considerable consternation over whether outside involvement is wise."

Melissa squirmed uncomfortably.

"Ah-ah, Dr. Kelley."

She heard the button pop on the intruder's holster.

"I can't help it!" she protested.

"Try harder. You wouldn't be nearly as attractive with a hole in your forehead. Besides, I'll detain you only a few minutes longer."

"What a shame."

"You should know, Miss Kelley, that there is someone on your team with, shall we say, divided loyalties."

"What is that supposed to mean?"

"Some might use the word 'traitor,' but 'saboteur' is perhaps more accurate."

"You mean someone on the team wants to ruin the project?"

"Exactly."

"Who is he?"

"Very clever, doctor."

"Come again?"

"Trying to prod me into revealing the gender of the mole so you could narrow the possibilities. I expose your attempt only so that you know you're no match for someone who's played this game hundreds of times. Actually, I have no problem telling you that your infiltrator is male."

"Why don't you just tell me who he is, if you're so concerned about the project?"

"I never said I was concerned about the project, only that I'm here to help you. I'm withholding his identity simply because I haven't figured out yet if he's my adversary or a potential ally. I'll only tell you who it isn't: Dr. Scott is in the clear."

"Why single him out?"

"You forget—I know all about him, too. Of all the people on this team, he'll be the most trustworthy if you run into a problem."

"I thought you were my knight in shining armor."

"I can't be everywhere."

"What a disappointment."

"Perhaps this small token of my affection will comfort you. Be advised that no one must know you have it." The mysterious figure reached into his lapel pocket. He tossed a badge onto the bed near Melissa's head.

"What's that?" she asked, squinting at the object in the faint glow.

"It's an access override card. It will get you into any room in the Facility that doesn't require a palm or retina scan. You don't need to punch in a code, just swipe the card. Use it *only* in an emergency. All the Group members have access to any of the rooms, including, of course, your own and those of your colleagues, so usage would not necessarily engender suspicion. The cards are all the same, so it isn't directly traceable to me. Nevertheless, using it creates the risk that those who monitor security may grow suspicious if one among the Group seems to be too interested in the members of your team."

"I can't see how giving me this information or the card benefits you in any way," Melissa observed. "If I've learned anything about your type, it's that you don't do anything for free."

"You needn't worry about what I'll gain. My motives and rewards are of no concern to you."

"Right."

"One last warning, Dr. Kelley. I'll be taking my leave now. Remain as you are for three minutes. If you open your door in an attempt to identify me, our next meeting will be much shorter, and far less pleasant— and I'll know if you comply when I check the security logs. Is that clear?"

"Crystal."

12

Technological progress is like an axe
in the hands of a pathological criminal.

—*Albert Einstein*

Despite the unpleasantries of the morning, Brian was eager to get back to business. He could understand the resentment expressed by others, but his curiosity had overruled his own umbrage at the way the oaths were handled.

"We have quite a team for this project," Dr. Bandstra said, addressing his audience. "I'll make this brief, though, since we have a lot of ground to cover. Please acknowledge your presence to the rest of the team when I reach your name.

"First we have Dr. Malcolm Bradley. Malcolm earned his masters and doctoral degrees in pathobiology from the University of North Carolina and was hired as a full-time researcher at MIT upon the completion of his graduate education five years ago."

"Seated on my right," Neil continued, turning his attention to the bearded, red-haired scientist, "is Dr. Mark Chadwick. Mark is one of the nation's authorities on bovine biochemistry, having earned both a PhD and doctorate in veterinary medicine from Montana State University six years ago. He has been the recipient of several National Science Foundation grants, and has assisted the FDA on a number of studies associated with bovine hormonal stimulation, reproduction, and pathology."

Brian listened intently as Neil continued to read the abbreviated resumes of the panel assembled in the room. In addition to the gregarious Malcolm and Chadwick, the third scientific specialist on the team was Kevin Garvey, a Harvard graduate in epidemiology employed by the CDC. Among the non-scientists there was Deidre Harper, whom no one would have any trouble remembering. She was the team's only foreign doctorate, having recently received her PhD from the University of Edinburgh in psychology for her work on group hysteria. She'd also been heavily involved in antiwar demonstrations during the Gulf War and a host of other activist causes.

Brian could not help being struck by the apparent lack of a common denominator among all these disciplines, not only as they stood in relation to each other, but also in relation to his own field. It was positively mystifying. If the others were not thinking along the same lines by now, they surely would be once Neil got to him. His thoughts were interrupted by Dr. Bandstra's recognition of the stunning and outspoken Dr. Kelley.

"Seated to my left," Neil motioned as he flipped a page, "is Dr. Melissa Kelley. Melissa's bachelor's degree is from the University of Notre Dame and included double majors in religion and history. She moved on to the University of Pennsylvania, where she earned her PhD in American studies with an emphasis on American religious history. Her dissertation was on apocalyptic religious beliefs among militia groups in the United States, but her specialty includes apocalyptic beliefs of American religious groups in the nineteenth and twentieth centuries. She recently authored a book on this subject.

"To Dr. Garvey's left is Father Andrew Benedict. Father Benedict was at Loyola University in Chicago, intending to go into physics. About half way through his MA program, however, he felt called to enter the priesthood. He finished his master's degree, then joined the Jesuits. Shortly after taking his vows and receiving ordination, Father Benedict was sent to Rome to study at the Pontifical Biblical Institute. While there he earned a master's degree in intertestamental studies and then completed a PhD in canon law. More recently, he has been active in the Diocese of Tucson, Arizona, and as an adjunct professor of religion at the University of Arizona."

"Lastly, and to the Father's left, we have Dr. Brian Scott." Neil said, putting down his papers and fixing his attention on his friend. "Brian is a creative young scholar, whose career I have followed since we met at Johns Hopkins University twelve years ago. Brian earned his bachelor's degree in Near Eastern studies, where he excelled in Biblical Hebrew and in the primary languages of the ancient Near East, such as Akkadian cuneiform, Egyptian hieroglyphs, Aramaic, and Sumerian. His academic record at Hopkins earned him a Century Fellowship at the University of Chicago's Oriental Institute, from which he earned his MA and PhD in the study of the Hebrew Bible in its ancient Near Eastern context. Brian is proficient in the translation of a dozen ancient languages and has authored several peer-reviewed articles on Semitic grammar, archaeology, and Old Testament interpretation. He's also a man whose friendship I would never want to lose, and one of the few people whom I can honestly say changed my own life."

Brian felt a twinge of embarrassment at the introduction, but he nodded appreciatively at his friend.

"Thank you, Neil," the Colonel said, taking the floor. "It's time we got down to business. Ready, Kevin?"

Kevin Garvey sat quietly in his chair, leaning forward, his arms resting on the top of the table. He made no effort to answer the Colonel, by word or action. By all appearances he was meek to begin with. Kevin's diminutive build, stooped shoulders, and impish mouth gave Brian the distinct impression that, although certainly brilliant, here was a man who had spent more time being seen than heard. Even during the heated exchange over their security oaths, Kevin had barely spoken. But his pensive expression conveyed more than preoccupation or shyness. Garvey looked scared.

"Kevin?" Neil broke the silence.

"I know this isn't going to make any difference," the scientist finally spoke, picking his words carefully and with pronounced deliberation, "but I'd like it stated for the record that I think this is a bad idea."

"We've had this discussion before, and the decision has been made," the Colonel answered grimly. Brian could tell he didn't like being second-guessed.

"Bringing scientific neophytes into this is something we're going to regret," he continued, looking around the table. "This is life altering."

"The Group is confident that they're right for the job."

Dr. Garvey tempered his response, as if resigned to his fate. "I guess this is where we find out if that means anything."

13

The significant problems we face cannot be solved at the same level of thinking we were at when we created them.

—*Albert Einstein*

Dr. Garvey looked apprehensively around the table. Brian could feel his heart pounding. Suspicious expressions formed on the faces of several team members. "You win, Colonel ... as usual," he sighed.

"As you know," he continued, "I'm an epidemiologist—a scientist who specializes in the study of public health, particularly crisis health issues. That's what this is about ... at least my contribution, anyway. The fact is that the U.S. military brought me here nearly a year ago to form an action plan that will help us save our population from an unstoppable threat to our food supply and economic viability. It might be useful to think of it as another plague."

"What sort of plague?" asked Deidre, a hint of anxiety in her voice.

"I assume you've all heard of mad cow disease, bovine spongiform encephalopathy, or BSE?"

Everyone nodded.

"How about its human equivalent, Creutzfeldt-Jakob disease, or CJD?"

The response was the same.

"According to what the public has been told, there have only been a handful of cases of cows infected with BSE in this country. That's disinformation. What if I told you that we have data that suggest roughly half the cattle population in this country were infected?"

"No way," Melissa replied.

"Dr. Kelley," the Colonel interrupted, his eyebrows raised as though scolding a child, "I can assure you that the data is real."

"Well, excuse my ignorance, or maybe my lack of gullibility, *sir*, but I've read about every wacko conspiracy that's ever come down the pike.

I just don't believe something like this would go unreported. Someone would blow the whistle."

"People can't report what they don't know," the officer said coolly. "Our data is the property of the Department of Defense. We don't give it away. Furthermore, since the government is the entity that grants ninety percent of the money used by science, we can deflect private sector scientists from what we don't want studied—or threaten to pull their funding if they get too nosy."

"I know what CJD does to people," Deidre fumed. "So you stood in the way of saving people and their families from years of dementia and misery? I can only hope the fatherland was made more secure."

"Frankly, Dr. Harper," the Colonel answered, unfazed by her sarcasm, "what you think of our actions is of no consequence. What you imagine to be a logical course of action just isn't that simple. There's so much you don't yet know."

"Well, let's start with how we know any of this," Brian spoke up. "I'm betting Mark can shed some light on that."

The comment drew quizzical stares from everyone in the room. Only the Colonel appeared unsurprised.

"So, Dr. Scott, I see that your little excursion on the Internet last evening wasn't time wasted."

"I'm guessing it wasn't," Brian replied. Despite being told about the monitored computer use, Brian still couldn't help feeling spied upon.

"I hope you were able to follow Dr. Chadwick's article. Mark, why don't you satisfy Dr. Scott's curiosity."

"The data Kevin is referring to," Mark began, stroking his beard, "is based on three decades of research, the last ten of which I was a participant. Examinations of tissue, blood, and organ samples from cattle confirm the extent and transmission of BSE."

"Could someone translate that?" Father Benedict wondered aloud.

"Sorry. The military has been covertly tracking the progress of BSE and its human equivalents. Our primary data come from what our government would publicly call ... well ... violent animal slayings of indeterminate causation."

"Come again?" Melissa queried impatiently.

"Cattle mutilations," Brian answered, rolling his eyes. "Cattle mutilations."

Melissa glowered at Brian. He knew instantly she'd taken the unconscious gesture as an insult. He could almost feel her glare cut through him.

Melissa turned toward Mark incredulously. "You can't be serious."

"I most certainly am."

"What do butchered cows have to do with this plague Dr. Garvey seems to think is around the corner?"

"I'll say it again," Kevin interrupted. "This is a bad idea."

"Kevin, they've all been psychologically profiled," Neil reminded him.

"Profiled for *what?*" Melissa inquired in a concerned tone.

"For what?" Kevin repeated her words to himself, just loud enough to be heard. He looked at her with an uneasy smirk. "Only the end of the world as you know it."

14

"I wonder if this was really a good idea," Brian asked in jest, pulling his chair in at the small table for two. Father Benedict gave him an uncertain look as he seated himself.

"You know," Brian smiled, "whether it was best to dismiss us for lunch before or after we'd heard the cattle mutilation stuff. Somebody might lose theirs if they really get into the details."

"I'm sure the Colonel was only buying time to get all his materials together. I have to confess I have another matter on my mind."

"Well, if it's more interesting than this, I hope you can talk about it."

"Indeed," the old priest said softly, an eyebrow raised as he made eye contact with Brian. He quickly touched his forefinger lightly to his lips, beckoning for silence. To his young friend's bewilderment, Father Benedict proceeded to relocate the salt and pepper shakers and the napkin holder from their table to one across the room. He surveyed those present in the cafeteria. The only other team members in the room were Deidre and Melissa.

"Is there something wrong?" Brian whispered after he returned to his seat.

"No," he answered, "just a precaution."

"You think someone's going to be listening to us? Come on, Andrew."

Again, the priest let the younger man's question go unanswered. He proceeded to run his hands over the undersurface of the table, like a child looking for the piece of gum he'd stuck there earlier.

"I'll say grace, if you don't mind," he added, as though he'd done nothing out of the ordinary.

"Go right ahead," Brian answered, somewhat embarrassed by the priest's odd behavior. The two of them bowed their heads as Father Andrew crossed himself and prayed for God's blessing. The priest had hardly finished praying when he reached across the table and touched Brian's hand.

"Brian, you must understand that I believe the task that lies ahead of us is one of the utmost seriousness."

"Well, I would guess so, given the environment and how we got here." Brian crumbled some crackers into his soup. "But we haven't really learned anything about the project yet. You know something I don't?"

"Not specifically, but ..." Father Benedict paused as a uniformed officer passed by the table on the way to the exit. Brian watched the priest's eyes follow the man until he was clearly on his way down the hall.

"Andrew, what's the reason for all this ... paranoia? Should I check my burger for a wire?"

The priest sidestepped the question. "I can't help wondering why God brought me here at this precise time, to this precise place. Do you recall from the introductions what I was doing right before I came here?"

"I remember something about the University of Arizona."

"Right. More specifically, I was sent there for two reasons, one of which I knew before I went—evaluating the work of a certain Catholic astronomy professor—but the other was set before me by God a few months after I arrived."

"Astronomy? Anything in that area is way over my head. But what does that have to do with where we're at now?"

"I'm not sure, but I know there's some relationship—and what I was looking into would not be over your head. I always try to see God's hand—especially in unusual circumstances like this. I'm surprised you haven't wondered why He's brought you here, what, with your background and your article."

"Oh, yeah, my infamous article." Brian shook his head wistfully. "I can't imagine any relationship to that lost cause, unless the military is going to start providing jobs for unemployed biblical scholars."

"I'm curious," Father Benedict said as he wiped his mouth, "what exactly offended your detractors that motivated them to get rid of you?"

"Probably the whole premise of the article itself."

"Perhaps ... those in your neck of the theological woods are likely not ready for such a subject. Too suspicious ... and, I daresay, too much absorbed with the idea that everything that's real must be mentioned somewhere in the Bible."

"Yeah," Brian sighed. "That attitude really irks me when I think about it."

"Don't lose heart," the priest continued, his expression softening. "You have much to contribute. You are *not* here by accident. God is up to something."

Brian looked at Andrew's wizened face, now adorned with a faint but sly grin.

"Brian," he whispered, "my Order sent me to Tucson just under a year ago. Do you have any idea what's in Tucson that might link the Vatican and the U.S. military?"

"Not really."

"The Steward Observatory at the University of Arizona."

"I don't understand."

"The Steward Observatory is host to VORG—the Vatican Observatory Research Group. It's the stateside headquarters of the Vatican Observatory."

"The Vatican Observatory? Since when does the Vatican have an interest in astronomy?"

"Since 1582, to be exact."

"You're kidding."

"Not at all. Pope Gregory XIII commissioned a committee to study astronomical data as part of the reform of the calendar in that year. Did you realize that it was a Jesuit who first classified the stars according to their spectra?"

"No. That's really remarkable."

"Indeed. Credit for that achievement goes to Father Angelo Secchi. Pope Leo XIII founded what we know today as the Vatican Observatory in 1891. The observatory was housed near St. Peter's, at first, and then moved to its present location at the Papal Summer Residence at Castel Gandolfo, about thirty miles southeast of Rome. The library at Castel Gandolfo contains more than twenty thousand volumes, including the works of Copernicus, Galileo, Newton, and Kepler. A second research center, VORG, was founded in 1981. Twelve years later construction of the Vatican Advanced Technology Telescope, VATT for short, was completed at Mount Graham in Arizona. It's arguably the best astronomical site in the United States."

"This is sure a far cry from putting Galileo under house arrest."

"Yes, it is. Actually, another of the reasons for the observatory's original founding was to counteract the notion that the Church was opposed to astronomy."

"So what was the point of having you evaluate someone's work in astronomy?"

"I wasn't really evaluating his astronomy—heavens, I don't know much about that field. I was eager for the task for apologetic purposes. I was sent to evaluate his research in a related area. My charge, an astronomy professor, has become a strong advocate for panspermia."

"What's that?"

"Panspermia is the idea that life—all life, mind you—sprang up on earth due to biological seeding from space. There are two variations of it. The most common position is that this process is random and undirected, purely natural."

"Is this related to the Mars rocks—the ones that caused the big stir a few years ago that were supposed to have microbial life on them?"

"Yes. Since undirected panspermia is often described as something like cosmic dandelion seeds getting blown to a lifeless, primeval earth, some scientists were—and still are—thinking of the meteor as an example of foreign space material that somehow arrived to earth carrying life."

Brian dipped a french fry into the ketchup on his plate. "Well, if that idea were correct, it would mean that everything, including humankind, evolved from this space material. I can see how that would provide a mechanism for kick-starting evolution, but that would only bother traditional creationists. Christian scholars and scientists who accept evolution wouldn't see it as much of an issue."

"True, but that isn't what I'm dealing with—or what we're dealing with here."

"So what was this guy teaching?" Brian asked, wondering what the priest was angling toward.

"Brian," the priest said in a low, ominous tone, "you have to understand that there is a potent, tireless evil lurking in the Church—in my own Order, mind you—a force of superlative and uncompromising malevolence. I don't know about Protestantism, but it's likely the case there as well."

"What do you mean?"

"I don't know how, and I have no facts for you. We have yet to discern the *real* reason we're both here—especially you. This project will ultimately lead to your article and your dissertation, and then beyond. *I feel it in my bones.*"

Brian couldn't help notice that Father Benedict's hands trembled as he spoke. The fear in the old man's eyes was apparent, but controlled.

Brian didn't know how to respond, save to place his own hand lightly upon the priest's lean arm.

Father Benedict exhaled heavily and peered down at his plate. "I'm sorry," he whispered after few moments.

"It's not a sin to be afraid, Andrew."

"I know, but it's essential I maintain my wits."

"I only wish I knew what you were so afraid—" He paused, remembering something. "Wait a minute. The other version of panspermia ... what is it?"

"The sum of all theological fears," Father Benedict intoned soberly. Brian watched Andrew's expression closely as the priest distractedly swirled the coffee around in his cup.

"Ask yourself for a moment, Brian: Why would the Church build one of the world's most powerful telescopes?"

"I don't know. What could they be looking for? I don't see how that relates to us, though." Brian tried to hide his frustration. The conversation seemed to be proceeding from one non sequitur to another. His article and dissertation were useless here.

"*That*, my young scholar, is the question to keep running through your mind during these proceedings. For now, I can only tell you there are others asking the same question, and that it has something to do with astral prophecy—astrology of a sort."

"Astrology? Why is the Church interested in astrology?"

"I'm not talking about horoscopes, and don't look so startled, Brian. Faithful rabbis and early Christians used to be heavily involved in this sort of thing. Very few people, except for Gnostics nowadays, bother with the subject—how we might take Jesus' words about the signs in the sky literally. I asked a friend at Castel Gandolfo to look into some things for me, but I haven't heard from him in days. It's most troubling."

"Well—" Brian stopped in mid-sentence. "We have company, Father."

Father Benedict turned around in his chair. Melissa was headed for their table with a noticeably deliberate gait.

"I wonder what she wants," Brian mused, glancing briefly at her toned legs and shapely form. "She looks like she's on a mission."

"I'm sure she is," the priest said, returning to the remainder of his lunch. "I hope you're ready."

"Hi," Brian greeted Melissa as she approached them.

"Skip it," she snapped.

"What's the problem?" Father Benedict intervened, trying to ease the tension that had already surfaced.

"I wanted to tell my colleague here that I didn't appreciate his condescending attitude toward me this morning," she tore into Brian. "You'll learn pretty soon that I don't take any crap—especially from men who think the phrase 'female scholar' is an oxymoron. You looked at me today like I didn't have a brain in my head, and if it happens again, I'll make a spectacle of you that no one here will forget. Just who do you think you are?"

Brian sat dumbfounded by the tirade directed at him. He gave Father Benedict an embarrassed look, but he could tell the priest had bowed out of the confrontation.

"Well? Don't you have anything to say? You're not so quick when you don't have the upper hand, are you?"

Brian glanced down at the table for a moment, then looked Melissa in the eye. "You're right."

"What?" she asked, surprised by the swift surrender.

"I said you're right. I didn't mean anything by my expression, but this has happened before. I should be more conscious of it. I'm sorry. It won't happen again."

Melissa's flashing green eyes probed him suspiciously, trying to discern his motives. "Do you really think you can dismiss this whole thing that easily?"

"I don't know," Brian said, unsure of where the conversation was going. "I guess I could apologize to the team when we meet again this afternoon. Would that help?"

"Yeah, but then I want you to roll over and play dead."

Brian could feel his anger rising, but he caught himself by recognizing that she was trying to push his buttons. "Melissa—"

"*Dr. Kelley.*"

"Okay ... Dr. Kelley, are you going to accept my apology or not? Whether it ends the matter or not, my response isn't going to change. You're right."

"I feel so relieved," she mocked. "I know your type. Somehow you'll manage to get people to sympathize with your side. Just stay out of my way!"

Without waiting for another response, she whirled about and headed back to her table. Brian's disbelieving gaze followed her across the room.

"Boy, is she a piece of work," Brian said when he was certain she was out of earshot.

"She's much more than that, Brian," the priest said, becoming serious once more. "I don't know her past, but my experience tells me she must have been tragically hurt in some way. I've seen few people get so nasty in such a situation. She's a very bitter woman. It's a shame really; she's much too young to hold such resentment."

"What in the world could have made her so miserable?"

"I don't know. Just remember, God loves her—no less than you or myself."

The priest's words pierced Brian's heart. He'd been swept away by the events of the past few hours, thinking only of his own circumstances.

"You're right, Andrew." Brian reached for his iced tea. He tipped the glass to take a sip, but the unexpected eruption of an incredibly shrill security alarm made his whole body jump, dumping the cold drink onto his chest.

"What's going on?" he yelled above the intermittent siren that flashed and screamed just behind him. The volume was deafening.

"I don't know!" Andrew shouted back. "But don't move—remember the security rules!"

Brian nodded.

Suddenly the two of them heard an even louder, solitary crack pierce the air. Andrew's face was drawn with concern. He grabbed Brian's arm and motioned for him to get down. They peered anxiously at the hallway, visible from the cafeteria's only entryway. Both of them gasped as they saw the upper arm and head of a man suddenly hit the floor just outside the entrance. Incredibly, the man struggled to his knees and began to crawl into the cafeteria. Brian could see a thin stream of blood pouring from his chest. The man wore an Army T-shirt, now soaked with blood, and military fatigues. He collapsed on his back after crawling only a few agonizing feet.

Without warning, Father Benedict scrambled out from under the table to the motionless figure. The priest looked into his eyes. The dying man tried to speak, but coughed up blood.

"Be still," the priest mouthed calmly, and he cradled the man's head in his lap. He quickly began the last rites.

The man cleared his throat with a burst of unanticipated energy. Blood spattered on Father Benedict's neck and collar. The priest could faintly hear shouts and footsteps above the din of the repeating alarm. He watched the man's bloody lips moving and lowered his head to his mouth.

"Gott ..." the man gasped with as much force as he could.

"Yes?" Andrew coaxed, straining to hear.

"... lieb—" he gasped, and then he expired in the priest's arms.

15

In our obsession with antagonisms of the moment,
we often forget how much unites all the members of humanity.
Perhaps we need some outside, universal threat to make us
recognize this common bond. I occasionally think how quickly
our differences worldwide would vanish if we were
facing an alien threat from outside this world.

—*Ronald Reagan,*
September 1987 address to the United Nations

The silent, grim-faced figure swiped his card through the reader at a knobless door and mechanically punched an extended access code into the keypad mounted on the wall. The door slid open, then closed tightly behind him. He strode deliberately toward a flight of stairs and descended quickly. Another lengthy hallway greeted him at the bottom, and he continued with the deliberate gait of one who'd made this journey many times.

The next door bore no card reader, only a small, dark, glass rectangle on the adjacent wall five and a half feet from the ground. A large, bulletproof pane of glass provided two Marine MP's—one standing sentry on the other side of the door, the other seated behind a console—a clear view of his approach. Their eyes never left the object of their scrutiny, who, upon reaching the door, stood motionless, his face positioned directly in front of the rectangular object. The retina scan took only a few seconds, and, identity confirmed, the door's electronic lock released with a loud click.

The two MP's saluted Colonel Ferguson as he entered, signed in, opened yet another door, and then disappeared into a carpeted foyer. He advanced to the lone door on the wall opposite where he stood, inserted a key, and turned the knob. He closed the door behind him and looked carefully into the room, squinting in the dim lighting. The veteran officer straightened his uniform, removed his hat, and stood before the twelve seated men.

"Good afternoon, Vernon," a tranquil, yet authoritative, voice reso-nated from the chair situated at the middle of a long, rectangular table. "We've been expecting you."

"Of course."

"Today's events were of great interest."

"I imagine they were, General."

"Today's events," a third voice interrupted from the shadows, "demonstrated that we have the wrong man leading this program."

The Colonel stiffened with anger, but he held his tongue.

"Oh please, Lieutenant," the General acknowledged with an annoyed tone. "Spare us a repetition of your concerns. That soldier's actions were beyond the ability of anyone in this room to foresee. Vernon can-not be blamed."

"That soldier was one of *his* men," the Lieutenant sneered. "If the Colonel's screening failed here, what else can we expect—especially from outsiders?"

"There was a time," the General responded, "when you were an out-sider. You wouldn't be part of the Group now if several who are now senior members had not defended you."

"The fact remains, gentlemen," the Colonel reentered the discussion, "that we are still on track. Nothing was lost by today's unfortunate mis-hap. I'll of course offer an explanation to the team tomorrow morning. Of course, no one will be able to investigate it, but that would be no concern anyway. It will be completely coherent."

"We're *not* on track," the Lieutenant protested. "We've lost the better part of a day now that you've postponed the briefing until tomorrow morning. Your part of this may not suffer, but need I remind you that there are other aspects to the program that are far more time sensitive?"

"If anything," the Colonel replied with an air of confidence, "this incident will be a convenient tool for compelling their belief. Once they know what they'll be working on, they'll understand how people can snap."

"They *must* believe, Vernon," the General said, his voice noticeably less cordial.

"And they will."

"Remember, Vernon, all means necessary toward accomplishing our goal must be utilized."

"Do I understand you correctly, sir?"

"Adam is at your disposal if necessary."

The Colonel nodded.

16

There is a lurking fear that some things are not meant
to be known, that some inquiries are too dangerous for
human beings to make.

—*Carl Sagan*

"If you don't mind my saying so," Brian leaned over and whispered to Andrew, "you don't look quite ready for this. Couldn't sleep last night?"

The priest shrugged as he watched Colonel Ferguson boot up his laptop for the morning's briefing. No one on the team had forgotten the disclosure of only a day ago about the cattle mutilations, nor had the anticipation waned for learning what that had to do with why they were at this yet unknown location. The shooting had shaken everyone, though—even those who had not witnessed the gruesome spectacle.

"I just can't make sense of it," Father Benedict whispered. "Why would a dying man I've never seen before tell me 'God loves' with his last breath—*in German?*"

"You're a priest; he was dying. It may have been all his mind had left."

"But German? He was an American soldier. It makes no sense."

"Is that why you didn't tell the Colonel?"

"I don't trust anyone here except you. You'd be wise to take the same point of view."

The two of them cut short their conversation as the Colonel cleared his throat to bring everyone to attention. On the table in front of the podium behind which the Colonel was standing sat a stack of manila folders, each about a half-inch thick.

"Good morning. Let me apologize again for the events of yesterday," he began in a serious tone. "The victim was one of my own ... as was the man *he* killed only moments before his own death."

This new revelation made several of the team members squirm uncomfortably in their seats. Father Benedict sat motionless, his eyes squinting in concentration.

"He'd been back from Afghanistan only a few months, the only survivor of his unit after an ambush. One of the men he was working with said something ... unflattering ... about one of his buddies who'd been killed, and he just, well, started shooting. After he realized he'd killed someone, he tried to run. The MPs were alerted, and you know the rest. We can't plan for everything, it seems, even though I'd like to think so. Tragedies happen, even here."

"We're all sorry for your loss, Colonel," Father Benedict offered.

"Thank you, Father. We just have to press on. I don't want it to sound callous, but we have more important things to think about. I think after this morning, you'll all agree."

The Colonel dimmed the lights from the console at which he was standing. "I'm sure you're all wondering how cattle mutilations relate to BSE and why it's as serious a problem as we've asserted. We'll get to that in a moment. For now, just so everyone gets up to speed, we need to cover the mutilation phenomenon. I hope none of you is very squeamish. If that's the case, do the best you can to follow; I really can't excuse anyone. Please pay close attention—especially to what's removed from a typical specimen."

The Colonel handed the remote to Mark Chadwick, who took over the discussion.

"Mutilations are most common in states whose economies are geared toward the dairy and beef industries—states like Wyoming, Colorado, and Montana. They have, however, been discovered all over the globe. The typical mutilation has several characteristics. The dead animal is found totally or nearly totally drained of blood, but with a complete absence of blood found anywhere on the ground around the body. You'll notice from the slide that various incisions are always found on the corpse as well.

"In some cases, body parts like the nose, lips, and tongue are removed. Sometimes one eye and several teats are also missing. But in nearly every case, the rectum and vagina are *cored out*. Here's a good close-up."

The next slide appeared, drawing gasps from several team members. The photo showed a very deep hole in what used to be the heifer's rectum. Incredibly, the hole was perfectly circular and smooth, as though created with some kind of unthreaded, hollow drill. There was no sign of tearing anywhere around or in the wound.

"Mother of God, who would do something like that?" Father Benedict said, staring at the slide.

"Some mutilations are performed by cults for use in satanic rituals," interrupted Melissa. "The sexual organs are the most desirable for those purposes. The rest have been attributed to animal attacks."

"Those are nice theories, Dr. Kelley," Mark responded, "but they're little more than desperate explanations. Does the picture on the screen look like an animal attack? Where are the teeth marks?" He clicked to the next slide, a close-up of the hairs at the edge of the rectal core. "These cuts are made with surgical precision. There's no gnawing such as would be indicative of a predator—not even tracks leading to or away from the body. Many cases have bones so clearly bisected that there is no visible bone fragmentation, even under magnification, and where internal organs or structures have been removed, no surrounding musculature was disturbed. What you're looking at gives every indication of extremely rapid, efficient, and precise cutting."

"I could produce hundreds of pages from licensed veterinarians and other professionals that would testify to animal attacks," Melissa countered. "I've been down this road before."

"No doubt you could produce such research," Mark acknowledged. "If you're interested, the next time you look into the subject, let me know if you find my name on any of those reports. I've issued several that reached the same conclusion, only I lied."

Melissa wasn't the only one surprised by the admission. Mark's scientific colleagues appeared especially startled.

Mark shrugged. "It was my job. I was hired by the military to both participate in the cattle experimentation program and to provide alternative explanations for what was going on. The cult and predator explanations were understandable to the general public, and convenient."

"Did you say you were hired to *participate?*" Deidre asked in disbelief. "There was some government program to go around and slaughter cattle?"

"So you just lied?" Malcolm burst forth in a contemptuous tone before Mark could respond to Deidre's question. "What kind of scientist lies to the public?"

"A very good one," said the Colonel in Mark's defense. "I know Mark can speak for himself, but I see nothing wrong with the approach we took. The public interest was our primary concern."

"Of course—the military always takes the moral high road," quipped Deidre.

"To answer your question, Dr. Harper," Mark replied, visibly annoyed, "yes, I was hired to do this kind of work. That's why I know it wasn't animals or cultists. I know how it sounds, but this is serious businesses, and I'm proud of my work."

"The reason this kind of work was necessary," the Colonel interjected, "was because we had to have a means to study BSE in cattle and track its geographical progression without public knowledge. We couldn't do that by raising our own herds and quarantining them. We had to know if it was spreading through the normal course of herd life, butchering, transport, and so forth. We had to maintain secrecy because if it became known that these kinds of diseases were running unchecked through the nation's food supply, it would have led to panic. We assumed you wouldn't believe much of this at first, so we prepared some proof."

The Colonel left his seat and distributed the manila folders around the meeting table. "What you have here is the record of our involvement in these mutilations and a couple dozen photocopied articles that prove that BSE is the root problem behind the nine thousand percent increase in Alzheimer's disease since 1979. As we've told you, we've been conducting a covert scientific study on this issue for decades. All this will become public soon, and we're trying to control that process so we can minimize the crisis. Everything you'll hear today has been peer reviewed and is a matter of utmost seriousness."

The Colonel sat down and motioned for Mark to continue.

"Bovine spongiform encephalopathy, or BSE, refers to a brain disease in cattle where the brain is riddled with tiny holes that give it a spongy appearance. The disease makes cattle behave in bizarre ways—hence, the public knows it as mad cow disease. The disease is caused by unconventional pathogens called prions, which are infectious proteins. Because of their unique molecular structure, prions are practically invincible. They can even survive incineration."

"How do cows get this disease?" asked Brian.

"Most likely by eating diseased sheep infected with the sheep version of BSE."

"Since when do cows eat sheep?"

"Since sheep are ground up into the meal that's sold to sheep farmers for their herds. It's been going on for decades—still is, in fact. And that's one of the problems."

"Wonderful."

"In humans, prions can cause Creutzfeldt-Jakob disease, CJD for short, which is a human spongiform encephalopathy. The disease is fatal, and death is preceded by severe dementia. CJD has been known for decades—well before anyone ever heard of mad cow. Some cases of

CJD seem to have genetic contributing factors, but other cases occur spontaneously in about one in a million people every year. Those cases are referred to as sporadic CJD. There's a new form of CJD that differs from the sporadic CJD. The scientific community has known for some time now that this new form—called variant CJD—is caused by eating beef from cows infected with mad cow disease. The mad cow scare in Britain made that clear."

"So what's the big secret?" wondered Melissa.

"Each form of CJD has identifiable traits under the microscope, so to speak. The public has been told its food supply is safe since there have only been a couple confirmed cases of variant CJD in the United States. What the public hasn't been told is that BSE prions can produce a molecular signature in infected humans that is *indistinguishable* from sporadic CJD. The point to all this is that what doctors think is sporadic CJD may not be. It may actually be variant CJD caused by eating infected beef—or venison, pork, or veal."

"But if sporadic CJD is so rare," Melissa asked, "and it's partly genetic, wouldn't these mirror infections just cause the statistics to spike? Doctors would know something is going on when a one-in-a-million disease starts showing up in one out of ten people."

"You're absolutely correct," said Mark. "But there's no spike to sound the alarm."

"Why not?"

"Because the excess cases have been misdiagnosed as Alzheimer's disease—which, of course, has gone through the roof. And we know that Alzheimer's disease can actually be a misdiagnosis for variant CJD. Studies at Yale and the University of Pennsylvania where autopsies were performed on victims of Alzheimer's found that a significant percentage of the victims actually had CJD."

"You should also realize," Kevin broke in, "that CJD is not an officially notifiable disease in the U.S. The CDC does not actively monitor for it. Autopsy rates in the U.S. have dropped from fifty percent in the 1960s to less than ten percent right now. Neither CJD nor the possibility of misdiagnosed Alzheimer's is properly surveiled. And since the usual incubation period is decades long, we won't know the real death toll for years to come."

"To play the devil's advocate for a moment," said Brian, "so what if I have these prions in me? If the incubation period is, say, thirty years, by the time I start losing my mind, it'll be my time to go anyway. Where's the crisis?"

"In the last five years, five people under the age of thirty have died of CJD," answered Mark. "In the twenty years previous to that, only one person under thirty died. That's a huge increase in terms of annual percentage, and it will only get worse."

"Surely the government is doing something about this," said Father Benedict.

"Only if you count nothing as something. Freedom of Information documents show that in 1991 the government considered taking pre-cautionary measures to do the kind of monitoring we've been talking about. They decided against it because the cost to the livestock industry would be too much"

"It's always about the money, isn't it?" said Deidre.

"That it is," agreed Neil. "A handful of scientists know all this, but the public doesn't. Even more importantly, the public has no idea as to the extent. That's where we come in. Our guess is that the majority of the nation's meat supply—beef, pork, veal, and venison, to be exact—is already infected. That's just the start. Once you factor in the dairy industry going belly up, along with all the residual industries that extend from the meat and dairy trade, millions of people will be out of work.

"Naturally, that will cause the already overstressed government relief programs to implode. Then wait till the insurance companies won't want to cover CJD-related illnesses, or people try to sue any government agency remotely connected to the problem. After that we can talk about the country losing hundreds of millions of export dollars and the job losses resulting from that collapse. I hope you're all getting the picture ... and that isn't the worst of it."

"Our monitoring program began in the mid-1970s in Colorado," the Colonel said, taking control of the discussion. "As the material in your folders will demonstrate, northeast Colorado was cattle-mutilation central back then. In just two counties we killed over two hundred head between 1975 and 1977. It isn't a coincidence that the same region would later be identified as the epicenter of BSE cases."

"But how do you do it?" Brian asked. "I've read a little about the typical mutilation, and Mark's description was familiar. No blood, no footprints—how is it done?"

"Excellent question," said the Colonel. "I think Mark was just getting to that."

"Right," Mark agreed. "Basically, we employ standard wildlife sampling techniques. For example, we use helicopters to get to the cattle—though ours were black and unmarked, and we typically worked at night, but not always. We were obviously trying to minimize the risk of detection and identification."

"Well, that's consistent," commented Melissa. "There are hundreds of anecdotal reports about black helicopters in the vicinity of an abduction. The only thing missing is the aliens."

Melissa's remark drew some chuckles, but the Colonel and Neil were noticeably not amused.

"The reason there is no blood at the discovery site is easy to explain," Mark resumed. "We capture a specimen by tranquilizing or euthanizing it first, hoist it on board the chopper, remove the blood and whatever else we want while on board, and then drop the specimen off a few miles away. When it's discovered, there are naturally no footprints, tire tracks, or blood. We try to use chemicals that are difficult to trace for the capture as well. Sometimes we were careless. I showed up to 'investigate' a couple cases where I could see abrasions caused by our hoists, needle marks, that sort of thing. A couple times I've seen the cow's legs were broken as a result of our drop-off. Once we even forgot a needle used for exsanguinations, but usually it was a flawless procedure."

"I've read that other animals don't go near mutilations. Is that true?" asked Brian.

"Yes, and the reason for that is the unnatural odor of the formaldehyde we use. Formaldehyde prevents scavenging, which was important to limit the spread of any prion-infected specimen."

"Why the weird cutting?" asked Deidre. "I mean, why tunnel out the rectum and take the sexual organs? It's kind of sick if you ask me."

"It's also necessary for our research. Beginning in the 1980s, researchers in the private sector discovered something we already knew: that aside from the brain, abnormal prions tend to concentrate in the mouth, esophagus, and large intestine—hence the coring of the rectum and removal of the lips and tongue. The reproductive organs are important for detecting the likelihood of passing the prions on through offspring. We often took eyes because prions are known to accumulate in the lens. Believe it or not, that's very common with human CJD. There are cases where human CJD was passed on by corneal implants."

"Speaking of eyes, Mark," said the Colonel, "show them the next slide."

"I think we're at the end."

"Actually, we're not," the Colonel informed him. "I've added a couple of slides since you last gave this presentation."

Mark hesitated, unsure what to make of the Colonel's comment.

He squeezed the remote.

"Whoa ... what would do that?" asked Brian. "The heifer's eye is powder blue."

"Radiation," answered Mark, eyeing the slide curiously, "and a high level at that. I don't think this is one of my specimens," he added, glancing at the Colonel.

"Keep going, Mark; there's another one."

Mark advanced to the next slide.

"Pardon the pun, people," said Malcolm, "but holy cow—what's that *thing?*"

The team members gazed in startled fascination at the macabre sight before their eyes. A close-up photograph of the inside of the chest cavity of a dead cow showed a bulbous beige-colored blob, covered with whitish specs and globules. There was no blood, but the blob appeared to have a moist covering. Mark stared slack-jawed at the picture.

"That," explained the Colonel, "is the specimen's heart ... or what used to be its heart. This picture is from a 1998 case in north-eastern Utah."

"What do you mean 'used to be its heart'?" asked Father Benedict.

"The heart is completely shredded; it's basically the consistency of lumpy gravy."

"It doesn't look that way," said Brian.

"That's because it's still inside the pericardium—the thin sac that surrounds the heart. In this case, the pericardium is intact, yet the heart has been jellified."

"How is that even humanly possible?" asked Father Benedict, a look of alarm on his face.

"It isn't," replied the Colonel.

"What's that supposed to mean?" asked Mark in an irritated voice.

"It's quite simple," the Colonel replied with an air of superiority. "We don't know how it was done because we didn't—and couldn't—do that. Mark isn't aware of this, but we aren't the only ones who were studying the problem. We had ... company."

17

Some military officials are seriously considering the
possibility that UFOs are interplanetary ships.

—*FBI memo on UFOs, 1952*

"Just what does *that* mean—'we had *company*'?" Deidre pressed.

Without a word, the Colonel reached underneath the top of the podium, withdrew a telephone, and pressed a single button. "Ferguson ... it's time. Tell Marcus and Lindsay their presence is mandatory in two hours."

The Colonel hung up the phone and looked out across the table. There was a queer mixture of anxiety, enthusiasm, and determination in his eyes. "The crisis about which you've been briefed is very real, but Mark has given you half the predicament. He doesn't know the rest."

The room fell completely silent. Brian turned his attention to the Colonel, who by now was enjoying the moment. A chill ran down his spine. *Is this for real?* His mind raced as he glanced first at Father Benedict, who had turned pale, and then at Neil, whose countenance had abruptly become careworn and troubled.

"I believe Dr. Bandstra has something to add," said the Colonel.

Neil removed a handkerchief from his lapel pocket and wiped the tiny beads of sweat that had surfaced on his upper lip. "I was brought on this project," he began, clearing his throat, "at the Colonel's request and by approval of the Group. The reason was simple: The matter before us concerns national security. The individuals who have been co-monitoring the prion diseases understand how much of a threat they are to us ... so much so that they're threatening to accelerate the infection cycle. Right now the only plant life of concern are the fields where the cows graze. It's well known that clean herds can get BSE by eating the vegetation from infected herds. Our adversaries are threatening to spread the infectious prions to our own food crops. Frankly, we have no choice but to meet their demands."

"Screw that!" Malcolm suddenly exploded. "We're Americans, and we don't surrender to *anybody!* Whoever these wackos are we should book their reservations in hell right now. Nuke 'em if we have to."

"Malcolm!" Deidre exclaimed.

"Hey, if it's us or them, I don't care."

"Actually, Dr. Bradley," Dr. Bandstra paused, wiping his brow once more, "the nuclear option is part of our strategy."

"Whoa," said Melissa, "how did we go from mad cow disease to nuclear war?"

"The naked truth is that we can't stop what they intend, but we can make the outcome undesirable for them."

"Neil ... just who are '*they*'?" Brian asked apprehensively.

"I think you know, Brian. They're the reason you were brought here ... the reason all of you are here."

"Neil ... do you mean to say—"

"Yes, Brian; I do. Our problem is the result of a deliberate act on the part of an extraterrestrial intelligence. *They* are here, and they've been here for a very long time."

18

The phenomenon of UFOs does exist,
and it must be treated seriously.

—*Mikhail Gorbachev,*
Soviet Youth, May 4, 1990

The team sat stunned around the table like speechless mannequins, Neil's words reverberating in their ears. Brian could feel his heart pumping wildly as he tried to process what he'd just heard. Suddenly Melissa regained her composure, and her mood hadn't changed.

"Little gray aliens?" Melissa Kelley asked mockingly. "This is all about the little gray guys we see on TV? Do we look like fools?"

"I understand your skepticism, Dr. Kelley," Neil responded calmly, "but I can assure you that this is no joke—and no lie. The extraterrestrial reality is our country's most closely guarded secret. Nothing is classified any higher."

Melissa just shook her head.

"In view of our study and its results," the Colonel offered, "the Group deemed it necessary to recruit outside experts to advise us on how to acclimate the public to the fact that we aren't alone—on either this planet or in the universe—not to mention the crisis they've created. All of you have certain areas of expertise that are relevant to a careful and successful handling of a public disclosure of this information. Surely you can see how your expertise in apocalyptic cults fits into this picture."

Melissa folded her arms and sat back in her chair.

"What about you, Dr. Harper? I would think your mind would be a bit more open."

"You ought to know I need more than your say-so."

"So just what is Dee's special expertise?" Malcolm asked.

"Your colleague has very quietly established herself as an expert in the alien abduction psychology—specifically in terms of profiling

73

and psychotherapy."

"No way."

"It's true," she answered abruptly. "That doesn't mean I believe in aliens, though."

"Neither did I," Neil broke in, "until I saw the proof. It's why I asked for Brian to be included on the project. He's one of the few religious scholars in the world to address this in an academic paper, and the apologetic angle he took will be quite useful toward persuading even the most conservative Christians that their paradigm will remain intact if ET is here."

"Thanks, Neil, but don't forget, it got me fired."

"I know, but most Protestants wouldn't react so impulsively. In terms of Catholicism, someone of Father Benedict's stature is indispensable. In addition to being a top bovine biochemist, Mark is an authority on cattle mutilations. Malcolm and Kevin are here because of their command of biology and disease control. We believe you're all the best combination of minds we could have to deal with the visitors."

"Visitors?" challenged Kevin angrily. "You make it sound like these beings are on a camping trip playing arts and crafts! If this is true—and mind you, I'm not buying it either—then we're dealing with incalculable human suffering."

"We don't believe their activities are ill-intentioned," the Colonel replied, "at least not from their point of view. None of you have met Dr. Marcus yet. He's spent a lot of time with them, and he feels the same way."

Malcolm interrupted. *"Spent time with them?"*

"Dr. Marcus is the leading authority in the world on intelligent extraterrestrial life, at least in terms of anatomy and physiology."

Melissa rejoined the discussion. "You know, this sounds more absurd the longer you guys go on. I'm personally insulted by your estimation of my gullibility. For all we know, you guys will wheel a bunch of Muppets in here and pass them off as alien bodies."

"I think we need to get back on track here," Neil said. "If we don't all get on board, we're going to lose critical time in dealing with our situation. This is a chess match we cannot afford to lose."

"Assuming this is true, Neil, why is it that you seem to think there are no other options?" asked Brian.

Neil looked at his friend in surprise.

"To be honest, I'll need to see whatever proof you saw in order to be convinced. Hope you're not offended."

"No, I understand completely, and you'll have it later this afternoon.

To answer your question, these aliens have been surveiling earth steadily since the thirties. They appear to have initiated a concentrated effort to learn about our planet and about us. We believe their intent has been to discern how workable a compromise plan for living together would be. Confirmation of their existence came in the form of several crashes and subsequent retrievals."

"Retrievals?" Malcolm eyed Neil skeptically over his glasses.

"Yes," Neil replied. "Despite the material remains in our possession, we really didn't know what we had on our hands until the fifties, when the visitors initiated contact and let us know their goal was coexistence."

"You say 'initiated,'" Father Benedict finally spoke up. "Are you implying that we couldn't have done the same—or wouldn't have?"

"The former."

"Can we communicate with them now?"

"Yes," the Colonel volunteered. "They have no vocal cords, so they communicate telepathically. It's an odd sensation at first, but you get used to just thinking without talking."

"You've engaged in one of these 'conversations'—with an extraterrestrial?"

"I haven't," Neil replied. "But the Colonel has."

The officer nodded in agreement.

"Getting back to the point," Neil continued, "our own civilization resisted any attempt at integration with the visitors because we feared the social, religious, and psychological upheaval disclosure would bring. This was the fifties, remember; we were confident that people just couldn't process it, especially since the country was so conservative, religiously speaking. In essence, we followed the recommendations of the Brookings Report and stalled for time."

"What's the Brookings Report?" asked Melissa.

"It was a study done for Congress in the early 1960s that, in part, dealt with the presumed socioreligious impact upon Americans should the reality of intelligent extraterrestrial life become factually known. To put it mildly, the presumed impact was deemed catastrophic by Brookings. As I recall, Brian dealt with it in his paper."

Brian nodded.

"The visitors weren't pleased with our recalcitrance toward mutual existence. Quite frankly, they didn't understand it. They grew more insistent with time. We suspect that the planet holds something they desperately need for survival, but we aren't sure what it might be."

"If these 'space aliens' are so technologically advanced," Dr. Garvey said with a smirk, "why don't they just get rid of us like so many household pests?"

"They certainly could if they wanted to," the Colonel interrupted. "The only thing forestalling something like that is our nuclear capability—and today, our biological weapons."

"Our government made a tactical error in that regard, as well," Neil resumed his discussion. "We made it very clear that if there was any attempt to circumvent our desire that public contact be postponed, or if they made any aggressive move, we'd use our nukes."

"Brilliant," said Deidre.

"Just so you and everyone else doesn't misunderstand the point, Dr. Harper, we didn't intend on using weapons against the visitors."

"Huh?"

The Colonel continued. "We'd never be able to touch them with our weapons. Their vehicles are too fast, and the larger ones are too remote to be touched. We informed them that we'd essentially nuke the planet."

"So our policy was MAD?" asked Melissa incredulously.

"Correct—mutually assured destruction. Exactly what it was with the Soviets in the fifties and sixties, except from a more aggressive posture. We had enough nuclear capability to destroy the earth and its resources, which is what they need."

"They would have to know we would never do such a thing. It doesn't make sense," Melissa replied.

"Well, they apparently did. I guess they've witnessed human beings kill enough of their own species and willfully pollute their own life-giving resources to think we'd do it."

"My estimation of their intelligence just went up a notch," Malcolm deadpanned. "Are the boneheads on our side who created this policy still around?"

"No, they've all since passed away. However, there are those in the Group who still believe in the policy—or did until the visitors trumped us."

"And how did that happen?" Father Benedict asked nervously.

"The visitors took matters into their own hands and decided to force us into population integration. They know that we have no cure for BSE or a way to forestall its spread—right now, anyway. They've threatened to infect every herd on the planet, and to spread the prions to crops we use for our own consumption. Their strategy is that no matter what we eat, huge segments of the population will be infected—then, they wait us out. They figure that we wouldn't act to hasten our own demise with nukes— that we'd fight and try to find a cure or a way out of check, as it were.

"They also think that when BSE becomes a plague, people will demand to know how and why it came about. And when we tell them, we'll be too busy coping with the crises of an ET revelation that we won't have the resources to solve the problem—and that the MAD policy will get out, with chaotic results. We've concluded that population integration, as risky as it is, is the better option."

"I don't follow," the priest responded. "How does it serve their purpose to jeopardize the planet's food supply?"

"They are immune from BSE. It wouldn't affect them in any way. Besides, they're scientifically way ahead of us. Speaking of which, as of a week ago, they dangled a carrot for us to convince us to agree—but it's only on the table for a month."

"And what might that be?" Brian could tell by his intonation that Andrew was suspicious.

"They've offered to take care of our ozone problem. We know they can do it, too."

"Aren't we at risk of contracting some sort of virus from them?" asked Mark.

"We can't be one hundred percent sure, but we've studied the alien bodies we have very thoroughly. There have also been exchanges of humans and aliens to study compatibility, but ... they haven't always followed the guidelines we agreed on."

"Meaning?"

"They take people ... actually, a good number of them."

19

I am completely convinced that
UFOs have an out-of-world basis.

—*Dr. Walther Reidel, Research Director and Chief Designer at
Nazi Germany's rocket center
at Peenemünde, LIFE Magazine, April 7, 1952*

Kevin Garvey groaned and swore under his breath as his alarm clock rudely informed him that his late morning nap had come and gone. He lay for a few moments in his bed, gazing at the ceiling, pondering what lay ahead for him and his colleagues. His mind rehearsed the events to this point. He closed his eyes and cursed again.

He sat up and swung his legs over the side of the bed. He reached for his shoes, but something else caught his eye. A single folded piece of paper lay just inside his door. His surprise turned to fear when he realized that someone had to have access to his room in order to leave such a thing. He sat for a few moments staring at the paper, assuring himself that it must be from the Colonel or Dr. Bandstra. He walked over to the door, picked it up, and unfolded what was in fact a short, typewritten message:

> *Your distrust of the project is well placed. I can provide
> you with evidence that all is not what it seems. Tomorrow
> morning after you are adjourned, go directly to the sixth door
> from the meeting room at the end of the corridor. This door is
> locked, but it will be overridden for fifteen seconds at exactly
> 6:35, allowing you access outside the restricted zone. You
> must be there at the precise time. Memorize the directions
> below to the next door indicated. It will be overridden for
> fifteen seconds as well, at exactly 6:40. Only you have the
> wherewithal to understand what you will see in this room.
> The exit will be overridden at 6:55, at which time you must*

leave. If you want to get back to your area without detection,
retrace your steps by the same time intervals. Destroy this
note so that it cannot be recovered.

Kevin stared at the paper in his hand. "Tomorrow morning, huh?" He stuffed the note into his pocket. "Wonder what this afternoon's performance will be like."

20

I know that neither Russia nor this country has anything even
approaching such high speeds and maneuvers. Behind the
scenes high ranking officers are soberly concerned about UFOs,
but through official secrecy and ridicule many citizens are led to
believe that the unknown flying objects are nonsense ... To hide
the facts, the Air Force has silenced its personnel.

—*Admiral Roscoe Hillenkoetter,*
former Director of the CIA, 1962 NICAP
press conference in Washington, D.C.

"Good afternoon, everyone."

Despite the attempt at politeness, Brian could see that the Colonel had only said it to get everyone in their seats. It wasn't necessary. As soon as Neil had arrived with the two heretofore missing team members, no one was interested in any delay.

One of the newcomers, a short, sandy-haired man adorned with the familiar white lab coat but sporting a very conspicuous paisley bowtie, was obviously Ian Marcus, who had been touted as an expert on alien life forms. The other was Air Force, and judging from the decorations on his uniform, he was a long-time officer.

"I'll dispense with the small talk," the Colonel began. "Time is of the essence. I'm proud to introduce Dr. Ian Marcus and Major Gordon Lindsay. Dr. Marcus was a student of Carl Sagan's at Cornell, where he earned a PhD in astrophysics. After a lengthy stint with NASA's Astrobiology Institute, he joined our operations at the Facility six years ago. It is no exaggeration to say that he's the world's leading astrobiologist.

"Major Lindsay is a career military man and the Air Force's chief archivist and historian with respect to U.S. relations with our alien visitors. Original documents and photographs of everything Major Lindsay shows you today during his presentation can be examined at the Facility archive. Your badge ID's have been added to the access permission log, and there are directions to the archive in your email accounts as we speak. Gordon, the floor is yours."

Major Lindsay was short, stocky, and sported a crew cut. He appeared to be on the cusp of retirement age. His sunken eyes and complacent expression gave him the look of a stern, humorless man—of someone who had resigned himself to the burden of secrets to which he'd been overexposed. He stroked an unsharpened pencil as he began to speak.

"You must all understand that every document I'll mention has either been declassified through the Freedom of Information Act or leaked to the public with my authorization as part of a slow acclimation process. We've been trying to condition the public to the reality of ET life for the past fifteen years. We didn't start out with that attitude, though."

"Meaning?" Malcolm asked.

"Meaning our intelligence community was scared witless when the visitors started invading our airspace. It started back in February of 1942, when the good citizens of Los Angeles were awakened by air raid sirens and antiaircraft fire. We were trying to shoot down one of twenty-five silver objects flying in V-formation near Long Beach. After over 1,400 rounds were fired and thousands of dollars of damage to homes and public buildings, nothing was shot down."

"How could you miss 1,400 times?"

"We didn't. The saucer didn't even move part of the time. It just hung there while the shells just bounced off or exploded all around it. Here's a picture of it and the *LA Times* newspaper headline the following day." Major Lindsay tapped a key on his laptop with his pencil, and the slide appeared on the screen. "Notice anything?"

"Yeah," Mark began, "the paper says five people were killed ... by falling shells!"

"Why in God's name did they start shooting?" asked Deidre.

"This was February of 1942. It was just three months after the Japanese bombed Pearl Harbor. Authorities thought they were under attack by some kind of wingless flying machine belonging to the Japanese."

Major Lindsay poked his keyboard again. "Two years later President Roosevelt wrote this memo. Notice in the last paragraph, the second line, that FDR refers to—and I quote—'*coming to grips with the reality that our planet is not the only one harboring intelligent life.*'"

"Good Lord," Deidre muttered, adjusting her glasses so she could make out the print.

"By the mid to late 1940s, our pilots—stateside and in occupied territory during World War II—began to report unusual craft in the sky.

Eventually Generals Douglas MacArthur and George Marshal established the Interplanetary Phenomenon Unit to investigate these phenomena. That organization operated under the aegis of the Director
of Counterintelligence."

"Did you say '*Interplanetary* Phenomenon Unit'?" Melissa repeated.

"Yes, you heard correctly."

Brian watched with curiosity as she scribbled something down on
a notepad.

"They could have just asked the Nazis," said Brian, swiveling his chair in the Major's direction.

"So you're familiar with Operation Paperclip, doctor?" asked the Major.

"Yes. When I was doing research for my journal article on extra-terrestrial life, I came across a lot of UFO stuff—and Operation Paperclip seemed to come up all the time."

"What's 'Paperclip'? And what's this crap about Nazis?" asked Mark, glaring at the Major.

"Operation Paperclip was our government's secret program, initiated under Harry Truman to recruit Nazi and Japanese scientists for our own use."

Mark and Kevin looked at each other, dumbfounded.

"Is he serious?" Melissa asked incredulously, looking at Brian.

"Absolutely."

"We'd been recruiting Nazi scientists prior to Paperclip, but the official program stepped up the operation. The program was officially disclosed to the public on October 1, 1945 as an effort to employ German scientists. What wasn't mentioned was the fact that most of the scientists brought over here were members of the Nazi party.

"Our military originally intended only to debrief these men—particularly since we had come into possession of thousands of documents from Peenemünde, Germany's top-secret rocket facility—and then send them back to Germany. We soon realized the extent and value of their knowledge, and what a waste it would be to just send them back. When we discovered their arsenal included flying disks, the War Department determined that we needed to control this technology. The only problem was that it was expressly illegal to offer Nazis immigration status, and President Truman was not of the mind to change that."

"So how did the project get off the ground?" asked Kevin, intrigued. Brian noticed Mark was playing with his beard again.

"Truman eventually did approve Paperclip, but he explicitly forbade including anyone who had been a member of the Nazi party or an active supporter of the Third Reich. The War Department's Joint Intelligence Objectives Agency soon figured out that most of the guys we really wanted couldn't pass this test. A deal was eventually brokered between a Nazi intelligence expert, Reinhard Gehlen—who had deeply infiltrated the KGB—and then CIA director Allen Dulles.

"Dulles thought that he could gain two things by dealing with Gehlen: Paperclip scientists and an ally—albeit a known Nazi for spying against the Russians. The result was that the dossiers of the scientists we wanted were sanitized—cleared of references to party membership, Gestapo ties, and any evidence of human experimentation. Even Werner von Braun had been initially labeled as a threat to our national security. Who'd have thought that the guy who served as one of Walt Disney's experts on the 'World of Tomorrow' used to work for Hitler?"

"I'm devastated!" Malcolm cracked. "One of the Mouseketeers was a Nazi!"

Brian and a few others couldn't help laughing.

"You have such an ... unusual way of putting things, Dr. Bradley," the Major said stoically. "May I continue?"

Malcolm sat back in his chair, still enjoying the moment.

"I'm sure you and the other scientists have all heard of Viktor Schauberger—correct?"

The three men nodded.

"Schauberger, of course, was an Austrian scientist kidnapped by the Nazis for the purpose of tapping his technological expertise. During his employ under the Nazis, Schauberger designed a number of flying disks powered by cutting-edge electro-magnetic propulsion."

"Why weren't these disks destroyed during the war?" asked Father Benedict. "I'm old enough to remember when the British destroyed Peenemünde in 1943."

"That's only partially correct, Father. It's true that Peenemünde was bombed, but most of it was underground, so it was relatively undamaged. Even so, Dr. Hans Kammler, the SS's *Obergrupenfeuhrer*, who was in charge of the Nazi weapons technology program, decided after the attack to distribute the various weapons projects at the facility to other locations throughout Germany. I should point out here that, eventually, the SS, under the direction of Heinrich Himmler, was given complete oversight of this technology and financial independence by Hitler. In effect, the secret weapons technology overseen by Kammler became what we would call in this country a 'black op'—a project whose funding is secret and independent of governmental oversight."

"Sounds familiar," said Deidre.

"In case you forgot, Dr. Harper, you're being paid under such an arrangement now."

"Whatever."

"I've never heard of any of this," Mark commented. "Didn't anyone ever get discovered?"

"On occasion. Take Arthur Rudolph, for example. Rudolph was operations director of the Mittelwerk factory at the Dora-Nordhausen concentration camps, where twenty-thousand workers died from beatings, hangings, and starvation. If you look at his Paperclip file, it reads that nothing objectionable about him was detected. Rudolph became a U.S. citizen and designed the Saturn 5 rocket used in the Apollo moon landings. His true record, however, was discovered in 1984, and he fled to West Germany to escape prosecution."

"This is all fascinating—and somewhat disturbing, I might add," said Father Benedict. "But I'd like to know what importance Brian is attaching to it."

"I think it's the explanation for basically the whole myth of UFOs and alien visitations."

Major Lindsay stared at Brian with a mixture of amusement and annoyance.

"There are two fundamental problems with that thesis, Dr. Scott. On one hand, you'd have to explain the Los Angeles case and the memo you've just seen—they both occurred before Paperclip. Second, I suspect that you know that in the late 1940s our military was wetting their collective pants over what you think were our own aircraft."

"Depends on what you're referring to."

Major Lindsay sat back in his chair. The egotistical look on his face exuded the superiority complex of one whose entire career had revolved around seducing people to beg for information that only he could dispense. Even now, as he divulged the secrets most guarded by himself and his peers, he enjoyed being in complete control. He tapped his pencil lightly on the table as the team awaited a response.

"Ever heard of Roswell?"

21

I believe that these extraterrestrial vehicles and their crews
are visiting this planet from other planets, which obviously are
a little more technically advanced than we are here on Earth ...
For many years I have lived with a secret, in a secrecy imposed
on all specialists and astronauts.

—*Colonel L. Gordon Cooper,*
Mercury and Gemini astronaut,
address to the United Nations, 1985

"Who's Roswell?" asked Kevin.

"Good God, Kevin, are you serious?" Deidre exclaimed. "Roswell is a *place*—a town in New Mexico. Haven't you ever seen *Independence Day?*"

"No," Kevin replied coolly. "I do research, not watch movies. Someone has to do real science while you practice your abduction pseudoscience."

"So the less informed we are about what we don't agree with, the more our own work increases in validity? Maybe you ought to take a timeout from playing with your calipers and get acquainted with pop culture."

"Forgive my ignorance as well," Father Benedict said apologetically. "I fear I'm not much better informed. Major?"

"Of course, Father. As Dr. Harper noted, Roswell is a small town in New Mexico, most famous for what is certainly this country's most controversial UFO incident. Since it is essential for appreciating all the secrecy that has characterized our UFO policy since then, all of you will need an introduction.

"On the night of July 2, 1947, a bright light in the sky was reported by several people near Roswell. A local rancher, Mac Brazel, heard a loud explosion minutes later. The next morning, Brazel discovered a debris field approximately 300 yards wide and three-quarters of a mile long in an adjacent pasture. Brazel decided to collect someof the debris. He put

a large, circular piece into a shed on his property and showed the rest
to his neighbors, the Proctors. Brazel celebrated the July 4 holiday at
home, and on July 5 took a trip to nearby Corona to tell some acquaintances about what he'd found. The morning after that, he decided to
take some of the smaller pieces into town for the local sheriff, George
Wilcox, to see."

"What did he think he had?" asked Melissa.

"He wasn't a scientist, so he had no real idea. He just knew that something had crashed. Roswell was home to an Army Air Force base, so he
suspected it was some kind of plane. Anyway, early that afternoon, Sheriff Wilcox and Brazel decided to contact the Roswell Army Air Force base
and report the find. The base commander, Colonel William Blanchard,
the base intelligence officer, Major Jesse Marcel, and a Captain Cavitt drove to the sheriff's office to have a look and talk to Brazel. Colonel
Blanchard eventually took a piece back to the base and alerted Brigadier
General Roger Ramey in Fort Worth, Texas. That evening, Marcel and
Cavitt returned with Brazel to examine the piece in his shed; the piece
Blanchard had was flown to Fort Worth at that time, as well. They stayed
the night and went out to the debris field the next morning."

"Was there anything unusual about the pieces?" Father Benedict asked.

"Yes," the Major answered. "According to what Major Marcel said afterward, the material was very lightweight and incredibly strong—they
tried to bend it by pounding it with a sledgehammer, but couldn't do
it. The smallest and thinnest pieces could be crumpled in the hand but
returned completely to their former state. The material was also imper-
vious to scratching and heat, and several pieces had some unidentifi-
able imprinting.

"Marcel and Cavitt spent the entire day at the site, and by nightfall
they had loaded the trunks of their vehicles with fragments. Major Marcel got home around two o'clock A.M. and showed the debris to his wife
and son. Later that morning, at seven thirty, base officers met regarding the debris, and guards were assigned to the access roads leading to
the field. A couple of hours later, troops arrived at the sight to begin a
cleanup. Then, at eleven o'clock A.M., Colonel Blanchard made a decision that earned Roswell enduring fame."

"What was that?" wondered Malcolm.

"He ordered the base public relations officer, Lieutenant Walter
Haut, to issue a press release to the local radio station, KGFL, and the
town newspaper, that the 500th Bomb Group of the Eighth Air Force of

Roswell Army Air Field had recovered a flying saucer. The story spread all over the world."

"What was the reaction in the town?" asked Father Benedict.

"Chaotic. Phone lines at the base, at the sheriff's office, and at the newspaper and radio station were completely tied up. The sheriff tried to send some deputies to the site, but by then the MPs had their orders to block access to the site to anyone except military personnel. They didn't want anyone to see anything, especially the bodies."

"Bodies?"

"Yes," the Major replied. "One of the craft occupants had apparently been thrown from the craft, but the others were inside. One was still alive. They were each about four feet in height, had light gray skin, heads that seemed disproportionately large for their bodies, and large black eyes. You're all familiar with the description by now because of media saturation. The bodies are certainly a problem for Dr. Scott's view."

"At least that's how it's come down to us," interjected Brian.

"I have a laptop full of scanned documents that provide the proof, but let's just look at three." It took Major Lindsay only a few seconds to search for what he wanted. His pencil went into action again.

"This first document makes it clear that there was indeed a saucer recovered at Roswell, and that it wasn't a U.S. military experiment as Dr. Scott would have us believe. Notice the statement to that effect a few lines from the top. Moreover, the memo demonstrates that since flying saucers were not Army or Navy, the FBI should get involved. Someone at the Bureau disagreed in the second typewritten paragraph, but look at the handwritten note under that paragraph. Clyde Tolson wrote, 'I think we should do this' and then sent it on to its final reader—which was who? Look at the handwriting at the bottom."

"Hmmpf ... none other than J. Edgar Hoover himself," Deidre said, shaking her head.

"Correct. Now look at what the Director said in response to the memo and Mr. Tolson's suggestion. It's a little hard to read: 'I would do it, but before agreeing to it we must insist upon full access to discs recovered. For instance in the Sw case the Army grabbed it and wouldn't let us have it for cursory examination.' Take special note of the references to 'disks' and the 'Sw case.' Does anyone know what 'Sw' might—and I can say certainly does—stand for?" he asked.

"Southwest?" offered Melissa.

"Quite correct," the Major replied, "as in New Mexico—as in Roswell. In fact, there was a second crashed disk nearby that few people know of.

Hoover was miffed he wasn't allowed access. Kind of strange if it was one of our own."

"Oh boy," mused Malcolm quietly.

"Still doesn't prove they're extraterrestrial," Brian noted.

"We're not done yet, Dr. Scott. Two more to go."

"The second memo is called the Twining White Hot report. You'll notice the first page is dated September 19, 1947, but it refers to activity on July 9, 1947—just days after the Roswell crash."

Brian glanced at the slide. "Okay, so what's in the document?"

"Glad you asked." Major Lindsay hit his space bar. "Take a good look, Dr. Scott."

Brian peered at the screen, carefully picking his way through the grainy yet readable document. The document described the recovery of four humanoid bodies whose physiological features suggested a non-human origin.

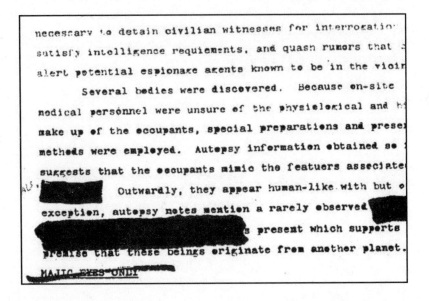

"Roswell is more than folklore, Dr. Scott, as you'll soon discover," the Major said with a defiant stare.

"I'm sure Brian has heard about the bodies before today. I'd like to hear his explanation, if he has one," said Deidre, her curiosity piqued.

"Before Dr. Scott volunteers his wisdom, let's take a look at the last document, the Eisenhower Briefing of 1952." All eyes were riveted on the screen as another slide flashed into view.

"In many ways, this is the proverbial smoking gun. The Eisenhower Briefing document details a secret recovery operation initiated on July 7, 1947—Roswell. As the Twining memo noted, four dead bodies were recovered, and the wreckage was moved to several locations."

"Amazing," Mark thought aloud, stroking his beard. "The clinical description of the victims is just so matter-of-fact ... human-like beings that apparently evolved differently."

"Yes," the Major agreed. "What's your explanation, Dr. Scott? What did the people who wrote these reports see if not aliens? Surely you don't accept the cover story we concocted."

"No thinking person would."

"What was that?" asked Mark.

```
            TOP SECRET / MAJIC
            EYES ONLY
            ...............
            * TOP SECRET *
            ...............

EYES ONLY                              COPY ONE OF

A covert analytical effort organized by Gen. Twining and
Dr. Bush acting on the direct orders of the President, res-
ulted in a preliminary consensus (19 September, 1947) that
the disc was most likely a short range reconnaissance craft
This conclusion was based for the most part on the craft's
size and the apparent lack of any identifiable provisioning
(See Attachment "D".) A similar analysis of the four dead
occupants was arranged by Dr. Bronk. It was the tentative
conclusion of this group (30 November, 1947) that although
these creatures are human-like in appearance, the biologica
and evolutionary processes responsible for their developmen
has apparently been quite different from those observed or
postulated in homo-sapiens. Dr. Bronk's team has suggested
the term "Extra-terrestrial Biological Entities", or "EBEs"
he adopted as the standard term of reference for these
creatures until such time as a more definitive designation
can be agreed upon.


Since it is virtually certain that these craft do not origi
ate in any country on earth, considerable speculation has
centered around what their point of origin might be and how
they get here. Mars was and remains a possibility, althoug
some scientists, most notably Dr. Menzel, consider it more
likely that we are dealing with beings from another solar
```

"During a 1997 press conference during the 50th anniversary of the Roswell crash, an Air Force colonel explained that the bodies were really test dummies used by the Air Force as part of a secret weather balloon project called Project Mogul. The problem was that the Air Force, by its own admission elsewhere, did not use those dummies until the early fifties. They were also very human in appearance, blue, and over five feet tall."

"Didn't anyone at the conference know the explanation wasn't workable?" Malcolm asked.

"That's the kicker," Brian responded. "One reporter did. He asked the officer in charge of the conference to explain the contradiction. It's still hard for me to believe, but he said that all the witnesses of the Roswell event had apparently suffered from what he termed 'time compression.'"

"Say what?"

"He was saying that they had all remembered an event that actually happened in the early fifties as having happened in 1947."

"Right," said Malcolm, holding back a laugh.

"He's not making it up," Deidre backed him up. "I saw the same conference. It was truly unbelievable."

"I know Colonel Haynes," Major Lindsay broke in. "He's a good, loyal officer. He was told what to say—to back up the Air Force's written report no matter what. And that report insists that the bodies were those dummies. But your intuition is correct—the conference was actually part of a planned conditioning program. By putting forth an explanation that lacked real explanatory power, we created the suspicion that there really were aliens involved, thereby conditioning more people to the idea. So, Dr. Scott—your view?"

"I think the Roswell event is best understood in light of what Major Lindsay began with in terms of his history—Operation Paperclip. One of the questions that would have inevitably surfaced in regard to the recovered technology was the effect that G-forces created by the incredible speeds and maneuvers at those speeds would have on human beings. In my view, the Paperclip recruits—known Nazis, mind you—argued successfully to their superiors that human beings should be placed in the crafts to see what would happen to the human body. It's no secret that the Nazis did this in Germany; human experimentation was a given. I think that, as they did in the 'Fatherland,' these scientists selected human undesirables—in this case, mongoloid children, maybe progeria victims—for their experiments, hence the size and appearance of the corpses. No one who saw them—and it would only have been for seconds—would ever expect that humans were in the craft, since we weren't supposed to have such a craft.

"What do you think would have been the fallout if the *Roswell Daily Record* had discovered that this craft was developed by Nazis and was being perfected by Nazis on our own government's payroll right after the war, and that the ongoing research involved sacrificing the most unfortunate members of human society? I'd say the alien angle was more palatable, and the ensuing cover-up fixed the American attention on the extraterrestrial hypothesis in our psyche. No one would ever think there was anything the government would want to keep under more secrecy than a crashed alien ship. I'm suggesting there is. There you have it."

"That's awesome," Malcolm said with admiration. "It makes sense—it really does."

"It's a fascinating alternative," Deidre said thoughtfully.

"Imaginative, is how I'd describe it," Major Lindsay said dismissively.

"This is all very entertaining," said Kevin, unconvinced, "but I have to agree with Brian. I need more evidence than these memos, as amazing as they are. Quite frankly, until I actually see a live alien being, I'm not going to be convinced. I don't know what bodies Dr. Bandstra saw, but in today's world, anything can be faked."

"Colonel?"

Without another word the senior officer withdrew a cellular phone from his briefcase and hit the speed-dial. "Hello … yes, this is he … tell Dr. Yu we're on our way."

The Colonel stood up, as did Major Lindsay and Dr. Bandstra. The rest of the team got the hint and did likewise, still unsure as to what was next. The Colonel walked quickly around the table and approached the door leading out of the conference room.

"From this point on," the Colonel warned them sternly, "it is imperative that you stay close to the rest of the team, since we will be venturing well beyond those areas where you have unescorted access. As long as you're with me, the MPs won't be alarmed. If you try to move about independently, your actions will be viewed with suspicion. Our security will shoot to kill should there be any hint of an escape from this portion of the base. Is that clear?"

The members of the team acknowledged the warning.

The Colonel proceeded through the doorway to the conference room and out into the hall. They followed him about fifty yards down the now familiar corridor in the direction of their living quarters, and, aided by the Colonel's pass card, exited the main corridor through one of the windowless doors lining the passageway. There were two small trams on the other side, waiting for their transport, and the Colonel and Major Lindsay each got into a driver's seat, the Colonel taking the lead vehicle.

The ride lasted longer than Brian expected it would. There were corridors, ramps, and tunnels that seemed to all look the same. He wondered to himself if they weren't being led in circles just for the sake of creating confusion.

Finally the trams came to a halt in front of a guardhouse, adjacent to which was a knob-less door. The small hut was heavily armed, a row of assault rifles having been mounted on the wall inside. Two dark blue sheets of glass about eight inches square were positioned next to the door, the lower about three feet up the wall, the one above it about five and a half feet from the ground. They reminded Brian of a checkout scanner at the grocery store.

The Colonel stepped from his driver's seat and stood at the door, waiting until everyone was gathered around him. He nodded to one of the MPs inside, who looked down at something where he was seated. The Colonel pressed his right palm to the lower square, which lit up at his touch. He kept his palm fixed in position for a few seconds, until the light went off. Next, he removed his hat and stood, slightly stooped, in front of the higher pane, touching his nose to the glass. A light quickly scanned his right eye, after which everyone heard a loud click.

The door slid open slowly, and the team passed through into a short corridor, adjacent to which was the open guardhouse. The MPs gazed at each of them earnestly, as though intent upon memorizing their faces for future reference. The Colonel traversed the corridor, at the end of which was a door identical to those in each member's room, a simple card reader fixed above the handle. The Colonel removed his identification card and paused.

"Remember, please stay together at all times. You'll soon see that those things that make up our everyday preoccupation, the things whose safe-keeping we've been entrusted with for the sake of our nation, deserve all the security we give them. You may not understand everything you see here, but the Major and I will do our best to satisfy your curiosity. Oh, and one more thing," he smirked arrogantly, "you'll also finally find out exactly where it is you've been staying."

He quickly swiped the card, and the familiar access light went off. "Welcome, everyone," he announced as he held the door open, "to Dreamland, the United States Air Force's Groom Lake Facility—or, as it's most commonly known, Area 51."

22

It's kind of fun to do the impossible.

—*Walt Disney*

"My God ..." Deidre whispered in awe as the team, led by Colonel Fergu-son, descended an iron flight of stairs to the ground level of a cavern-ous hangar.

There were no jets or other aircraft on the tarmac, but there was a great deal of bustle along the perimeter of the floor space. White-coat-ed men and women were busy traversing in and out of dozens of rooms built into the walls, detectable only by virtue of the clustered windows that allowed visual access to the hangar. Technicians wearing coveralls drove small flatbed trams laden with equipment and machinery back and forth between several large work areas whose contents were par-tially concealed by translucent tarps draped over the surrounding scaf-folding. Brian also took note of several stern-faced MPs, equipped with side arms and accompanied by large, thick-shouldered German shep-herds.

"This place must take up at least a square mile," Melissa remarked, rendered nearly breathless by the shocking expanse. "I can't believe we've been next to this for all these weeks."

"Actually," Neil responded casually, "you've been on the floor above it. We're roughly a half-mile underground."

"Incredible." Kevin grinned and followed the Colonel.

Brian caught up to Neil as the team reached the floor. "A hangar underground? How can you test anything? There's no runway or a way out—"

"We don't need them," the Colonel interrupted with a cryptic smile, having overheard the question. "This way," he directed the team. "I know the pathways are narrow, but please observe the markings at all times."

"Please stay within the lines," Malcolm cracked under his breath as he let Mark and Father Benedict pass on in front of him. "Single file!"

"Must you, Malcolm?" Deidre complained good-naturedly.

"I still don't understand," Kevin fussed, just ahead of Brian and Neil. "Granted the ceiling is pretty high, but how can you test any jets in this environment?"

"Who said anything about jets?" Brian said, his voice quivering with excitement. Despite his doubts about extraterrestrials, the prospect of seeing a UFO up close was sheer ecstasy, regardless of who built it. "Does that look like any jet you've seen recently?" He pointed to the image now emerging behind the tarpaulin.

Kevin's pace slowed, and he finally stopped. He stared, mouth agape, at the perfectly round silver craft resting atop a small tapered platform at the heart of the restricted area.

"Kevin," Dr. Bandstra nudged him gently, "you need to keep going; we don't want to put too much distance between us and the rest of the team."

"Yeah ... right."

The group soon arrived at the slit that allowed access through the tarpaulin. Brian couldn't take his eyes off the saucer. It was the perfect blend of elegance and technology. A middle-aged Asian man emerged through the opening and handed the Colonel a clipboard, the contents of which the Colonel proceeded to inspect.

"Good afternoon, everyone," the Asian man said jovially. His round face beamed as he placed his pen into the lapel pocket of his lab coat. "It's so nice to have some outsiders."

"You mean earthlings?" quipped Malcolm. Several of the members laughed, but the Colonel greeted his jest with only a scowl.

"You'll have to get used to Dr. Bradley."

"Now, now, Colonel," the scientist interjected. "You must all excuse the Colonel," he added, turning toward the team. "He's under a great deal of pressure, much of which is unfortunately caused by myself. We can be notoriously slow."

"He means meticulous," the Colonel offered, his countenance brightening slightly, "and we wouldn't have it any other way—in fact we can't allow it to be any other way."

"You look familiar, sir," Kevin remarked to their greeter, peering through the small crowd. "I'm Kevin Garvey—have we ever met?"

"Not personally, Dr. Garvey. You may have seen me during your graduate work at Cal Tech. I taught there before coming here a few years ago."

Kevin nodded pleasantly.

"This is Dr. Michael Yu," the Colonel began his introduction, "formerly employed, as you just heard, at Cal Tech. Dr. Yu's PhD is from MIT. His specialty was particle physics. He's in charge of propulsion systems here."

"And back-engineering alien technology?" Mark asked seriously.

"Not much," Dr. Yu admitted. "Most of that was before my time. I'm standing on the shoulders of giants."

"You're far too modest, Mike," Neil contradicted him with the compliment.

"Ready when you are, Colonel." Dr. Yu smiled again.

"Good, give us a few minutes." The Colonel turned and headed for a door located about fifty yards from where they were standing. Neil motioned for everyone to follow him.

"Where are we going?" Father Benedict asked.

"To get a better view," Neil answered.

Once through the door, the team began ascending a flight of stairs, which was in turn followed by another, and then yet another, each of which turned to the left. The third set, however, was clearly makeshift, and not part of the permanent structure of the building. It led to an undersized entryway, barely five feet in height. The words *"Observation Deck"* were stenciled above the opening. Brian ducked inside and emerged into a spacious room, which he estimated was roughly half a basketball court in size. Two rows of cushioned chairs faced a large open window, from which the expanse of the hangar was plainly visible. There was no view of the work area they had just visited.

"Take a seat, everyone," the Colonel directed. "There'll be enough room, since Dr. Bandstra and I will be standing."

Brian moved toward the final seat on the first row, next to Melissa Kelley. But as he sat down, she abruptly stood and, with a glare, made her way past the others already seated and sat down in the back row. Father Benedict quickly filled her space and placed a hand on Brian's shoulder.

From the seat next to Father Benedict, Deidre leaned forward and gave Brian a curious glance. "You two have a fight?"

"I think it has something to do with the fact that I have a pulse."

"Ignore her," Father Benedict whispered.

Brian sighed.

"Oh, yeah! Will you take a look at that!" Malcolm exclaimed, sitting up in his seat.

The words were barely out of his mouth when the shiny hull of a classic "flying saucer" floated in front of the window, arresting the view of everyone. Brian wasn't sure, but it looked to him like the very bottom of the craft, which emitted a strange, bluish hue, was spinning.

The Colonel picked up a phone hanging on the wall next to a panel of small lights and buttons. His only words were, "We're ready," and he hung up the phone. A few seconds later, the craft went into a series of maneuvers. They began simply, with several brief horizontal and vertical trips to each side of the hangar and from floor-to-ceiling.

"How does it do that?" wondered Kevin incredulously. "There's no evidence of exhaust, no engine ..."

"There's no sound either," commented Mark. "Just that weird glow underneath."

Suddenly the craft stopped in a dead hover at its original position. Without warning, it accelerated to the far end of the hangar at an incredible speed, covering the distance in under a second. It was as though it had been shot out of a gun, yet still visible to the naked eye.

"It's coming back—right for us!" Kevin bellowed before the group could process what they had just seen. "Everybody down!"

Only Neil, Major Lindsay, and the Colonel resisted the perfectly natural inclination to take cover.

"Relax, people," the Colonel said with a grin. "What's the problem?"

Mark Chadwick picked himself off the floor and peered cautiously out the window. The saucer was hovering silently as before, although this time much closer to where they'd been seated.

"Hope you guys have fun scraping the pilots off their windshield after that stunt," Kevin griped, irritated and embarrassed.

"Completely unnecessary," the Colonel said cockily. "Take a look for yourself."

The craft slowly rotated 180 degrees before them, revealing two large, rectangular portals, one above the other. The upper panel slid open to the side slowly as they watched. Dr. Yu and two pilots waved to the team from where they were seated inside the craft.

"How is that possible?" Melissa wondered aloud. "He doesn't even have a hair out of place."

"They should have been atomized," Kevin argued. "I'm not going to believe this isn't some kind of sleight-of-hand stunt until I fly in one of those myself."

"We thought you might say that." The Colonel smiled mischievously and pressed one of the buttons on the panel next to the phone. A thick pane of glass appeared at the side of the open window and slid slowly across their line of sight.

"Wait a minute ..." Deidre said apprehensively. "Does this mean what I think it does?"

"Mother of God, we're inside one!" Father Benedict exclaimed in an agitated voice and rose hurriedly from his seat.

"Please sit down, Father," Neil requested in an understanding voice.

"But my heart—I'm much older than the rest of you," he said, his breathing becoming labored.

"There's nothing to fear," Major Lindsay assured him, coming to his side. "You'll feel nothing, believe me. The only precaution any of you need take is to keep looking straight ahead. Otherwise you may get nauseous. There's no danger."

"No danger!" Andrew protested.

"Easy, Father." Deidre took his arm and led him back to his seat next to her. "You guys better let him calm down first," she demanded, staring at the Colonel.

"Of course."

Father Benedict sat back in his chair, closed his eyes, and took a deep breath. After a couple minutes, he nodded for the Colonel to proceed. The Colonel picked up the phone.

"You're clear for maneuvers, Captain."

The team members braced themselves for acceleration, but felt nothing happen. Suddenly the panorama of the hangar changed drastically—up, down, sideways—the visual perspective changing in only a fraction of a second, like watching a television while channel surfing. The craft then went into a slow 360-degree circuit, whereupon the team was able to watch the entire perimeter of the hangar pass before their eyes.

As soon as the saucer completed its rotation, the far wall of the hangar appeared to rapidly come into view before their eyes and then disappear, like separate frames of a slide show, albeit one that kept reappearing in alternating sequence over and over. Their craft was accelerating from end to end, as they had seen the first one do. The experience was disorienting at first, but no one became ill.

"He'll slow it down now," Colonel Ferguson prepped them, "so that you can see you're actually in motion and not being visually deceived. Some of you may find this frightening, but you're in no danger. If you start to feel sick, just close your eyes; there will be no sensation of motion, so you needn't worry about that."

The craft repeated its end-to-end pattern, each time decelerating. The visual effect this time was like going forward and backward on a roller coaster, but at ten times the speed. There was no sense of gravitational force. Colonel Ferguson picked up the phone again and paused.

"Set her down."

The saucer landed a few hundred yards from where the craft had been docked earlier. In a few minutes they were all outside, and the Colonel was escorting them to the perimeter zone. The team was abuzz with amazed curiosity. Dr. Garvey was especially talkative and tailed the Colonel like an enamored schoolboy.

"How can G-forces be totally eliminated?" he inquired excitedly. "Where did we get antigravity?"

"I think we've already told you where we got it. We'd like to take credit for it, but we can't."

The Colonel led them to a door on the near wall of the hangar, which opened into a small lounge. The cheery Dr. Yu arrived a few minutes later.

"Hello again, everyone—I hope you all feel okay."

"How do those things work?" Kevin blurted out. "It just seems impossible!"

"How many of you remember the 1997 experiment where British and Dutch scientists levitated a frog? It was a pretty hot news story across the nation."

"I do," Malcolm acknowledged. Several others did as well.

"Good," Dr. Yu continued. "The way they accomplished this feat was to put the frog inside a magnetic cylinder and then create a magnetic field at least a million times stronger than that of the Earth. The idea was to create a field strong enough to distort the orbits of electrons in the frog's atoms. The result was that the magnetic field pushed the frog away from earth's magnetic field, which made the frog float."

"What does that have to do with UFOs?" asked Deidre.

"Pardon, me, doctor," the scientist said pleasantly, "but this craft is *not* unidentified." His gentle correction drew chuckles from around the room.

"Okay, you got me."

"The connection between the frog experiment and what you just experienced goes back to Einstein's theory of general relativity."

"I don't recall Einstein working on antigravity," Kevin said.

"The technically correct term is 'gravity modification.' According to

Einstein, spinning objects can distort gravity. Until 1989, it was thought the effect would be far too small to measure in the laboratory."

"What happened in 1989?" Father Benedict asked.

"In 1989, Dr. Ning Li of the University of Alabama in Huntsville predicted that if a magnetic field were applied to a superconductor, lattice ions within the superconductor would begin to spin rapidly and create a miniscule gravitational field."

"Well, I lasted thirty seconds," Brian lamented.

"Hold on—keep listening. In 1992, two scientists, Podkletnov and Nieminen, tested some of Dr. Li's ideas. They discovered that spinning a superconducting ceramic disk at five thousand rpm can produce a two percent reduction in the weight of objects placed over the spinning disk."

"And Einstein," Malcolm thought aloud, "realized gravity and acceleration were indistinguishable in certain experiments. That would mean modifying gravity could also modify the effects of acceleration. Hence, no G-forces."

"That's right," Dr. Yu confirmed Malcolm's musing.

"So that spinning-light thing we saw under the saucer was a superconductor—that actually *repelled* the craft away from earth's gravity?" asked Melissa.

"Yes, pretty much," he answered, pleased at a novice's ability to see the connection. "There are technical problems with the way you've stated it, but that's basically it. The phenomenon is known as the Meissner effect. Basically, the repelling effect serves to create a gravity-free area around the craft. Once the craft escapes the pull of earth's gravity, the gravitational shield around the craft actually functions to *pull* the craft through space at speeds close to the speed of light, rather than propelling it. The craft simply goes in the direction the shield is concentrated. Human scientists like Dr. Ning Li at the University of Alabama-Huntsville were on to the principle, but we had to have the help of the visitors to generate the magnetic field for large craft."

"Yeah," sneered Deidre, "they helped us in exchange for our looking the other way when they decided to use our people as guinea pigs. You might look at them as heroes, but to me they're just demented, celestial proctologists. They disgust me, frankly."

"I understand your feelings—" Dr. Yu began.

"Do you? How could you, unless you've been a victim?"

"Well, I haven't been a victim, as you put it, but I do think you're being unreasonable—and hypocritical," Dr. Yu countered, never losing his genuinely pleasant persona.

"And how's that?" Deidre shot back, her voice more intense.

"Honestly, doctor," the scientist intoned with deliberation, "if you knew that the path to saving your race went through the door of human experimentation, would you cease your work? Would you really sacrifice the future of your people in order to avoid the distasteful?"

"I'd look for other ways to—"

"That isn't the question," he stopped her. "Would you condemn the rest of us in this room and our children to extinction to keep your own moral sense intact? After all, that is the dilemma from the aliens' perspective. They need a place to stay—is there room at the inn?"

Deidre squirmed in her chair, as Dr. Yu and the others waited for a response. Brian glanced at Father Benedict, whose face bore an expression of deep reflection.

"Well?" Dr. Yu pressed.

"I guess not—but I'd trust my own motives before I'd trust an ET."

"If they in fact exist," Brian added.

A hush fell over the room. Dr. Yu cast a confused glance at the Colonel. "Is there a problem?" he finally asked.

"We've told them about the visitors and about our problem—the reason they're here," the Colonel responded, "but a number of our members can't seem to accept that the visitors are real."

"Oh ... I see," he said thoughtfully. "That's not surprising. Have they seen Dr. Marcus' lab?"

"We have a date with Ian tomorrow morning at eight o'clock."

"Very good."

"I'm looking forward to it," the Colonel said, eyeing Brian. "It's always stimulating to breathe life into myths."

23

It is my thesis that flying saucers are real, and that
they are space ships from another solar system.

—*Dr. Herman Oberth, father of modern rocketry,*
The American Weekly, October 24, 1954

Kevin glanced at his watch nervously as he stood inside his room at the door. Six thirty A.M. He debated with himself whether following up on the note he'd received was worth the risk—or even necessary, after what he'd just seen and heard.

Dr. Yu had been most impressive, answering each question he or any of the others had offered with aplomb. The technology was exponentially beyond anything he'd ever heard of in graduate school or read in professional journals. It was truly otherworldly, from his perspective. *What could I possibly see now that would change my mind? What would make me doubt the project?*

He looked at his watch again. Exactly two minutes had passed. If he was going, he'd have to go now. It would take a minute or two to reach the proper doorway. Kevin held his breath and carded out of the room.

He arrived at his checkpoint with thirty seconds to spare. He looked ahead at the cafeteria. A dim light shone from its entrance. He was alone in the hallway. He watched the seconds pass one by one through the LCD of his watch. The wait was intolerable.

As soon as the minute expired, he tried the door handle. It released as though it had been expecting his touch, and he passed through silently. He hurriedly set the timer on his watch and followed the directions he'd committed to memory as instructed, glancing only at his watch to track his time. He had no way of knowing, however, how close he was to his objective.

He quickened his pace to a trot as he saw his remaining time drop under one minute. The illusory footrace ended with only a few more strides. His eyes widened as he read the phrase on the door: *Auroral*

Research Observation. Winded initially by apprehension but now by anticipation, he impatiently watched the seconds tick past six forty. He placed his hand on the latch. Again the door yielded.

Kevin found himself on the upper tier of an expansive, auditorium-style room that reminded him immediately of the old Mission Control center he'd seen on television as a child during the NASA Apollo missions. He silently descended onto the main floor via a carpeted set of stairs to his left. True to his unknown informant's word, the room's four computer consoles were unoccupied.

Once on the bottom, he gazed, mouth agape, at the massive view screen. All the earth's continents and oceans were displayed on adjacent panels, arranged in a panoramic display. Bright white lights studded the continents, marking major cities. Wind currents, color-coded according to altitude and atmospheric layer, were superimposed holographically on each continent, their pathways and directions being updated at thirty-second intervals. Ocean currents were likewise indicated. Symbols and data readouts on each panel informed onlookers of current weather conditions, wind velocity, temperature, and barometric pressure.

His watch shone 6:47. *Great.* He had only eight minutes left. He moved deliberately from console to console, trying to determine what it was that he was supposed to glean from this excursion. Suddenly a high-pitched beeping sounded. Kevin stepped away from the computers, fearful that he'd triggered an alarm. The beeping stopped after only a few seconds. He eyed the door nervously, but nothing happened.

Four minutes left. He turned back to the view screen, and his eye immediately took note of a small, blinking red light situated on the screen in south-central Alaska. He stepped closer and noticed the time readout in the lower left hand corner—8:49. *What?* He looked again at his watch and then realized the clock on the screen was oriented two hours behind the time zone he was in. *Two hours? That's ... Alaska.*

Kevin looked up at the red blinking light he had noticed a few minutes ago. He was close enough that he could read the city names. *Gakona, Alaska.* He knew he'd heard of it before. Suddenly he remembered. He looked incredulously at the screen, taking in all its data tracking. *No way—this is impossible.*

In a flash, Neil's words of barely two days before came flashing back: *"They promised to take care of our ozone problem."* Instantly Kevin understood why he'd been directed to the room, why he'd been singled out—and how the team could be deceived.

Who sent you here? A voice suddenly invaded his mind.

Kevin whirled around, but his senses were suddenly overtaken by an invisible force, his mind commandeered by an unseen intruder. His forehead began to throb violently. His eyes rolled backward, deep into his skull. The sensation of being levitated off his feet never registered in his brain.

I don't like being deceived, the voice continued.

Kevin's body dangled in midair for a few more seconds, then stiffened tightly for just a moment before his limbs began to flail wildly and involuntarily. His head jerked violently from side to side. Blood began to trickle from the corner of his mouth and his ears. Then, just as abruptly as the assault had begun, his limp body fell to the floor with a dull thud. The assailant turned silently toward a neighboring wall and passed through it effortlessly.

24

It's done routinely.

—*Comment of an unidentified NASA technician to Donna Hare,
former subcontractor in the photo labs of the Johnson Space Center
in Houston, in her April 9, 1997 testimony to the U.S. Congress that
she watched the technician airbrush
a UFO out of a space satellite photo*

"It's ten after eight. Where's Garvey?" the Colonel demanded impatiently, surveying the team. "He knows better than this. *Well?*"

"No idea," Mark replied uneasily, taken back by his friend's uncharacteristic tardiness.

The Colonel scowled and took the phone from its resting place on the table. Malcolm glanced curiously over at Mark while the Colonel barked orders that Kevin's room be accessed on the double and that he be escorted immediately to the conference room. The team waited tensely in the awkward silence, anticipating their colleague's arrival and the ensuing tirade.

Several minutes that seemed like aeons passed as the Colonel paced behind Major Lindsay's chair. Instead of the expected sound of the door's security latch, the phone rang. The Colonel stared at it for a moment, puzzled, and then picked it up.

"Well then, where is he? Check the logs!" the Colonel bellowed, his anger turning into exasperation. "Oh, I see. Get your butts to those checkpoints, then. If he doesn't turn up, I want every inch of this base searched! And instruct the guards not to shoot!"

The Colonel slammed the phone down on its base and spread his hands on the shining, mahogany table. Silently he hung his head down in concentration. The wide-eyed team members sat speechless.

"I should never have approved your request to remove cameras from the corridor," he grumbled in a low, angry voice, turning his gaze toward Neil.

"What is it, Vernon?" Neil ventured after an awkward moment.

"It appears," the Colonel growled, "that Dr. Garvey was a little too impressed yesterday ... or that he's become bored with our company."

"I'm afraid I don't—"

"He checked out of his room this morning at six thirty," the Colonel shouted, "and apparently got out of the secured corridor!"

"*What?* How is that possible?"

"How should I know?" the Colonel snapped. He clasped his hands behind his back and looked toward the floor in concentration. "Someone let him out into the base. Security lapses simply will not be tolerated."

The Colonel began slowly pacing back and forth, assessing the possibilities. Brian cast a glance at Father Benedict, who appeared deep in thought, his chin on his chest.

The Colonel suddenly stopped and raised his head. He looked at the wall. "Have any of you been contacted by anyone outside this project? If you have been, and don't tell me right now, you run the risk of my considering such a future revelation as a violation of your security oath. I can and will make your life a living hell if this project is in any way compromised."

No one spoke, but they watched each other carefully for any hint that an answer might be forthcoming.

The Colonel lowered his head once more, watching the team out of the corner of his eye. "Major, we have to press on. There have been too many delays already. Let Ian know we're on our way."

***

Kevin's eyes opened lazily, and his consciousness was immediately filled with intolerable pain. Every joint, every muscle, every fiber ached mercilessly. He could feel the blood in his mouth, the nausea in his stomach, the erratic heartbeat in his chest. As his vision cleared, he took note of the analog clock on one of the view screen's panels: 6:55. He had to leave a message; he had to warn the others.

Mustering all his strength, he began to roll toward one of the computer consoles, each revolution producing crushing pain. Breathless, he reached the stool and desperately pulled himself on top of it, gasping and wincing with each inch of elevation. He came to rest on his side, his torso clumsily thrown over the seat.

He smiled to himself weakly as he recognized he could navigate his way to the Facility's email program using the team password. Using his right index finger, he typed an address and then tabbed to the subject line.

Without warning, his chest was suddenly seized with terrific pain. He clutched at his heart with his right hand, his body writhing in agony. He felt himself losing his balance and grabbed at the keyboard, bringing it crashing to the floor with him as he toppled from his makeshift perch. Panting, he pulled the keyboard toward him.

In silent, dark elation, he took note of the small green light that told him it still functioned. The room slowly began to spin, but he gritted his teeth where he lay, trying to clear his mind. His fingers stumbled through fifteen keystrokes. He grabbed the mouse, which was dangling by its cord from the tabletop. He placed it on his leg, navigated to the send button, and clicked. With his last ounce of strength, he jerked the keyboard's cord from the computer. A defiant grimace creased his mouth as the blackness claimed him.

25

I was called one afternoon [in 1948] to come to the Oval Office—the President wanted to see me ... I was directed to report quarterly to the President after consulting with Central Intelligence people, as to whether or not any UFO incidents received by them could be considered as having any strategic threatening implications ...

—*General Robert B. Landry,*
Air Force Aide to President Harry S. Truman

"Sorry it's so cold in here," Dr. Marcus apologized to the group huddled together in front of him, "but here in the morgue everything needs to be properly stored and temperature controlled. There are extra lab coats in the locker if it will help."

Emotions of excitement and anxiety fought for dominance in Brian's mind. Were there really the remains of alien beings behind those stainless steel doors? How could he know for sure? Despite his theoretical handle on the situation, he knew that this truth could potentially redefine every religious sentiment in the Western world. But, after all, that was why he was here—to defend his contention that serious theology could quite easily accommodate the existence of other worlds, the reality of other sentient beings.

His mind wandered momentarily to the paper he'd written about the subject, the one that had cost him his teaching position. He knew he was right, that his exegesis was sound, that those who'd passed judgment on him had never seriously thought about the subject. *So why am I scared?*

"We'll start with a brief overview of the bodies," Dr. Marcus informed them. "If you want to see the actual forensic examinations, we have them on film. Two of the corpses were filmed on 16mm, due to the late forties date, so the quality isn't that great. The third is on standard VHS and DVD and is about a year old."

"A year old!" Mark blurted out. "How did you get the body?"

"Things die, Dr. Chadwick. The aliens gave us the body for further study; it isn't like we have a whole bunch of these, and the ones we do recover on our own are usually mutilated or burned, since they are invariably retrieved from crash sites. We looked at it as a gesture of good-will on their part."

"What killed it?" wondered Melissa. "What if it died of some extra-terrestrial disease? I can't help thinking of the *Andromeda Strain* right about now."

"Then I wouldn't be standing here talking to you. I performed the autopsy myself, and I haven't had so much as the sniffles since. Really, people, you have to get over the Hollywood approach to the visitors. They aren't here to dispose of us like some pathogen."

"At any rate," he changed the subject, unlocking the handle release on the middle drawer with a key, "behind you we have several micro-scopes and drawers of literally hundreds of slides if you feel inclined to check them—tissue samples, bodily fluids, toxicological analyses, that sort of thing. I've done a full genetic workup with DNA sequencing, and the internal organs are also stored here. You may examine what-ever you wish, and I'll answer your questions to the best of my ability. The only thing I ask is that you do not touch anything unless you're wearing the proper gloves and facial gear. I don't want anything con-taminated. That being said ..." His voice trailed off as he popped the latch on the drawer.

Gasps punctuated the silence as Dr. Marcus drew the metallic slab out of its sheath in full view of the team. Gingerly, the team members approached for a closer look. It was an impeccable specimen. All the familiar visual features that had seeped into culture through a host of media were there: the chalky-gray skin; the bulbous cranium, dis-proportionate to the underdeveloped torso, with the narrow, tapering jaw; the black, opaque, almond-shaped eyes; the spindly limbs. But this wasn't television.

The lifeless figure peered up at them in an emotionless, unnerving gaze. The signs of autopsy were evident, the Y-incision on the torso hav-ing been neatly sewn up. The skullcap had also been carefully returned to its original position, and both eyes had sporadic, delicate stitching on their perimeter. Deidre looked away momentarily, fighting the gag reflex brought on by the overpowering odor of formaldehyde. Brian's pulse quickened, but the anxiety of the moment had passed; he was en-tranced.

"You can compare this specimen to one from Roswell," Dr. Marcus said, unlatching the drawer to the left of the first corpse. The team's attention was immediately drawn to the second drawer as it yielded its contents. "It was injured in the crash, and there's been some discoloration due to age, but it's still worth a look."

As Dr. Marcus had noted, one of the legs had been mutilated and badly burned. There were various smaller lacerations on the corpse. The face was contorted in an expression of acute pain. It was evident that it had suffered greatly in the moments before it succumbed to its injuries. The autopsy had not been as careful, and the specimen had been left in varying stages of dissection.

"Height and weight ranges from three and a half to four and a half feet, and sixty-five to ninety pounds," Dr. Marcus began his introduction. "The black 'eyes' are actually not eyes at all; they're protective coverings. Here," he said, retrieving what resembled a dental pick from a nearby drawer, "let me show you."

Dr. Marcus carefully inserted the end of the instrument under the edge of the left eye of the more recent corpse. The black casing gave way with little effort, revealing a pale, pupil-less, milky ball. "We're not sure how their eyes work, to be honest."

"You mean without the covering?" remarked Melissa.

"Right."

"There are lenses within, but without a pupil it would seem that light can be absorbed through the entire ball. If that's the case, they'd need the protective black layer to prevent overexposure to light rays."

"Why the stitching around the eye?"

"An entryway into the sinus cavity. The nasal openings and mouth are extremely undersized, so that's the best way to avoid disfigurement or splitting the head open."

"Oh."

"You'll also notice," Dr. Marcus continued, peeling back a loosened flap of skin on the creature's throat, "that they don't have vocal cords."

"And no discernible outer ear," added Mark, intrigued, as Dr. Marcus gently turned the creature's head, "only tiny apertures."

"The Colonel said that they're alleged to—I mean, known to—communicate telepathically," Deidre reminded him, peering skittishly over his shoulder.

The Colonel and Dr. Bandstra, who glanced at each other, did not miss her rewording. She'd been won over.

"Do you know how they do that?" Malcolm asked, gaining Dr. Marcus' attention.

"I'll show you what we think they use to do it," Dr. Marcus offered.

Mark stepped away from the slab, and Dr. Marcus opened the drawer adjacent to the one on which the body lay.

"These are the internal organs," he noted, pulling the slab a few feet into the room. "Of particular interest is the brain. What do you notice immediately?" he asked, holding a fluid-filled glass canister aloft, its spongy contents visible to the group.

"Wow," Mark whispered in amazement. "It's got a third lobe."

"Precisely," Dr. Marcus replied, pointing to the globular mass situated between what otherwise looked like the two halves of a human brain. "We know from the ongoing work on ESP at Stanford and Princeton that the human brain is capable of projecting and receiving thought from an external source. We figure that's the use of the extra lobe, since the rest of the brain is remarkably similar to our own."

"Have you considered the possibility that they aren't true extraterrestrials?" Melissa inquired.

"What do you mean? What else could they be but extraterrestrials? The evidence is staring you in the face," the Colonel asked with some exasperation.

"I'm thinking in terms of evolution," she explained.

"I still don't get it," said Neil.

"I believe Dr. Kelley is wondering whether I've considered that these beings may have evolved from humans, or some other earthly life form—correct?"

She nodded.

"I have in fact explored that option," said Dr. Marcus, "but I've ruled it out. Granted, there are genetic correlations between our DNA and theirs, but—"

"Doesn't that suggest evolution from a common source?" she interrupted.

"Common source would not mean they evolved from us. If life here were seeded from space—the old panspermia idea—and the same kind of microbes started life on their planet, then common source would be an explanation, but the visitors would still be genuine ETs. The real problem with your idea, though, is the utter uniqueness of several anatomical features."

"Such as?"

"Take the stomach, for instance."

"Yes, I noticed it was extremely small, even for their body weight."

"Precisely. In all the specimens I've autopsied, I've never discovered stomach contents. Reports of earlier autopsies are the same. I know they can eat because I've seen them do it, but it seems they don't have to. From their 'blood work'—if you want to call what they have 'blood'—their bodies do have the sufficient nutrient and mineral content to maintain their metabolism and general health. I suspect they have some kind of osmotic ability to draw what they need from their environment by absorption. In other words, their skin functions like a filter. It would have to be bidirectional, too, since they have no excretory system that I can discern."

"Aha," cracked Malcolm, "that's why they're so interested in proctology." The Colonel glared at him. "Just a thought," Malcolm said whimsically.

"So you see, Dr. Kelley," Dr. Marcus concluded, "I can't see how the process of evolution can account for the virtual absence of digestive and excretory systems. If the process moved in this direction, how could the organism survive it?"

"You know what else they don't have that sort of makes it hard to explain them as evolved humans?" Malcolm piped up again.

"What?" asked Melissa, nonchalantly.

"Genitals. How do these critters get it on?" He looked at Dr. Marcus.

Mark volunteered an answer. "They reproduce asexually."

"We don't think so."

"Huh?"

"I believe they reproduce artificially. In fact, from what we know of their genetic expertise, I wouldn't be surprised if they just cloned themselves. After all, they're pretty much exactly the same. Every specimen I've examined is basically a carbon-copy of the others."

The team spent the next half hour questioning Dr. Marcus and examining the results of his work. The team's scientific personnel were particularly thorough. They made sure that between them they handled or viewed everything at their disposal. Brian followed the questioning as best he could, but it was difficult for someone without the necessary background. Thankfully, Neil was eager to talk and soon made his way over to his friend.

"You look pretty calm, Brian," he began.

"Why wouldn't I be? You know my thoughts on the issue."

"It's just that when it really hits you, it kind of rocks your world. I have to admit, I went through a few days of doubt about all I'd believed about the Bible, creation—even God."

"Why?" The depth of Neil's struggle took Brian aback. "You read my paper. We'd even talked about this sort of thing before I ever put anything into writing."

"I just found it unnerving that the only thing keeping me grounded was your words on a piece of paper. I'm relieved you can take all this in and still be so confident."

"God doesn't owe us an exhaustive history of everything He's done since the beginning of time."

"Right," Neil smiled, "but that isn't your main argument."

"True. A correct understanding of the image of God is critical. I hope I won't be wasting my time when I present my work. Most of our audience doesn't care about religion anyway."

"I'm glad you mentioned your presentation. I don't know if he's mentioned it to you yet, but the Colonel has scheduled it for tomorrow at eleven o'clock A.M."

"Sounds fine. I'm more or less going to lecture through my paper. I'm ready."

"He isn't concerned about your being ready," Neil confided to him. "He wants to give Andrew the evening."

"I didn't know he was presenting anything."

"He isn't. The Colonel doesn't think he's taking things so well. The only thing he's done since seeing the bodies is pace around like an expectant father. There's something wrong."

"Would you like me to ask him?" Brian offered.

"It's worth a try. Uh-oh, here he comes."

Brian watched the old priest approach. A distracted look creased his face.

"Seen enough, Father?" Neil asked gently. "It seems everyone is convinced but you."

"Not everyone is convinced, Neil," Brian corrected him.

"What are you saying?"

"Just being honest," Brian said in a low voice. "I can see why you were convinced, but—"

"Why *I* was convinced?" he asked incredulously, being careful to keep the conversation private. "What about you?"

"I was convinced until Melissa's question about evolution from humans."

Father Benedict's distant gaze disappeared, his attention now fixed on the conversation.

"What?" Neil marveled.

"Let me explain. It was her question—it was stupid."

"Now you've lost me."

"She knows how evolution is supposed to work," Brian replied. "There's no way she would have overlooked the fact that the stomach couldn't have sustained the creature. And if it drew nutrition in an 'alien' way, pardon the pun, she would have known there could be no evolutionary link between them and us. Plus, it's perfectly obvious that any trait supposedly evolving over millions of years couldn't have been transmitted generationally in these beings, because they have no sexual organs. She'd have to be blind not to have noticed that. She's just too smart not to make the connection. There's no way they could have evolved from *Homo sapiens*."

"I'm still not sure I follow."

"In evolutionary thinking, the loss of an organ is due to its disuse; an organ becomes vestigial and then eventually disappears. But to evolve, you need transmission of genetic change through reproduction. You can't have both; they work against one another. She'd never have overlooked that. There are only two other options. One is that these beings have never reproduced sexually, but always 'naturally' by another means, as asexual organisms on earth do. That in itself disqualifies them as being directly related to us. Your other choice is that some other being *created* them sexless but with the intelligence to perpetuate themselves through technology like cloning."

"Brilliant!" Father Benedict exclaimed under his breath.

"But, if you're correct," Neil questioned, "why would Melissa have even asked the question?"

"That's the point—I don't know," Brian replied, shrugging. "But she did it for a reason. She's after something, and if she's not convinced, neither am I. I don't know if you've noticed, but she's developed a preoccupation with Marcus' autopsied corpse. She's been standing there staring at it for the last ten minutes."

Neil peered over Brian's shoulder discreetly. As he'd said, Melissa stood over the body, arms folded, chin on her chest, staring at its face.

"Have you asked her about her question?" Neil inquired, turning his attention back to Brian.

"I've been fighting the urge."

"Why?"

"She pretty much despises me, and I don't want to cause a fuss and draw attention."

"If she really is fishing for information, she wouldn't show her hand that easily. Too smart."

"I hate it when you use my own logic against me."

"So?"

Brian sighed. "All right."

He took a deep breath and walked over to where Melissa stood transfixed in thought. If she'd noticed his approach, she showed no interest. He hesitated.

"What is it, Melissa?" he whispered. "What do you see?"

She maintained her silence.

"Come on, Melissa," he persisted. "I know you're on to something. What is it?"

She looked up from the corpse and gave him an annoyed glance. The two of them looked at each other but said nothing. Suddenly, the words of her mysterious assailant came back to her: "*He's the only one here you can trust.*" She flushed with anger, not only at the recollection of the incident, but at the very thought of trusting a man—especially this one. *Just you wait. I'll expose you like all the others. All in due time.*

"Stuff it," she snapped, and walked away.

Brian hung his head in frustration. He felt a hand on his shoulder and turned to see Father Benedict's friendly, but concerned, face.

"You must keep your wits about you, son. Your time is now." He paused, as if overtaken by some dramatic realization. "And you must be single-minded."

"What do you mean?" Brian wondered where Andrew's prophet imitation had come from.

"You weren't brought here by those arrogant fools. *God* sent you here. The final pieces of the puzzle are coming together for me. I've pursued them most of my life, but God has shown me that it will be given to you to expose them. I'll help you all I can, but after tomorrow, my days will most likely be numbered."

Brian didn't know what surprised him more, the priest's language or his ominous declaration. "Andrew, what—"

"*Your dissertation*—I keep telling you! It holds the answers to our questions, especially now."

Brian was confused.

"Look at its face," the seasoned scholar whispered, taking Brian's shoulders and turning him toward the alien corpse. "Look at it and think about what you just said to Neil! Look at it and remember: '*And behold, one of the Watchers appeared fearsome—like a serpent.*'"

A chill ran up Brian's spine as the priest repeated the text of the Dead Sea Scroll fragment so familiar to him. He looked down in startled disbelief at the gray figure.

"It can't be."

"It is."

"It makes no sense."

"It will. Look at its hands."

Brian's eyes moved haltingly from the creature's face to the shoulder, and down the emaciated arm to its hands. He closed his eyes tightly, his mind racing to process what Andrew was driving at. He opened them and looked again. He swallowed hard. He hadn't noticed before. He looked up at the priest, frightened by the connection the old man had made.

The alien's hands each had six fingers.

26

Congressional investigations are still being held
on the problem of unidentified flying objects, and the
problem is one in which there is quite a bit of interest ...
Since most of the material presented to the Committees is
classified, the hearings are never printed.

—*Congressman William H. Ayres, 1958*

"This is exactly how we found him, sir," the MP informed the Colonel.

The Colonel looked down at Kevin's stiffened body resting atop the computer keyboard.

"The doctor suspects massive internal bleeding, Vernon," Neil informed him as he walked over to where the Colonel stood. "He's guessing it was an aneurysm."

"Any history of that in his files?"

"He thought he recalled reading it two or three generations removed, but he's going to check."

The Colonel nodded.

"What do you suppose he was doing?" Neil asked.

"Looks to me like he sat down here to work on the computer when it happened," observed the Colonel. "He took the whole keyboard with him when he seized—ripped it right out the back," he noted, inspecting the connecting prongs. "We'll have the hard drive checked." He paused, then shook his head. "What a loss. How are we supposed to replace him on such short notice, Neil? He was absolutely key."

"I'll start going through the files. We have to move fast."

"Who let him in here? Did we recover an override badge?"

"No. It looks as though the doors were accessed remotely."

The Colonel shook his head. "Just what I didn't want to hear. Wait till I tell the Group."

"I'll tell the team."

"Thanks."

***

Mark lay in his bed looking at the ceiling. It had been nearly three hours since Neil had assembled the team and given them the terrible news. Mark had met Kevin ten months ago, and the two had spent nearly every day since working together. He didn't look like much, but Mark had grown to respect him. Restricted to the room, pending an investigation, he'd tried to sleep, but he couldn't. It just didn't make sense. *An aneurysm?*

Mark abruptly rolled out of bed. *Maybe they know more by now.* He sat down at his computer and accessed his email, recalling Neil's promise to email everyone with details as soon as he had them. *Nothing.* He moved his mouse in disgust to close the program but stopped, his eye falling on a nonsensical subject line.

"Can't even avoid spam at Area 51," he muttered, opening the transmission. There was no message. Confused, he looked back up at the subject line.

"What the ... "

The line contained thirteen characters:

gakonaakharpkev

Mark stared at the odd, cryptic notation. He knew intuitively that the last three letters stood for Kevin, but he could make no sense of the rest. The time on the email indicated Kevin had sent it just a few minutes after he'd left his room. Mark closed the program and shut down his computer. If it were an aneurysm, it must have happened as Kevin was typing. The message was pure gibberish.

27

It suddenly struck me that that tiny pea, pretty and blue,
was the Earth. I put up my thumb and shut one eye,
and my thumb blotted out the planet Earth.
I didn't feel like a giant. I felt very, very small.

—*Neil Armstrong*

The alarm clock beeped annoyingly from its perch on the nightstand next to the bed. Melissa reached lazily toward the sound, clumsily fingering the assortment of buttons on top of the electronic nuisance. She located the snooze button and pressed it firmly. Peaceful silence filled the room, and she pulled the covers up to her chin, rolled over, and began drifting back to sleep.

"Rise and shine," a voice unexpectedly intruded.

Melissa's eyes flickered open in alarm.

"Don't move, Dr. Kelley," the voice commanded. "The rules of engagement haven't changed."

She recognized the voice. "What are you doing in my bedroom?" she bristled angrily. "I have a mind to—"

"To what?" he cut her off in a sarcastic tone. "Do what you're told, and you'll live to hate me another day. You really ought to change your attitude. I'm not here to hurt you, remember?"

"It must have slipped my mind. What is it now?"

"I'd like a few answers, then—"

"Then you'll throw me another information bone?"

"Really, doctor, the analogy is most unfitting. I actually find you quite attractive. You'd expect that, of course."

"Shut up and get to the point!"

"I'd like to know why our little slideshow didn't convince you of the reality of extraterrestrial life."

"How would you know whether I believed it or not?"

"The good undersecretary informed the Colonel, and the Colonel briefed the Group last night. We all believe heartily in the free flow of information, you know."

"I never said anything to Dr. Bandstra."

"Correct—technically. Dr. Scott suspects you aren't convinced," he added, and he summarized Brian's suspicions for her.

"Since when does Dr. Scott speak for me?"

"He doesn't, but your demeanor has convinced him you're on to something ..."

"So what?"

"So your own uncertainty has tainted him. I believe his exact words to his friend, the undersecretary were, 'If she's not convinced, I'm not convinced.'"

"Sounds like he's just trying to keep up," she said, drawing some satisfaction from the idea.

"If that's what you think, you couldn't be more incorrect. You don't know Dr. Scott as I do."

"Oh, that's right—you know everything. Sorry, I forgot."

"You know, there are multitudes who would kill to see what you've seen. What makes you smarter than them?"

She didn't answer.

"Don't play games with me," he warned. Melissa smiled under the covers, enjoying his irritation.

"Well?"

She maintained her silence.

"If you don't help me," he said in a more controlled tone, "I can't assure you of my help when you might need it. Now, tell me why you think the bodies aren't real."

"I never said I didn't think they were real," she said coyly.

"I'm intrigued. Go on."

"Of course they're real," she continued, choosing her words carefully, "they're just real fakes. That's all I'll tell you."

"Clever girl," he said with an unseen smirk. "I can see my choice of you has been totally justified. You're wrong in what you think is the truth, but close—closer than any of the others."

"What do you mean, I'm wrong?" she asked defensively. "I haven't told you what I think."

"You've told me enough—told me what I wanted to hear. You see, no one else would have understood your comments."

"Why is that, O omniscient one?" she asked bitterly.

"Because," he continued confidently, unfazed by her sarcasm, "I know how you spent your time during what should have been your first semester of college. No one else here does, because it isn't part of your record."

Melissa's eyes widened in horror. He really did know everything.

"Your self-training during that time has put you ahead of the others," he droned on while she remained silent. "Nevertheless, you're wrong. But take heart, you'll soon see something that will perhaps help you put the pieces together."

"If you know all these things," she blurted out vengefully, "why the mind games? If you know we're being taken for a ride again, why not just tell me and get it over with?"

"It's just more fun this way."

"You're hiding something."

"Yes ... I am," the figure said with a thoughtful sigh. "But what I'm hiding will only help you. As I said before, I'm acting out of self-interest. That shouldn't be hard for you to swallow."

Melissa was taken aback by his change of tone. His words made him seem less contemptible somehow. "So, when am I going to receive this epiphany?"

There was no answer. After a few seconds of indecision, she decided to sit up in her bed. As soon as she did, she heard the familiar click of her door's locking mechanism. He was gone.

She breathed a sigh of relief and looked over at the clock. Brian's presentation would begin in a couple hours. She was actually looking forward to it. It was time to start laying the groundwork to bring him down.

28

"As the Colonel has already told you," Brian began, "my part of this project concerns how to make the news of an intelligent extraterrestrial reality palatable to the conservative Protestant religious community. To say the least, it's going to be a hard sell. I'm hoping to explain why and how people who'd object to the idea can be put at ease with such a disclosure. Please feel free to interact at any time."

The Colonel interrupted. "Let's clarify what you mean by religious conservatives first."

"Okay. When I use that term, I'm thinking of people who believe that the Bible is the only source of truth and that it must be interpreted literally. If something can't be fit into that box, then it can't be true. Logically, then, to those of that mindset, if ET showed up, their faith would be shaken quite a bit, and if our team just told them ETs were real without undeniable truth, they'd assume we were trying to undermine their beliefs and consider us the enemy."

Melissa scoffed. "Just great—some real thinkers." She put away her pen and tablet. Brian got the impression she'd only taken it out for that moment anyway.

"That attitude doesn't seem too difficult to address," said Mark. "This gets a bit personal for me since my parents would fit into this lot. There are lots of things that aren't in the Bible. I don't know much about it, but things we take for granted like electricity and gravity aren't going to be in some Bible verse."

"I agree, and that's how I'd approach the basic objection—show them they already accept things that aren't in their Scriptures, so ET is just another one of those items."

"We'd hardly need an expert here if it were that easy, though. What else don't they like about the idea?"

"I'm sure you're all acquainted with the controversy over evolution for many people of faith."

Heads nodded.

"Believe it or not, that battleground gets dragged into this issue, too. Some religious conservatives think that an ET reality supports an evolutionary view of human origins. Anyone who thinks like that would resist the idea."

"Why would that be?" asked Malcolm. "I had some colleagues at MIT who were pretty religious, and they didn't seem to care about evolution at all. They just said God created it—like He was the mechanism for getting it started. I thought they were a little weird, but they were good scientists."

"There are a lot of scientists who are theologically conservative and take that view. An ET reality wouldn't matter to them. They would just say God created ET and move on."

"A lot? Oh, come on," protested Melissa. "I can't believe there are many people who fit that description. It sounds to me like they were filtering their science through their religion. In my book that shows a lack of objectivity, and they shouldn't be taken seriously. They're just closet creationists."

"Actually, Christian and Jewish scientists who don't mind evolution are also pretty open about their creationism, but they don't hold a literal view of the Bible. And despite what Melissa thinks, they deserve to be taken seriously. Melissa, do you know who Frances Collins is?"

"Not off the top of my head. What's the point?"

"He's head of the Human Genome Project and a serious Christian. If you think he doesn't do real science, you're the one who shouldn't be taken seriously. And I doubt he'd be accused of filtering his findings through anything."

"Whatever. It's all bull." She stared defiantly at Brian, waiting for the next volley.

"I think we'd best stay on track here," the Colonel broke in.

"No problem." Brian smiled. His point had been made. "There are three more substantive obstacles to getting those who share this worldview on board with an ET reality. The first is the idea that if ET is real, and he is a sentient being capable of religious interests, then Jesus would have to go to his planet, die, and rise again so ET could be redeemed."

"Sounds silly," said Deidre.

"It is. This view forgets that, in Christian theology, the only reason humans need atonement for their sins is because they are morally guilty before God as a result of Adam's fall. The New Testament teaches that Adam's guilt was transferred to all humans, and therein lies the loophole. ET, as a nonhuman, isn't in need of forgiveness since he wasn't the species punished by the fall. He'd suffer the effects of the fall, like the rest of creation according to the New Testament, but he wouldn't need personal forgiveness.

"ET would benefit from the atonement in a general way. That is, he'd either be part of the new heaven and new earth that Christianity teaches will appear some day when Christ returns, or he'd be completely peripheral. And ET having religious interests doesn't undermine my argument, since the Bible teaches angels have that and are not included in the atonement. The objection is completely baseless, but it's very common."

"Interesting," said Deidre, cleaning her glasses. "What's number two?"

"I'll call it the 'image of God objection.' In a nutshell, the book of Genesis teaches that when God created humans, He created them 'in His image.' According to biblical theology, the image is that which makes humanity unique among all created things. It's clear that this can't be physical appearance because the Bible elsewhere teaches that God is spirit and genderless."

"So what does the Church teach on this?"

"Theologians of Judaism and Christianity have taught for centuries that the image of God refers to things like intelligence, consciousness, communication capability, morals, the ability to commune with God, and the like. If any of those or some combination are correct, then an ET that had the same abilities would prove the Bible is wrong on this point and that humans aren't the apple of God's eye, so to speak. You only need to remember how the Church reacted to Galileo when he proved the earth wasn't the center of the solar system—that it wasn't anything special. This objection fears the same thing would happen with humanity—we'd be nothing unique."

"Father Benedict?" the Colonel prompted the priest, who had been a spectator to this point.

"I don't think the Catholic church would react this way, especially since the Vatican has stated publicly that they aren't troubled by evolution or the idea of extraterrestrial life. Muslims wouldn't care either since the Qur'an teaches that Allah could have created other worlds. Conservative evangelical Protestants are another story. Brian's concern is valid for those people."

"So how would you handle that group, Dr. Scott? Is this a serious obstacle?"

"I think the objection is completely misguided. And if you want me to speculate on why my article caused such a stir with my former employer, a small evangelical Protestant college, this is probably the issue."

"How is that?" asked Malcolm.

"Oh, I said a couple things that didn't exactly endear me to the establishment. I wrote that the Church had fundamentally misunderstood the Old Testament concept of the image of God, and that if it staked its position on the traditional explanations, the Church should abandon its pro-life position. That sort of thing."

Deidre chuckled. "That would sure win points with the religious right."

Mark sat back in his chair and folded his arms. Brian could see he wasn't following. "I don't see any connection between this image thing and abortion. What are you getting at?"

"If the image of God is some quality we have—intelligence, language, even the ability to be self-aware or commune with God in our minds—a fetus, especially in the first trimester, doesn't have any of those abilities, which in turn would require the conclusion that it lacks the image, which leads to the contents of the womb being subhuman by biblical standards. So why be against abortion?"

"Got it."

"My solution to the image obstacle is based on a point of Hebrew grammar in the text of Genesis 1:26, the primary biblical verse concerning the image: 'And God said, "Let us make humankind in our image." ' I don't believe the image of God is a *thing* put into us by God that makes us unique, but rather it's something we do or are. It's not a quality; it's a *function*. We don't possess God's image; we *image* God."

"How do you get that?" Melissa interjected with a sour expression on her face, challenging him. "That doesn't seem to be what the verse says."

"Think what you want, Melissa. Grammatically, the phrase 'in the image of God' should be translated something like '*as* the image of God,' meaning we function in the capacity of God's representatives on earth, no matter what our abilities or handicaps."

He went on. "The English preposition has the same nuances. If I say, 'Put the dishes *in* the sink,' the preposition denotes location. 'I broke the vase *in* pieces' refers to result. If I said, 'I work *in* medicine,' I mean I work *as* a doctor or nurse. That's the meaning of Genesis 1:26. The phrase means we're here to take care of the earth and run things the way God wants them run in our position *as* God's representatives."

"I say we shouldn't give these Neanderthals a second thought," Melissa remarked. "If the truth upsets their myths, who cares? They'll have no choice but to adjust. And I have to say that your work on this tells me you're just as desperate to preserve your own beliefs."

The comment drew quizzical expressions from both Neil and the Colonel.

"The text is what it is. I just go with what it says. In case your memory is short, I didn't win any congratulations for what I wrote," Brian replied.

"And you won't get any from me."

An awkward silence filled the air, but it was soon mercifully broken by Malcolm. "So, in your view, if ET is out there, and he's a lot smarter or more powerful, it doesn't matter because he wasn't given the same status?"

"Correct. There's no need to forfeit the image of God, and hence the doctrine of the uniqueness of humanity, in accepting the reality of sentient extraterrestrial life. The two are mutually exclusive concepts. The result is that Jews and Christians alike who take their faith seriously have no reason to be alarmed should intelligent extraterrestrial life ever become part of our worldview."

"That sounds quite useful for reaching people who'd react negatively to the visitors for religious reasons," noted the Colonel.

Melissa glanced at Brian with a plastic smile. "While we're on this fascinating subject, I have a question. There's something in that Genesis verse I've always wondered about, but I've never gotten a satisfying reply."

Okay, what's the punch line? "And what's that?" Brian asked, fighting the urge to give her the scrap she seemed to so desperately want.

"Why are there plurals in the verse? You know, 'Let *us* make man in *our* image'—why isn't the singular used if there's only one God? From the research I've done on apocalyptic cults," she added with an air of superiority, "if the visitors showed up and quoted this verse, it would be 'praise the Lord and pass the ammunition' time. It literally sounds like humanity was created by a group of cosmic beings ... like maybe God delegated the job."

29

For who in the clouds can be compared to the Lᴏʀᴅ?
Among the sons of the gods who is like the Lᴏʀᴅ—
a God greatly feared in the council of the holy ones,
and more awesome than all who are around him?

—Psalm 89:6–7 (Hebrew, 7–8), the Bible

Brian paused, more in response to the expression on Father Benedict's face than to collect his own thoughts. The elderly priest appeared filled with eager anticipation, as though this was the moment he'd been waiting for.

Melissa smirked. "It's okay if we move on. I wouldn't want to embarrass anyone with polytheism in the Good Book."

"Your question is hardly uncomfortable. This is actually my expertise since it was the focus of my dissertation. And it actually relates to a third potential objection to ET from conservatives, so I was planning on bringing it up anyway. Thanks, Melissa."

Melissa's flummoxed expression almost made him laugh out loud, but he quickly reminded himself where this was going. He sensed this was what Andrew had been thinking all along, why the priest had kept referring to his dissertation, why he'd quoted the long lost scroll in Marcus' lab. *It's only about what other people could think. It doesn't have to make sense to you.*

"First of all, I'd like to be clear that Melissa is partially right in two respects. First, I agree that the verse in question is best understood as indicating the Hebrews believed there were other gods. Second, the divine plurality found in the Old Testament may require an altogether different view of an ET presence."

"What?" Neil was startled. "Am I hearing that you don't think Judaism was monotheistic and that it has something to do with ETs?"

"Not exactly, Neil. This will take some unpacking. This wasn't part of my paper, as I'm sure you know."

"Yes, by all means."

"Most Christian interpreters have traditionally argued that the plurals in Genesis are references to the Trinity, the idea that God is three persons in one essence, or that they are a literary device known as the 'plural of majesty,' as if to emphasize the one God's greatness by referencing Him more than once. I don't buy either of those explanations. The first is simply reading the New Testament back into the Old, and it leads to heresy on its best day. The second is a grammatical device that applies only to nouns, not verbs like we have here. Hebrew grammarians dispensed with the second view decades ago—not that theologians were watching."

"How does seeing the Trinity in that verse lead to heresy?" Neil asked. "I've heard that before from people who certainly weren't heterodox."

"It's pretty simple. Seeing the Trinity in Genesis 1:26 would work if that were the only verse like that, but there are other passages where the Trinity is impossible as an explanation. Take Psalm 82:1, for instance. Although English translations have camouflaged the Hebrew of that verse, the text is crystal clear: 'God stands in the divine assembly; in the midst of the gods he passes judgment.' There is a single word translated both 'God' and 'gods' in that verse—*elohim.*

"The word *elohim* is plural in form, but it is used for Israel's singular God over two thousand times in the Old Testament. It's sort of like our English word 'deer'—you can't tell if it's singular or plural in *meaning* until you see it in context. In Psalm 82:1, the first occurrence of *elohim* is singular, so it is translated 'God.' We know that because the verb it goes with is singular. But the second *elohim* must be plural because of the prepositional phrase. You wouldn't translate that God 'stands in the midst of God'—that would be nonsense; you don't stand in the *midst* of one. The verse proves point-blank that Israel had a pantheon."

Deidre chuckled and shook her head. "This is your dissertation? You're into Jewish studies, and you did a dissertation on a Jewish pantheon? You never really wanted to teach, did you?"

Brian smiled and shrugged. "I just love Israelite religion. Anyway, I think the plurals of Genesis 1:26 are there because God is speaking to His council. Melissa is right that people could look at it and say a group of gods—or ETs—created humans, if it were assumed that the ancient people of biblical days mistook aliens for their gods or angels. In terms of the text, though, that view isn't accurate.

"Grammatically, the pluralization here is called the 'plural of exhortation.' English does this, too. If I say, 'let's go for pizza,' but I drive and pay for all of you, I just used the plural of exhortation—I exhorted you to agree with my idea, but the actions that produced the pizza, so to speak, were mine alone. In Genesis 1:26–27, all the verbs for the creative acts that follow are singular."

"Nice job, Brian." Neil smiled. "Makes sense."

"But I still haven't answered your question. Psalm 82:6–7 has God judging the other gods of the pantheon for being evil and corrupt and telling them they will die like men. The plurality there can't be the Trinity or you'd have evil members of that Trinity sentenced to death by God the Father for their corruption. That's heresy. You can get away with a Trinity in Genesis only if you ignore all the other divine plurality passages."

"So much for the blessing of monotheism," said Melissa. Brian certainly hadn't forgotten her tantrum in the cafeteria, but she seemed unusually determined to embarrass him.

"This isn't a theology class. Let's remember why we're here," said the Colonel. "Now what about the ET issue?"

"In a minute. I need to correct that comment as well." Brian tried to ignore her scowl. "The Old Testament does assume the existence of other gods, as references to the sons of God show very clearly. Consider the Ten Commandments. The first one tells Israelites not to worship other gods, but it never denies they exist. The fourth and thirty-second chapters of the book of Deuteronomy tell us God divided up the nations—a reference to the Tower of Babel story—and put the nations under the authority of the sons of God—the ones mentioned in Psalm 82:6."

Brian continued, eager to make his point. "Psalm 29:1 tells the other gods to worship Yahweh. In Exodus 15:11 Moses says no other gods can compare to the God of Israel—a worthless theological statement if the beings he's comparing Yahweh to are as fictional as cartoon characters. Even Israel's creed, 'Hear O Israel, the Lord our God is one,' just tells us something about *Israel's* God without denying the reality of others. What made Israel's faith distinct in ancient times was the uncompromising belief that their God was 'species unique.' Yahweh was an *elohim*, but no other *elohim* was Yahweh, or ever could be."

"How was He unique?" asked Neil, who didn't look quite as disturbed.

"He was regarded as uncreated, all powerful, and the creator of all the other gods. You must realize that monotheism as we think of it—the denial that there are any gods but one—is actually a seventeenth-century term imposed on an ancient culture. Israel's faith doesn't fit our preconception of that term. Israelites believed in many gods but only one Yahweh, who was intrinsically superior."

Brian looked at the Colonel, who was motioning for him to get on with the ET issue.

"How all this might relate to an ET disclosure concerns the other gods in Psalm 82:6 called the sons of the Most High. Elsewhere they're called the *beney ha-elohim*."

"The what?" asked Deidre.

"Sorry for the Hebrew—*'the sons of God.'*"

"Angels?"

"No—they're actually what the text says—gods. They outrank angels. The Hebrew word for angel is entirely different."

"Are they demons then?"

"Not exactly. They're fallen, but they outrank demons, too. We don't want to get lost in the details, though. For our purposes, the most important passage you'll find them in is Genesis 6:1–4, which kicks off the story of the great flood. In some books that didn't make it into the Bible, like the book of Enoch, they're sometimes called Watchers. I might as well read the story since the religious right is going to be thinking along these lines." Brian got out his Hebrew text and began flipping pages. He read aloud.

> *When mankind began to multiply on the face of the earth and daughters were born to them, the sons of God saw that the daughters of mankind were beautiful. And they took them for wives any they chose. Then the* Lord *said, "My Spirit shall not abide in mankind forever, for he is flesh: his days shall be 120 years." The Nephilim were on the earth in those days, and also afterward, whenever the sons of God came in to the daughters of man and they bore children to them. These were the mighty men who were of old, the men of renown.*

Father Benedict interrupted. "None of you probably realize this," the priest began, "but this biblical story echoes stories found in every major religion and culture around the world. Mesopotamians, Greeks, Egyptians, African tribes, Native Americans, Asians—they all have a story of beings from the sky or the heavens that came down, had sex with human women, and produced unusual offspring—divine human hybrids—who were given the divine right to rule over humanity."

"I don't see the point," the Colonel objected.

"I do." Deidre stared at the table, lips pursed, unconsciously rolling her pen between her forefingers and thumbs.

"You of all people should," Brian said. "I've read enough UFO books to know that the people who write them try to argue that the prescientific people of biblical days mistook alien visitors for these sons of God, which would mean—"

Deidre interrupted. "Which would mean that people could easily conclude that the visitors we're supposed to get them to accept are these fallen sons of God."

"So we go with your first view," the Colonel sparred. "Like I said before, I for one have never detected any hostility from the visitors."

"It's not quite that simple. Because of Hollywood, most people are somewhat familiar with alien abductee testimony, which frequently describes sexual contact—harvesting sperm, female eggs, even forced intercourse. If they knew this part of the Bible and had read some abduction literature, they'd think we were in league with the devil. They'd crap their pants."

"There's also an apocalyptic element to this," Brian added.

"Isn't there always?" droned Melissa.

"When the disciples asked Jesus when He would return, Jesus linked the events prior to the great flood to His second coming. Matthew 24:37 pretty much says it all, where Jesus says point blank that, 'As it was in the days of Noah, so it will be at the coming of the Son of Man.' "

"I didn't hear anything about aliens in there."

"It's true that most religious people would think Jesus was referring to a culture engaged in sinful living on an unprecedented scale in that passage, but sooner or later they'll notice that Jesus mentions 'marrying and giving in marriage' in the same passage. The only ones doing that in the Genesis 6 description are the sons of God and the human women. What you want to market as a friendly living arrangement with ET could be viewed by many as the harbinger of the apocalypse."

"This just can't ... be right," Neil said haltingly, aghast at what he was hearing.

"It isn't," the Colonel objected. "What proof do you have that any of this religious mythology has anything to do with the visitors? Besides, they hardly look like angels or anything else divine."

"That's true ... but their appearance *is* a concern." Brian looked at Father Benedict. "I can't say it makes much sense to me ... but ... well, it's just that there are some weird coincidences when it comes to their appearance ... among other things."

"Like what?"

Brian hesitated, unsure of how to proceed. The ancient scrolls and texts with which he was so familiar flooded his mind, but none of them seemed to make sense.

Father Benedict prompted him in an almost clairvoyant way. "Go ahead, Brian. It doesn't need to make sense to you. Just tell us what you see as problems."

Brian nodded. "Well, for starters, there's the whole matter of the so-called serpent in the garden of Eden."

"Satan?" Melissa started to laugh, and Mark joined her.

"Sort of."

"Sort of? So-called?" asked Neil.

"The word 'Satan' isn't actually used as a proper name in the Hebrew Bible. The term just means 'the adversary' and isn't actually used of Helel, although the New Testament makes that connection."

"Who's Helel?" Neil asked.

"According to the prophet Isaiah, that's the name of the heavenly being who rebelled against God some time before humans were created, the one the New Testament later connects with the garden of Eden episode. His full name is *Helel ben-Shakar*—it means 'Shining One, son of the dawn.' According to another one of those ancient Jewish books that was never considered part of the Bible, *The Life of Adam and Eve*, Helel fell from grace when he refused to worship Adam after he was created. He didn't think Adam should have authority over him."

"He was pissed because God put the newbie in charge?"

"A wonderful way of putting it, Malcolm. I'm sure you all know the biblical story of Eden. Haven't you ever wondered why Eve wasn't surprised when the serpent spoke to her?"

"Because it's a fairy tale?" Melissa mocked.

"No, but thank you for playing, Melissa. The real answer is that she wasn't surprised because she wasn't talking to a serpent—she was speaking to the *nachash*."

"What do you mean?" asked Neil. "Are you denying the story?"

"Far from it. The word translated 'serpent' in Genesis 3 is *nachash*. It's a fairly common word, and it can, of course, be translated as the noun 'snake.' Having a snake in Eden doesn't fit the two other passages in the books of Isaiah and Ezekiel that talk about the same episode—no snakes in their accounts."

"What do they say happened?"

"I'm getting to that. Back to *nachash*. Besides 'snake,' the word can have three other meanings in the Hebrew Bible, one of which means 'to shine.' The Hebrew word for 'shining brass' is related to it."

"I think I know where this is going," Deidre murmured and looked up at him.

"Anyway, *nachash* in Genesis 3 can just as well be understood as a substantive participle rather than a noun."

"A what?" Mark asked, annoyed.

"Sorry for the grammar. What I mean to say is that the word *nachash* can be translated as—"

"The Shining One," Deidre finished his sentence, a disturbed look creasing her face, "the same meaning as the Helel guy ... or thing."

"This is ... amazing," Neil interjected. "How do you know your reconstruction is right?"

"Isaiah 14 and Ezekiel 28 confirm that understanding. The prophets have a heavenly being expelled from the garden along with Adam and Eve—not a mere snake. My own view is that Helel had a serpentine appearance, and that Eve saw him and his type come and go all the time in Eden—it was the place the divine council met since its description in the Bible matches divine council courts in other ancient Near Eastern literature. She wouldn't have been surprised at all if one spoke to her. It probably happened a lot."

"What about the sons of God, the Watchers? Do any ancient texts say what they look like?"

"Yeah. There's a Dead Sea Scroll that describes one—4QAmram to be exact. It describes the Watcher as *'fearsome—like a serpent.'* " He looked over at Father Benedict, who was occupied with watching the reactions of the others.

"These are just myths, people," Mark spoke up. He looked at Brian. "At least I hope you don't actually believe they present us with reality. And besides, why would a human woman want sex with a serpent creature? It makes no sense ... as if it could."

"I think we'd all agree that until a few days ago we'd have said aliens were a myth, too. All I'm suggesting is that the Bible and other ancient religious texts tells us that, in reality—to use your wording—there's a supernatural world that interacted with the human world. Those supernatural beings, call them inter-dimensional if it makes you more comfortable, can manifest physically in flesh, and the Bible references some of these occasions."

He went on. "Then again, ancient books outside the Bible say they can shape-shift. The book of Enoch says that in general terms, and one of the Gnostic Coptic texts from Nag Hammadi in Egypt discovered sixty years ago specifically says that's how Genesis 6 happened."

"I suppose the shape-shifting stuff is in UFO books, too?" asked Malcolm.

Deidre nodded.

"Just so I'm clear, there are a lot of reasons to not equate these beings with genuine, mortal ET beings, but a lot of religious people will make that connection. Our problem is that the sacred books of Judaism and Christianity have these beings as fallen and evil. Even Muslims might think that. The Watchers of Jewish texts are the *Djinn* of the Qur'an. Many people could think the visitors are demonic."

"Man, this Genesis 6 stuff is right out of abductee therapy sessions. I've heard a lot of weird stuff, but you're freaking me out, Brian. The reptilian aliens my patients talk about are especially nasty—and huge. Abductees describe them as seven or eight feet tall. If religious people make the connection, we'll look like we're in league with the devil."

"Deidre, there are no reptilians," the Colonel insisted. "Believe me, I'm in a position to know. The only visitors are the Grays—and they don't match any of these descriptions."

"Well, Colonel, you may think or even know that, but my patients wouldn't. Some of them have told me they believed the Grays were like bio-bots, created by the reptilians—in their own image, so to speak. They—"

"Now you're freaking me out," Brian interrupted. "Two more things just popped into my head. The sons of God of the heavenly council share the image of God—remember the plurals. The image refers to ruling status, something the Watchers had before humans were created. When mankind was created, God gave the authority over earth to humans."

"We've heard all that already." The Colonel glared at Brian, who couldn't miss his agitation.

"Right, but I didn't mention that in order to rule, humans—and the Watchers—were given abilities, one of which was creative power. We have that and use it all the time—in science, engineering, genetics, and so on. The point is, they likely could do anything we could do—I'm thinking of cloning here—and do it better. And in Gnostic material, it specifically has them creating humankind. I'd never really thought about that as it relates to the ET question before ..."

"This is ridiculous!" the Colonel suddenly exploded. "We're here to talk about how to solve problems, not make the difficulty any greater!" He stopped and took a deep breath. "Look, my concern is that whether we like it or not, they're here, and they're coming out. We've got to be ready. There's a lot at stake here."

"We understand," offered Father Benedict. "I'd suggest Brian finishes his remaining thought and then we take a break."

The Colonel nodded.

"Okay," Brian sighed, "but it's more of the same. That Gnostic text, *The Apocryphon of John*, has a different version of what happened at the flood right after the Genesis 6 episode with the Watchers."

"Yes, and ... ?"

"Instead of people being saved by riding out the flood in the ark, that text has them escaping ... in a cloud—a glowing one."

30

Brian snuggled comfortably under the covers, his sleep disturbed briefly by his body's internal rhythm. He smiled to himself at the realization that, for a change, he had nowhere to go and nothing to do. The Colonel had informed everyone after his presentation the previous day that another meeting with an attaché from the Group was being arranged, but the earliest opportunity for such an engagement would be in two days. All the day held for him was the bliss that only a warm pillow and a darkened room could offer.

He sighed with contentment, shifting his position, and instantly froze in terror. His foot, now consciously held motionless, had come to rest on the hairless, smooth, warm skin of another body. His heart raced, the pace rising with his sense of bewilderment. His memory raced through the events of the previous evening, but he could recall only going to supper with Andrew and reading himself to sleep.

His mind was soon invaded by another frightening thunderbolt: He was nude. He never slept naked.

The few seconds that passed before he gathered his wits seemed like hours. The figure next to him had not stirred. Grabbing the edge of the blanket atop him, he mustered his courage and bolted out of the bed, scurrying out of the bedroom and into the living room. He stood there in shocked dismay, wrapped in the blanket.

What had he done? His mind groped helplessly for an explanation. Whoever was in his bed wasn't dead, and that left only one plausible alternative. Suddenly, the possibility that he'd been dreaming came to him, but he dismissed it quickly. He was awake, and by anyone's interpretation of the scene, guilty as sin.

He surveyed the environs of his quarters. Everything appeared completely normal; nothing was amiss in any way, as far as he could tell.

Why shouldn't it be? With a sigh of resignation, he walked noiselessly back into the bedroom, prompted by the morbid sense of curiosity he was sure a perpetrator felt when returning to the scene of the crime. He gazed briefly at the figure, her exquisite, naked body, partially covered by the bed sheet, lying peacefully on her stomach. Her face was turned toward the wall, but the tussled auburn hair told him all he needed to know. His heart sank.

Silently he opened several drawers and took the items he needed. There could be no recovery from this. His reputation was ruined. The two people he'd counted as friends, Andrew and Neil, would never look at him the same way. Thoughts of what they would say—and worse, what they would only think to themselves—coursed through his mind. *Hypocrite.*

Brian showered somberly. He typically used this time to pray and think through what he needed to accomplish for the day, but there was no sense of communion now, no eagerness to be productive. By the time he turned off the water, he couldn't remember if he'd even washed his hair. He was in an inescapable fog. Guilt came over him in waves, as did the maddening awareness that he remembered nothing about being with Melissa. He dressed in the living room and then reentered the bedroom, only to discover that she was already gone.

He turned to leave, but stopped. His senses told him there was something different about the room, but he couldn't put his finger on it. He turned around and stood in the doorway, unsure of what it was that had drawn his attention. After a few seconds of silence, it dawned on him. *What's that smell?*

He took a few steps into the bedroom, sniffing at the air. Although faint, a queer, sweet-smelling aroma had circulated about the room. Brian walked over to Melissa's side of the bed. To his surprise, he could clearly discern the distinct outline of her body. He bent down and touched the bed. It was warmer than Brian imagined it would be, but what took him aback even more was the fact that the surface of the sheet was moist.

He sat down on the edge of the bed and peered closely at the vague silhouette, baffled by the traces of her presence. *What of it?* he chided himself sarcastically, then lapsed into a daze. He wondered how long it would be before this secret got out. *It'll be the first thing out of her mouth.*

An unexpected knock at the door stirred him from his gloom. He didn't move, hoping his caller would go away. After a few seconds another series of knocks came, and then a third. Brian rose slowly and took his time getting to the door, opening it in a spirit of resignation.

"Hey, man, are you goin' to breakfast or what? It's almost ten o'clock, and I don't want to be the only one draggin' his butt this morning," Malcolm greeted him jovially.

"Come on in," Brian said in a monotone, his mood immune to even Malcolm's infectious smile.

"Whoa," Malcolm said in a more subdued tone as the door closed behind him, "what's up? Your dog just die?"

Brian walked over to the room's lone chair and collapsed in it, not caring to respond. He stared at the wall behind his colleague.

Malcolm looked at him carefully. "Is it Melissa?"

Brian shot a startled glance at the lanky, bespectacled figure. "What do you mean?" he asked, trying not to appear panicked.

"You know," Malcolm explained, "she's made a habit of trashing you whenever she can and in front of as many people as possible."

Brian shook his head.

"No, I didn't think so. No way you'd have seen her this early. Even she wouldn't come over just to insult you."

"Let's go," Brian said abruptly and stood up. It was the only thing he could think of to change the subject.

"Wait a minute." Malcolm stopped him as he approached the door. "Man, what's that weird smell?"

"I don't smell anything out here," Brian answered, "but I know what you mean. Your nose must be real sensitive."

Malcolm looked at him curiously.

"In the bedroom."

Malcolm strode deliberately into Brian's bedroom and emerged a few seconds later. "Man, that's funky. Are you burning incense or something?"

"Nope."

"So what is it?"

"Honestly, I don't know," he answered, thankful that Malcolm had not noticed anything else.

31

Malcolm and Brian put their trays down on the table next to Father Benedict, who was just finishing his breakfast.

"Well, it seems everyone slept in this morning," he said, his face bearing a cheerful expression that Brian hadn't seen in days. "I trust both of you got a good night's rest?"

"You bet, padre," Malcolm answered, pouring syrup on his pancakes.

Brian stared at his plate.

"And you, Brian?" the priest persisted.

He shrugged.

Father Benedict wiped his mouth, eyeing his young friend carefully. "I'm surprised. You were in such a good mood last evening, what with the pressure of your presentation removed. I know the seriousness of this, but—"

"It isn't that," Brian interjected, cutting him off, his gaze unwavering.

"Then what is it?"

"I ... I can't say ... not now anyway."

"I doubt you have anything to say that I haven't already heard, Brian. I am a priest, you know."

"Yeah, I know."

Father Benedict looked across the table at Malcolm, who could only cast a quizzical expression in return, his mouth already stuffed.

"We need to talk, Andrew," Brian suddenly admitted. "It's just ... I've done something terrible."

"Not you, man," Malcolm said, swallowing. "What could you do that's so bad? I think God'll forgive you for oversleeping."

"I'm serious ... it'll just take me awhile bef—"

141

"Mind if I sit down?"

The three of them acknowledged Deidre's presence. None of them had noticed her approach.

"Go right ahead," Father Benedict gestured. "Good morning."

"I saw you guys jawing away over here. Looked pretty serious."

"It is," Malcolm offered. "Brian here seems to think he's offended the Almighty."

"Let's not get into it."

"Nobody's perfect, Brian," she said, a hint of sympathy in her voice.

"I'm well aware of that."

"Maybe we should let the man go for now," Malcolm suggested.

"What?" Deidre questioned. "That doesn't sound like you, Malcolm. I'd think you would be the one who'd want the scoop before anyone."

"I do—but just trust me, it's time to change the subject. Don't turn around, Dee, but I think you'll agree with me when you find out who's coming—unless you like hearing Brian trashed."

"Do you mean what I think you mean?" she asked.

He nodded and proceeded to butter his toast.

"Do I want to be here for this?" She smirked and pushed herself away from the table.

Brian looked up from his plate and over Deidre's shoulder. Melissa was making her way over to their table, a fierce scowl on her face.

"Thanks for the thought, Malcolm, but it won't matter a few minutes from now," he intoned somberly.

Melissa sat down amid the group, not bothering to ask permission. "Good morning, everyone," she said in a saccharine voice. "I trust everyone had an enjoyable evening—especially you, Brian."

All eyes at the table were upon him, a few with eyebrows raised in curiosity, but still he refused to speak. Brian stiffened for the inevitable.

"It seems I've finally left you speechless," she continued cattily. "I would think you would at least have given me a thank you after last night."

Brian could feel the blush coming over his face. He eyed the stunned expressions of the small audience sheepishly.

"No way!" Malcolm gasped.

"You mean ... you two ..." Deidre gawked.

Brian looked down at his plate again. Deidre remained where she stood. Andrew held his peace.

"Look," Brian said in a halting voice, "I apologize."

"Are you trying to insult me?" Melissa retorted. "I've had a lot of different morning-after reactions, but never an apology."

"I don't know what to say," he struggled. "I just don't remember a thing. One minute I was with you," he added, finally looking at Andrew, whose face was drawn, "and the next I was in my room reading, and then this morning I woke up with you in my bed. I guess we must have—"

"You just don't know when to quit, do you?" Melissa fumed. "You've got to be the most arrogant man I've ever met. I don't know what you're trying to pull here, changing the story, but—"

"I'm not changing anything! I woke up, and you were in my bed, okay? Let's let everyone know!" Brian challenged her, raising his voice in agitation, throwing up his hands.

"I wasn't in your bed, you idiot. You were in mine!"

"What?"

"Is there something wrong with your hearing?"

"No, and nothing's wrong with my eyesight, either. You were in *my* bed this morning. I don't know how you got there, but you were definitely there. Believe me, I noticed!"

"I'm not letting you weasel your way out of this," she came right back, her voice trembling with rage. "You had me last night *in my bed!*" She punctuated her statement emphatically. "And as for not remembering, cut the crap. Nobody sleeps with me and forgets it! For my part, I can certainly justify not recalling your performance. Now that I think about it, I don't feel like eating anymore."

The two of them stared each other down, oblivious to the nonplused expressions of their audience.

"I think I'll stay a bit longer," Deidre said to no one in particular and pulled in her chair.

"God knows I don't want to get into any of the prurient details," Father Benedict intervened, "but I'd like to hear your version of what happened, Melissa."

"I know you're a priest, but you can't be that ignorant."

"Indulge me."

"Well," she began, "I left supper about the same time as everyone else, and then I went back to my room for a glass of wine."

"With Brian?"

"No, he wasn't with me then."

"Quite right. He was with me. When did Brian come to your room?"

"Andrew, I didn't go—"

The priest waved him off. "Let's hear it, Melissa. When did Brian come to your room?"

She hesitated. The others at the table eyed her suspiciously.

"I don't know," she answered. "I can't explain how the wonderful Dr. Scott got into my room, but I do know he was there this morning!" she added defiantly.

"I see," the priest mused. "Can you remember any details of the, er … encounter?"

Melissa sat back in her chair with a sigh, again hesitant to respond.

"It's important, Dr. Kelley," he pressed her.

"No … I can't," she confessed. "He was just there."

"Did you speak to him this morning when you awoke?"

"No, I just screamed at him and threw a pillow at him, but he never moved."

"Did he awake at all?"

She shook her head.

"Brian," he continued, diverting his attention momentarily, "did you speak to Melissa this morning?"

"No," he replied, his curiosity aroused. "It's pretty much what Melissa just said. I woke up and felt her in the bed next to me, then got out of there as fast as I could. She never stirred or said anything."

"You make it sound like an escape."

"I didn't mean anything negative. It's just that … that I would never do a thing like this—at least I never thought I would. I can't remember a thing about it. I just assumed the worst."

"The worst?"

"It's an expression, Melissa."

"What's with you? You make it sound like being with me was something detestable. You should consider yourself lucky."

"Here, here!" quipped Malcolm.

Deidre glared at him.

"What Brian is trying to say," Deidre explained, "is that it's part of his beliefs that sex is for marriage. Right?" she questioned him.

Brian nodded.

"You mean you're a virgin?"

Brian said nothing, knowing he'd given her yet another occasion to mock him.

Melissa laughed and shook her head in disbelief. "No, there are no alien life forms around here!"

"If you could suspend the hilarity," Father Benedict said seriously. "What we have here in point of fact are two people who insist that each woke up in the other's bed, neither of whom can remember any contact with the other. Is that about right?"

Brian and Melissa looked at each other, the latter trying to contain her amusement.

"One of you has to be wrong," Deidre concluded.

"You mean lying," Brian clarified.

"Actually," Malcolm interjected, this time with a thoughtful expression on his face, "they could both be telling the truth."

"How is that?" Deidre asked.

"Melissa, do you remember anything unusual about your room this morning?" Malcolm asked. Brian could see his mind was probing through the details.

"No," she answered in a more earnest tone.

"You answered too quickly. Take a minute and think about it."

"I know where you're going with this, Malcolm," Brian said. "I doubt whether that has anything to do with this."

"Whether *what* has anything to do with this?" asked Deidre.

Malcolm held up his hand for silence, taking note of Melissa's now perplexed countenance.

"Come to think of it," she began, "there was something strange. I noticed this peculiar smell in my room. I emailed the service provider about it just before I came here."

Malcolm and Brian looked at each other. "Let's go, Melissa," Malcolm said, standing up hurriedly.

"What?"

"We need to get into your room—*now.*"

"What's the meaning of all this?" Father Benedict queried.

"I don't know, but I noticed the same thing in Brian's room when I stopped by this morning. I want to see if it's the same smell."

"It was just an odd smell—what could it mean?" Melissa demanded, still seated.

"Like I said, I don't know, but it might be important. Come on!"

The five of them left their trays at the table and hastened down the hallway to Melissa's room. She carded the door and punched in her access code. Malcolm was the first to enter.

He motioned for Brian to follow him. "You smell that?"

Brian nodded, a pleased but bewildered look etched on his face.

"Is it perfume?" asked Father Benedict.

"Please!" replied Melissa.

Brian walked into the bedroom and tore back the covers.

"You can make that up when you're done doing whatever it is you're doing," Melissa informed him curtly. "Bring back any memories?"

"As a matter of fact, yes," Brian answered.

"What's up?" asked Malcolm, entering Melissa's bedroom.

"I didn't want to say anything when you came over this morning," Brian explained, "since I felt so ashamed, but I noticed that there was some kind of imprint of Melissa's body on my sheet, and it was also warm to the touch, and moist over the entire impression—even close to an hour after I got up."

"An imprint of her body, huh?" Malcolm noted, his eyes darting in Melissa's direction. "If it's still there, can I keep the sheet?"

Melissa rolled her eyes.

"Can't you stay serious for more than five minutes?" Deidre chastised him.

"What's this on the sheet?" Brian asked, peering closely at several small spots.

"Blood," Melissa answered.

"Blood?" Deidre queried, her attention arrested.

"Yes—I've been having some bleeding lately."

"Forgive me for my ignorance," Brian interrupted, "but if it's your time of the month, wouldn't that interfere with your version of events?"

"It isn't my time of the month," Melissa retorted.

"Then why are you bleeding?" Deidre wanted to know.

"I've had it happen before, usually at times when I'm under stress—prelims, dissertation defense, that sort of thing. I guess my body feels that having my life disrupted and career threatened is sufficient reason to do it again."

"Okay. Get it checked."

"Which side did you think I was on?" Brian asked, changing the subject.

"You were on that side," she retorted, pointing to the spot nearest the wall.

"There does seem to be some discoloration," Father Benedict perceived, "but it's hard to tell if there's really a shape there."

The others agreed.

"At any rate," the priest continued, "Malcolm says the scents are the same."

"Maybe you're just trying to protect your buddy," Melissa accused sarcastically.

"Listen, sweetheart," Malcolm rebutted, "Brian can take care of himself. As far as I'm concerned, if he did nail you, more power to him. The only thing I'd want is the details, *comprende?*"

Melissa sighed and left the bedroom.

"Thanks—I think," Brian said, unable to suppress a grin.

"No problem. For the record, I'd say nothing happened between you two."

"I would concur, under the circumstances," Father Benedict added, feeling the mattress.

"What a surprise," Melissa cracked from the other room.

"We could have Dr. Bandstra check the door logs, then we'd know when anyone went in or out," Deidre suggested.

"We would only know if the door opened," Father Benedict reminded her. "Only your own card can open your door from either the outside or inside. We'd have no way of knowing if the person who opened the door would have let someone in."

"Wait a minute," Brian suddenly remembered, "when I got out of the shower this morning, Melissa—or whoever it was—was gone. She couldn't have gotten out without my card."

"I didn't get out, because I wasn't there!"

"Well, then, how did I supposedly get out of *your* room?"

"You could have used my card."

"I don't know the code."

"So you say."

Brian gasped in exasperation. "I could just as easily say you know mine and are hiding it. Your stubbornness is pointless."

"Maybe it was someone else—in both cases," Malcolm thought aloud, "and these other individuals had cards that overrode all others."

"Why would anyone go through the trouble of pulling a stunt like this?" Father Benedict asked, his confusion building.

Melissa remained silent as the others pondered his question. Her mind drifted back to her last conversation with her unknown "benefactor." He'd hinted that she would be exposed to some clue that was important to the real truth of the project, but she couldn't fathom learning anything from this strange incident. His advice that Brian could be trusted came rushing back to her as well. Should she tell the others? If she exposed her source now, would she be in danger?

Malcolm's voice broke her train of thought. "What if the logs indicate nothing? What do we have then, ghosts?"

"Who knows?" Deidre threw up her hands. "I just think we need all the information we can get. We should have the logs checked."

"Agreed," Father Benedict sided with her.

"How do we get the information? You know how paranoid this bunch is. Anyone asks any questions, especially about room access, and they're bound to get suspicious."

"Dr. Bandstra should be able to get us that information. I'm sure he'll be eager to clear his friend of any indiscretion."

"I have a confession to make," Melissa suddenly spoke up.

The others waited, unsure of what was coming. She proceeded to tell them about her unknown assailant and his visitations, recounting as best she could remember what he'd told her, omitting only the detail that she had a second access card.

"I can't believe it!" an incensed Deidre exclaimed. "Somebody from the Group tells you that someone on the team is dirty, and you don't think of telling us? We could all be in danger—we have a right to know!"

"Like I told you, I wasn't sure how he'd react ... and I'm still not. I don't know what he'll do, and I never know when he's going to show up."

"How is he going to find out?" asked Brian. "No one here will breathe a word."

"You *swear* you don't know this guy?" Deidre demanded, still visibly upset.

"I have no idea who he might be. Nothing about it makes any sense."

"What about the others?" Malcolm asked.

"We could tell Mark, but I'd keep my mouth shut around the Colonel and Dr. Marcus—and Neil, for that matter," Deidre opined. "Sorry, Brian, but he's too close to the inside."

Brian hesitated to respond. He didn't like the idea of any conspiracy against his friend.

"I'm afraid I have to agree with Dr. Harper," Father Benedict said.

"Okay," Brian acquiesced. "I won't spill the beans."

"So what about this bedroom fiasco?" Deidre wondered.

"I'd say that there must be some connection to what Melissa's visitor divulged," Father Benedict reasoned, "even though we haven't the foggiest idea what that might be. Unless something else happens that Melissa feels is a more likely fulfillment of his words, I don't think we have any other choice than to make that assumption."

"For what it's worth," Melissa said, turning her attention to Brian, "I'm willing to believe Brian—if he's willing to believe me."

"Of course."

"Consider yourself undefiled then."

"Gladly."

32

The simplest questions are the hardest to answer.

—*Northrop Frye*

Brian sat back in his chair and stretched, yawning loudly. The day off had turned out to be emotionally and mentally exhausting. After the strange goings on of the morning, he'd concerned himself with going through his dissertation in an effort toward seeing it through Andrew's eyes, trying to discern the connections between the ancient descriptions of a heavenly host of gods and the contemporary mythology of UFOs and alien beings. The notion made his head spin.

He looked at the clock, which read ten o'clock P.M. He was hungry again, despite the fact that he'd eaten heartily at lunch and dinner. Lunch had proven most interesting. Father Benedict had made it a point at that time to inform each team member privy to the events of the morning that the security logs revealed no door activity after Melissa and Brian had entered their own rooms the evening before.

Andrew had approached the steward with what he called a "security concern" that Melissa's and Brian's cards were not operating correctly, saying that he'd overheard the two at breakfast discussing it. The steward had cooperated with his request to check the logs for malfunctions. Andrew could only tell them that the steward did not contact Neil and the Colonel in his presence, and he hoped they weren't told after he'd left.

While it had cleared Brian personally, the new information only deepened the mystery. If no one had entered the rooms or been granted admission, what was the explanation for what he and Melissa had experienced? Regardless of the bizarre turn of events, he was relieved that the episode was over, his reputation still intact. He had no teaching position, no money, no woman in his life, and no realistic prospect of filling any of these voids. When everything was said and done, his integrity was really all he had.

The hard part was that Melissa was as hot as she was miserable. He'd lapsed into imagining himself with her several times during the day. It would always start off innocuously enough, with the simple pleasures offered by a woman that he'd never experienced firsthand: the soft feel of a small, smooth hand sliding into his, an affectionate embrace, a lingering kiss, a smile meant just for him. The daydreams would inevitably become more intense, moving naturally toward more sexual fantasies. He knew the daydreaming was useless and spiritually counterproductive, to say the least, but he longed for companionship. The familiar shroud of terrible loneliness had descended upon him again. It would pass—it always did. The fact that she hated him so much was almost comforting.

A firm knock at the door interrupted his thoughts. Brian got up and opened the door. It was Neil and Father Benedict, both of whom wore serious expressions.

"Got a few minutes?" Neil asked.

Brian wondered immediately if Neil had learned of this morning's events and glanced at Father Benedict as he entered the room. As if anticipating the unspoken question, the older man quickly shook his head.

"We need to talk." The undersecretary got right to the point. "I dropped by Andrew's room, and he suggested the three of us chat before we meet with the Group's representative."

"About?"

"Your presentation."

"I noticed you looked kind of disturbed at points."

"Of course! You can't sit through something like that and come away unfazed—especially if you're me."

"Meaning?"

"Meaning I have no idea what to do. I wanted you here to help me reconcile the existence of these beings with my faith, and your first offering was everything I'd hoped for. Your second was like my worst nightmare. The Colonel was pretty angry. Afterward, between the two of us, he went on and on about how what you said would undermine the project."

"Am I in trouble?" Brian asked. "Lord knows it wouldn't be the first time."

Neil shrugged.

"Well, if he wants to send me home, I'll of course honor the security oath."

"You're not going anywhere. There's no way you're expendable now, especially to me. The three of us need to re-strategize this whole project."

Brian looked at him curiously.

"What Neil means," Andrew broke in, "is that he needs to come up with Plan B for his and our welfare if ET turns out to be in any way evil. You already know what I think."

"I have a lot of questions floating around in my head, Brian. I know we don't have time tonight to get into all of them, but I can't wait until we can."

"I have something to talk to you about as well, but the under-secretary's questions are more pressing, I'm sure."

"I have a little time before finishing my preparations for our trip tomorrow. Let's get some coffee at the cafeteria and talk."

"Sounds good. I'm kind of hungry anyway. Father?"

"Yes, I'll tag along."

The three men strolled down the hallway toward the cafeteria. They passed the door to Melissa's room, engaged in conversation. None of them noticed when, a few seconds later, Melissa slowly cracked her door and watched their figures turn the corner.

She looked the other direction, then back again. Satisfied no one was watching, she silently made her way the short distance to Brian's room. She took out the card her assailant had given her and stared at it momentarily, calculating the risk one more time. *It'll be worth it.* She passed the card through and held her breath.

The door opened promptly, without the need for a code. She quickly went inside and closed the door behind her carefully, as though the empty room had ears. She looked at her watch and then began strolling around the small quarters, gazing at his library. She bent over his desk and took note of the large book that lay open. Guessing correctly that it was his dissertation, she dispassionately read a page or two, but then carefully returned to the page at which she'd begun, leaving everything exactly as she'd found it.

She checked her watch again. Ten minutes ought to be enough time. She extracted the card from the pocket of her jeans and strode to the door, passing the card through the reader as before. At the familiar click, she opened the door slightly and held it for a few seconds before she let it close on its own weight. *That should keep you from getting too much attention, whoever you are.* She began unbuttoning her blouse, her lips curled in a deceitful smile. *At last.*

33

If a man does his best, what else is there?

—*General George S. Patton, Jr.*

"So fire away, Neil. What is it you want to ask me?"

"Well, for one thing, I seem to recall that there's some verse somewhere in the Bible that says angels can't have sex? Or maybe that there's no sex in heaven—is that right? That would seem to contradict a literal view of Genesis 6."

"You're thinking of Matthew 22:30," Brian answered. "Many scholars think that when Jesus made the statement that there is no marriage in heaven since we'll be 'like the angels,' He was teaching that angels can't have sex. That isn't what it means, since that isn't what it says. The verse doesn't say that angelic beings *can't* have sex; it just says they don't."

"That's a pretty weak response."

"I agree, but it's a legitimate interpretive option. I prefer to handle the objection by pointing out that the verse says the angels *in heaven* don't have sexual relations. You should recall that the sons of God in Genesis 6 were not in heaven—they were on earth. We know from elsewhere in Genesis that when these heavenly beings came to earth, they took on real, unmistakable, corporeal form. For instance, in Genesis 18 and 19, the two angels accompanying the Lord when He visits Abraham were able to eat, and they also physically grabbed Lot and pulled him into the house when the men of Sodom threatened him."

He continued, "I would say angels don't need to eat in heaven either, as we won't—as far as the Bible tells us—but on earth they could and did. There's no reason to suppose that the same isn't true for other physical abilities, such as sex. And as Paul wrote in 1 Corinthians 15, there's such a thing as celestial flesh—flesh of a different kind than we have now, but flesh nonetheless."

"That's seems more coherent. Second question: Aren't there other views of Genesis 6 besides such a literal one? If there are, why don't you accept them?"

"The short answer is yes, there are other views. Some say the sons of God are really the godly lineage of Adam's son Seth, who intermarried with the ungodly line of Cain. The text doesn't say that anywhere, though, and if you ask me, it's rather chauvinistic. Why are the women considered to represent ungodliness? All the text says is that they were the daughters of men.

"It also implies that no other human lineages were God-fearing, which is absurd. That view and any other one ignores the fact that all the other ancient Near Eastern civilizations had some version of this story, and in some cases, the Hebrew terms are linguistically related to terms in the literature of those other people."

He went on. "The comparative material is a strong reason to take it literally, but I have others. Peter and Jude did so in their writings in the New Testament, and all Jewish and Christian interpreters before Augustine did as well. He didn't like the literal view because of his disagreements with a group of early Christians called the Manicheans. He was originally in that sect but had a falling out. He left them, came up with the Sethite view, and his influence made sure that most of the Church adopted it. The rest is history."

"I see." Neil looked at his watch.

"Dr. Bandstra," Father Benedict asked softly, "I know you have to go soon, but I'd like to know something. Have you seen one of these larger alien creatures—the reptilian kind?"

"No, thank God. If I had, I'd be hustling all of you out of here now. Like I said before, I've never even seen one of the little ones alive. The Colonel has."

"Could he have lied when he told you that?"

"I've known him almost ten years, and even though most of the time we haven't seen eye to eye, I've never known him to lie. I can't think of a reason he'd want to. I've been privy to everything you all only learned incrementally."

"How about the Group?"

"I've never met any of them—except, again, for the Colonel, but he's more of a liaison than anything."

"Maybe we'll get some answers the day after tomorrow," Brian suggested. "This other Group representative—do you know who it is?"

"No. All I can tell you is that our destination is on the East Coast."

"Where?" the priest queried.

"A place called Mount Weather—you might remember hearing about it after the September 11 tragedy. One of the things we use it for is continuity of government protocols. Members of the chain of command are secured when we need to make sure the president and vice president should not be traveling together."

"I recall hearing about it," Father Benedict said. "What are we going to do there?"

"I can't say more right now. We'll leave the morning after tomorrow, and will meet our contact the same evening, though I'll be behind you a couple of hours since I have to take a different flight. Which reminds me"—he paused and looked at his watch again—"I'd best be going. I'll probably only see you again at Mount Weather."

"Assuming nothing else funny happens," Brian quipped. Andrew looked at him in a panic. Brian instantly knew he'd slipped.

"What do you mean?" Neil asked.

"Oh ..." he stalled, trying to cover his gaffe, "you know ... maybe if Melissa has her problem again."

"What's that? I didn't know she had one."

"I overheard her telling Deidre this morning that she was having a bleeding problem."

"Bleeding? You mean menstrual bleeding?"

"Sort of," Brian continued, relieved that he'd thought of something convincing. "It wasn't the regular female thing. She said she'd had the problem before in graduate school when she was under a lot of stress. She didn't seem worried about it—more annoyed than anything, which suits her."

"Has she had it checked?"

"I think so. Deidre insisted on it."

"Good. Well, I'll see the two of you when possible. Good night."

"Good night," Brian and Andrew echoed as Neil left the cafeteria.

Father Benedict breathed a sigh of relief. "That was close. You must be more careful."

"I know—do you think he suspected anything?"

"No."

"By the way, what was it you wanted to talk about?"

"I've had a troubling afternoon, Brian."

"What is it?"

"Do you recall my mentioning that a friend of mine at the Castel Gandolfo was doing some work for me related to astral prophecy?"

"Yes."

"I got tired of waiting for some response from him—it's been weeks, which is most uncharacteristic. I spent the afternoon online going through some Italian newspapers in Rome. My friend is dead."

"Dead? How?"

"The paper said it was a heart attack, but he had no heart condition."

"Well, that isn't unheard of."

"True ... but I can't shake the notion that there's more to it."

***

Neil strolled quietly down the hallway, his mind still reeling from Brian's presentation. He wanted to believe there was no cause for alarm, that his questions would be answered. Brian's answers tonight didn't help, since they keep the door wide open for a supernatural explanation for the visitors. He found it ironic he had reached a point where he was praying the visitors were genuine ETs, whereas a few weeks ago the idea had shaken his faith.

He also felt uneasy now about continuing to keep his friend in the dark. But if Brian was right, then the things Neil knew about the project—that the team members still did not know—needed to be kept from all of them. Brian hadn't changed. He was still his unfailingly analytical self, even in the face of Melissa's constant harassment.

He froze at the thought of Melissa, riveted in the middle of the silent hallway. He paced back and forth several times, hands on his hips, rehearsing Brian's words during their conversation. *They wouldn't!* He stood still, deep in thought; a few moments passed, and his face flushed with anger. *Why would she be singled out? Whatever the reason, I can't allow it!* He whirled about and headed for the security monitoring station.

***

Brian carded himself into his room and turned on the light switch. His late-night snack and the conversation had combined to induce drowsiness, but he sat down at his desk to finish reading the dissertation chapter left uncompleted as a result of the earlier interruption. He sleepily turned the page, but was jolted into full consciousness when the light in the bedroom behind him suddenly came on. A chill ran up his spine as he quietly got to his feet. He crept cautiously toward the bedroom and peered inside.

"Not again," he groaned, staring in disbelief at the redheaded form lying motionless in his bed, face toward the wall as before.

"No ... this is the real thing," the familiar voice answered seductively as Melissa gracefully turned on her side and came to her knees on the bed, wearing nothing but a mischievous smile.

34

Compassion is the antitoxin of the soul:
where there is compassion, even the most
poisonous impulses remain relatively harmless.

—*Eric Hoffer*

Caught completely off guard, Brian stood in the doorway, mesmerized by the sight of Melissa's naked body. A voice inside him beckoned him to turn away, but the vision of her fleshly perfection muted the inner pleas. She was everything he'd ever fantasized about ... and never had.

"Are you just going to stare, or are you coming to bed?" Melissa purred, stroking the surface of the bed next to her. The sound of her voice awakened him from his stupor.

"Wh—what are you ... doing here?" he finally asked, the words barely escaping from his dry throat. He swallowed hard, his eyes running the course of every curve of her shapely form.

"I'm here for you."

Brian didn't respond, transfixed in the moment.

"You know, Brian," she said softly, tilting her head to one side, "I've been really hard on you. I want to make it up to you ... and this is the best way I know how."

"How did you get in here?" he mumbled weakly.

"I asked a guard to let me in," she lied. "I told him it was your birthday and I wanted to surprise you. He got the hint," she added playfully, her perfect mouth breaking into a sly grin as she slid her feet onto the floor.

Brian watched her approach him, her body moving rhythmically across the short span that separated them. She gently draped her arms around his neck and looked into his eyes, the intoxicating scent of her perfume numbing his senses. "I understand how you feel about your standards, but it's just one night. I don't want the others to know, either, so this will be our little secret. Let me make your first time something you'll always remember," she whispered, then kissed him lightly.

They locked eyes once more. "Now, how do you want me?"

Brian didn't move. He could feel himself careening to the point of no return, his desire building. Melissa pressed herself against him and backed him against the wall adjacent to the doorway to the bedroom. She could feel his heart pumping furiously, her cheek resting on his chest. She warmed herself by the heat of his body. *You're mine.*

"I know you're a little nervous," she whispered again, running her hands down the length of his arms, caressing his muscles. "There's nothing to be afraid of," she soothed, drawing his arms around her bare waist. "Touch me ..."

Brian began to slide his hands around her hips, but hesitated. The fight within him had resumed, but the unfamiliar, exciting sensation of her warm, silky skin under his palms summoned him further.

Suddenly she took hold of his face and kissed him hungrily. Instinctively, he reciprocated, his lips seeking her warm, sweet mouth. His conscience screamed at him to stop, and he reluctantly pulled his head back.

"Don't think about it," she gasped, locking her arms around his neck. "Just let it happen." She kissed his neck softly, and then his chin. "Haven't you been wondering what it would be like?"

His silence gave her the answer. Brian closed his eyes, trying to get his bearings.

"Take me and find out, Brian," she coaxed him, stroking his hair. "I don't know about you, but I've been thinking about having you all day long."

Brian struggled to focus. He had thought about her that day, dozens of times, and he wanted her—right now. There was no denying it.

I've been thinking about having you all day long. Her words burned in his mind as he remembered how he had made love to her in his thoughts. But no sooner had the deed entered his mind than he remembered his relief at retaining the respect of the others, the wonderful release of the guilt. He felt Melissa slowly unbuttoning his shirt. *This makes absolutely no sense—why would she ever want someone like me?*

His senses were jolted back to the present by the glide of Melissa's hand over the hair of his chest. She looked at him longingly with her deep, green bedroom eyes. "I'm going to undress you," she informed him. "Don't move."

"No—" Brian protested hoarsely.

"Trust me," she replied, pulling his shirt from the top of his pants, "you'll enjoy what I have in mind."

"No ... I mean ..." he stammered. "Lie down on the bed."

She pulled his shirt apart and pressed herself against his chest. Brian could feel his will numbing again, but she quickly broke the embrace. "Whatever you want," she said compliantly, with a toss of her head. She turned and stretched herself out on the bed. She rolled over to meet him and gasped. He was gone.

Immediately, she jumped out of the bed and hurried into the living room, where Brian was fumbling with his card, trying hurriedly to pass it through the locking device. She quickly subdued her anger. As she saw him begin to punch in his code, she lunged for him.

"Don't leave, Brian," she pleaded, and snatched his hand away from the keypad. She quickly put her arms around him again. "What's wrong?" she asked innocently. "I know I came on pretty strong, but it's just that I want you in bed—tonight."

"Give me a break," he replied, out from under her spell. "This is *me* you're talking to."

"I know." She smiled.

"Yeah, right. Get dressed."

"You know," she said, biting her lower lip for a moment, "we wouldn't have to go all the way. There are other ways I can please you," she added, a sultry grin returning to her face.

"It'd be just as wrong."

She reached for his belt, ignoring his refusal. He grabbed her arm and squeezed it tightly.

"What is it with you?" he demanded indignantly. "Ever since that first meeting you've treated me like a fool, belittling me in front of anyone who was within earshot, making fun of my looks, my standards—and now I turn you on?"

"I just want to make all that up to you," she insisted.

"No, you don't. For some reason, you want to ruin me, to bring me to shame. What kind of a twisted slut are you?"

"Twisted!" Melissa exploded, "I'll tell you what twisted is. Twisted is you peddling your religion in front of real scholars! Twisted is portraying yourself as more pure than anyone else! Well, I know better. I *know* you want me. You're not what you make yourself out to be. Your kind are all the same: controlled, thoughtful, and kind on the outside, but on the inside you're just as corrupt, ready to drop your pants and your precious standards—but in this case, you'd get caught, so you hide behind your sickening self-righteousness!"

Brian felt the anger welling up in him, a fury like he'd never known. "Let me tell you something, Miss Kelley," he seethed. "I don't feel aroused, I feel *pity*—pity you're so weak that the only way you can cope with whatever's made you so angry is to try to make other people as miserable as yourself."

"Why you—let me go!" she snarled, trying unsuccessfully to jerk her arm from his grasp.

"I'm not finished!" Brian shouted. "I have something else—"

He stopped in mid-sentence, his gaze having fallen on the tears welling up in her enraged eyes. The paradox jolted him for a moment, but his surprise was soon replaced by a wave of realization.

"Go ahead!" she blustered, but held her bearing.

"If you ever do anything like this to me again," he said calmly, looking squarely into her moistened eyes, "I'll listen."

"*What?*"

"I'll listen," he repeated himself. "I don't know what you've been through, but I'm going to find out."

"Is that so?" she sneered.

"Yes ... it is," he replied, still holding her arm. "I may not ever be of any good to you," he continued in a gentle but firm tone, "but you're not going to leave this base without knowing God placed someone in your life who at least wanted to help you deal with whatever was done to you. When you're ready to talk, I'll listen." He released her.

Melissa appeared ready to engage him again, but her expression changed, as though his words had hit their mark. The silence was broken by the clamor of shouting and bootsteps in the hallway.

"Get dressed," Brian said and proceeded to button his shirt. Melissa disappeared into the bedroom just as an MP carded his way into the room, his pistol drawn.

"Hands in the air!" the gunman shouted at Brian, who by this time had taken a seat on the couch. He complied. Another MP entered the room and headed for the bedroom. The Colonel followed as a third Marine held the door open, just in time to see Melissa emerge from Brian's bedroom, jeans and bra in place, but no blouse, hands behind her head, escorted by the security detail.

"What's going on here?" the Colonel demanded.

"What does it look like?" Melissa asked sarcastically.

"Melissa was just leaving," Brian explained.

"You mean I was just undressing for you."

"No, you were just leaving."

The Colonel eyed both of them suspiciously. "I don't know what the two of you are up to, but you'd better come clean right now.

The security system didn't make up the alarm it just relayed. What's going on here?" he bellowed.

"Let me in, soldier!" a voice demanded from behind Brian's cocked door. Neil pushed his way inside, a panicked expression on his face.

"You!" he shouted when he saw Melissa. "What do you think you're doing breaking into—" He stopped when he saw her state of undress. "Never mind. I think I can guess."

"I was invited!" she shot back.

"Shut up!" Neil shouted, startling Brian. He'd never seen his friend angry before. "You can stuff your story right now! I know Brian better than that."

"Maybe you don't."

"If he was so willing, why the override card?"

"What's this about an override of security?" the Colonel inquired with a panicked expression.

"The security logs will explain everything. She has an override card."

Melissa said nothing and refused to make eye contact.

"Let's go, Dr. Kelley," the Colonel said in an ominous tone.

"Can I put my shirt back on?"

"Do you want it back on?" Neil spoke bitterly.

"Hurry it up," Colonel Ferguson ordered, and Melissa finished dressing.

The three of them left the room, leaving Brian alone, but not for long. A knock came only seconds after his door had closed behind the Colonel. It was Father Benedict. Over his shoulder, Brian could see the rest of the team members huddled together trying to peek into his room.

"Come on in everybody," he sighed.

One by one, they filed inside. Brian shut the door and collapsed into his chair.

"Are you all right, Brian?" Father Benedict asked.

"I've had more uneventful evenings."

"Man, we all get rousted out of bed, and the next thing we know, Melissa's getting her lovely tush hauled off to detention, away from your room," Malcolm observed. "So what happened?"

Brian briefly relayed the episode to the dumbfounded audience.

"That woman has real issues," Deidre said, shaking her head.

"Her behavior is just ... irrational," Mark remarked, mystified.

"What have you got that I haven't got?" Malcolm wondered aloud.

"Malcolm!" Deidre started in on him.

"Sorry."

"This is very upsetting," Father Benedict reflected. "How did she get the card?"

"Most likely from her mystery visitor," Malcolm deduced. "Makes you wonder, doesn't it?"

"What?" asked Mark.

"If anyone else has one."

35

I would rather feel compassion
than know the meaning of it.

—*Saint Thomas Aquinas*

"You sure you don't mind waiting, ma'am?" the MP asked Melissa.

"I'm in no hurry. Just get my bag there in one piece."

"Move it out!" the Marine ordered the driver, and the tram rolled out onto the tarmac toward the transport jet a few hundred yards away.

She wasn't looking forward to the flight, but at least she'd gotten away from the catacombs of the Facility. It had been almost a month since any of them had seen the surface, and the simple pleasure of seeing the sunrise was well worth the five o'clock A.M. rising time. The warmth of the sun felt exhilarating.

Melissa watched the drab green vehicle get smaller and smaller as it headed east in the direction of the early morning sun. It zipped past the stalled jeep that, along with the tram, had been intended to carry all of them to the plane for boarding. The tram couldn't hold all of them, and the MP had asked her to wait for his return.

She'd actually chosen to stay behind for another reason. Brian hadn't shown up with the others, and the Colonel had radioed for someone to check his room. She was determined to show him that she hadn't been taken in by his feigned concern. *He's just full of himself.* She would show him who was weak.

She scanned the buildings situated at various locations about the airfield. It was amazing how innocuous the base appeared. The hangars were large but unimpressive. Who could imagine the secrets awaiting far below the surface? It seemed odd that the only sign of life was a solitary plane slowly creeping toward the beginning of a runway, and another MP with two German shepherds.

Though the MP was about a hundred yards away, she could tell he was watching her closely as he guarded the door through which she and the team had come only a few minutes ago. Whatever. She heard the door behind her open and saw Brian emerge, carrying his familiar backpack and wearing a typically unfashionable pair of plain shorts and a T-shirt. He was escorted by a Marine, who spoke to Brian briefly and then went back inside. Melissa smiled to herself as she saw Brian start out in her direction, only to halt when he recognized her. She enjoyed knowing she made him uncomfortable.

Brian walked up to where she was standing but passed her without uttering a word. He set his bag down against the side of the building and looked out over the tarmac, which seemed to stretch for miles. The sight was uplifting; it was so good to be outside. *If only the company were better*, he thought to himself, but instantly felt a pang of regret at his unspoken sarcasm. He allowed himself another brief glance at her small form.

Despite her behavior last evening and her malicious spirit, he found himself still wanting to drink in her form. She looked as unflawed as ever in her white shorts and powder blue tank top. But he knew all too well what lurked inside her, and the realization quickly took the edge off the attraction. Whatever lay behind Melissa's crass attitude, she was its prisoner. He knew he couldn't let her hostility toward him dictate how he treated her.

"Guess I shut my alarm off by accident," he said, turning in her direction.

"Guess you've mistaken me for someone who cares," she replied, holding her hand above her eyes, searching for the tram. It was nowhere to be seen.

"I meant what I said last night," he reminded her.

"I'll bet."

"I want to help. You can trust me."

Melissa cast him a frustrated expression and said nothing, choosing to communicate her feelings for him with her middle finger. Brian didn't push.

Melissa resumed scanning the horizon for the missing vehicle. The plane was still there, but their means of getting across the expanse was mysteriously gone. She also noticed that the other plane was by now nearly out of visual range, and that the surface had become eerily quiet. It was as though they were completely alone.

"Melissa."

She refused to look at Brian.

"Melissa."

She heard him again, but this time there was a sense of urgency in his voice. She looked to her left where he was standing, but he did not return her glance. Instead, he was peering over her shoulder. It took only a few second to read the alarm on his face. She turned in the direction of his gaze and her eyes fell on the two German shepherds she'd seen a few minutes ago. The guard was gone. The dogs were unrestrained. As soon as they made eye contact with Brian and Melissa, they bolted toward them.

"Run!" Brian commanded her. "Over there!" He pointed to a jeep about fifty yards away.

"Wha—"

"Just do it—run!"

36

Brian grabbed Melissa's arm and pushed her into motion. "Head for the jeep! Get under it!"

He started running as well, and almost immediately outpaced her. After a few more strides, he looked back over his shoulder. The dogs were dismayingly fast for their size and were rapidly gaining on them. He thought he could make it, but there was no way Melissa would.

Brian suddenly whirled about and sprinted toward Melissa. "Keep going!" he yelled as he flew past her.

Bewildered, she paused and looked behind her at Brian, who was now heading straight for the dogs as fast as possible. In amazed horror, she watched as he slowed his pace, timing the leap of the first animal, and caught the dog in midair. The impact nearly toppled him, but he managed to keep his balance. Then, in a remarkably swift, deliberate motion, he altered the path of his momentum, the first dog still in his arms, and dove into the second animal. She turned and ran for the jeep, too afraid to witness what would surely follow.

Brian immediately began pummeling the head of the dog pinned on its side underneath him. The shepherd went into a frenzy. Brian out-weighed the dog by a good seventy pounds, but it was all he could do to keep the animal in a prone position.

The second animal lunged and hit its mark. Brian cried out as the fangs penetrated deeply into his exposed calf, but he held the dog beneath him fast. He had no choice; there was no way he could protect himself against both animals simultaneously. Desperately, he dug into the pinned animal's eye socket with his thumb, trying to ignore the pain shooting through his leg. The dog beneath him yelped in enraged agony and jerked violently, managing to loosen its hind legs, which he immediately set to fending off the man on top of him.

Suddenly, Brian felt the shepherd's sharp teeth release his leg. Without warning, a second attack came from the side and inflicted a vicious bite on his shoulder. The animal did not lock on, though, choosing instead to go for its victim's throat. Brian caught a glimpse of the charging animal out of the corner of his eye and had no choice but to release his grip and surrender his arm to the second dog's gaping maw.

Melissa made it to the jeep and scrambled underneath the stalled vehicle. She lay prostrate, panting heavily, more from panic than exertion. She'd heard Brian's scream as she'd reached safety. A piercing yelp punctuated the air next, and she maneuvered her body into a position where she could see what was happening.

The battle was raging about thirty yards away. She flinched as one of the dogs latched onto Brian's left arm and shook it violently. Brian yelled in pain again but managed to get to his feet, the dog firmly attached and standing on its hind legs. The other dog seemed momentarily disoriented, walking in circles, shaking its head, blood streaming from one of its eyes, but it soon got its bearings and circled behind its quarry for a counterattack. Brian frantically jammed his thumb into the eye of the yet unwounded dog, which instantaneously released his arm as it whined in distress and retreated.

Run for it! she screamed in her mind, but, to her astonishment, Brian made no move toward the jeep. Instead, incredibly, he went on the offensive, diving on the shepherd he had first injured, pinning it to its stomach. Sitting atop the dog and straddling it, he quickly grabbed a forelimb, placed his knee upon the joint, and jerked the paw upward with all his might. The second dog charged at him as its partner howled bitterly, knocking Brian from his position, but not before he'd succeeded in maiming the first animal.

The shepherd scratched furiously at Brian, now on his back, who tried to deflect the buzz saw of claws and teeth with his arms. Brian spun onto his side and quickly got on his feet. The dog lunged at him and, as if by design, found Brian's bleeding arm and seized it in its jaws again. Brian gasped in anguish. The dog twisted his head repeatedly, gradually reducing the muscle of Brian's forearm to raw meat.

For a brief moment, Brian caught sight of its bloodied muzzle, its eyes rolled back into its head, maddened by the taste of his blood. Brian felt his knees buckle, but he managed to stay on his feet. He knew if he hit the ground again, it would be for the last time. He tried punching the shepherd in the face, but his strength was weakening. The dog refused to relinquish his grip. Finally, as if by impulse alone, he grabbed the dog's ear and yanked it hard; but rather than releasing his arm, the dog became more enraged, tightening its toothy hold on its fading prey.

Suddenly, in a flash of insight, Brian let go of the ear and kicked the canine viciously between the legs where it stood. Still he could not free himself. He kicked again, and then a third time. The dog gasped for air, and Brian's arm fell free from its jaws. Summoning his strength, he fell upon the panting animal and, as with the other, broke its foreleg. He rolled off the fallen beast and watched it writhe in agony, its body contorted by the pain.

Brian looked down at his arm, a bloody, shredded mass with fingers. He could only raise the limb halfway, and as he clenching his fist, the excruciating pain shot through his arm to his shoulder. His stomach heaved at the gruesome sight, and dizziness swept over him.

Melissa's scream jolted him into alertness. He turned toward the sound. The first wounded dog had hobbled to the jeep and was trying to get at Melissa. Brian tried to run, but stumbled and fell in disorientation. He toiled clumsily to get to his feet and finally succeeded. He trudged toward the unsuspecting shepherd, now preoccupied with snapping at Melissa's kicking feet. Gritting his teeth to fend off the pain, he abruptly seized the animal's hind legs and pulled him from beneath the side-panel of the jeep. In a swift, calculated motion, and with a loud, tormented gasp, he spun the animal around, airborne, smacking its head into the fender. Then Brian slumped onto the tarmac on one knee.

The maneuver spent him, but it also accomplished its purpose of stunning the dog. He crawled to the stricken animal, but not before it had recovered. Brian's feeble offensive was met with two rows of teeth. He cried out as the dog's mouth found his mangled arm. Blood spurted as the canine's teeth ground to the bone, and Brian gasped and began to cry. Suddenly, adrenaline surged through his body as he saw his own blood spurt through the teeth of the enraged animal. He realized in a panic that an artery had been severed.

He quickly grabbed an ear as before and, pulling the animal upright, tried to disable it as he had done the other, by kicking it between the legs. After half a dozen well-placed blows, the dazed shepherd still clung tenaciously to his victim, but more out of instinct than anything else. Brian tried to pull his arm away, but the pain nearly caused him to black out.

Finally, out of desperation, he placed his other arm firmly around the back of the exhausted dog's head and, mustering the last of his strength, jerked the animal's head back. The sickening crack of the beast's neck was muffled by Brian's own anguished scream. The two combatants collapsed to the tarmac, Brian's twisted limb still in the mouth of the dead, twitching animal.

"Brian!" Melissa frantically called to him, "Get up! You can make it— it's only a few yards!"

Brian could hear her plainly, but he couldn't move. A pool of blood began to form next to him. His breathing slowed as his body began to lapse into shock. A peculiar dark circle began to appear at the periphery of his vision. Melissa's voice faded, but not before being replaced by a low, threatening growl. Brian knew immediately he was going to die, but he felt strangely calm.

He turned his head to face the other crippled, partially blinded assassin. The dog was badly injured but had fared better than he had. The wounded shepherd limped awkwardly but purposefully toward him, teeth bared, his lone good eye seething with rage. Brian prayed for a merciful end. He closed his eyes as the dog closed in for the kill. But instead of feeling unforgiving jaws closing about his neck, he heard a dull thud, followed by a whimper. He slowly opened his eyes and watched Melissa, tire wrench in hand, barely three feet from where he lay, rain down blow after blow on the dog's skull until it gave way.

Melissa dropped her weapon and rushed over to Brian. She pried his arm from the dog's mouth and then gingerly turned him over onto his back. She tore frantically at his belt and, upon removing it, quickly applied a tourniquet around his upper arm. She cradled his face in her hands and looked into his eyes, now drenched with tears of agonizing pain. She quickly glanced behind where she knelt and then back down to him.

"Can you hear me?"

He couldn't speak.

"Help's on the way," she said, her lip quivering. "Just hang on."

37

Whatever is begun in anger, ends in shame.

—*Benjamin Franklin*

"I want to know what happened out there this morning, and I want to know *now!*" Colonel Ferguson exploded.

The twelve men in front of him remained silent.

"Cowards!" he challenged. "I don't know what's a more gutless deed, arranging a murder like this or refusing to take responsibility for it."

"Colonel—"

"Don't interrupt me!" the Colonel bellowed.

"Vernon," the large man at the center of the table intervened, "I think it would be wise to exercise some restraint here. I understand your concern and anger, but—"

"But what? The Group isn't used to being spoken to in such a way? Who cares!"

"You will," a thin, nattily dressed man informed him calmly, "once you're removed."

"Then you might as well kill me," he retorted unflinchingly. "The agenda is more important than you or me—more important than all of us collectively. I will not allow decades of planning and research to be washed away because one of you doesn't like outsiders on the team."

"That can be arranged," another voice said from the shadows.

"Do you think you can intimidate me?" the Colonel asked defiantly. "How dumb do you think I am? I haven't lasted thirty years in this game without knowing how to protect myself. I know your identities, where you live, who your children and grandchildren are. I've been gathering information on all of you for years. If I so much as come down with a cold, I'll expose all of you. Try and take me down. You'll only get one chance."

"So this is your trusted friend, eh, General?" a third voice resonated in the silence of the Colonel's tirade.

"Yes," he answered coolly, "he is. And knowing Vernon as I do, he'll do exactly what he's said."

"Then he's the traitor here," a voice accused.

"No," the Colonel objected. "Anyone who'd allow our work to be threatened and not be outraged is the one guilty of treachery—or spinelessness. Now, who wanted Dr. Scott and Dr. Kelley dead?"

"This is ridiculous!" the well-dressed man exclaimed and began to rise. "I'll not be bullied in this manner! We've all committed our lives to the success of this plan; none of us would jeopardize it for any reason."

"Sit down! No one but those of us in this room could have arranged this. Who else could get to the surface to try this?"

"Or be armed," the General added. "Do we know yet when the MP Dr. Kelley reported to be on the tarmac was killed?"

"Judging by the body, probably minutes before the incident," Colonel Ferguson replied, still visibly agitated.

"That would mean he was the one who released the dogs," the General reasoned thoughtfully.

"Are we sure about that?" asked the Lieutenant. "Maybe someone shot him so that the dogs would get loose, then moved the body later. Would anyone on the team itself want these two dead?"

"No one," a voice emanated from off to the side of the large table.

"Hmmpff," the thin man sniffed. "I suppose you think we're guilty as well."

"The thought had crossed my mind."

"What a shock," he scoffed.

"I may be a newcomer here," the speaker retorted from the shadows, the anger rising in his voice, "but I am far from being a mere follower. The Colonel may be in the minority, but I side with him in the matter. One or more of you is trying to scuttle the plan, and I have no qualms over personally dealing with whoever it is. Don't let my appearance mislead you."

"Yes," the thin man droned, "we're all well aware of your reputation. Some of us question your allegiance. Perhaps your loyalty has become divided."

"My allegiance has not wavered and never will. You simply will not face the reality that everyone on the team was accounted for. Each member was already on the plane, except, of course, for Dr. Scott and Dr. Kelley."

"Including yourself?"

"Of course."

38

Make the most of your regrets …
To regret deeply is to live afresh.

—*Henry David Thoreau*

Melissa exited her room and walked hurriedly down the hallway away from the cafeteria. After a few steps, she paused and hastily unzipped her purse and peered inside. Satisfied that its contents were secure, she continued on her solitary journey. About halfway, she stopped at one of the doors leading beyond the restricted confines and tapped gently on the door. The door opened as if programmed. The MP on the other side, posted to allow passage, visually confirmed her identity. She acknowledged the guard with a glance and continued on her way, a second MP at her side.

It had been two full days since the attack. Except for Father Benedict and Melissa, the team had already been transported as planned to its new destination. It was perfectly understandable that he had stayed behind until Brian could travel. After all, he was a priest and friend. On the other hand, Melissa had needed to beg for the privilege. Neil and Father Benedict had been dead set against it, but to her relief, the Colonel had finally relented after her repeated requests.

Melissa and her military escort turned what was by now the familiar last corner of the walk to the Facility's infirmary. She'd come every few hours since Brian had emerged from surgery, but he'd been deliberately kept under heavy sedation. She could only sit beside the bed in the silence, stricken with guilt, running the events of the past month—and especially the past few days—through her mind.

Why had she done those things? Why had she so doggedly pursued the ruin of a man she barely knew, a man who had repaid her unrelenting hostility by saving her life nearly at the expense of his own? She of course knew the answer, but now the remembrance of her own pain did not revive her determination to strike back. She felt only an abiding sense of shame as she approached the door to Brian's hospital room.

"Thanks," she said quietly to the MP, who turned and walked a few yards away to his designated post, joining a second armed guard. She paused briefly, looking at the door. The moment she'd both yearned for and dreaded had arrived. She took the knob. To her surprise, it turned in her hand. The door swung outward, propelled by Father Benedict. The priest put his finger to his lips and closed the door behind him.

"I was told he was awake," Melissa said in a hushed tone.

"Oh, he's awake," the priest answered quietly, taking her arm and guiding her a few feet from the door. "I just don't want him to hear this conversation." She looked at him curiously.

"Don't act so surprised, Melissa," he said abruptly.

"I wasn't acting."

"Of course," he said condescendingly. "So the huntress now looks for compassion from her prey," he observed with a cold stare. "For some reason, since he awoke, he's asked about nothing other than how you are. I'd say it was delirium if I didn't know him as I do."

"Listen, Father," she said, bowing her head, "I don't want to argue with you again. I—"

"You'd just like to forget this whole thing ever happened, wouldn't you?"

She held her tongue.

"Well it *did* happen, and now you—and Brian—must live with the consequences!" he said angrily through clenched teeth.

She looked up at him, his eyes now aflame with contempt. She made no attempt to engage him.

"Haven't you anything to say?" he growled.

"There's nothing to say."

"There's *plenty* to say!"

"I know how you feel about him, Father, but—"

"How could you know how I feel about anyone," he interrupted her again, "especially him?"

"I'm sorry. I misspoke."

"You're responsible for a great deal more than a poor choice of words," he accused. "I've never in all my years met such an uncaring soul. You've done nothing but ridicule him since you've been here, and now we're supposed to accept your remorse as genuine and not self-serving? Are we really supposed to sense grief after what you did the other evening? Tell me, how are you planning to use this latest incident against him?"

The old priest's words pierced her through the heart. No anger welled up inside her, only shame. She stood before him, spiritless, and made no effort to defend herself. Andrew beheld her, an implacable expression on his wizened face.

"I know you must have suffered in some terrible way to become so spiteful," he continued, "but you aren't the only person who has experienced great hurt. You have no idea, not that you would actually care, what this man has endured in his short life. Yet through it all, he's clung to his faith, consciously refusing the path you've trodden for years. God forgive me for saying it, but it seems far more just for you to be suffering than him."

"I'd like to see him now," she said quietly and turned toward the door.

"I'm not through," Father Benedict warned, grabbing her arm tightly. She stopped, refusing to look him in the eye.

"Listen very closely to me, Dr. Kelley, because what I have to say won't be repeated. Do I have your undivided attention?" he asked, yanking her in his direction. She fixed her gaze on him and shook her arm free of his grasp.

"Good. If I so much as hear a single unkind word directed at him from your mouth, I swear by my calling I'll make you pay for it dearly. You may take me lightly, young lady, but you do so at your own peril," he threatened, drawing closer to her. "There is much more to me than meets the eye. You would do well to remember that."

"I will," she said edgily, taken back by his demeanor.

"Don't be so surprised, doctor," he said, noting her startled gaze. "It isn't that I enjoy wasting my time on revenge; I'm simply devoted to his welfare. I suspect you'll never comprehend how important he is to the future. Brian Scott is worth a little extra time in purgatory. You, on the other hand, are not."

Father Benedict abruptly turned and walked away, leaving Melissa alone outside Brian's door. She sighed, a feeling of disgrace filling her as she watched the priest disappear around a corner. Her shame was momentarily pushed aside by the realization that Andrew had left the area unescorted. She looked at the MP, whose gaze was riveted on her, and shrugged it off. There was no question who was under more suspicion.

39

If we could read the secret history of our enemies,
we would find in each person's life sorrow and
suffering enough to disarm all hostility.

—*Henry Wadsworth Longfellow*

"Hi," Melissa ventured cautiously as she entered the room.

"Hi," Brian reciprocated with a weak but sincere smile.

Melissa pulled up the chair that had become hers over the last two days and sat down at the side of the bed, where Brian was propped upright.

"You're okay," he sighed. "What a relief. I couldn't get any specific information about you out of anyone this morning. I don't know what the big secret was."

"Brian, thank you—" she began, biting her lip.

"You don't need to say anything," he stopped her. "I'm okay."

"You're alive, but hardly okay," she disagreed, her eyes scanning the half dozen or so scratches on his face and neck, and then proceeding finally to his left arm, which lay in front of her, the lower portion of which was heavily bandaged and in a protective cast. "You lost a lot of blood, Brian. I'm amazed you made it."

"Yeah, I was surprised to wake up here. God was good. I have you to thank, too."

"But your arm ..." She cupped her hand over her mouth and turned her head away, trying not to cry in front of him. "Didn't they tell you?"

"Yeah. The doctor showed up right after I woke up. He gave me the whole description of the surgery and the reconstruction. Kind of neat the way they fixed the artery, but he lost me about half way through it, to be honest."

"But you have nerve damage," she said, clearing her voice. "He had to tell you ... that you'd probably never use your hand again."

"He did. We'll see," he sighed.

"He was serious, Brian."

"So am I."

She marveled at his stubbornness, but her attention was quickly drawn to his still-swollen thumb protruding from the cast, now twitching haphazardly. Brian felt nothing but followed her glance.

"It does that from time to time ... might be a good sign."

Melissa burst into tears, overcome by the guilt inside her. Brian watched her for a few moments, her body trembling with grief.

"Melissa ..." he said softly.

"It's my fault!" she wailed, her face contorted with sorrow.

"How would it be your fault? You didn't do this to me, and you certainly didn't make me do anything."

She shook her head.

"It's not your fault," he said, trying to comfort her. "You aren't to be blamed."

"Why did you do it?" she sobbed.

Brian thought for a moment. "It was just ... the right thing to do. I knew you weren't going to make it to the jeep."

"It makes no sense," she said through her tears. "I've treated you horribly—deliberately, too. You were right the other night, you know. I wanted to ruin you, to make you a hypocrite in front of everyone. I've thought about it every day since the first meeting. And then you take everything I've dished out and do this. You should have let me die."

"That's absurd," he replied. "I made the right choice, and would do it again."

"Didn't you hear me?"

"I heard you."

"You must be high," she sniffed. "Nothing you're saying makes sense."

"From my view it looks as though God had me at the right place at the right time. I overslept, which is pretty rare; we wind up topside together ... I don't see anything to blame you for. As far as the other things you've done since we've been here, well ... look at me."

Melissa hesitated but lifted her head and looked into his eyes. There was no anger in them, only compassion and sincerity.

"Are you listening?"

She nodded.

"I forgive you." He smiled.

She closed her eyes and dropped her head.

"Look at me," he insisted again.

She complied, reluctantly.

"Did you hear me?"

She nodded again.

"Just so we're clear, and can leave all this behind," Brian added, "I want you to know I'm not holding onto any of it; it's forgotten. We're stuck here together, so when we see each other, I don't want you to feel ashamed. If you've learned anything about me at all, you can believe me when I tell you that I forgive you—completely."

Melissa closed her eyes once more, squeezing the tears from them. She rose from her chair and threw her arms around his shoulders and embraced him tightly. She sobbed openly, her head pressed to his chest.

Brian hadn't expected the display of emotion and was uncertain how to respond. Cautiously, he placed his good hand on her head and stroked her thick, auburn hair softly, waiting for her to regain her composure.

After a few moments, her anguish subsided, and she lifted her head and looked into his eyes. "I'm so sorry ... thank you," she whispered, touching his face.

"You're welcome," he acknowledged quietly, his skin flushing at the sensation.

"I've never met anyone quite like you," she continued, in the same position. "You're not like—" She abruptly stopped. A distant gaze appeared on her face, followed quickly by a painful frown, and she pulled away from him.

"I'm listening ... you can trust me."

"I know. I guess I owe you an explanation."

"You owe me nothing. You better remember that or be prepared to put up with my reminding you all the time."

"Okay." She forced a smile and sat back in her chair, looking at the wall across the room.

"You really don't have to tell me anything. I just thought it might help."

"I was eighteen," she began, not even hearing his last comment, "and it was a few weeks into my freshman year at Penn State."

"I thought you went to Notre Dame?" he noted, puzzled.

"I did. I just didn't start there."

"Neil didn't mention it in your introduction."

"That's because he doesn't know about it. I left after three weeks, and I had no permanent record."

"Go on," he encouraged.

"My parents were totally against my choice. They wanted me to go to the fundamentalist Christian college they had gone to. They were missionaries."

Brian's eyes widened with interest.

"I know it's hard to believe, considering what you've experienced of me. I was born in Ireland during the first year of their ministry and lived there until I was fourteen, when we moved back to the States."

"Why did your family leave the field?"

"They decided to live in the U.S. while I attended high school. I was an only child, so they planned on returning once I entered college. I went to high school in this country and was a National Merit Scholar. I got the best scholarship offer from Penn State, so that's where I went."

"Was that the only reason you made the choice?"

"No." She paused. "I have to admit, I was a little rebellious—although not in an overt sort of way. There was a guy from my high school whom I'd been dating, and he was going there as well on an ROTC scholarship. My parents liked him since he convinced them he shared their beliefs. They had no problem with him; their problem was that I was going to the university."

"Why was that an issue?"

"We were members of a very strict church, and one of the unspoken litmus tests in the church for parental success was to have your child in a fundamentalist college. Turned out my scholarship only shamed them. It was just ... bizarre."

Brian sighed and shook his head. She glanced at him curiously. He motioned again for her to continue.

"Two weeks into the fall semester, my boyfriend told me we'd been invited to a party," she said, now looking down at the floor, clasping her hands. Her voice slowed, as though confessing to some crime. "He had a few friends on the football team, and they'd invited him to their frat house for what turned out to be a drunken orgy. I'd never been in that kind of environment before ..." Her voice trailed off. Brian remained silent.

"I went to the party with him, but when I saw what it was, I insisted on leaving. He told me we didn't have to drink, that he wouldn't if I wouldn't—that we could have fun anyway. I bought it, and that was my second mistake."

"I take it he got you drunk."

"Drugged, actually. Ever heard of Rohypnol?"

Brian shook his head.

"It's the so-called 'date rape' drug. It's odorless and colorless. I had no reason to ever suspect him of any harmful intent. I was hopelessly naïve—at least at the start of the festivities," she said cynically, the bitterness creeping back into her voice.

"I think I know where this is going," Brian interrupted. "You really don't have to go any further."

"Oh, but I do—you can't imagine where this all ended."

"Okay," he said uneasily.

"To make a long story short, my date and his friends took turns having their way with me. I have no way of knowing how many there were, maybe half a dozen. I woke up on the floor inside the lobby of my dorm. At least they put my clothes back on."

"Please tell me they're serving time somewhere." Brian flushed with anger.

"Of course not. I left school a few days afterward and went back home. I lied and told my parents I'd made a mistake and didn't want to go to college there. It was easy to sell them on the notion that I'd go where they wanted me to the following fall."

"Why didn't you tell them the truth?"

"Are you serious? They'd have been ashamed of me."

"Ashamed of you? You were raped!"

"It didn't matter."

"What do you mean?"

"A few weeks later, I began feeling ill. My mother took me to a doctor, and he discovered I was pregnant. My parents were beside themselves, to say the least. I told them what had happened, but they didn't believe a word of it. My father insisted that I'd gone to Penn State just to sleep around with my boyfriend."

"I'm sorry for saying this, but what kind of father would treat his daughter like such trash?"

"The kind who depended on financial support from the people involved. My father felt compelled to take the word of a rapist over his daughter's, since the rapist's dad happened to be the pastor of the largest contributor to the good ol' boy network affectionately referred to as our Mission Association," she seethed, reliving the injustice.

Brian was stunned.

"The pastoral staff at my boyfriend's church suddenly 'saw the light' that abortion was permissible in cases of rape. Greg's dad told me that if I didn't have the abortion, my father—which meant my family—would lose financial support. He also said he'd lobby to have dad's ministerial credentials yanked. Not only that, but should I ever bring charges against his son, he promised he would counter sue for false arrest or defamation of character.

"My dad told me it was the best thing to do for everyone concerned, and that God wouldn't hold me accountable—at least not for *that* sin. I didn't want to do it, but I was eighteen and scared for my parents, especially my mom. I had the abortion."

A hush came over the room; only the beeping of one of the monitors to which Brian was hooked up could be heard.

Brian broke the silence. "What did your mom say when it was all over? At least you had her for support."

"Not quite," Melissa scoffed. "That's the best part. Shortly after the abortion, I overheard my parents arguing about the whole episode. My father blurted out something to the effect that it served my mother right to have this happen after what *she* had done. I confronted the two of them on the spot, and we had a huge blowup. It was worth it, though. I learned that day that my mother had cheated on my father while we were in Ireland. From the sound of things, I got the distinct impression that my father wasn't sure if I was even his daughter. Eventually the whole combination of events drove my mother over the edge and destroyed our family."

"What do you mean?"

"Mom wound up in a mental hospital. She never left, either. She died there a little over a year after her admission. My father committed suicide a few months after that. I didn't have any firsthand knowledge of all this, mind you. I left home for good the summer following my assault and never told my parents where I was going. I found out years after the fact from old friends in my hometown. So there you have it. God's surely been good to me. Thank you Jesus for screwing up my life."

"Melissa—"

"Don't lecture me about God, Brian, or even blasphemy for that matter."

"I had no intention."

"What is it then?"

"Come here, please." He motioned with his right hand after a moment of hesitation.

Melissa stood up and moved to the other side of the bed. Brian took her hand and looked up at her. "I know you know this, but I think you need to hear it from someone else."

"What's that?"

"None of it was your fault. God would never hold you accountable for any of this."

"I know," she acknowledged, somewhat irritably, and tried to pull her hand back, but Brian did not let go.

"That's not all," he said nervously, mustering the courage to say what was on his heart. "I'm sorry for what was done to you. If I had been there, I'd have been on your side, no matter what. You've overcome so much to make a success of yourself. I admire you."

"Oh, Brian, if you only knew ..." She paused. "You have no idea who I am."

40

The 'medical examination' to which abductees
are said to be subjected, often accompanied by sadistic
sexual manipulation, is reminiscent of the medieval tales of
encounters with demons. It makes no sense in a sophisticated
or technical framework: any intelligent being equipped with
the scientific marvels that UFOs possess would be in
a position to achieve any of these alleged scientific objectives
in a shorter time and with fewer risks.

—*Dr. Jacques Vallee, Confrontations*

Malcolm made his way noiselessly down the unfamiliar hallway, hugging the wall as he moved. There were no guards that he could see, a fact that brought no comfort, only suspicion that he'd been set up. He wasn't even sure who or what had beckoned him to venture out of his quarters this night. *What am I doing here?*

His breathing suddenly became uneven, and he felt the first of dozens of small beads of sweat on his forehead trickle down the side of his face. He'd never done anything like this, especially when the stakes were so high. Suddenly a light shone from behind him, its flickering beam moving from side to side as it progressively crept toward him. He panicked.

Resigned to the fact that he'd be detected no matter what he did, Malcolm broke into a reckless run down the hallway and made an abrupt turn to the right, a decision that placed him in the midst of a maze of intersecting corridors. An alarm shattered the stillness, and the beleaguered scientist was suddenly seized with the realization that he had lost his sense of direction; he had no idea where he was or where he was going.

Disoriented and winded, he stopped, trying to get his bearings. The echo of distant footsteps rapidly dispersing through the hallways reduced him to near hysteria. He curled up on the cold floor, trembling, awaiting discovery and the fate that came with it.

Unexpectedly, his eye caught the emission of a soft glow from underneath the door across the corridor from where he lay. It seemed warm and hospitable, even inviting. For reasons he could not grasp, he felt drawn to its source. He stood erect, suddenly energized, and crossed over to the door. He turned the knob, sure the door would be locked. Amazingly, it swung open.

The light blinded him at first, and he quickly closed the door behind him to keep the glow from escaping into the hallway. Turning once more, he beheld a surprisingly vast room. He quickly put his hand to his mouth to muffle a frightened cry at the even more shocking contents. Before him were positioned dozens—perhaps hundreds—of sterile, glimmering, stainless steel gurneys. Atop each one, to his horrified fascination, was a perfectly intact alien corpse.

Compelled by some unseen force, Malcolm made his way to the closest body. Compared to those he had seen in the Facility, the specimen was flawless. The feel of its skin was soft and fleshy, not the rough, grainy texture he'd expected, as with the aged, desiccated epidermis of the autopsied bodies in Dr. Marcus' lab. Despite its macabre appearance, to Malcolm it seemed a work of art.

Without warning, a familiar but anomalous sensation intruded upon Malcolm's transfixed awe. It was the queer aroma he'd detected in both Brian's and Melissa's rooms. He took a deep breath, filling his nostrils with the odd bouquet. Yes, he was sure of it. He hadn't noticed it at all when he'd entered the room. He looked around the cavernous chamber, hoping to detect the source of the emission, but could find nothing that suggested a source.

He looked back down at where the corpse before him lay, and to his horror, it had vanished. Anxiously, he surveyed the gurneys in the room, and then stumbled backward in terror. Half of them were empty. He wanted to get out of the room, but he couldn't move.

Suddenly the remaining bodies became animated and sat upright, as though somehow brought to life by his fear. They quietly and robotically shuffled toward him. In utter dread, he finally managed to move his feet, each of which seemed to weigh as much as his entire body. He fell and was instantly immobilized, as though the floor itself held him in a fingerless grip. The aliens closed in, unmoved by his frantic screams.

A voice broke into his mind, its source unknown. *Malcolm! Malcolm!*

"Malcolm!" Mark shouted in earnest, shaking his bunkmate.

Malcolm shot upright in his bed, his T-shirt drenched with sweat, his heart pounding in his chest.

"You okay, guy?" Mark asked, crouched at the side of his bed.

"Yeah ..." he said, checking his surroundings.

"Some dream."

"Yeah ... right. It seemed so real."

"Tell me about it. You woke me up out of a sound sleep, and that's something. What were you dreaming about?"

"Aw ... just weird stuff. It was freaky."

41

To be wronged is nothing unless
you continue to remember it.

—*Confucius*

"So educate me," Brian replied.

"You don't want to know."

"It's up to you. It might be good for you."

"I guess it doesn't matter," she sighed. "Like I said, I stuck it out at my parents' house the rest of that school year—not that we were a family anymore, mind you. I decided I wanted to go into medicine, so I spent the year studying, both to prepare for the premed programs I'd applied to and to take my mind off of what had happened, which didn't work.

"I became angrier every day. I quit going to church and basically told my parents where they could shove their phony religion. When I left, I told them in a letter that I would never be back and that I wasn't going to tell them where I'd decided to go to school. I even went through the trouble of getting my own post office box so they wouldn't see any of my mail while I was applying to other schools. As you now know, I wound up at Notre Dame. I ended up changing my major during my first semester there."

"Why was that?"

"I discovered the joy of exposing Christians for the frauds they were."

Brian didn't know what to make of the statement, and waited for her to continue.

"You look confused," she said, still clasping his hand.

"I am," he confessed.

"During orientation week, I ran into one of those Campus Crusade nuts trying to convince me I needed Jesus. He invited me to an ice cream social, and I told him I'd go if he took me. I don't know where I got the idea, but I wanted to see if he had the same thing on his mind as my rapist boyfriend and God-fearing mother. We weren't alone twenty minutes before we were doing it in the back seat of his car. That wasn't the enjoyable part; that came when I saw him a few days later at their literature table and announced to his friends what we'd done. He was crushed. I'd found my coping mechanism. Since then, every guy who has tried to pass himself off to me as some sort of spiritual giant has failed the 'Melissa test.' It didn't matter if they were married, either."

"I can hardly believe no one ever resisted."

"Some did, but never for very long. Gradually these small-scale humiliations weren't enough. I decided to major in religion and dedicated myself to demonstrating that these people were just as screwed up as anyone else. They were empty-headed simpletons who had no answers, only pious platitudes they used to manipulate everyone else."

"So you would have tried to seduce me again?" he asked, a saddened expression on his face.

"No ... you were different," she said, the shame returning to her voice. "Like I said, you weren't the first to say no, but you were the first to sort of see through why I was doing it. I knew there would be no point in coming after you again. It made me furious, actually. It was only after you'd nearly gotten yourself killed that I thought about what you'd said. So how about it? You can't think of me as anything other than despicable."

She uncovered his hand, inviting him to release hers. He did, but Melissa stayed at the bedside.

"You're right," he said thoughtfully. "What you've done is terrible. You should be ashamed of yourself—are you?"

Melissa opened her mouth to answer, but halted. She'd been taken back by the question. Brian waited for her answer.

"Yes," she said dejectedly and looked down at the floor, averting his gaze.

"Do you plan to do it again?"

"No," she said solemnly, looking at him once again.

"Why not?"

"What do you mean, why not?" she asked, again surprised.

"You tell me. Why wouldn't you keep doing it? I'm sure you'd find more men who'd fall for you—so why not do it?"

"Because it's wrong!"

"So how did you justify it in the first place?"

"How do you think? It felt great to expose those hypocrites ..."

"But ..." Brian prompted, sensing her hesitation.

"But ... it hasn't really helped."

"And it never will. You need to forgive them."

"I don't know if I can."

"But you want to."

"I don't know that either."

"Sure you do. You just told me that your hate for the people who did this to you hasn't helped at all. As I see it, not wanting to forgive them is like saying you're content to stay as you are. You can't have it both ways."

"Okay, Socrates. I guess my problem is that I don't believe I can really do it. But will it really do any good? I know your faith is important to you, but why does God make us suffer? I hate to say it like this, but look at you. You've been faithful to your beliefs and kind to me—but look what it's gotten you."

Brian closed his eyes, her brutally honest words echoing in his mind. He'd thought the same thoughts himself, of course. His mind traversed through the memories of his own angry conversations with God in the hope of finding something that would comfort her.

"Sorry if I offended you." Melissa's apology broke his concentration.

"You didn't," he assured her.

"What is it then?" she asked.

"I used to think," he sighed, "that with the talents God had given me, I was going to be something special. I wanted more than anything to make a contribution to my field, to do something noteworthy for the right reasons. I've had to learn that those things aren't going to happen. God must have other plans."

"That isn't very encouraging, if you don't mind my saying so."

"I think the real answer to your question," he continued, "is that you aren't—and I wasn't—asking the *right* question. The question isn't what will make us happy, but how should we spend our lives for the greater good, no matter where we are."

"Are you fulfilled, then?"

"No, not yet, but I believe that somehow I will be. Right now I have to confess I don't know what's going on in my life, probably because I have no life to speak of."

"You've mentioned losing a teaching position a couple of times. Tell me about it."

"It's a long and fairly convoluted story ... small potatoes compared to what you've been through."

"Didn't any of your colleagues defend you?"

"No, I wasn't trusted from the get-go. I was an outsider. Most of these small religious colleges hire people who are known by someone already connected to the school. What's more, I was pretty open about disagreeing with interpretations of the Bible that I knew just weren't correct. I was a prime candidate for pariah status even before my infamous paper."

"I'm sure your friends and parents were supportive."

Brian didn't respond. Melissa realized she'd inadvertently touched a nerve. Her curiosity was piqued. Brian had certainly earned her respect, and his character had already shown itself in some unforgettable ways, but she knew next to nothing about him. She studied his face, now turned toward the wall.

He took a deep breath, collecting himself. She could tell by his expression that he was calculating how to extract himself from this position of vulnerability. She sensed that the pain to which Andrew had alluded had somehow surfaced inside him. His guard was up. She wanted to know what made him tick—for the right reasons this time—but hesitated, not knowing how to proceed.

"Neil was upset," Brian finally offered, turning his attention from the wall to his lap. "He hasn't always been available when I needed someone to talk to, what with his job and everything, but I know he's in my corner."

"He seems very devoted to you," she stepped carefully, "but I can't help wondering why you answered the way you did. You singled him out and didn't mention your parents. Do you mind if I ask why? If you do, I'll understand."

"I don't know how to say this without sounding like a charity case," he replied, "but I don't have any other friends. It's my own fault, for the most part."

"Oh, come on."

"Seriously. I've had some acquaintances, but no one other than Neil who I really consider a friend, a confidante—you know, the kind of person who would call you for no other reason than to see how you were doing, or who'd invite you over to eat or watch football. I'm an only child, too, and all through high school I more or less kept to myself. I was quite overweight, but I wasn't too bad at sports, so I was at least tolerated by the guys. After games everyone else went out partying or had dates. I went home and read or watched TV. I didn't fit in and really didn't care to, either.

"By the time I hit college, I knew what I wanted to do and what it would take to get into a prestigious grad school, and I gave myself totally to my studies. I've never had anything you'd call a social life. Neil got on my case about that at college. He tried to get me to 'participate in life' more, but I pretty much wore him down. I had better things to do, or so I thought."

"You sound as though you regret not listening."

"I do—a little, anyway. Once you adjust to being by yourself, you basically begin to work best that way."

"You mean it became a comfort zone."

"Yeah … something like that. I didn't even stay in the dorms at college. I rented a room. I've lived by myself since I was eighteen."

"Are you sure you aren't exaggerating a little? You make it sound like you were a hermit."

"I'd say that's the exaggeration," he replied somewhat defensively. "It isn't like I avoided people *completely*. They left me alone, so I left them alone."

"You never went out?"

"I've been to a mall, if that's what you mean," he joked nervously.

"You know what I mean, like to a concert with friends, or better yet, your prom—everybody goes to their prom."

"Skipped it."

"Oh, brother—why?"

"It's customary to go with someone, which was beyond the realm of the possible for me. Trust me, you haven't lived until you've overheard your mom and dad asking themselves if you're gay because you've never had a date."

Melissa couldn't help let out a chuckle at the comment, but she quickly suppressed it when she noticed the memory had darkened Brian's mood considerably. "You okay?"

"Yeah … I shouldn't let things like that bother me; they usually don't, but then again, I don't really think about them either. That event was one of several turning points in my relationship with my parents. I should have just lied and told them I was meeting someone there and gone. It would have made them happy."

"I'm sure they got over it."

"I'd like to think they did."

"What do you mean? Don't you know?"

He shrugged.

"You never asked them?"

"I didn't get the chance," he lamented. A tear rolled down his cheek, and he looked away, embarrassed.

Melissa quietly rose from her chair, moved to the bedside, and sat down on the edge. She gently touched his face as before and turned his head back toward her. She wiped the small droplets away with her thumb. "I'd like to hear your story," she said softly and waited.

Brian nodded faintly, and, after several minutes' delay, took Melissa through the events of his upbringing, his gradual estrangement from his parents, and their eventual turnaround before their deaths. Melissa was captivated.

"I can surely understand the part about them thinking you'd made bad choices. It's terribly severe, though, for them to just emotionally write you off. It had to be devastating for you," she said sympathetically.

"It was."

"But it sounds like they eventually came back."

"I think they did. I'd just have liked to hear it."

"You haven't said yet how they died ... do you mind?"

Brian shook his head. "They were murdered ... gunned down at a gas station a few blocks from campus. I had to identify the bodies."

"Oh my God!" Melissa gasped. "How horrible! It must have been awful ... I just can't imagine it."

"It was ... but having to watch the store videotape was worse. The guy just came barging in while they were at the counter and shot them both in the head like they were—" He stopped, unable to continue. Melissa took his hand.

"He killed the clerk too," Brian continued haltingly after a few minutes, "right after he opened the cash drawer."

Melissa closed her eyes, a wave of shame sweeping over her. The memory of her cruelty toward him came rushing back. Andrew's earlier accusations swirled about in her mind.

"Melissa," Brian looked up at her, sensing her thoughts, "I meant what I said."

"I know," she whispered. "It's just so terrible. I hope he rots in jail."

"The police never caught him. Incredible."

"How could that be?" she wondered in exasperation.

"Because for some reason ... God allowed it," he answered with conviction. "I know it's not the most soothing answer, but I believe it's the right one. I believe everything happens for a reason ... and I see what happened here the same way. I'd do what I did for you again in a heartbeat. It's easily the most meaningful thing I've ever done."

Melissa leaned forward and embraced him again. Brian could feel her warm body shiver. She was weeping, and the realization moved him to tears again as well. He put his arm around her, and the two of them held each other without exchange, overcome by emotion. Finally, Melissa silently released him and pulled back just far enough to behold his face. They looked into each other's reddened, tear-soaked eyes.

"Boy, we're fit for duty, aren't we?" Brian smiled sheepishly.

Suddenly the door, located behind Melissa, creaked open. "Time to feed the inmates," a nurse announced jovially as she awkwardly pushed a cart into the room. "I ... uh ... hope I'm not interrupting anything."

"No." Melissa sniffed and wiped her eyes with a tissue. She looked at the wall clock. "I guess I'd better go for lunch, too—oh, I almost forgot!" she said, sliding off the bed. She picked her purse up off the floor next to the chair, but waited to open it until the nurse had set everything up for Brian and gone on her way.

"I brought you something—and don't laugh."

"Okay," Brian agreed, growing curious.

"There's no place in this godforsaken Facility to get any flowers, but I managed to scrounge this up," she said proudly, extracting a single white carnation, the stem bent in two places, from her purse.

"Thank you." Brian grinned. "I've never gotten a flower before."

"Maybe you still haven't; it's pretty hammered. I sort of borrowed it from the arrangement in the cafeteria."

"It's great," he said appreciatively.

"I need to get going."

"Are you planning on coming back?" he asked, hoping.

"Of course. Do you want me to bring anything from your room? Maybe a book? The Colonel has given the MPs permission to let Andrew and me do that under their supervision."

"No ... we can just talk."

"About what?"

"Anything."

42

Half the work that is done in the world
is to make things appear what they are not.

—*E.R. Beadle*

Brian shut off the water, patted his toothbrush dry with a towel, and placed it into his travel bag. He looked self-consciously into the mirror, his only attire the ragged athletic shorts he habitually wore to bed. He toweled his hair once more and tried in vain to sculpt the tussled mass into a form he deemed presentable, but soon gave up.

He carefully raised his cast-encased left arm and, with his right hand, slid the bottom of the sling hanging from his neck around the cast. Glancing once more at his image, he self-consciously decided to drape a towel over his shoulders before leaving the room.

"Needless to say," he said to Melissa as he emerged, "I was surprised to see you this morning."

"I thought you might need some help," she answered, too cheerily for the ungodly hour, leaning atop his desk. "You know what happened the last time you overslept," she added, beholding him with transparent amusement.

"Hope you can make yourself useful, then," he said, returning her glance with a smile as he passed her on the way to his bedroom. "Give me a minute."

"How does the arm feel, anyway?" she asked loudly enough to be heard in the next room after a short interval of silence.

"A little achy," he answered, "but I only woke up once or twice during the night."

"Did they give you any pain medication?"

Melissa waited for an answer, but none was forthcoming. After a minute she walked to the doorway of the room and peered inside. Her heart sank as she silently watched him struggling with the polo shirt he'd selected for the day. Brian had no clue he was being watched, but was instead fully absorbed by his predicament. The sight would have been funny had she not still felt responsible for his plight.

"This is why I came over this morning," she reminded him as she stopped him, took his arm, and gently guided it through the short sleeve.

"Thanks," he said, a little embarrassed, "but I'm going to need to learn how to do this by myself."

"You will," she replied, "and when there's no pain, I'm sure it'll take only seconds—but if you want to eat breakfast, we need to keep things moving."

"Right."

"What were you thinking, anyway?" she asked, "There's no way you could get yourself and your things in order in time this morning. You should be glad I'm here."

"I am, but I had already asked Andrew to come over this morning."

"Why didn't you ask me?"

"Come on," he responded, grinning, "having a woman help me get dressed? It's kind of awkward."

"You seem to be managing," she replied, smiling. "But, if you prefer his company ..."

"You can tie my sneakers if you feel slighted," he quipped. A knock on the door reverberated through the room. "That would be Andrew."

"Great." Melissa rolled her eyes.

"What's the problem?"

"Let's just say I'm not his favorite person."

"He'll get over all this," Brian assured her. "I didn't see as much of him yesterday. Are you avoiding each other?"

"Hardly."

"My card's in the top drawer." He nodded in the direction of his bureau. "Would you let him in?"

"If I knew your passcode," she said, retrieving the card.

"2929."

"You aren't supposed to tell me that; you'll have to get it changed now."

"I don't think so," he said, slipping his sneakers on. "You'd better let him in before he thinks something else has happened to me."

"He'll most likely call security the moment he sees me," she muttered, disappearing into the living room.

Melissa opened the door, and, as Brian had guessed, it was Father Benedict. The priest appeared startled, but then his expression settled into disdain. He entered the room without a word.

"He's in the bedroom," Melissa informed him.

"Is he decent?" the priest said coldly.

Melissa turned and went into the bedroom without acknowledging the barb. Seated on the bed, Brian looked up at her; her expression told him the priest had arrived. Without a word, Melissa knelt in front of Brian and tied his shoes for him.

"How are you going to do this on your own?" she asked, as though nothing had happened.

"Velcro ... I'm way ahead of you. Good morning, Andrew," he called. The old priest stood in the doorway.

"Good morning," he responded. "It seems my presence isn't required as you expected."

"Melissa's been here since three o'clock A.M. She knew I'd need some help."

"How thoughtful."

"It was," he smiled, catching her glancing at his face to see his reaction. "What's with the four thirty A.M. departure anyway? I know they want us out there as fast as possible, but this is crazy."

"Major Lindsay told me a few minutes ago that our transport wasn't used during the daylight hours."

"Why is that?" Brian asked curiously. Father Benedict shrugged with ignorance.

"What's he doing up this early?" Melissa wondered aloud.

"He and the MPs will be escorting us to the hangar."

"Makes sense," Brian noted, grabbing his backpack.

"Shall we go to breakfast then?" the priest asked.

"Absolutely."

43

At no time when the astronauts were in space were
they alone: there was a constant surveillance by UFOs.

*—Astronaut Scott Carpenter, who photographed
a UFO while in orbit on May 24, 1962.
NASA still has not released the photograph.*

"I hope the food's as good where we're going as it is here," Brian commented, having eaten his fill. "I think the infirmary gets the trainees. That's the best meal I've had in, what is it, five days?"

Andrew nodded.

"The Major should be here in about fifteen minutes," Melissa reminded them. "I forgot something back in my room that I'll need—don't leave here without me, okay?"

"We'll be here," Brian answered her.

"I'll take your tray back, Brian ... and yours as well Father. Do you mind?"

"No," the priest answered casually, "thank you very much."

The two men watched as Melissa cleaned up their area and disposed of everything. She smiled briefly at Brian as she quickly departed for her room.

"Are you sure you're up to traveling, Brian?" Andrew asked once she was out of earshot.

"Do I have a choice?"

"Not really, I guess. We do need to get the show on the road, as they say. I'm sure the rest of the team is going stir crazy by now, what with this delay."

"Anyway, to answer your question, I do feel pretty good—at least as long as the painkillers do their thing."

"Are you aware your physician will be accompanying us?" the priest asked.

"He mentioned the possibility yesterday."

"I received a copy of the email the Colonel sent to the Facility concierge yesterday confirming it. The Colonel is anxious to have the team back together, and I must say, so am I. We have much to do, and too little time in which to do it. Hopefully the change of venue will be an adequate protective measure."

"Accidents do happen, Andrew."

"Accidents? Do you seriously think this whole incident was an accident? You don't know the details yet. Apparently Melissa used good judgment for a change and refrained from discussing them."

"Well ... I just figured it was due to negligence. The dogs did what they were trained to do and had no supervision for some reason."

"The reason was because someone wanted you dead. The MP holding the dogs was murdered."

The revelation forcefully assailed Brian's mind. He wondered what else he hadn't been told.

"But why?"

"We haven't come up with a reason yet. Supposedly everyone here at the Facility knows how important the team is, but accidents don't happen in places like this. It was premeditated and arranged."

"It's weird. Why would we be targets?"

The priest shook his head. "By the way, you're using 'we' a great deal, Brian. How exactly would you assess your relationship with Melissa? The two of you have been basically inseparable since you awoke. One of the reasons I haven't been in your company is I can't seem to get any time with you without her being present."

"Why is that so important?"

"Because I don't trust her—and if you're wise, you won't either."

"You're misjudging her, Andrew, at least now. Your initial instincts were correct. She's been through some tragic circumstances and had a lot of anger to resolve. A week ago I'd have said you were right on target."

"*Had* a lot of anger? Has she told you something that's convinced you she's dealt with it?"

"More like she's promised to try, and I believe her. Ultimately I hope it will restore her faith."

"Her faith?"

"It's a long story, and one I'll need her permission to share. You'll just have to trust me for now."

"Very well," he replied. "Are you certain Melissa isn't thinking in terms of a different kind of relationship? It wouldn't be the first time—"

"Actually, it would," Brian interrupted.

Andrew shrugged. "I've seen romances derive from similar situations, especially during a hospital chaplaincy I once held. The doctor saves a woman's life, and she becomes emotionally and romantically attached to him. Most of the time it doesn't last."

"And at no time did it involve me—and as long as Melissa's eyesight is functioning properly, there's no danger of that happening in this case. I'm still me, Andrew, and in case you hadn't noticed, my appearance wasn't exactly improved by the incident."

"Your cynicism aside, I just don't want to see you sidetracked. You must remain focused."

"Yes, Obi-Wan."

"I'm quite serious."

"I won't get sidetracked."

"I think you already have been."

"How is that?" Brian asked defensively.

"Melissa's misgivings about the alien corpse. Have you taken the opportunity to ask her about it, now that you're on speaking terms?"

"Well ... no. I hadn't thought of it."

Father Benedict cast a knowing glance in his direction. "What have you talked about then?"

"Oh ... just stuff ... you know."

"I'm afraid I don't."

"Just getting to know each other a little better. We've talked about our families, each other's areas of expertise, gotten into some theological subjects ... that kind of thing."

Father Benedict said nothing, but his dubious expression spoke for him.

"Really, Andrew, you needn't worry," Brian sighed. "I'll confess, I do enjoy her company, but futility is an effective teacher. I won't avoid her and won't try to spend less time with her. Somehow, I think I can help her deal with her past, and I don't want to do anything to drive her away."

"And I won't allow anything to deter you from your task," Father Benedict responded. "My gut tells me that these 'beings' are the evil divine ones, and we must prepare the Church. You may still doubt it, but you know far more about this than I do. I've just shown you the foundation; it falls to you to erect the edifice. You're the only one who can see the forest for the trees."

"So you don't put any credence in the Colonel's explanation that we're being blackmailed by the Grays with the goal of coexistence?"

"None. Biblical history is repeating itself, as our Lord said it would. If you don't get the truth out, even the faithful will be deceived into believing."

44

I think there may be substance in some of these
UFO reports ... I believe the American people are entitled
to a more thorough explanation than has
been given them by the Air Force to date.

—Congressman Gerald R. Ford, March 1966

"I just noticed something odd," Father Benedict whispered to Brian as the small contingent zipped through the tunnel on its way to their flight.

Brian glanced at Major Lindsay, who didn't appear to be listening. "What is it?" he asked quietly as the tram turned a corner and stopped at an inordinately large closed doorway.

"The email I received from the concierge," Father Benedict answered, "mentions that we'll rendezvous with the team less than two hours after our flight is scheduled to leave." He showed Brian the page as the door rose vertically before them. "There's no way we'll be on the East Coast that soon."

"Must be a typo," Brian offered as the tram drove through the gateway.

"No," Melissa disagreed loud enough for everyone to hear. Brian peeked at her curiously, but soon followed her wide-eyed gaze to the center of the cavernous hangar. "It's not a typo," she finished her sentence in an awestruck tone.

Brian stared at the mammoth triangular vehicle toward which the tram was headed. As tall as a three-story building, each of its sides were easily the length of two 757s set end to end. Brian could scarcely believe anything so large could fly. He watched dumbfounded as several flat-bed trailers were being cleared of the last of their payloads, without so much as a conventional forklift or pallet jack. He gazed hypnotically as the work-crews affixed some type of disk under each pallet and simply pushed the cargo off the trucks and floated it inside the immense craft.

"You can pick your jaw off the floor now, Dr. Scott," Major Lindsay said as their tram came to a halt. "It's the same technology that powers your transport, just a different application. See the bluish lights on the underside of each tip?"

Brian could see the faint hue reflecting off the floor of the hangar directly underneath the end of one of the triangle's tips. He nodded with recognition, recalling the antigravity propulsion unit of the craft they'd been in earlier.

"How fast will we be going?" Father Benedict asked nervously, still apprehensive of the technology.

"Your flight will last about thirty minutes. By the way, Dr. Scott, if you think this one is large, you should see the ones *they* have," he said, enjoying the stupefied expression of his young adversary. "We're putting you on a cargo flight," he added, turning to Father Benedict and Melissa. "We don't like to make unnecessary trips—our way of trimming the federal deficit," he droned facetiously. "Hope you don't mind."

None of them answered, absorbed by the immensity of the sight.

"Good. Some people prefer the sportier model," he joked. "Dr. Hastings is already aboard. Have a nice flight!"

45

"We need to talk," Melissa informed Brian in a hushed tone, her eyes darting about the cabin so as to judge its volume. Both Father Benedict and Dr. Hastings were seated a short distance from them and were already engaged in conversation. "We only have a few minutes before we arrive," she reminded him.

"I think I know what's on your mind," he whispered. "The bodies?"

She nodded.

"Why don't you wait till we level off? Andrew should hear this."

"Don't bother him; you can always tell him what I said."

"He wouldn't feel bothered."

"No," she persisted, then hesitated as she appeared ready to explain.

"Why not?"

"I'm just not comfortable around him," she admitted. "He doesn't like me, that's for sure."

"It's true—he doesn't trust you. Can you blame him?"

"No, but that isn't it altogether."

Brian looked at her curiously.

"There's something else about him ... I can't put my finger on it."

"Women's intuition?"

"That and his own words. You know, he threatened me outside your hospital door just before I came in to see you."

"Seriously?"

"Absolutely. I never told you about that until now, so how did you know he doesn't trust me?"

"We talked while you went back to your room."

"Do you trust me?" She looked at him earnestly.

"Yes," he reassured her. "Now tell me what's on your mind. What was it about the corpses that left you unconvinced?"

"The fact that they may have been human, for starters."

"What?" he gasped.

She motioned for him to keep his voice down.

"How can you say that?"

"You figured out part of it on your own—at least that's what my mystery visitor told me after the alleged 'unveiling.' You noticed the problematic link between a possible evolutionary development of the 'creature' and the tiny stomach and absence of sexual organs."

"How did you know what I thought about that? I only told Neil and Father Benedict."

"My visitor told me."

"You didn't mention that conversation to the others."

"I didn't want anyone to know. You know that means Neil reported it to either the Group or to the Colonel, don't you?" she asked.

"Yes, but he told me he would have to tell them. There's no secret there."

"Interesting ... I hadn't realized that."

"What about the idea we threw around that these beings are real and just reproduce themselves asexually by cloning?"

"We don't have that kind of technology, Brian."

"If they exist, maybe they do."

"Well ... all right. I'll concede that's a possibility. Anyway, those two observations made me guess that somehow the corpse was possibly faked."

"And how was that done?"

"The corpse may actually be a human fetus whose growth in certain anatomical points has been selectively allowed to continue, or which was actively stimulated—you know, to keep the head disproportionate to the body but let the arms and legs grow, that sort of genetic manipulation or inhibition."

"Can we do that today?"

"Sure. If I'm right, then the eyes have also been surgically altered to make them appear slanted—not just to get into the sinus cavities, as Dr. Marcus claimed. I've seen pictures of this sort of thing, albeit on a far less dramatic scale, in human embryology textbooks. The result is a human that looks nonhuman."

"What about the sex organs, or lack thereof?"

"They were simply removed and cosmetically obscured."

"Boy, Andrew is gonna hit the roof when he hears this."

"Why?"

"He believes they're real, that they're creations—part of my sons of God scenario."

"Do you believe you're correct?"

"Nothing I've seen so far makes me believe there are really aliens here. The technology can be very advanced, but still manmade, and if the corpses are a fraud, that speaks for itself. Then again, if there really are Watchers here, it's a good bet they've mastered this sort of technology and given it to humans."

"So what are you going to do as far as the project is concerned?"

"I'm willing to write up my first view, but I also at least want the second to be part of the record. On the other hand, it would really trouble me if the corpses were fakes. What would be gained by deceiving us again—and in a far more elaborate way? What could the point be?"

"I have a question of my own, too," noted Melissa.

"What's that?"

"Why wouldn't Mark have caught any of this?"

"Good question; that does seem odd."

"I'd like to think he may never have had a course on human embryology. It isn't a class you'd normally take in his field. I picked up all of this studying on my own during what should have been my freshman year. On the other hand, maybe he did notice and said nothing, which would be very unlikely, given his reaction to the previous ruse."

"Right. Or maybe ..."

"Maybe he wasn't supposed to say anything *that* time."

46

Every dogma has its day.

—Abraham Rotstein

"Ouch!" Brian complained.

"You'll thank me later," Dr. Hastings replied with an amused expression, removing the needle from Brian's stricken arm. "I won't be available when the last one wears off while you're in your meeting. It's a little early, but it won't matter."

"Yeah, but does it have to *cause* pain? You usually give it to me in the rear."

"I think this is more appropriate for being in a car with Dr. Kelley present," he replied, putting the syringe back in his bag.

"What a wimp," Melissa teased him.

"Are we ready, sir?" the MP behind the wheel asked, peering into his rearview mirror.

"Drive on, soldier."

"Yes, sir."

The car pulled away and sped across the tarmac toward the gate, which was already opening for their departure. The occupants of the vehicle couldn't help admiring the beautiful sunrise that was just beginning to illuminate the rolling, green hills. Compared to the dusty red of the Nevada desert, the scene before them was almost Edenic.

"Reminds me of Pennsylvania," Brian said, gazing out the window.

"Close," Father Benedict informed him. "We're in northern Virginia, actually."

"How do you know that?" Melissa wondered.

"Dr. Bandstra told us we'd be moved to Mount Weather; that's where it's located."

"Mount Weather, huh," she mused. "Home of the 'shadow government' in the wake of September 11. Can't be too much of a secured hideaway if it's on a mountain."

"Actually, it's *inside* the mountain," Dr. Hastings replied.

"Great, another underground base," Brian complained. "So how much longer do we have to look at the sun?"

"About an hour," Dr. Hastings answered from his seat in the front of the car. "And be advised, no conversation about the project is allowed until we're inside."

"Wake me up when we get there," Brian yawned, suddenly drowsy.

"You don't drool, do you?" Melissa asked jokingly.

Brian opened one eye and smiled mischievously. "Too late to change seats now."

***

"Are you sure everything will go as planned this time?" the thin man seated at the long, oak table inquired accusingly. "We can't have any more miscalculations, Colonel."

"I think I'm aware of that."

"Don't get testy with me. It's your flawed oversight of this project that has nearly cost us our life's work—and it may still, if Scott cannot be convinced."

"After today there will be no doubts. Dr. Scott will have no choice but to believe."

"Is Adam ready?" The thin man turned his attention toward the General, seated as always at the head of the table.

"Absolutely. Dr. Scott is as well."

"This had better work," the gaunt figure complained nervously, looking at his watch. "It's not like we've done this before. If you screw up, everyone will know and eventually comprehend. And you'll be a dead man," he threatened, reaching for a glass of water.

"Careful, Dietrich," the Colonel cautioned, smiling wryly. "You don't know who poured that."

The thin man looked into the glass, back at the Colonel, then drained it defiantly.

"What about Dr. Kelley? She isn't convinced either," another voice reminded the small assembly.

"She'll believe, and the team will be ready to work with a vengeance. The deadline is still attainable. The project will succeed, and you'll have your precious legacy," the Colonel pronounced confidently.

47

The truth is rarely pure, and never simple.

—*Oscar Wilde*

"Man, it is so good to see you again!" Malcolm beamed, entering the room, shaking Brian's hand, and slapping him on the back. "I can't tell you how good!"

"Thanks, Malcolm," Brian said appreciatively.

"Ditto that," a familiar voice from behind Brian said. A grinning Deidre was peeking inside the door to his new quarters. "If Mark hadn't looked out the window at just the right time ... I don't want to think about it."

"What do you mean?"

"I saw the dogs attack you," Mark explained, entering behind her. "Everybody else was busy talking or trying to go back to sleep while the plane did a turn toward the runway. I looked out just before the plane rotated my line of vision away from where you and Melissa were waiting."

"Yeah," Malcolm laughed, "he started hollering like a banshee, and the Colonel got the pilot to stop. From what we heard afterward, you'd have bled to death."

"Thanks." Brian reached for Mark's hand and shook it firmly.

"Craziest thing I ever saw anyone do," Mark said, shaking his head, hands on his hips, "especially considering who you were trying to save. Just plain nuts, if you ask me."

"Really!" exclaimed Malcolm. "I know you'd risk your butt for me, and maybe even Dee, but Melissa?"

"I'm thrilled to see all of you, too," Brian said, trying to steer the discussion in another direction.

The four of them had their attention diverted by a gentle tapping on the still-open door. Awkward silence filled the room. An embarrassed Melissa let herself inside.

"I just dropped my things off at my room, and ... I wanted to see if you needed any help," she said to Brian quietly, trying not to look at the others. "I can see you don't," she observed, then turned to leave.

"Wait," Brian called to her.

She hesitated, then turned back to him.

"There is something I need. Come over here, please," he requested, patting the space on his bunk next to where he was sitting.

Melissa reluctantly complied.

"I'm also alive because of Melissa's quick thinking," he praised her, "and I'm very grateful. I know it's been pretty apparent we haven't gotten along that well—"

"We?" interrupted Malcolm, "I'd say it was her problem."

Melissa started to rise, but Brian took hold of her arm.

"He's right," Melissa acknowledged uncomfortably.

Malcolm and Deidre exchanged surprised glances.

"We need to get something out in the open," Brian said, taking charge of the conversation, "I hold nothing against Melissa, and I won't be happy if I have to listen to anyone cut her down. She said what she said to me because of some of her own issues that needed to be dealt with, and we've been through them. We've had little else to do in the last few days but talk, and things between us have changed a lot—all for the better. What's done is done; I forgive her, and if I can do it, I expect all of you to do the same."

The room fell silent once again. Brian surveyed their faces expectantly. No one seemed ready to take the initiative to respond.

"Nice try," Melissa said sincerely, patting Brian's hand, which was still clasped to her arm. "I'd like to go now."

He released her.

"Hold on," Malcolm finally spoke to her. "I know Brian wouldn't lie to us, and if that's the way he feels, it's cool. I'm sorry for my attitude a moment ago. I have a habit of just saying whatever pops into my head."

"What a revelation." Deidre rolled her eyes.

"Thanks, Malcolm." Melissa managed a smile.

"No problem."

Mark looked at her a little dubiously, but finally nodded his approval.

"Good to have you back." Deidre gave her a hug.

"I missed you, too," Melissa replied, feeling relieved.

"I hate to interrupt this Hallmark moment," Malcolm cracked, "but we need to get Brian up to speed before the big meeting."

"When is it?"

"About twenty minutes," Mark replied. "I take it you haven't seen Dr. Bandstra or the Colonel yet?"

He shook his head.

"The Colonel told us when we got here that the purpose of this little excursion was to show us irrefutable proof that he was telling us the truth—finally—that we really have been visited by extraterrestrials, and that they're calling our bluff on disclosure."

"So what was the proof?" Brian asked.

"We still haven't seen it," Malcolm whined. "Five days later."

"You haven't been exactly bored, Malcolm."

"What does that mean?" Melissa asked.

"Malcolm's managed to see just about everything in reasonable walking distance."

"The security here isn't as aggressive as at the Facility," Malcolm explained with a wink. "You'd be amazed how far our badges get us around here."

"It isn't like there's much to see," Mark griped, "unless you're fascinated by food stockpiles and forklifts."

"What exactly is this place used for besides hiding politicians?" Brian inquired.

"Mount Weather is about fifty miles west of D.C. It's the nerve center for FEMA's underground empire," Deidre replied in her familiar sarcastic tone.

"FEMA—the Federal Emergency Management Agency, right?" Brian asked.

"Right. FEMA runs nearly one hundred underground command posts, or if you prefer the political doublespeak used at our briefing, 're-location centers.' This one's the biggest and, from the looks of it, the most well-supplied."

"Relocation centers? Who are they planning on relocating?" Melissa wondered suspiciously.

"Good question, isn't it?" Deidre smirked.

"Most of these places were built in the event of nuclear war," Mark explained.

"The government wanted a place where top officials could preserve their behinds," Deidre continued, "while the mere mortals on the outside fended for themselves. I know it sounds incredible, but they have a complete alternative government-in-waiting down here. Everyone from the president down through cabinet-level secretaries has a counterpart. A complete parallel federal apparatus. It isn't just about hiding the people we know about who've been elected."

"Is she serious?" Melissa queried incredulously, looking at Malcolm.

"You bet," he confirmed. "If all our top government officials were killed in some catastrophe, their secret stand-ins would all be alive and ready to go, right here."

"All duly unelected, of course, and they have no term limits, either. The mirror government also has representatives of five federal agencies—the FCC, the Federal Power Commission, Selective Service, and the VA—a complete network," Deidre chimed in. "This base isn't even in FEMA's published budget."

"How did you know that?" Malcolm quizzed her. "That wasn't part of the briefing."

"Our briefing wasn't the only source of information I've had on Mount Weather. FEMA is under no congressional oversight; it answers only to the National Security Agency. That alone should make all of us leery of this place."

"What do they do here day to day?" Brian asked.

"Several things I'm sure you would find interesting," Deidre answered. "FEMA exists to manage national crises. They also play war games, studying various crisis models. But according to what I've read, they primarily collect and process data on U.S. citizens. They have files here on over millions of Americans, and the place is networked to all the other national relocation centers. Mount Weather is basically one big database for those who survive."

"Survive?" There was alarm in Melissa's voice.

"Yeah," Malcolm picked up the discussion. "They monitor something called the 'survivor's list' here. The government actually has a list of around six thousand people deemed vital to the survival of the nation in the event of a catastrophe. Names, addresses, the works."

"Do I know anybody on it?" joked Brian.

"Look in the mirror," Deidre answered.

"Get real."

"It's the truth," Malcolm said cheerily. "The Colonel told us we're all on it. I feel more secure already. If anything happens to good old mother earth—that is, if ET all of a sudden wants to play nuclear chicken—we're on the dole. It almost makes me want to plug my ears when I hear that sucking sound of our tax dollars getting vacuumed down the black hole we call the federal budget."

"Typical," Deidre said cynically. "Even if we fail in helping society transition to a peaceful existence with the Grays, the government will still pay us. What a system."

"It may be a money pit, but it's impressive," Mark admitted. "The accommodations may not be modern or plush, but it's a virtually self-contained facility carved right out of solid granite. There's an on-site sewage-treatment plant, a 250,000-gallon water supply, and a purification system for processing the underground ponds. The place has dozens of private apartments and dormitories, cafeterias, hospitals, mass transit system, communications network, and even its own power plant."

"Yes, ladies and gentlemen," Malcolm dutifully noted, "among the government's underground facilities, this is the Hilton."

"That's probably why we were only supposed to be here a day; we can't be too comfortable." Deidre sighed.

"Only a day?" Brian wondered.

"Initially," Deidre elaborated, "we were all supposed to make the trip, stay a day, and then go back to the friendly confines of the Facility. Then you had your ... accident. Was it really an accident?" She looked first at Brian, then at Melissa.

"Apparently not," Brian answered, observing their reactions.

The room grew quiet.

"Any clues?" Mark asked, a bit shaken. "This could mean none of us are safe."

"No. We'll tell you what we've heard later. Anyone seen Andrew?"

"Probably in his room," Melissa offered. "I saw the MP let him in and give him the key."

"No," Malcolm answered, glancing at his watch. "He's probably on his way to this meeting to end all meetings, and we should be too."

"Where is it?" Brian asked.

"Bottom floor of this building. Go down the stairs and head toward the main lobby, but keep going past it to the end of the hall. It's the last room on the left before you reach the end. They've configured the door with a card reader. Your old one from the Facility will get you inside."

"Why don't you all go on ahead," Brian suggested. "I need to use the restroom."

"Er ... uh, Brian ... ?" Malcolm began his question awkwardly, but with his trademark grin.

"Yeah?"

"Can you manage ... what with the arm and everything?"

"Yes!" Brian laughed along with the others.

Brian hurried to relieve himself while the others filed out of his room.

Exiting the bathroom, he was surprised to see Melissa still present.

"Malcolm's quite a character, isn't he?" Brian said with a smile. "It's good to be around him again."

"I'm sure he's glad to see you," she said quietly.

"Meaning?"

She sighed. "Thanks for what you said to them. It was very kind."

"You think he didn't mean what he said?"

"They all said what they did for your sake. It would be a different story if you weren't here. It's okay; I know I deserve it."

"It's not okay, and you don't deserve it. They have no context for understanding you."

"Neither did you, but you were still good to me."

"You need to give them the benefit of the doubt ... and some time. I'm sure you're up to the challenge, aren't you?"

Melissa let out a little laugh and shook her head. "How can I say no to that? You sure know how to corner me."

"I have confidence in you. You aren't the type to be so easily beaten."

"Do you always know the right thing to say?" She smiled.

"Actually, no," he said, returning the expression and grabbing his backpack. "Most of the time I'm fairly clueless when it comes to situations like that. I usually end up saying nothing, but I've tried to be better since my parents died. You never know whether you'll get a second chance to say what needs to be said. Coming?" He headed for the door.

Melissa followed him to the door but stopped him before he opened it. He looked down at her in curiosity.

"Well said," she congratulated him, her voice lowering. "Thank you again for defending me; it certainly would have been easier not to."

"I don't want you to be uncomfortable around the others," he said good-naturedly.

"You're a wonderful man," she smiled back, and then, without warning, reached for him and kissed him softly on the cheek.

Brian froze.

"Come on," she coaxed and reached for the handle.

Brian didn't move. She scanned his face closely, trying to judge his hesitation. To her surprise, his countenance had changed to one of anxiety. He looked positively distraught.

"What's wrong?" she asked, concerned by the transformation.

"I don't ... I think it would be best not to do that again."

"Why not? I want you to know you're appreciated. To quote my favorite theologian, 'It was the right thing to do.' "

"I just ... I just don't want things to change."

"What do you mean?"

He paused, gathering his thoughts. "It's been wonderful to have regular company over the last few weeks, especially these last few days," he said, struggling to maintain eye contact. "To tell you the truth, I didn't realize how much I missed it all these years. I don't want that to change ... especially with you."

"Why would it change? I didn't exactly slap you. You're not making sense, Brian."

"I can't explain. When we go back to the Facility and get down to work, I was hoping things could stay like this. I know you'll be busy— we'll all be busy. I just don't want anything to happen between us that would make you want to write me off, okay?"

"Well ... sure ... I had no intention, but—"

"Thanks," he said, visibly relieved, and opened the door. "We need to go. We can't be late for this."

"Right," she said, still puzzling over his response.

The two of them scurried down the stairs, entered the conference room, and sat down next to each other at the far end in the two remaining seats, positioned adjacent to Neil and Father Benedict. Brian expected to get a warm reaction from his friend, but Neil could only manage a respectful nod, his face etched with apprehension. Brian thought it curious that both Ian Marcus and the Colonel were absent, but no sooner had the thought crossed his mind than the latter appeared at the doorway.

"Good morning, everyone. Good to see you, Dr. Scott."

Brian nodded.

"I'm quite sure you're wondering just what it is we'll be doing this afternoon, particularly in light of my earlier comments. Our assembly is physically whole once more, but there is still the matter of the intellectual unity we'll need to carry out our mission. After today, that, too, will be a reality."

Brian and Melissa exchanged skeptical glances. The Colonel checked the time on the wall clock. As if on cue, someone knocked at the door behind the Colonel where he stood.

"Right on time, Ian," the Colonel welcomed Dr. Marcus, who peered into the room. "How is Adam?"

"Still a little shaky sir," the scientist answered without entering.

"We have a special guest with us today." The Colonel turned his attention back to the team. "He's traveled a great distance to be here.

He's been advising us on the project for several years, but only occasionally in person. You'll have to excuse his condition at the present; it takes him a while to adjust when he does make the trip."

"Nasty case of jet lag?" Malcolm guessed.

"An ironic choice of words, Dr. Bradley," the Colonel smirked. "Gravity happens, you know. And, for our theologians present, please forgive the name. Ian?"

Dr. Marcus ducked out of view for a few seconds, and then the door swung open wide.

Startled gasps and scattered expletives punctuated the air. Some of the team members stood at their chairs to get a better look. The gaunt, diminutive object of their awe shuffled slowly into the room, bobbing clumsily on spindly, atrophied legs and bare feet that protruded from what were obviously a child's pair of sweat pants, supported by the arm from behind by Dr. Marcus. The whitish-gray color of his skin contrasted starkly with the blue NASA T-shirt that hung over his lean torso. The scene would have been comical if the figure had not been so emotionally and intellectually compelling.

"Mother of God ..." Father Benedict mumbled in a stupefied voice.

Adam stopped a few feet short of the near end of the table, gazing at the team through his large, milky-black eyes.

48

Seeing is not always believing.

—*Rod Serling*

The frail gray being turned its head slowly toward where Colonel Ferguson stood. The military man, whose concentration was temporarily focused on gauging the initial responses of those in the room, suddenly behaved as though he'd been tapped politely on the shoulder. He turned to Adam with his full attention. The two of them gazed at one another for a few seconds without the slightest hint of expression on the part of either. The Colonel nodded, then turned to the wide-eyed audience.

"A few words of introduction are in order before Adam gets to know all of you," he began, visibly pleased by the astonished reactions of the team. "Adam is, as you can see, one of the mythical creatures to which I've been referring for some time now. He's part of the ongoing exchange program to which I've also alluded. He and a few other Grays, as they've been categorized, visit us rotationally on a regular schedule. Their duties include technical assistance and, now that we've agreed to their insistence on disclosure, compliance with that agreement. We send our own counterparts to them as well."

"Where?" a flabbergasted Mark Chadwick blurted out.

"Their base of operations is on the other side of the moon right now. As far as exchange programs, we use the underground base in Dulce, New Mexico; Area 51 and its sister location S-4; and our base in Pine Gap, Australia. This is the first time Adam has been to Mount Weather."

"How does it communicate?" Malcolm asked eagerly.

"Please don't use the word 'it' around Adam. The military's sexist predilection being what it is," he urged, eyeing Deidre, "we've assigned male names to all the visitors. As you know, they are sexless, but they are sentient, have a range of emotions, and can be offended. They normally don't wear anything, either; the clothes were our idea."

"Sorry. The T-shirt's a nice touch."

"Why does he walk so strangely?" Melissa asked.

"Gravity. It takes him time to get used to earth's gravity, particularly in the context of his delicate anatomy. Which reminds me," the Colonel continued, "Adam does not speak as you and I do. He communicates telepathically. He can receive messages from you mentally—you can think in words, since he has the English vocabulary of, roughly, a teenager. It should go without saying, however, that he's considerably more intelligent. It's far better to conceive concepts or visualize, but that takes a lot of practice on our part. He can also receive conversation verbally, again with the same vocabulary limitations. When he 'speaks' to you, he will use both words and images. And one last—"

The Colonel suddenly stopped and abruptly turned toward Adam, whose gaze was riveted on Deidre. The small creature turned again toward the Colonel, who then glared at the psychologist in consternation.

Deidre looked at the Colonel smugly, then glanced around the table. "Yep, he can read minds all right. He got my message loud and clear."

"Need I remind you to whom you're talking?" the Colonel asked, flushing with anger.

"Nope. He just needs to know there are some of us here who are less than thrilled with him."

"What did you say to him?" Mark asked uneasily.

"It's just between him and me," she answered with a determined expression. "I don't know what you have planned here, Colonel, but I don't want the sucker touching me."

"That goes for me as well," a pale Father Benedict echoed.

"You needn't worry, either of you," the Colonel said in a calmer tone. "As I was about to say, you should all be aware that Adam may periodically scan your mind, rather than conversing—at least that's what we call it. Don't be alarmed; there are no ill effects."

"Other than him knowing everything you've done behind closed doors, you mean," Malcolm said apprehensively.

"Not necessarily. He isn't likely to be interested in mundane things. He usually wants to know the basics of who you are and if you have any knowledge that's of use to him. They don't use it aggressively; it seems to be just something that's done when they meet a new person, or when they deem it necessary—sort of their version of a handshake.

"As far as what I have planned, I have nothing in mind. The time is Adam's, to do with as he sees fit. Feel free to ask him questions, but he may or may not choose to answer. We may be here an hour or five minutes; I don't know what he'll do. I'd only ask that you make your questions relevant. Adam knows nothing of trivial cultural items, such as sports or television shows. He's a scientist and, in the most dramatic sense of the word, an anthropologist."

With that, the Colonel stepped back toward the wall and motioned to the strange entity that he was through.

The team scrutinized Adam intently, unsure of what to expect. Ian Marcus released his arm, whereupon the alien began to gingerly navigate toward the left side of the table where Malcolm was seated. The bespectacled black scientist closed his eyes, and the two figures remained motionless for nearly a minute. Finally, a wide grin creased Malcolm's face.

"That's it!" he said excitedly, eyes still closed. "Just awesome, dude." He opened his eyes, and Adam began to move again.

"He just gave me the answer to a question I missed on my prelims—it was great!" Malcolm exclaimed, answering the question on everyone's mind.

Not everyone was touched by Malcolm's usually infectious enthusiasm, though. Brian, Melissa, Father Benedict, and, most notably, Deidre—in front of whom Adam now stood—could not disguise their apprehension.

Deidre eyed the creature coldly, as though trying to discern its motives, its own hidden thoughts. Her distrust of the entity was solidified by years of interviewing hundreds of traumatized abductees. She was determined to keep her wits about her, to keep the upper hand. Her effort was short-lived. A few seconds after facing off, Deidre's body stiffened, then began trembling. Her eyes rolled back in her head. She had been rendered completely helpless.

"Tell him to stop it—*now!*" Father Benedict shouted.

No one moved.

"Colonel, get that thing away from her, or I will!" he almost shouted, rising from his chair.

"Easy, Andrew!" Neil beckoned, restraining him. "She isn't being hurt. It only looks bad because she tried to resist."

"Listen to yourself!" the priest scolded him angrily.

The commotion did not appear to faze Adam in the least.

"Look!" Melissa tried to get Andrew's attention. He turned just in time to see Deidre's body relax, a sorrowful but calm look on her face. A tear trickled down her cheek. She nodded in agreement to an unheard question.

"Thank you," Deidre said unconsciously in a subdued voice.

A few of the room's occupants exchanged bewildered glances. The confusion was not missed by the creature, who suddenly turned his attention to the opposite side of the table, briefly scanning Mark and Neil, both of whom made every attempt to submit to the process. It wasn't clear whether there was any intercourse between either of them and Adam, who quickly moved on to Father Benedict, an altogether different kind of subject.

"Where do you come from?" the priest asked aloud for all to hear. Adam gazed at the elderly face for a few seconds. Father Benedict's face took on a troubled appearance, creases of anxiety stretching across his brow. "How old are you? What is love? How did you get here? Who is your god?" the priest rapidly peppered him.

Brian was struck by Father Benedict's seemingly fragmented line of questioning. He watched the old man's face carefully for some hint of emotion, some disclosure of what was going through either his mind or Adam's, but there was nothing. The encounter ended with Adam simply turning aside, as though he'd lost interest.

Brian watched with a weird mixture of horror and exhilaration as Adam diverted his gaze to himself and Melissa. For several seconds the gray being glanced from one to the other, then inexplicably looked back over his shoulder at the Colonel, who offered no visible response.

Melissa abruptly let out a startled gasp and grabbed the arms of her chair. Adam was reading her, though his vision was still directed at the Colonel. Melissa gradually relaxed, a serene expression forming on her face. She seemed at peace, almost enjoying the experience. Again there was no hint of conversation.

Brian suddenly felt Adam's mind probing his own, filling his consciousness with flashes of his past, things long forgotten as well as things unforgettable. He had the sensation of falling but could still feel his physical surroundings. He closed his eyes; somehow, doing so helped ease the sensation. The presence in his skull was benign, not threatening; inquisitive, but not invasive; intense, but not sinister. Then a voice penetrated the inner silence.

Do not be afraid.

I'm not, Brian thought back.

Your arm—are you in pain?

Sometimes ... not now.

How was it injured?

Rather than using words, Brian tried to recreate the events of the attack in his mind as best he could, following the Colonel's advice. Adam remained completely passive, apparently unmoved by the gruesome, violent event. Then, as quickly as his mind had been seized, it was released.

Brian slowly opened his eyes and found himself face to face with Adam, his eerie countenance only inches from his own, having advanced to where he was sitting. Somehow he had known what he would see and was not alarmed in any way. He watched in transfixed fascination as the being moved back a step and then extended his gnarly palm toward him, the six delicate fingers—each no wider than a string bean—coming to rest on his own exposed hand. Adam bent slightly to inspect the crippled limb and remained in this position for nearly a minute.

Brian moved his eyes rapidly across the room. The others on the team stared at the spectacle, like unblinking, mystified, sentinels.

All at once, Brian detected a warm, prickly stimulation just below his elbow. It quickly dispersed throughout his lower arm down to the fingertips. The sensation felt like his arm was asleep, but he could feel a steady rise in temperature. He felt a twinge of pain, but before he could voice any alarm, the discomfort dissipated. The warmth, however, was constant.

"What's happening?" Melissa rose from her chair in concern to get a better look at the arm.

"I—I don't know," he struggled for an answer. "It just feels all warm and sort of bubbly. It almost tickles."

Without warning, Adam reached for Melissa as he had Brian moments before. She pulled back, startled, but the voice inside her head reassured her. Still uncertain, she allowed the creature to take her hand and place it in Brian's. He raised his head and stared at Brian.

Take the female's hand.

"I can't," he protested audibly. He had tried to command movement from the now useless appendage for days and knew it was pointless.

Squeeze the female's hand.

Brian complied. The hand obeyed his mental command effortlessly. Melissa covered her mouth in shock. Brian repeated the simple yet unthinkable task half a dozen times, breathlessly watching the formerly unresponsive fingers caress Melissa's.

"I can't believe it!" he exclaimed and found eye contact with Father Benedict's astonished face. He looked back at Adam, whose blank features hadn't changed.

"Thank you!" Brian gasped, but Adam turned away un-ceremoniously, this time heading for the door and the waiting Dr. Marcus. He paused for a few seconds and looked at the Colonel, and in another moment, he'd departed, like a mere apparition, leaving his small audience dumbfounded.

"I've seen them do some pretty wild things," the Colonel said, advancing toward Brian, "but never this," he finished, shaking his head.

The other members of the team quickly gathered around the elated Brian to share his joy firsthand. Only Father Benedict remained detached, slumped in his chair, overwhelmed by what had just taken place.

"It's a miracle!" he overheard Deidre rejoice.

That's exactly what people will say, the priest thought, his head cupped in his hand.

49

Flying saucers are real. Too many good men
have seen them, that don't have hallucinations.

—*Captain Eddie Rickenbacker,*
American "Ace of Aces," recipient of the Congressional Medal of
Honor, and Commander of the 94th Aero Pursuit Squadron in
World War I.

"Over here, girl," Deidre waved.

Melissa maneuvered her way through the crowded cafeteria toward the undersized table at which she and Neil were seated.

"I don't know about you two," Melissa said lightheartedly, "but I can hardly wait to get back to my cell at the Facility and get to work on my research. It's just so exciting being part of something like this! I mean, I know this project will change human belief systems forever, and may cause terrible upheaval, but—"

"You don't have to explain," Deidre said, cutting her sandwich in half. "I feel the same way. What about you, Neil?"

"I'd have to say that my own conflicts have been resolved," he answered in a reflective, almost somber tone.

"You've undergone a bit of a change on your own then," Deidre reminded him. "You didn't look so upbeat after Brian's second idea about these beings."

"Things are much clearer now," he replied, sipping his coffee. "I'm curious, though. Do either of you care to share your own experience with Adam?"

"He didn't really say anything to me," Melissa jumped in. "I hate to sound drippy, but I just felt this overflowing sense of love ... like there was some sort of fondness for me. I can't really describe it any other way. What about you, Deidre?"

"Well ... it was pretty personal," she confided. "This is going to sound crazy, but take it in the context of my research ... I've always had this fear that I'd been abducted myself, and that someday it would happen again, and that my daughter would be taken. I've coped with it by telling myself that my subconscious has absorbed too much of my subjects' testimonies."

"Why didn't that take care of it?" asked Neil. "Sounds plausible to me."

"My mom once told me it had happened to her—and abductions tend to run in family groups. Her testimony was another factor that compelled me to go into the subject. I knew my mom—she was an avid churchgoer, almost a saint in my eyes. She wasn't one to lie or make up something like that."

"Wow," Melissa voiced her surprise.

"Anyway, Adam caught all that."

"And ... ?"

"He admitted that he knew of my mother—that was the hard part, but at least he told me the truth. He promised me that neither my daughter nor I would ever be touched. His words, if the term applies, were, 'Does this help you?'" Deidre paused to gain her composure, the emotion of the moment still vivid in her heart. "That's when I started to cry," she sniffed. "I've just had this overwhelming sense of dread, that I'd stepped into something in my research that would someday cost me dearly. It was just what I needed to hear."

"Remarkable," Neil said reflectively. "That was just as special to you as Brian's healing was to him."

"Where is Brian, anyway?" Deidre asked, looking at Melissa.

"What makes you think I'd know?"

"Just a guess," she said slyly.

"He went right to the hospital and had the cast removed. He was so excited, he and Malcolm went to lift weights to try out the hand. I'm so thrilled for him!"

"I'm even happier to hear that," Neil commented. "I'm sure you're quite relieved."

Melissa looked down at her tray, trying to contain herself, but to no avail. "Why must everyone keep saying things like that?" she burst forth. "It seems Brian's the only one around here willing to really forgive me!"

She stood up to leave, but Deidre stopped her. Neil continued his meal.

"Well?" Deidre demanded, looking at the undersecretary.

"It was just an observation, not an attack," he said calmly. "I will admit," he continued, "that I'll be watching your attitude toward him with some healthy skepticism."

"Thanks—for nothing," she shot back.

"Don't misunderstand me, Melissa. I can see you've changed, and I trust Brian's judgment. It's just that you can't undo your unrelenting nastiness in a few days. You have to earn my respect. I can only promise that if you earn it, I won't withhold it. Do we understand each other?"

"Yes," she said, stung by his remarks, the blush receding from her face. "Seems fair to me," she grudgingly conceded. "Still, Brian's shown me a no-strings-attached kindness."

"He would," Neil noted thoughtfully. "He has a profound capacity for forgiveness. Still, I wish he'd have allowed me to help him more with his own weaknesses. He's very hard headed at times."

"When you say weaknesses," Melissa inquired, intrigued, "what do you mean?"

Neil eyed her dubiously, silently questioning her motives.

"I know you have a right to be suspicious, but I'm asking for the right reasons, if that's what you're wondering," Melissa intuitively responded to his delay in answering. "We've spent a lot of time together over the last five days, and I've learned more each time we talk, but there are areas I just can't seem to penetrate. His guard goes up a lot. It's very frustrating."

"He's a man, honey," Deidre joked.

"I'll have to ask you what you mean," Neil challenged.

"For instance," Melissa elaborated, "every time I steer the conversation beyond the tragedy of his parents or how he was fired, or anything academic—you know, trying to get at what makes him tick, his feelings, his fears, that sort of thing—he changes the subject. Sometimes he doesn't even bother trying to be very deft about it, either. He just won't talk about himself in ways that reveal anything deeply personal."

"Don't expect it to change," Neil cautioned, "and don't take it personally. I know him better than anyone, and there are parts of him that really are impenetrable. He's really only confident when it comes to his areas of expertise, not in relationships. He has a pretty low self-image when it comes to anything else but academics. I'm no psychologist, but I've no doubt it also has something to do with being emotionally disowned by his parents."

"He's mentioned some of that," Melissa commented, "but I still sort of thought he was exaggerating."

"It's not that he's socially inept, although he is rough around the edges. It's just that he never did anything in terms of a social life. For sure there are worse habits to pick up in college than studying, but he seemed to me very imbalanced. I tried to get him to open up, but it was pretty much a futile exercise. If you asked him if he ever had fun, he'd say he did whenever he opened a book."

"Did he ever accuse you of pestering?" Deidre asked.

"No. My wife and I invited him over a couple of times to get him to mix with other people, but he'd typically just start reading something in my library."

"I can see him doing that," Melissa agreed.

"There was nothing good-natured about it, either," Neil continued. "He suggested next time we try St. Mary's School for the Blind. It was just over the top."

Melissa and Deidre laughed out loud.

"Well," Deidre noted, becoming serious again, "for sure someone with healthy self-esteem isn't going to act that way, but it's not like he's let that area of his life turn him into an underachiever. He knows what he's good at and has the drive and passion to set high goals and meet them. He may still come around."

"I wish I could be as optimistic. In all the years I've known him, I don't recall him ever being involved in or mentioning a close relationship with anyone."

"What about his friendship with you?" Melissa asked.

"I imagine he's about as close to me as he's capable of getting to anyone, but there are still walls between us. There are things he simply will not talk about, to me or anyone else."

"It's pretty obvious to me that the issue is vulnerability—he doesn't like it," concluded Deidre.

Dr. Bandstra reflected for a moment. "That's interesting ... I've often wondered whether he might genuinely enjoy being alone and doesn't need the kind of closeness most people do."

"No," Melissa dissented thoughtfully, "that isn't true."

"How would you know?" he inquired.

"He told me so," she notified them, "earlier today, just before the meeting."

Neil appeared surprised.

"Yeah," Deidre recalled, "you lagged behind with him after we left his room; you guys were almost late."

"We talked for a few moments and then caught up."

"What did you talk about?" he asked.

"I wanted to thank him for something he said ... to the rest of the team."

"Yeah," Deidre jumped in, "it was good he said what he did. He pretty much brought up the whole issue of Melissa's attitude before the attack."

"So what did he say that got your attention?" he asked.

Melissa balked at the question, not wanting to relate any specifics.

"Well?" Neil persisted.

"He deflected a compliment I gave him. He made it sound like I was going to get upset at him if I did it again. No offense, but it was odd."

"Now, that's something I haven't seen," Neil replied. "What do you think, Deidre?"

"It's kind of odd," she said, pondering the episode, "but nothing pathological, I'm sure," she winked.

"Regardless," Neil declared, a change in his demeanor apparent, "I'd like you to keep your distance."

"I can't say I like your tone," Melissa took offense.

"Get used to being disappointed, then. You've got a long way to go with me, Melissa, and when it comes to Brian, I won't let anything slide. The guy has been through enough. I love him like the son I never had."

"You can't keep me from talking to him."

"Actually, I can, but I won't. But if you pull anything even remotely like your little exploit of recent memory, I'll make sure you regret it."

"You and Father Benedict," she retorted.

"Oh?"

"It seems you two fine, upstanding, Christian gentlemen have a thing about threatening women. You're both hypocrites," she said angrily, having had enough at last. "Or maybe Brian's the only real one in the bunch."

Neil flushed with anger as well as embarrassment, but he wasn't about to apologize. "I think it's time for me to leave," he said, rising from his chair, picking up his tray.

"Oh, Neil," Deidre asked politely, but trying to take the edge off the tension, "you haven't touched your french fries—do you mind? I'll take your tray back."

"Sure," he replied, scowling at Melissa, who glared back in return. He set the tray back on the table and left without another word.

"That could have ended better," Deidre said, unperturbed, reaching for a fry.

"I hope you're not talking to me," Melissa fumed. "He has no right—" She stopped, caught short by Deidre's knowing stare.

"Okay, he's got a right," she admitted, "but he ought to just keep it to himself."

"I can agree with that," Deidre allowed. "Let's face it, it's personal with him."

"Oh well," Melissa dismissed the observation.

"Hey," Deidre changed the subject, "it appears the good undersecretary didn't touch his pie—chocolate cream, honey."

"So what?" she answered, still stewing.

"So the pie doesn't care who its owner's been. No woman I know can withstand chocolate. Go ahead, you'll feel better."

"I'm trying to watch my figure."

"Oh yeah, you really need to keep an eye on that."

"What is this, food therapy?"

"I did learn something in grad school. Speaking as a professional, there are clinical studies that suggest—"

"Stuff the infomercial," she interjected, smiling distractedly, "you talked me into it."

"I guess the Colonel's a happy camper now, what with all of us on the same page," Deidre mused while Melissa took a forkful. "Good, huh?"

"Very," she said, taking another bite.

"I know we'll only be here tonight, Melissa, but you and Brian should spend some time getting acquainted with this place. Malcolm said he was going to suggest it to you once you guys got here. There's some really weird stuff here. That building over there," she said, pointing as she looked through the glass of the cafeteria, "it's full of—"

Her explanation was cut short by the sound of Melissa's fork hitting the floor, rapidly followed by agitated gagging.

"My God, Melissa, what is it?"

Melissa cast a distraught expression at her colleague, but she was unable to speak. Deidre could see, through the fingers clutching at her neck, that Melissa's throat had bloated with alarming swiftness. The woman gasped ineffectually for air. She lunged for her purse, toppling their drinking glasses and scattering their utensils. No sooner had she unzipped the top than she collapsed to the floor, suffocating, her complexion already evincing a bluish hue.

Deidre rushed to her colleague, dodging Melissa's arms, which were now flailing hysterically. She tried in vain to clear her airway. "Get a doctor, quick!" she shouted at the small crowd that had gathered. She hurriedly tried to clear an airway, but Melissa's throat had swelled shut.

Unsure of what to do, her eyes fell upon Melissa's purse. She quickly grabbed it and dumped the contents onto the floor. Her eyes immediately recognized what her colleague had attempted to find. Without hesitation, she pulled the top off the injection device and jammed it into Melissa's thigh through her slacks.

50

What is now proved was once only imagined.

—William Blake

"The arm looks great," Malcolm said, beaming, "hardly a scratch left. I'd swear you could see the scarring disappear if you watched close enough."

"It feels great, too," Brian grunted through his last bicep curl before releasing the bar. "Just incredible!" he said jubilantly, squeezing his once-crippled hand, rotating the wrist back and forth. "I can't remember the last time I honestly enjoyed working out. I wish I could start all over again!"

"How do you think he did it?" asked Malcolm.

"I have no idea." Brian took the bar from its stand and began pumping the weight rapidly, ecstatic at the completeness of the restoration. He was sure it was his imagination, or maybe the sense of exhilaration, but he seemed stronger than before the injury.

"Save some of that for the Olympics," Malcolm said with a broad smile as he took the bar after Brian's last rep and carefully replaced it on its stand. "Makes you wonder what else the little dude can do, doesn't it?" Malcolm asked.

"Yeah, it does."

"Hard to believe. A few days ago I'd never have wanted to see one of those metallic midgets."

"Why is that?" Brian asked, laughing.

"I had the weirdest dream a couple nights ago," he began.

"What was in it?"

"Lots of Grays. They were dead at first, or asleep or something, and then they all came after me like one of those zombie flicks."

"Tell me about it."

Malcolm proceeded to relate the details of his dream to Brian, who couldn't contain his amusement until Malcolm mentioned one specific detail.

"You mean you were in this room with all these gray aliens, and the smell was there too?"

"Yeah, but not at first. It was only after I'd turned around and some of them were missing."

"Are you sure it was the same smell?"

"Absolutely, man. Why do you ask?"

"It's just odd. Remember how Father Benedict seemed to suspect that the smell and what Melissa's unidentified visitor said were somehow connected? It still doesn't make sense."

"We'll have to talk more about it later. Right now, there are things you need to see here at Mount Weather that I'm sure you'll find interesting, and we have only this evening to do it."

"What kind of stuff?" Brian wondered.

"This place is like a survivalist's factory outlet, man. You wouldn't believe the stockpiles of food, water, medical supplies, fuel, batteries, seeds, baggies to crap in—you name it, they've got it, and *lots* of it."

"Well, it's FEMA's nerve center, like Deidre told us. They're supposed to have all that stuff, for the survival of the government."

"Brian, according to Mount Weather's published PR, they're supposed to have enough supplies for two hundred people for several months. I'm no logistics expert, but I can show you now that they've got stockpiles in here that will last for years, and for thousands, maybe tens of thousands of people—and that's just what I've seen so far."

"Are you sure?"

"Yeah, and that's not all." He motioned to Brian to draw near enough to hear him whisper, "They've got bio-weapons here too—anthrax and some lethal pollutants."

"How do you know?"

"It's my expertise, man. I've handled the stuff in grad school. Believe me, I know what it looks like and how to read the labels. The freaky thing is, our clearances allow us to get to it. Now you tell me how that stuff is used in disaster relief."

"I would think if it had some sinister purpose, then they wouldn't have let you just go snooping around for it."

"Well," he checked his voice, "they didn't exactly give me directions to where it was. Once I saw we had some weight around here, I just hitched a ride on a few trucks and rode around all day. You'd be surprised what you can do with one of our badges and a clipboard—not to mention an expression that convinces people you know where you are and what you're doing. While everybody else has been sitting around playing cards or picking their noses, old Malcolm's been up and about town. I've been to some of the storage areas that are way back inside the mountain; that's where they have the real interesting stuff."

"So what's your theory?"

"I haven't got one, but I can say two things with confidence."

"Yes?"

"One, they know something's gonna happen that we don't, and it'll be real nasty when it goes down; two, I'm glad we're on the survivor's list. Maybe they'll make me the new EPA head if I behave."

"Only you could put things quite that way."

"C'mon," Malcolm grinned, "we need to get our butts in gear. We can pick up Melissa afterwards. She'll want to see some of this too."

The two of them showered and dressed quickly, then exited the exercise area. They covered only a few yards of the short distance to their accommodations before the sight of flashing red lights ahead distracted them.

"What's over there?" asked Brian.

"The cafeteria—one of them anyway."

"Looks like something's going on."

"Can't be anybody getting their stomach pumped," cracked Malcolm, "the food's too good here."

"Want to take a look?"

"Yeah, but just for a minute."

As they neared the cafeteria, they suddenly saw the familiar form of Deidre breaking through. She didn't see them, but they could plainly make out her expression.

"Not to be unscientific or anything," Malcolm said seriously, "but I've got a bad feeling about this."

"Dee!" Malcolm called. She turned and, upon recognizing them, trotted out to them.

"Now, Brian," she warned, putting her hand on his chest, "this is going to look much worse than it is."

"What is it?" he asked, a feeling of dread building inside him.

"It's Melissa."

"What happened?" he demanded fearfully.

"She's going to be all right. It was a close call, but she'll be fine."

"What—" He stopped in mid-question as the crowd parted for the stretcher carrying Melissa. Brian ran over to the side of the stretcher before Deidre could stop him. The attendants paused long enough for him to see her pale, slightly bloated face, partially obscured by an oxygen mask. She looked at him briefly through heavy eyelids but was only semiconscious.

"What happened?" he insisted again as Deidre and Malcolm approached from behind. "Why is her face so swollen?"

"Some type of allergic reaction," Deidre guessed, then related the details of the incident to the two of them.

"What do you think she reacted to?" asked Malcolm. "I've seen people look like that after bee stings, but it was never life threatening."

"I'm not sure, but I'm going to find out. The only thing that saved her was that I found her epinephrine injector and knew how to use it. I had a patient during my psych practicum who carried one for a food allergy. We had our sessions right after the lunch hour, so he showed me how to use it in case he ever had a reaction and went into anaphylactic shock during a session. Melissa's reaction was incredibly fast; she must have a severe allergic condition to something."

"Where are they taking her?" Brian asked.

"The main infirmary is a few blocks from here. That'd be my guess."

"Then let's go."

"Brian, let them do their job and treat her."

"But there isn't much time."

"I don't think you'll have to worry about leaving tonight," she remarked. "Once the Colonel hears about this, he'll want an investigation."

"For an allergy?" Malcolm said incredulously. "The man's paranoid, but not that much."

"Well, even if he does want us to leave, you can join me in some civil disobedience. I'm not going anywhere until I get some answers."

"What is it, Deidre?" Brian inquired, sensing she was troubled.

"She had a reaction all right, but I don't think it was an accident."

"What?" the two men echoed in unison.

"I'm going to find a few people I want to question. I'll meet you guys at the hospital in an hour or so."

"Wait a minute," Malcolm demanded, grabbing her arm. "What are you suggesting?"

"What doesn't make sense?" Brian urged impatiently.

"I can't explain it," she responded, looking at Brian, "but I just have the feeling that someone tried to kill Melissa."

51

It is possible to make large sections of any
population believe in the existence of supernatural
races, in the possibility of flying machines, in the
plurality of inhabited worlds, by exposing them to a
few carefully engineered scenes, the details of which
are adapted to the culture and superstitions of a
particular time and place.

—*Jacques Vallee, Passport to Magonia*

"Why do I have an overwhelming sense of *déjà vu?*" the thin, well-dressed man sniped sarcastically. "We were eager to congratulate you, Colonel, but it appears you're trying to snatch defeat from the jaws of victory once again."

"Shut up!" the Lieutenant exploded. "You've known for weeks we have a saboteur among us. For all we know, it could be you. Why else would you be so consumed with making the Colonel look incompetent?"

"How dare you?" the older man seethed. "We know where your sympathies lie."

"We? I don't see anyone leaping to their feet to join you. It seems everyone else can keep their heads, especially when we've achieved our goal."

"We've achieved nothing until their research has been disseminated and the disinformation believed, you twit!"

"Gentlemen, gentlemen," the General drew their attention. "I share both your beliefs and concerns, and I suspect that Colonel Ferguson will prove yet to be more than a match for our adversary. Vernon?"

"Yesterday's occurrence was indeed a scare, but we believe we know who's been trying to terminate the project," he said, not caring to conceal his satisfaction.

"So, what are you doing about it?" the thin man demanded. "Eliminate the problem!"

"Oh, I will—and personally, I might add. We just need one hundred percent confirmation, and that will come in a few hours, a day at the latest."

"What about the team members? Have they been confined to their quarters?"

"None of our researchers are involved," Colonel Ferguson replied. "Let them wander around; this will be their home in the near future anyway. Whatever they find they'll thank us for later."

***

"How're you doing?" Brian asked. He smiled and leaned over the freshly-awakened Melissa.

She blinked a few times, clearing her mind, and looked about at the familiar faces surrounding her bed: Brian, Deidre, Mark, Malcolm, and—to her surprise—Neil and Father Benedict.

"Okay," she sighed, then winced. "I've got a winner of a headache, though."

"You've been asleep for a couple of hours. Do you remember anything?"

"Before or after I hit the floor?" she muttered, moving her head from side to side, trying to relieve the tension.

"Anything at all," Deidre said.

"Let me sit up," she requested, activating the mechanized berth. "I do have something to tell you ... it's pretty strange, actually."

"I think we're getting used to that," said Mark.

"Well," she began, "I remember taking some of Dr. Bandstra's pie, and then all of a sudden I couldn't breathe. It's my fault, really; it was so careless."

"Could you explain, Melissa?" asked Father Benedict.

"I have a nut allergy."

"You never broke out in hives around Malcolm," Brian quipped. The others laughed.

"You're learning from the master, Grasshopper."

"Ow," Melissa groaned, flinching again. "Don't make me laugh; it hurts."

"Go on," encouraged Neil.

"Like I said, I'm allergic to any kind of nut—peanuts especially. I have a severe allergy to anything made with peanuts or peanut oil, or any peanut product."

"Which explains the epinephrine," Deidre noted. "The pie crust was made with peanut oil. I checked."

"Death by chocolate cream pie ... hmm," Malcolm remarked.

"Why didn't you tell anyone about your allergy?" Brian asked.

"I didn't think I had to," she answered. "The food preparers at the Facility had the specifics as to my dietary requirements. I never thought about tasting the pie since I assumed everything was kosher here as well, so to speak. It was terribly careless."

A few of the team members exchanged worried glances.

"What's wrong?" Melissa wondered, observing their demeanor.

"All that information was forwarded to the cooks here, Melissa," Neil informed her. "They knew all about your allergy."

"But how ..."

"Deidre thinks that someone tried to kill you," Brian informed her soberly. "She also thinks the attack by the dogs wasn't an accident either."

"What?"

"I guessed food was probably the reason for your reaction," Deidre began unraveling her theory, "so after they loaded you onto the medical cart—"

"Oh, Deidre," Melissa broke in, "thank you so much ... I would have died. I saw you keep me breathing after you stuck me. It seems like I'm a calamity waiting to happen." She glanced at Brian.

"How did you know I gave you CPR?" Deidre exclaimed, hit by a sudden realization. "You were unconscious by then."

"That's the weird part ... I saw you working on me from above. It looked to me like I was floating above my body. I saw you two guys, too," she said to Malcolm and Brian, "walking toward the cafeteria."

"Oh boy," Mark said, shaking his head.

"What else did you see?" Deidre asked, her interest and focus sharpened.

"I'll tell you in a second," she said with renewed vigor. "Right now I want to hear what makes you think someone is trying to get rid of me—and even more importantly, why."

"Deal. After you were on the cart, I told Malcolm and Brian what I suspected and went to talk to the Colonel. He assembled the food prep staff for this section of the base, and we questioned them. That's when we discovered that the information on your allergy had been forwarded. It was sent by email the day after Brian got out of surgery, well ahead of your arrival."

"Where is the Colonel, anyway?" Melissa asked.

"He's launched a full-scale investigation. Man, I thought I'd seen him at his worst, but he went positively berserk when he found out what had happened. Whoever did this better pray the MPs get to him first."

"Wait till you hear the rest," Brian told her.

"Once we found out that they knew better than to make a pie with peanut oil, we wanted to find out who made it."

"Should the staff really have been expected to be that careful?" asked Father Benedict. "There are hundreds of people who eat at that cafeteria."

"People with peanut allergies can't be around nuts at all," answered Melissa. "Whole schools have been forced by legislation to stop serving nut items or recipes prepared with peanut-based materials. Even major airlines will refuse to serve those little peanut snacks when they know someone with a nut allergy is on the flight. If they had the information, they knew better."

"We learned from the staff on duty for today," Deidre continued, "that the pie was just sitting out with the rest of the items to be placed in the dessert case, but no one would admit to making it."

"What a surprise."

"We also found out from the menus on the kitchen's computer that chocolate cream pie has never been served here before."

"But it's listed in my dietary information file among the desserts that can be prepared at no risk, along with a lot of other chocolate desserts," Melissa noted. "Maybe someone had access to my file and figured I'd be partial to one of those desserts."

"He was right then," Deidre noted. "Unfortunately, anybody on staff could have seen that sheet, and they're not going to admit to making the thing."

"I'm no cook," said Neil, "but I've never seen my wife make pie dough with peanut oil."

"Ordinarily, you wouldn't put anything like that in dough," Melissa answered him.

"Which tells us," Father Benedict broke in, "that such preparation was deliberate. The pie was intended for you."

"But it seems like such a random act," Brian commented. "One pie isn't going to go very far; anyone could have taken a piece, and Melissa would never have had the opportunity."

"Actually, it may not have been so random, Brian," Neil offered, recalling something. "I saw the pie put out while I was in line. I took a piece, since it's one of my favorites as well. Melissa was only four or five people behind me—and she didn't even take a piece. She was certainly in a position to get one, which must have been the intent of putting it out there, but she didn't. She had the reaction to my piece."

"How did she get yours?" Father Benedict wondered aloud.

"I left in a huff ... we had an argument."

"It was my fault."

"Hopefully the Colonel will turn up something else," Brian said optimistically. "I'd like to hear about your experience now, Melissa."

"Brother ... it was really weird," she said in a disbelieving tone. "I've heard about NDEs and OBEs, but I never put any credence into them."

"NDEs? OBEs? Translation please," Mark inquired.

"Near death experiences and out-of-body experiences," Deidre responded. "Melissa didn't have a pulse for two or three minutes. Tell us about it."

"Well, like I said, I had this floating sensation, and I could see you trying to revive me. After a few seconds, I guess, I decided to go look around. I went outside the building and was just looking around at all the activity when ..." She stopped.

"When what?" asked Father Benedict.

"I can't believe I'm saying this," she said, flustered. "After I floated—or whatever I did—outside, I felt some sort of presence. I never saw whatever it was, but he, or it, told me in my head to follow him. I did, and on the way to where I was being led, we passed Malcolm and Brian, like I said." She paused then. "I just realized something."

"What?" asked Deidre.

"We could fly around, but instead of going above the buildings, my guide led me by way of the streets here inside the cavern. We'd follow one, then turn right; then another, and turn left. It was almost like—"

"Like it wanted you to remember where you were going," Brian perceived.

"Right. Maybe it was just a dream," she speculated.

"Maybe," offered Deidre. "Was there anything else?"

She nodded. "We got to a building and went in through the door—and I mean right through the door. Once we were inside the building, we passed through a few checkpoints, came to a place where two hallways intersected, and turned right. A few feet away there was a solid door. It opened as if commanded, and I saw a room with lots of shiny tables in it, like the slabs the alien bodies were on."

Brian immediately shot a startled glance at Malcolm, who, unlike a moment ago, appeared uncharacteristically serious.

"Did you say shiny tables?" Malcolm asked weakly.

"Yes."

"Would you say there were hundreds of them?"

"Yes, that would seem right, but I didn't count them or anything."

"Was there anything on them?" he asked, swallowing hard.

"No."

Malcolm breathed a sigh of relief.

"There was one other thing about the room," Melissa added. Malcolm stiffened to attention. "It seemed permeated with that strange aroma that was in my room—and Brian's."

"I need a drink," Malcolm said woozily.

"What's the problem, Malcolm?" Neil asked.

"Better let him sit down in one of the chairs," Brian cautioned before relating Malcolm's nightmare and its obvious overlap with Melissa's experience to those present.

"*That*," Melissa said emphatically after Brian had finished, "is just bizarre. Do you think it means anything?"

"It has to, but I have no idea what. Father?"

"I agree—and from the look on your face, Deidre, I'd say you concur."

"I've been exposed to too much of this to say I didn't think it had some meaning."

"Now what could that be?" Mark scoffed.

"Don't start in on me again with the pseudoscience crap," Deidre warned. "You still owe me an apology from the last time. Besides, I think we've all had our paradigms stretched today, thank you."

"I don't know about Brian," Father Benedict continued, "but I believe these experiences could be God's way of giving us information—but they could also be deceptions. Each experience as it unfolds must be evaluated against what we know can be relied on for sure."

"I agree," Brian remarked. "At the very least it deserves investigation. If we detect any falsehood in it, then we'll disregard it as anything meaningful. If nothing comes from it, there's no harm done. Was there anything else, Melissa?"

"Yes, two things happened. Right after I saw the room with all the tables, something in my head told me to go to a room down the opposite end of the hall. I did and went inside. The only thing that happened there was that I felt my guide—or whatever you'd call it—wanted ... oh, this sounds crazy."

"What?"

"I had the distinct impression I was supposed to get down on the floor."

"Did you?"

"No. After I hesitated, I was … transported—it's the only way I can describe it—to another location."

"Can you describe it?" Father Benedict asked urgently. He stepped closer to the bed and sat on its edge.

"It was a library, that much I know … and a small one at that. There was something on the floor … I mean, someone." Melissa stopped, her skin suddenly flushed and moistened with perspiration. "It was a priest, or at least he looked like one, in a dark robe. He was dead. I can't describe what he looked like because he was lying face down. I think he had a beard, though. Then I woke up in my body … if that's the right way to put it."

"What's the second thing?"

"I don't know if it's related, but when I came to, I kept thinking about a saint. I'm not even Catholic, but I couldn't get him out of my head."

"Which one?" asked Father Benedict.

"Saint Gregory."

The priest stood up without a word. His eyes locked onto Brian's, but he remained silent. Brian held the connection for a few seconds but soon turned away, his thoughts racing.

"What's wrong? What's with Saint Gregory?"

Brian turned to Melissa. "I'm not sure yet. Do you think you could find this room, the last place you saw in your … experience?"

"I think so. They're going to hold me for observation until morning."

"We'll do it then."

52

We've had contact with alien cultures.

—*Astronaut Dr. Brian O'Leary*

"Take your time, Melissa," Brian said patiently.

Brian watched as Melissa stood at an intersection under the artificial light illuminating the huge expanse of granite far above their heads. It was an incredible sight, this bustling, underground town.

Save for the absence of the sun, the scene before them could have been played out in any small town or outdoor military base in the U.S. Vehicles of all shapes and sizes, most of them powered by electricity, moved in every direction, their progress impeded or authorized by stoplights. Pedestrians, alternately attired in military dress, occupational uniform, or civilian clothing, were busy with the day's demands. There were no buildings more than two stories high, and most of them were coated with the same dull beige paint. Down one direction they could see a barber shop, down another a PX station.

Guards were a rare sight, but they did serve as reminders to the team that they weren't in Mayberry. There was no sense that those who were employed at Mount Weather were in the business of hiding anything. If you were here, you were supposed to be here, and you were an active part of a massive preparation campaign—but for what?

"I'm sure this is the way," Melissa assured the group of seven following her. "It isn't far."

Melissa led the team across the intersection and two more blocks, pausing only occasionally to pick out a landmark for guidance. At the next intersection she turned right, then left at the next street. The group made its way on foot straight toward what would have been the edge of town had the installation been in the open air. As it was, they finally reached their destination at the foot of a large, factory-like building situated across from the "town" proper and adjacent to the mouth of the next gaping cavern. The well-worn road leading into the expanse attested that the cavern was regularly used. Nonetheless, there was nothing visible from where they found themselves.

"I've been in that cavern, and in one other," Malcolm informed Brian as he looked into the grotto.

"Anything about the building look familiar?" Brian asked him.

"Nope."

"Well, let's see if that holds true for what's inside."

The team made its way to what they guessed was the main entrance, a double-glass door equipped with the familiar electronic admission control.

"Allow me," Father Benedict said politely and swiped his card.

The door clicked open without incident. They entered and were greeted by an MP seated at a desk.

"Please sign in, sir," the guard instructed the priest, "and the rest of you as well."

The formality acknowledged, Brian motioned for Melissa to take the lead. She had no trouble discerning her surroundings and led them confidently through a series of hallways until she reached the crossroads she had mentioned from her bed the evening before.

"This is it," she said.

"It sure is," acknowledged Malcolm, somewhat apprehensively. "The playroom is right over there." He pointed to the right.

The team turned right, into the connecting corridor, and Malcolm and Melissa strode with deliberation to the third door on the left. Melissa tried the door. It was securely locked.

"Oh well," Deidre reacted in frustration. "This was a wasted trip."

"Not so fast," Neil chided her and withdrew a small set of keys from his rear pants pocket.

"How do you rate?" asked Malcolm.

"I'm the assistant project leader, remember? They gave me these keys when we got here, but I've only ever tried the one that's the master to our little dormitory."

Neil tried a few keys and eventually had success in unlocking the door. He opened it slowly and stepped inside the room, followed by the others. True to their colleagues' recollections, an enormous room filled with hundreds of shiny metal tables, each about five feet in length, immediately confronted them. All of them were empty. Brian couldn't help but hear Malcolm breathe a sigh of relief.

"Anybody notice the smell?" Mark asked.

"What smell?" asked Deidre, sniffing the air.

"That's the point. Smells like the only person who's been in here has been Mr. Clean."

"He's right," Brian agreed. "There's nothing unusual here."

"I don't get it," Melissa griped disappointedly. "I was sure we'd find some clue here."

"I don't think anyone doubts you," Brian said, inspecting one of the tables. "You did get us here without much effort."

"But what could it mean?" Father Benedict wondered aloud. "Why would Malcolm's dream and Melissa's experience be so similar?"

"Melissa," Deidre spoke up, "didn't you say that your guide sort of wanted you to go down the hallway in the other direction?"

"Yes." Melissa turned slowly in recognition. "It's that way." She pointed.

"Let's go," Father Benedict insisted. "We can't pass up any chance to learn from Melissa's experience." With that, the aged cleric headed down the hallway.

"He is an exorcist, you know," Brian said, eyeing Melissa with a nervous smile and turning to follow Andrew.

"Let's hope we don't need one," Neil said darkly, following right behind him. The others followed.

The team cautiously made their way down the opposing corridor. They carefully observed any signs on the rooms that lined the hallway. Each one was unlocked and empty, with the exception of the last room.

Neil got out his keys and, after finding the correct key again, unlocked the door and pushed it open. He peered inside and then turned the lights on. The others filed inside. The windowless room contained nothing of apparent value or secrecy, only a large, rectangular, polished oak table surrounded by thickly cushioned low back swivel chairs. The deep, plush carpeting that greeted their feet was the sole hint of luxury. The lone adornment was a striking but unspectacular black sun disk, its wavy rays pointing in all directions, fixed on the wall behind one of the long sides of the table.

"Nice ... but again, I don't see anything terribly interesting," said Mark.

Brian spoke up. "Melissa, were you at any particular spot when you had the sensation that you were supposed to get on the floor?"

"I went in and started to move around the table like this to my right and ... ooh ... I feel dizzy. Brian—"

Brian darted past Father Benedict just in time to break Melissa's fall. He gently laid her on the floor and felt her cheeks for warmth.

The alarmed team crowded around her body. Father Benedict anxiously eyed the door behind them. After a few moments Melissa's eyes flut-
tered open, alert as ever.

"What happened?" Brian asked, worry etched on his face.

"I'm not sure. One minute everything was fine, the next I had this
irresistible vertigo. I think I'd like to leave now—"

Melissa's attention was focused toward the floor, underneath one of
the air-conditioning vents that lined the room's paneled walls. "What
the …"

She quickly turned onto her hands and knees and reached underneath the vent. Pulling her tiny quarry from the darkened niche, she
blew the dust from the minute artifact she held between her fingers.

"Am I looking at what I think I'm looking at?" Deidre asked, un-
nerved by the revelation.

"You sure are," Mark confirmed with a glance.

"I have a bad feeling about this," Malcolm noted in a conspicuously
somber tone.

"Don't throw it away," Father Benedict charged.

"I'm not keeping it," Melissa refused. "You want it, you keep it."

"Fine." The priest reached out and took the object.

"We'd best be going," said Neil.

The seven filed out of the room, Andrew last in line. As he neared
the doorway, he looked back at the black disk mounted on the wall.
He stared at it momentarily.

"What is it, Andrew?" Brian asked as the others exited the room.

"I've seen this … symbol … before. I just can't place it. I know it means
something, and it's related to everything else we've learned in the past
twenty-four hours."

"You're giving me the creeps, Andrew."

"I would think Melissa's little discovery would be sufficient for that,"
the priest sighed. He took one more look at the tiny article and then
pushed the bloodstained human tooth deep into his pocket.

53

As a rule, we disbelieve all the facts
and theories for which we have no use.

—*William James*

"How in the world can you say you don't believe Adam was an alien?" asked Melissa, astonished at Father Benedict's judgment.

"I merely said," he began slightly above a whisper, eyeing the Colonel, Neil, and Ian Marcus seated a few rows ahead of him, "that I didn't believe he was extraterrestrial."

"Then what is he? I'm guessing your view has something to do with Brian's second view—the stuff about Genesis 6 and the sons of God."

"The Watchers—and you're correct. Your recent experiences and the tooth you found make me even more convinced. I'm anxious to hear Brian's thoughts on what you told us."

"Well, let's ask him."

Brian waved her off, eyes closed and head rested against the headrest in his seat, his brow wrinkled in discomfort.

"What's wrong with him?" asked Deidre.

"I hate flying," Brian answered for her. "It hurts my ears. I guess we can't expect the antigravity express every time." He shifted in his seat. "Give me a few minutes."

Melissa turned to Father Benedict. "What did I say that made you think of these Watchers?"

"Your apparent waking fixation with St. Gregory. I think it's an image planted in your mind by the presence you felt. The key is the word 'Gregory.' It comes from the Greek *gregori*, which means 'Watcher.' God works in mysterious ways, Melissa. I've witnessed this kind of thing before."

"But Gregory was known in medieval mythology as the one who killed the dragon, and I know the dragon was a symbolic title for Satan. How could a Watcher be an opponent of Satan and be evil?"

"Because there are good Watchers as well. In fact, the only biblical mention of them, the fourth chapter of the prophecy of Daniel, are of the good ones. Don't forget, the word 'Watchers' as applied to the fallen sons of God is found in Jewish Aramaic texts that never made it into the Bible."

"Maybe the presence was a good Watcher and that's why the word stuck with me."

"I don't believe so. You see ..." Father Benedict hung his head.

Melissa could tell he was fighting his emotions. "What is it, Father?"

The priest gathered himself and sighed. "I knew the dead man in your vision."

"What?"

"Father Mantello was a dear, trusted friend. He was the librarian at the Vatican Observatory at Castel Gandolfo."

"Are you sure it was him?"

Father Benedict's eyes began to tear up. "Please excuse me," he said, taking out a handkerchief.

"He's sure," Brian intervened and related what he knew of the details Andrew had discovered on the Internet.

"With all due respect, Father," Deidre asked once Andrew was ready, "are you certain it wasn't a heart attack? Just what were you asking him to research?"

"He had no heart condition whatsoever ... and I'm afraid I don't feel comfortable sharing my request right now. It needs to wait until we're back at the Facility."

"Well," Melissa offered, "let's assume all this *is* related to these Watchers—and I have to tell you all that I'm not convinced they even exist. How does that explain what we've seen?"

"I take it you believe more in Adam as an ET because he's physical?"

"Well ... I guess that's fair to say."

"Why couldn't Adam be a dimensional being who can take physical form if he wishes?"

"Well, seeing as how we don't know any differently, I guess I'll say that's possible. But if that's the case, why does Adam need to travel in a spaceship? Why is he subject to physical laws? I'm sure he has a determinate lifespan and has to sustain himself. Why would a dimensional being—and I'm sure you mean 'spiritual being' by the term—need these things?"

"That has two possible answers," Brian broke in. "On one hand, if he were a spiritual entity who could just take on flesh at will, he *wouldn't* need those things—but we should all remember that we've just been *told* these things about Adam. If someone is trying to deceive us, that could be part of a planned misdirection."

"But the technology—it's so far beyond what we're capable of," said Mark.

"Maybe. I'm no physicist, but even Dr. Yu told us that what we saw was just a large-scale extrapolation of technology already being developed outside the military. If the military had enough interest in exploiting a technology that derived from Paperclip, as I tried to suggest to Major Lindsay, they could throw enough resources at it to be way ahead of the normal R&D channels. We haven't taken a ride with Adam to the other side of the moon—we've just been told what we more or less expect to hear about him using saucer spacecraft."

"I'm not buying it. I know what I saw—and you were healed by him, for God's sake!"

"I know, and I have to confess that leads me to think he's the real Mc-Coy. But neither of us can prove the other possibility is wrong."

"True, but it seems less plausible," Mark said and turned his attention to the view outside the window.

"On the other hand," Brian said, thinking out loud, "getting back to Melissa's question, Adam could be a spiritual being, but when he takes physical form, he becomes subject to the limitations of the physical. I hate to draw the analogy, but consider Jesus. Christian theology has Him as true deity, but as an incarnate human being, He was subject to everything we are—He had to eat, drink, relieve Himself, go through puberty, learn to use a spoon, and so on. And He certainly aged and could be hurt. The New Testament describes Him as eating after the resurrection as well—something that may have been written down to draw an analogy with Genesis 18, where God Himself comes to Abraham in a body and has a meal. I don't see a corporeal presence and a spiritual reality as mutually exclusive."

"Speaking of Jesus," Deidre said, "my mom took me to church when I was little. She'd have a holy rolling fit if she heard you say that her Bible taught that Jesus wasn't the only son of God. I've been wanting to ask you about that—and Father Benedict, since he seems to like your work."

"It's actually pretty simple. Practically everyone has heard the Christian teaching that Jesus was the 'only begotten' son of God."

"Right. So what about the other ones?"

"Up until a century ago, scholars believed that the Greek word behind 'only begotten' came from a Greek verb that means 'to beget,' as in 'to bring forth' or 'to father.' That isn't true, though. Linguistic work in ancient Greek since the turn of the century has established that the word comes from another Greek word spelled almost the same way, and that word means 'class' or 'kind.' The word for 'only begotten' really means 'one of a kind' or 'unique.'

"There may be many sons of God, but Jesus is unique among them. In Christian teaching, His uniqueness stems from Him being equal to God's own essence but yet as another person. He's also God's uncreated co-creator. He's as 'species unique' among God's sons as Yahweh is among the gods."

"That answer sounds like it would irritate traditionalists and theological liberals," observed Melissa. "I'll say it again for Deidre, you didn't really plan on a teaching career. You just don't fit anywhere."

"I just call 'em as I see 'em ... and paint the bullseye on my chest later."

"But getting back to Adam. In the Old Testament story, these sons of God fathered ... what were they called again?" asked Deidre.

"*Nephilim.*"

"Didn't you say giants before?"

"That's what the word means—despite what most conservative interpreters want to say, I might add."

"Are you wearing another bullseye for this one?"

"Yeah. I'm in the minority even though the Hebrew morphology of the term eliminates all the other options."

"Morphology?"

"The formation of the word, its spelling, in a manner of speaking."

"What does spelling have to do with it?"

"The notion that the *Nephilim* are only human men is based on the unexamined assumption that the word comes from the Hebrew verb *naphal*. Allegedly, *nephilim* actually means 'those who are fallen,' as in warriors killed in battle, or as in fallen, sinful people in the sense of the fall in Eden. Saying the *Nephilim* were just spiritually fallen people also contradicts the comment in the book of Numbers that the Israelites were like grasshoppers next to the *Nephilim*, but no one seems to care."

"So what's the problem with those options?" Mark asked. "Any of those are better than having giants running around, especially if people want to believe this is real."

"Many on the religious right would agree with you, but I'm just being honest with the text. Most people who try to argue this way don't seem to realize the whole approach is flawed. If the word came from *naphal* and meant what they said it does, it would be spelled *nephulim* or *noph-*

elim according to the rules of the Hebrew language. It obviously isn't. The word is actually borrowed from the Aramaic word for giant, which is *naphil*."

"And in regard to giants, that isn't as far-fetched as it sounds," he continued. "We're not talking about people fifteen or twenty feet tall. Even taking Goliath's height literally—at least according to most Hebrew manuscripts of the Old Testament—puts him at a bit over nine feet. There have been modern people a few inches from that."

"But the biblical giants were a race, not just one person," said Melissa.

"Right. There were actually several giant races mentioned in the Bible beside the *Nephilim*—the *Anakim*, the *Emim*, the *Zamzummim*, the *Rephaim*. But there were races in the recent past and even now whose men regularly exceed seven feet tall—the Patagonians, the Yosemite Indians, the Watusi ... there are verifiable examples. According to the anthropological studies I've seen, the average height of people in ancient times was just over five feet. Someone around seven feet tall would have been a giant in those days."

"But do we really need angels or Watchers to have human gigantism? It seems like a complete fairy tale."

"I don't know—I'm just telling you what the text says."

"Well they goofed with Adam. He's as shrimpy as they come."

"I didn't mention this in my presentation, but there's another way to look at Genesis 6 that may relate to the Adam question—and Dee's research—that allows a completely literal view of the events without any sexual procreation at all."

"What?" Father Benedict asked, a surprised look on his face.

"Well, the writer of Genesis 6 was relating a story described by pre-scientific people. These beings from the sky show up, take women, and the women became pregnant. The ancient person would conclude that the pregnancy was the result of sex, not knowing there could be a technological alternative."

"Are you talking about cloning?"

"No, just artificial insemination like we practice it now. What if Genesis 6 were talking about what abductees describe—right down to the actual procedures—but written by someone who couldn't grasp that?"

"You know," added Deidre, "there are accounts in the middle ages that match abductee testimony perfectly, except there the culprits are referred to as demons. Sperm samples taken, female eggs harvested, it's just bizarre."

"I know it's far out, but I don't think it's farther out on the limb than aliens taking us and manipulating us genetically, which would seem to be the other view given what we've seen here."

"I don't follow."

"Well, we really have three possibilities with what we've all seen: One, Adam's an alien, and his kind have been abducting human men and women and harvesting genetic material from them for whatever purpose. Two, Adam's really a spiritual being—say a Watcher—who can take the physical form we know as Adam. He and his kind do what they do to people, again for reasons unclear. Three, Adam is a physical being that was made by some advanced spiritual being and does what he's told or programmed to do."

"But why giants then and not now?" asked Deidre. "My patients don't claim to be giving birth to giants. In fact, I've never come across a single case that says anything like that. Some victims believe they're 'breeders,' for lack of a better term, but not producing giants."

"I don't know. Maybe in ancient times the results of the Watchers' creative effort was gigantism. With Adam they just wanted a worker bee—who knows? It's all speculation, and it's only one of the three possibilities. My point is only that it still goes back to what you think they are, and we could be dealing with either a genuine alien or something altogether different."

"And worse," Father Benedict added. "I know you're trying to be honest, Brian, but what I'm hearing here doesn't move me from my position. Tell me, are you now willing to surrender your interpretation of the Roswell event?"

"No ... no, I'm not, but I don't think the Roswell incident and what we're dealing with here are necessarily related."

"You mean you *assume* that they aren't related. Why are you so willing to believe that at Roswell the military used the ET angle as a prop to cover up heinous dealings with Nazis, and yet so willing to believe there's a real ET presence here?"

"Because I was just healed by one! The thing scanned my mind, too. I know I can erect a scenario that has all this related to the Watchers, but I can't just ignore something so compelling. Maybe ET, the Watchers, and humans are all separate categories."

Melissa reentered the discussion. "How do you account for the mind scans, Father, and what happened between you and Adam?"

"The mind scans are irrelevant. If these beings are spiritual entities, such an activity is well within their abilities. The fact that they can do this sort of thing doesn't negate my view. Adam told me nothing and did nothing inside my head. In fact, his silence was disturbing. He couldn't answer any of my questions—questions that were basic to where he came from, to personhood, and to the universe's ultimate origin."

"Maybe he wasn't interested," Deidre suggested. "He's a scientist, not a philosopher."

"Aren't you, as a scientist, interested in those things?"

"Well ... yeah."

"Then Adam's evasion of the questions is telling, in my mind. Why avoid the questions or appear bored with them when they interest us?"

"Maybe he isn't Catholic," Malcolm jested.

Everyone enjoyed the joke except Andrew.

"Speaking of not addressing questions," the priest continued, unwilling to surrender, "Melissa, why would anyone want to kill you? And what about your earlier skepticism over the corpses we saw in Dr. Marcus' lab?"

Malcolm and Deidre looked at her curiously. Mark turned away from the window, redirecting his attention back to the discussion.

"It's true," she admitted. "Up until our meeting with Adam, I didn't think they were real."

"You still haven't shared what you thought with any of us," Andrew said, "except perhaps Brian."

"Brian and I did talk about it on the flight to Mount Weather. I'm no expert in anatomy or anything," she paused and deliberately nudged Brian to draw his attention to her remarks, "but I had my doubts. I'm surprised Mark didn't have some, too."

Melissa proceeded to sketch out her suspicions. Mark listened with interest.

"That would be quite clever," Mark admitted.

"Ingenious is more like it," added Malcolm. "I'm impressed."

"They looked real to me," Mark continued, "and everything I looked at under the slides checked out. I'm no expert in human anatomy—or humanoid, for that matter. I may not have been as dependent on Dr. Marcus for explanations of what I was seeing, but I did need some help. I only had one undergraduate class in human anatomy. If it has two legs, then I'm not your guy."

"What do you all make of Melissa's clandestine contact, the one who told her point-blank there was a saboteur among us? How does that factor in with what we've seen and been told?"

"And my dream," Malcolm added to the list, "not to mention what happened in Brian's and Melissa's rooms, and that weird smell."

"Doesn't all of this make any of you the least bit apprehensive about just believing what's been put in front of us?" Andrew asked them as a group. "Doesn't it give you less confidence about the neatness of the package you think you see?"

"I think we can understand your concerns, Andrew," Brian spoke up. "At least I know I can. But I think honesty requires admitting that your view is only an option. You haven't overturned the other possibility."

"And what about the bloody tooth Melissa found?" Father Benedict still wasn't giving up.

"Why would the tooth have any relevance?" asked Malcolm.

"The being in Melissa's experience wanted her to see it—the same one that showed her the body and put the *gregori* in her mind. I don't know how, but they must be connected."

"We have no way of knowing that," Mark objected.

"I think you all need to start seeing events through spiritual eyes," the priest sparred. "For myself, when there are loose ends to a matter, especially of the variety and significance of these, I suspect there's far more than meets the eye going on. I do hope I'm wrong on one suspicion, however," he disclosed, casting a worried eye on Melissa.

"What's that?" she asked uncomfortably.

"That whoever is targeting you will try again—very soon."

54

Victory goes to the player who makes
the next-to-last mistake.

—*Chessmaster Savielly Grigorievitch Tartakower (1887–1956)*

"So where've you been all day?" Melissa asked as Brian let her into his room.

"I went to the Facility archive this morning," he answered. Brian took visual inventory of Melissa as she made her way to the couch. She folded her legs underneath a wraparound jean skirt after she was seated. The white, short-sleeved pullover accented her bust line. White ankle-high socks and tennis shoes completed the casual ensemble. Brian tried hard not to look very long.

"Really? Why?"

"I had to check out something that occurred to me in the shower. I was on my way to breakfast, but it kept nagging me."

"What was it?"

"Remember that one document Major Lindsay showed us—the first one that mentioned the Roswell bodies?"

"Not in detail."

"I'll get it. The assistant archivist let me print it out." Brian rummaged through his backpack and found the document in a folder, which was jammed thick with other papers.

"Look at the handwritten comment in the left-hand margin."

```
     In the interest of National Security priorities it was
necessary to detain civilian witnesses for interrogation to
satisfy intelligence requiements, and quash rumors that could
alert potential espionage agents known to be in the vicinity.
     Several bodies were discovered.  Because on-site
medical personnel were unsure of the physiological and biological
make up of the occupants, special preparations and preservation
methods were employed.  Autopsy information obtained so far
suggests that the occupants mimic the featuers associated with
ORIENTALS.  ████████  Outwardly, they appear human-like with but one
exception, autopsy notes mention a rarely observed ██████████
████████████████████ s present which supports the
premise that these beings originate from another planet.
     MAJIC EYES ONLY
```

"Where it says 'Orientals'?"

"Yeah. This memo says the occupants of the craft had features that one would associate with an Oriental or Asian appearance."

"What are you thinking?"

"During our meeting, I said I suspected that the bodies were really human victims—Mongoloids or progeria victims. What if they were small Japanese—with or without progeria?"

"Come on, Brian, that's a stretch."

"I thought so, too, but then I remembered some things I'd read years ago about Operation Paperclip. There was a Japanese element to the program."

"Still doesn't prove anything."

"No, but wait till I walk you through what else I found in the archives. Ever hear of Unit 731?"

"No."

"Unit 731 was one of the more infamous atrocity mills of World War II. It was an officially sanctioned and funded bioweapons program unit headquartered in Harbin, Manchuria. Among historians of human rights abuses, it's become synonymous with human experimentation. They practiced live human vivisection and used human subjects to study the effects of frostbite and high altitude pressurization. Exposure to bioweapons, flamethrowers, and explosives were routine. And the experiments included U.S. POWs. Some of the people involved were brought to the U.S. under Paperclip."

"Go on," said Melissa, her interest growing.

"Unit 731 was intended as the potential source of the bioweapons the Japanese planned to use on the United States as part of the Fugo balloon project."

"Never heard of it."

"It was Japan's experiment in using high altitude balloons as weapons. The goal was to launch the balloons from Japan in such a way as to ensure that they would be carried by the winds over the western United States. Eventually they intended to put suicide pilots in them and arm them with lethal biotoxins."

"Oh my God ... did they ever do any of that?"

"Nine thousand Fugos were launched in the initial phase of the plan, equipped with small-scale explosive devices. A few reached U.S. soil, and there were several casualties. The press was put under a gag order so the Japanese would never know any of them got here. They never put bioweapons on them. We bombed Hiroshima and Nagasaki before they could."

"Incredible. But what does that have to do with Roswell?"

"Well, it got me thinking—or rather, a picture I remembered seeing got me thinking. Check this out." Brian drew a full-page photocopied photograph from his folder and placed it in front of Melissa. "This is actually a model used fifteen or twenty years after Roswell, but it's descended from what I think they used at Roswell."

Melissa shook her head in astonishment as she examined the picture of a perfect saucer-shaped craft with a high altitude balloon attached to it.

"Major Lindsay didn't mention it, but there are witnesses and physical evidence connected with the Roswell story for *both* a high altitude balloon and anomalous metallic wreckage. I think they used the balloon to pull the craft up to very high altitudes, then dropped it."

"Dropped it?"

"Yeah. Some of the early German saucer models were built to glide—the German Horten model in particular."

"But what about the bodies?"

"My theory is that we brought the Germans over here to continue their work but wanted to put an engine in their craft—a nuclear powered engine. There was a contemporary project called Nuclear Energy Propulsion Aircraft for just that purpose. Eventually, you'd need to pilot these things, and that would mean testing radiation shielding and the effects of radiation on humans would become necessary.

We brought the Japanese crews over here who were training to pilot the makeshift gliding cockpits of the Fugos. When it came time to test for radiation, those in charge used human expendables from Unit 731. One of them crashed at Roswell by accident in the storm witnesses describe happened the night before the wreckage was discovered."

Melissa eyed him suspiciously. "Wait a minute. You didn't just come up with this on your own. That's an amazing string of circumstances. What did you find this morning?"

"Something I don't think Major Lindsay wanted us to see. Here." Brian handed Melissa another sheet of paper from his folder. "Check the date and then read the description."

He watched as Melissa's eyes scanned the document, which was checkered with blacked-out sections but legible. Her eyes widened in disbelief. "This contradicts most of what the Major told us about the extraterrestrial nature of the Roswell crash. The craft was suspended from a balloon! We ought to take this to him and demand an explanation."

"There's more. You thought the Asian bodies with simultaneous progeria was a stretch. Do you know anything about progeria—ever come across it when you were studying for a medical career?"

"Only that it's very rare and makes people appear very old."

"Right, but progeria victims average between four and five feet in height, have enlarged bald heads, and are sometimes polydactyl."

"They have extra fingers and toes? No way."

"Afraid so. There's another type of progeria disorder, too, called Werner's syndrome. I did some checking online from one of the archive computers and discovered it affects adults and is the leading cause of premature aging."

"But that's most likely very rare as well."

"It is—in the U.S. Guess where eight hundred of the one thousand cases currently reported are found?"

"Not Japan."

"Bingo."

Melissa's eyes narrowed in concentration. Brian could tell she was probing everything she'd heard for weaknesses.

"I don't suppose you found anything that connects progeria sufferers with human experimentation, especially radiation testing, and then connected all that to Roswell or Paperclip?"

Brian smiled. "I love the way your mind works. So nice of you to ask." He handed several more pages to her. "I'm sure there's more. I just knew a few keywords on what to ask for and got some startling material."

Brian watched her skin flush and jaw tighten. He'd seen the look before.

"This report, dated one year before Roswell, in 1946, proves point-blank that the Army was using the German saucers just like you said. They were working with the Horten brothers."

"I know, but the next two were almost too good to be true—the FBI saying that flying saucers were a highly classified Army project, dated to August 1947 no less, and another 1947 document that talked about experiments on 'mutations' in extreme altitudes."

Melissa handed the pages back to Brian. She crossed her arms, unconsciously wiggling her foot, lost in thought.

Roswell
(1 page)

TELETYPE

FBI DALLAS   7-6-47   6-17 PM

DIRECTOR AND SAC, CINCINNATI   URGENT

FLYING DISC. INFORMATION CONCERNING.   HEADQUARTERS

EIGHTH AIR FORCE, TELEPHONICALLY ADVISED THIS OFFICE THAT AN OBJECT

PURPORTING TO BE A FLYING DISC WAS RE COVERED NEAR ROSWELL, NEW

MEXICO, THIS DATE. THE DISC IS HEXAGONAL IN SHAPE AND WAS SUSPENDED

FROM A BALLON BY CABLE, WHICH BALLON WAS APPROXIMATELY TWENTY

FEET IN DIAMETER.   FURTHER ADVISED THAT THE OBJECT

FOUND RESEMBLES A HIGH ALTITUDE WEATHER BALLOON WITH A RADAR

REFLECTOR, BUT THAT TELEPHONIC CONVERSATION BETWEEN THEIR OFFICE

AND WRIGHT FIELD HAD NOT   BORNE OUT THIS BELIEF. DISC AND

BALLOON BEING TRANSPORTED TO WRIGHT FIELD BY SPECIAL PLANE FOR EXAMINATI

INFORMATION PROVIDED THIS OFFICE BECAUSE OF NATIONAL INTEREST IN CASE

AND FACT THAT NATIONAL BROADCASTING COMPANY, ASSOCIATED PRESS, AND

OTHERS ATTEMPTING TO BREAK STORY OF LOCATION OF DISC TODAY.

ADVISED WOULD REQUEST WRIGHT FIELD TO ADVISE CINCINNATI

OFFICE RESULTS OF EXAMINATION. NO FURTHER INVESTIGATION BEING

CONDUCTED.

                    WYLY

END   RECORDED

CXXXX ACK IN ORDER   EX-29   JUL 22 1947

UA 92 FBI CI MJW

DPI M8

8-38 PM O

6-22 PM OK FBI WASH DC

OK FBI OK DC

SUMMARY REPORT
Report No. F-SU-1110-ND
Date   10 January 1946

HEADQUARTERS
AIR MATERIEL COMMAND
WRIGHT FIELD, DAYTON, OHIO

GERMAN FLYING WINGS DESIGNED
BY HORTEN BROTHERS

By

N. LeBlanc, Captain, Air Corps

Approved By:

Walter F. Nyblade

Walter F. Nyblade, Major, Air Corps
Chief, Aircraft Branch
Technical Section
Analysis Division
Intelligence (T-2)

For the Commanding General:

M. E. Goll

M. E. Goll, Lt Colonel, Air Corps
Acting Chief, Analysis Division
Intelligence (T-2)

1595

TO   :   D. M. LADD   DATE: August 19, 1947

FROM   :   E. G. FITCH

SUBJECT: FLYING DISCS

S.W. Reynolds

                                                             Aug. 19

        Special Agent ██████████ of the Liaison Section, while dis-
cussing the above captioned phenomena with Lieutenant Colonel ██████
of the Air Forces Intelligence, expressed the possibility that flying
discs were, in fact, a very highly classified experiment of the Army or
Navy. Mr. ██████ was very much surprised when Colonel ██████ not only
agreed that this was a possibility, but confidentially stated it was his
personal opinion that such was a probability. Colonel ██████ indicated
confidentially that a Mr. ██████ who is a scientist attached to the Air
Forces Intelligence, was of the same opinion.

        Colonel ██████ stated that he based his assumption on the
following: He pointed out that when flying objects were reported seen over
Sweden, the "high brass" of the War Department exerted tremendous pressure
on the Air Forces Intelligence to conduct research and collect information
in an effort to identify these sightings. Colonel ██████ stated that, in
contrast to this, we have reported sightings of unknown objects over the
United States, and the "high brass" appeared to be totally unconcerned.
He indicated this led him to believe that they knew enough about these
objects to express no concern. Colonel ██████ pointed out further that the
objects in question have been seen by many individuals who are what he
terms "trained observers," such as airplane pilots. He indicated also that
several of the individuals are reliable members of the community. He stated
it is his conclusion that these individuals saw something. He stated the
above has led him to come to the conclusion that there were objects seen
which somebody in the Government knows all about.

        Mr. ██████ pointed out to Colonel ██████ that if it is a fact
experimentations are being conducted by the United States Government, then it
does not appear reasonable to request the FBI to spend money and precious
time conducting inquiries with respect to this matter. Colonel ██████ stated
that he agreed with Mr. ██████ in this regard and indicated that it would be
extremely embarrassing to the Air Forces Intelligence if it later is learned
that these flying discs are, in fact, an experiment of the United States
Government.

        Mr. ██████ subsequently discussed this matter with Colonel L. R.
Forney of the Intelligence Division of the War Department. Colonel Forney
stated that he had discussed the matter previously with General Chamberlin.
Colonel Forney indicated to Mr. ██████ that he has the assurance of General

SWR:LL   EX-64   RECORDED   1 ∙ ∶ - 8 3 8 9 4
                                             INDEXED
1 SEP 29 1947 COPIES DESTROYED   14   31 SEP 23 1947
        270 NOV 13 1954

"Okay," she said after a few moments, "assuming the Roswell event wasn't extraterrestrial, and the government had Nazis on the payroll who were experimenting on the weakest elements of society, where does that leave us? If the Roswell bodies were human, that doesn't explain Adam, unless I'm missing some connection."

"No, you're right, it doesn't explain him. But what it does demonstrate is that we weren't given the truth during our briefing with Major Lindsay. I'd like to know why. After all, it's just like you said. Why not just say that Roswell was a Paperclip screw up like I suggested and follow that by saying that aliens were still real?"

"That question almost makes me question Adam's reality, but he was right there in the room scanning us, touching us. What if—"

"What if Andrew's right?"

"I ... I just don't know."

Melissa's train of thought was interrupted by a knock on Brian's door. Brian went to the door and opened it. It was Malcolm.

"Hey, Brian. Wait, she's here again?" he whispered when he saw Melissa over Brian's shoulder. "Man, I need to come over here and take notes sometime."

"Use the back of a stamp when you do," Brian muttered under his breath. "Come on in. I have something you'll want to see."

"Ditto. Either of you been online today?" he spoke up.

"Not on my room account. Melissa?"

She shook her head.

"Try it—*now*," he urged. "But you'd better sit down first."

55

All truths are easy to understand
once they are discovered.

—*Galileo Galilei*

"A page from the *USA Today* weather site? What's the big deal?" Brian wondered, looking away from his computer.

"I got the same thing in my inbox this morning from an unidentified sender. Look at the weather report."

"Hmm ... okay, two inches of snow ... *in Death Valley? Is* this for real?"

"Yeah, and that's not all," Malcolm said, looking at his watch. "Watch your screen ... it'll change in any second now."

"Whoa, what's going on?"

"What's the computer doing?" Melissa inquired, leaving the couch.

"It's some sort of executable file or pop-up that redirects your Internet browser to a specific site. There it goes!"

Brian watched closely as a second window opened, unsolicited, on his screen.

"And it wants us all to see this," said Brian, perusing the site.

A series of loud knocks echoed on Brian's door.

"I'll get it," Melissa volunteered.

"She knows your passcode?"

"Yeah, I gave it to her." Brian shrugged.

"I didn't get my wedding invitation."

"Cool it, Malcolm. Who is it, Melissa?" he called, still perusing the screen.

"You mean who isn't it," she replied.

Brian looked toward the door in time to watch the last of the civilian team members file into his room, including Neil.

"I was trying to find Malcolm," Mark spoke up. "He wasn't in his room, so I went down the row."

"We all came along when we realized we'd all gotten this," Deidre explained, waving the now familiar printout of the website.

"Give me a few minutes to read through it. Melissa can let you all in on what I discovered this morning. Neil, I hope you're ready for it."

Melissa shared the details of her conversation with Brian and his documentation while Brian read through the site sent to the team.

"This is incredible," said Neil, aghast at Brian's discovery. "But if Roswell was a prop—"

"What's HAARP?" Brian interrupted, turning toward the others.

"It stands for High-frequency Active Auroral Research Project," Neil said, his mind still reeling from Brian's revelation. "It's under my jurisdiction at the Department of Defense."

"I've heard of it," Malcolm declared. "The padre's suspicions on our plane ride back here just may be right."

"How is that?" asked Father Benedict. "What is this High-frequency—"

"HAARP," Mark said gravely, "the acronym is HAARP. I don't know much about it other than that, but when I read through the site, it scared the crap out of me."

"Wait a minute," said Neil. "I know what distresses *me* about it, but why are you so bothered if you don't know what it is?"

"Because of this," he announced, handing Neil the email he'd received from Kevin weeks ago. "Read it for everyone."

"There's no message, but the subject line reads g-a-k-o-n-a-a-k-h-a-r-p-k-e-v."

"What's 'gakonaakharpkev' ... however you'd say it?" Deidre asked, trying to put the letters together.

"It was from Kevin!" Father Benedict cried. "The last three letters are 'Kev.'"

"Right," confirmed Mark. "And the date and time show it was sent the morning he disappeared—and he was found in the High Frequency Auroral Room. Sound familiar?"

"Mother of God!" Andrew exclaimed.

"That isn't all," said Malcolm. "The date on our little weather report page is the same as that email. Kevin was obviously trying to tell you something—and we know what it was now."

Mark nodded. "The first eight letter are 'Gakona AK'—that's ground zero for HAARP. Kevin grew up in Alaska and knew all about HAARP. I'm guessing he misspelled the word in the next four consonants due to his trauma. He'd seen HAARP in action and was trying to warn us."

"What's this HAARP?" demanded Deidre.

"HAARP," Neil began, "is a ground-based Star Wars weapon system."

"Among other things," clarified Malcolm.

"One at a time, please," Father Benedict insisted.

Neil continued, "In the early days of what would become HAARP, the technology primarily focused on using the ionosphere as a sort of telecommunications shield. We discovered all our communications could be knocked out by magnetic storms, solar flares, or nuclear events, so we wanted a means to keep communication intact world-wide. Eventually, we developed the HAARP technology to protect us against that threat."

"So what's bad about that?"

"HAARP technology enables extremely low frequency radio waves to be sent through the earth itself, in addition to going through the iono-sphere. The goals in that case were submarine communications, as well as the ability to jam everyone else's communication abilities. It would also enable us to detect compliance with nuclear test bans worldwide."

"But it has other applications," said Malcolm. "My roommate at MIT was in atmospheric science and spent a summer internship in Alaska at the HAARP site. Like Neil said, it can send super-powerful radio waves into the ionosphere, an electrically-charged layer of the earth's atmo-sphere about forty or so miles above the earth's surface," Malcolm ex-plained.

"What does that do?" asked Melissa.

"When these radio waves are sent into the ionosphere in a very fo-cused beam," Malcolm elaborated, "specific areas of the ionosphere get heated up. These areas release electromagnetic waves back to the earth. The waves permeate everything in their path, whether it's dead or alive, and can cover a broad path or a very focused target."

"Depending on how the beam is manipulated," Neil broke in, "the electromagnetic pulse could be used as an explosive device."

"So, in other words," Brian rephrased his friend's explanation, "this antennae system I'm looking at on the screen could blow up large areas anywhere on the globe, or fire strategic pulses at other missiles in the sky—anywhere on earth?"

"Right—it's the Star Wars defense system, but on the ground."

"How powerful would these explosions be?" asked Deidre.

"Thermonuclear."

"I knew I shouldn't have asked."

"But what's the deal with the snow?" asked Brian.

"Well, what else happens up there in the atmosphere?" Malcolm asked rhetorically.

"Weather," Deidre droned. "It can affect the weather, can't it?"

"You got it."

"HAARP technology has been used experimentally for rain production and lightning and hurricane control," Neil informed the team. "Those projects were called Skyfire and Stormfury. Theoretically, it could also be used to heat the globe ... or damage the protective ozone layer over an enemy territory."

"Theoretically, my ass!" Mark snarled. "Kevin tried to tell us they had access to this thing here. They could cause or even fake any sort of climate disaster."

"But why would they?" Brian questioned.

"The point may not be the weather modification," Father Benedict said, his head lowered in thought. "They could kill crops and blame it on alien retaliation against our food supply."

"There are two other things HAARP can do—theoretically," Malcolm said accusingly, looking at the undersecretary.

"Dear God," Neil mumbled to himself, "I can't believe they'd do this." Before anyone could react, he turned and headed for the door.

"Neil!" Brian called. "What are you doing?"

"This has to end—today!" he said angrily and carded himself out.

"Look out, Colonel," Deidre said, shaking her head.

"So what else can this thing do, Malcolm?" Father Benedict urged.

"Well, it can cause perceptual distortion and mental disruption in humans."

"Mind control?" The priest gasped.

"That's a little strong," Malcolm said seriously, "but President Carter's former national security adviser, Zbigniew Brzezinski, did say he wanted to use it to create what he called 'a more controlled and directed society.' Scary stuff."

"This is unbelievable," Brian said, reading another portion of the site. "We actually have a machine that can modify weather ... and influence people's mental states?"

"You said two things. What else could they do with it?" Deidre pressed.

"There are scientists who have suggested that images could be projected on the ionosphere when you heat up."

"Images?" Mark wondered aloud. "Like in pictures?"

"Yeah ... you could sort of transform the sky into a screen ... theoretically. It's like something out of a Bond movie."

"So, what I'm hearing," Melissa said, "is that someone using this device could project whatever they wanted right onto the sky."

"Yeah ... and I think we're both tracking on what might be the double feature. Anyone for *Independence Day?*"

"I don't like how this is shaping up," said Father Benedict. "Ready-made catastrophes? Projecting images on the sky? Mental manipulation? ... *Mother of God, no!*"

All eyes turned to Father Benedict and his horrified expression. The priest seemed absolutely stunned.

"Benedict ... you blind fool!" the priest berated himself.

"What is it, Andrew?" Brian asked.

"*Gottlieb* ... The dying soldier wasn't telling me 'God loves' in German. He was giving me a *name!*"

56

Everything comes gradually
and at its appointed hour.

—Ovid

"You're telling me that the CIA had an official mind-control program?" Brian looked at Father Benedict skeptically.

"Believe it," said Melissa. "I've even read some of the congressional testimony on the program."

"It's true. It was known as MK-Ultra. Sidney Gottlieb was the former director of the program."

"Oh, God," gasped Deidre. "I know that name, too. Some of my military abduction survivors have used it. This is all going someplace I don't want to go."

Malcolm paced the room, head down, concentrating on a perspective that had begun to suggest itself in light of the new disclosures. "The bodies ... what about the bodies?" he asked, loud enough for the others to hear. He suddenly stopped, a disturbed look etched on his face.

"I hate to sound like I've turned to Father Benedict's side here," Malcolm said anxiously, "but what if the Roswell story and now this HAARP revelation aren't the only deceptions in play here? What if the biology is bogus as well? What if the bodies were phony?"

"No way," Mark objected. "We both went over the stuff in Marcus' lab. He let us conduct any inquiry we wanted. You can't fake DNA."

"Not in the sense of making DNA that isn't real DNA." Malcolm's energy grew as he thought aloud. "However"—Malcolm stopped and looked at Mark—"DNA can be created."

"You mean cloning?"

"No, I mean designing DNA to one's own specifications—not just replication." He resumed pacing around the room, engaged in a silent intellectual struggle.

"I've never heard of such a thing. You're dreaming, Malcolm."

"Then I'm in the right place," Malcolm mused distantly. "This is dreamland, isn't it?"

"Just what are you talking about?" Melissa pressed him. "Out with it."

Malcolm slowed his gait and then paused. He stared straight ahead at the wall he was facing, as though receiving some unexpected revelation from it, mentally locking the last pieces of the fantastic puzzle together.

"Nanotechnology," Mark finally said.

"What's that?" Deidre queried.

"In simplest terms, the science of the extremely small," he answered.

The team exchanged confused glances.

"Nanotechnology is a field that combines physics, chemistry, biochemistry, and engineering. It's the attempt to create machines that are no bigger than a molecule—or three or four of them across, the actual width of a nanometer—that's one-billionth of a meter."

"Are you serious? Can we really do that?" Deidre asked.

"Yes, on both counts. I took a couple courses in nanotech in grad school."

"You're telling us that we can actually build working, molecular-level machines?" Brian marveled.

"It's true—although the smallest I've ever witnessed was only as small as a strand of DNA."

"Oh, that's comforting," cracked Melissa.

"Your sarcasm is well-placed," Father Benedict said stoically. "If this kind of science is in our grasp, we'll be our own gods."

"What do you mean?" Brian asked.

"You have to understand what this kind of thing would mean if perfected," Malcolm explained. "Nanotechnology is molecular manufacturing, a process that involves building things one molecule at a time. Imagine a super computer no bigger than a cell. Theoretically, anything composed of matter could be assembled at that level artificially. Since we know how molecules are stuck together and in what combinations to form the elements, any chemical compound could be programmed into a computer the size of a nanometer, and the computer would assemble the compound. You could put some of these nanocomputers into a glass of water, and when the person drank it, the machines could be turned on by a remote control to, say, find a cancerous tumor in the stomach and zap it—disassemble the tumor into molecules and eliminate it."

"Or tell the little workhorse to manufacture nutrients in dead soil, producing arable land," Mark suggested, considered the implications, "or even materialize food on your table?"

"Yes! What's really wild is if such computers could be triggered by voice recognition software, you could just speak and things would materialize. 'Let there be pizza!' Nanotechnology is the principle behind the replicator technology in Star Trek. The possibilities really are endless."

"You could heal any disease, even reverse cell deterioration and hence aging," Melissa pondered. "It's positively ..."

"Godlike," Andrew said grimly. "Or how about putting the right nanoprobes into the air or water so that only people of a certain race would contract a fatal disease?"

"Always looking on the bright side," Deidre said facetiously.

"If I've thought of it," Andrew scowled, "I'm not the first. And I might add," he commented, "that this kind of technology is another artificial method of reproduction, in a manner of speaking."

Brian looked at the old priest, knowing where he was going with the observation.

"You're suggesting," Brian turned to Malcolm, his mind racing through the events of the past few days, "that the alien beings we saw were made of real organic ... stuff ... complete with unique DNA, all manufactured with the aid of this technology?"

"Only theoretically. Such advanced applications aren't reality yet."

"Yeah, like everything else we've seen around here," Melissa remarked.

"And these nanoprobes could be introduced to the body in a variety of ways—like ingestion, in your example?" asked Brian.

"Sure."

"Is there any obstacle to saying that nanotechnology could rebuild muscles and nerves?" he asked apprehensively.

"Nope. Like I said, anything that can be broken down to molecules could be reproduced if the atomic and molecular composition of the object was already known or determinable. You could manufacture anything out of thin air—although there would be more there than air; you just couldn't see it."

Brian looked at Melissa, whose speechless expression told him immediately that she had followed his thoughts, and then back at Malcolm.

"What would it take to materialize a human body?" he continued. His mouth had become suddenly dry.

"At least a thorough knowledge of the biochemistry of the human body ... the human genome ... a person's specific DNA sequence ..."

"I know we're in the realm of science fiction here—" Brian began.

"I think this place has a zip code there," cracked Deidre.

"—but the nanotechnology idea holds a lot of explanatory power for what Melissa and I experienced. I'm willing to bet that Melissa's visitor staged that brief demonstration to show us what could be done here. It certainly got my attention."

"That's wild ... but possible—if the technology exists."

"Would these nanoprobes be at all traceable?"

"Sure. All you'd need is an atomic resolution microscope that could image individual atoms. We have one here in the lab we use. Why do you ask?" He read the expression on Brian's face. "Oh, wow ... now that's a little less fantastic—and checkable."

"Let's go."

57

You get tragedy where the tree,
instead of bending, breaks.

—*Ludwig Wittgenstein*

Brian, Melissa, Mark, and Malcolm hurried toward the lab, moving as quickly but inconspicuously as they could, each of them filled with a mixture of expectancy and dread. Father Benedict had chosen to pass on the trip. The Gottlieb revelation had shaken him, and he needed time to think. He and Deidre had gone back to her room to look through her research on what abductees had said about being mentally controlled.

The small contingent arrived at the lab without incident.

"You're sure Hastings injected you in the left arm on the way to Mount Weather?" Malcolm asked, preparing to take some of Brian's blood.

"Absolutely—he stuck me when we got there, too. Every other time I took it in the butt. It had to be deliberate."

"Maybe. Only one way to find out ... make a fist."

Malcolm found a vein, inserted the needle into Brian's arm, and withdrew the sample.

"What do you think you'll find?" asked Melissa. "Do you know what you're looking for?"

"Anything unusual," he answered, mounting the slide. "We'll probably know right away."

"This would be unbelievable." Melissa shook her head. "Shooting into you nanoprobes that restored your arm? This place is starting to scare me. How do you know what's even real? What was Adam doing with you if you're right? He had to be real. I didn't imagine getting my head filled with a nonexistent presence. He was in there."

"Jackpot, folks," Malcolm said, peering into the scope. "Want to take a look at the impossible, Mark?"

"Amazing!" Mark exclaimed as he watched tiny, bumpy structures floating across the slide. "Those things are machines?"

"Nanomachines. Each bump is a single molecule. Not something you're born with, for sure."

"And their job is what?" asked Melissa, taking a look.

"My guess is that these reassemble muscle, tissue, blood, cartilage, skin—everything necessary for a functioning, restored appendage, and all programmed to put everything where it belongs."

"Fantastic!" Brian said.

"And proof," a voice behind them said, "that we've all been used." Neil closed the door behind him, having let himself in unnoticed. The undersecretary stood before them, unmoving, a look of bewildered desperation on his sweat-streaked face.

"What is it, Neil?" Brian asked, backing away from the microscope.

"Uh, Brian," Mark observed in a hushed tone, "your friend has a gun."

Their collective attention moved quickly down to the semi-automatic pistol in Neil's hand.

"It also has a silencer," Melissa managed quietly, her mouth becoming suddenly dry.

"I never intended for things to turn out this way," he said to Brian, his voice filled with regret. "I didn't know ... you have to believe me," he pleaded.

"I do, Neil," Brian said, trying to stay calm. "Why don't you put the gun away and tell us what the problem is? I think we'd all feel a lot better if you did."

"I believed the Colonel ... and the Group," Neil continued, recounting the events that had brought them together. "I needed you here. It was too much for me to handle, and I knew you would have the answers. Turns out you had too many ..."

"Why don't you tell us what you know," Brian said, trying to reason with him.

"I didn't know ..." Neil repeated, looking around the room, his eyes betraying an inner panic. "I'm so sorry."

"What kind of trouble are you in, Neil?" Melissa asked gently. "Let us help you. We need to stick together."

"Trouble? I'm in no trouble," he growled, suddenly turning antagonistic. "It's humanity that's in trouble ... all because of them ... and *you!*" he bellowed at Melissa.

"Me?"

"Neil, what are you talking about? We can deal with whatever crisis you see coming," Brian tried again, but he could see his friend slowly slipping toward the point of random impulse.

"No, you can't! You don't understand. She's the key to their plans."

"You!" Melissa blurted out. "It's been you all this time! You're the one who's been trying to kill me."

Neil hesitated, as though even at this point he could absolve himself of guilt, as though he could avoid the indictment of his comrades' gaze.

"I can't believe it!" Brian moaned in despair.

"It's true ... I never meant for you to get hurt, Brian ... you know that."

Brian could only stare in shock at the man who'd mentored him, who'd been his surrogate father, his friend.

"I'd arranged to take a later flight that morning ... I sabotaged the second jeep and ordered the MP to make sure you were the one left behind waiting," he said, staring at Melissa. "I knew I'd have to kill him later to avoid detection, but that was of little consequence compared to what I'd learned had to be done. I was inside ... taking care of the other MP with the dogs when the first jeep left. I thought you were on it, Brian. I had no idea you'd overslept. Once I'd let the dogs outside, there was nothing I could do."

"But why?"

"It's in here," he said, reaching into his lapel pocket.

Seizing the opportunity, Mark bolted for the armed man. Neil tried to sidestep his advance, but Mark deftly grabbed Neil's gun hand by the wrist. The two of them struggled for control of the weapon. Mark stuck his hand in the undersecretary's face and began to push him toward the wall, and the two of them careened into a table. His balance upset, Mark slipped and pulled Neil down on top of himself. Neither man surrendered his grip.

Neil suddenly gained the upper hand, rolling on top of Mark, but leaving his own back unprotected. Malcolm took a step toward the scuffling duo, but by that time Neil had jammed his free elbow into his adversary's face. The pain caused Mark to lose his hold for a few seconds, but it was all the opening his killer needed. The three onlookers watched in horror as the graying man fired off two rounds into the prone scientist.

"What are you doing?" Brian shrieked in disbelief.

Neil got to his knees and then his feet. He wiped his brow and staggered toward them.

"You just murdered a man!" Brian screamed at him. "Are you insane?"

"No ..." he gasped, catching his breath. "You'll understand when you read this." He reached once again into his suit coat and pulled out an envelope.

Brian didn't move.

"Take it!" Neil shouted.

Brian obeyed.

"Put it away, out of sight!" Neil insisted. "You mustn't let anyone see it."

Brian again complied, folding the envelope and inserting it into his pocket.

"Now," Neil said, straightening himself and gathering his resolve. "It's time to finish what they've started."

Neil raised his weapon and aimed it at Melissa, but before he could squeeze the trigger, Brian stepped into the line of fire.

"Get out of the way, Brian!" Neil demanded, lowering the weapon to his waist.

"No."

"I said get out of the way! They have to be stopped! You know the power they have."

"Neil, my arm wasn't healed by Adam—that's why we're here."

"I know that!" he snapped, becoming agitated once again. "I heard the whole thing. I'm not talking about that little charade, I'm talking about your research. You were right ... now stand aside!"

"I'm not moving," he said resolutely, feeling for Melissa behind him. "You'll have to shoot me."

Neil closed his eyes in anguish; terror and regret mingled in his face.

"I love you, Brian," he said, opening his eyes, "but it's better for only one more to die, even if it's you, than millions."

Brian swallowed hard. Neil raised the pistol and took aim. A shot pierced the tense silence, followed by an explosion of glass. Brian, Melissa, and Malcolm saw part of Neil's skull hit the wall adjacent to where he stood. Neil was dead before he hit the floor. The Colonel and his entourage carded the door and burst into the room.

58

One death is a tragedy.
A million deaths is a statistic.

—*Josef Stalin*

"I'm sorry for your loss, Dr. Scott," a disoriented Brian vaguely heard over the crunch of glass under the soldier's boots. "I know he was a good friend. I just wish I had an explanation for his behavior. We had no choice."

Brian wiped the tears from his face and looked up at the Colonel from where he sat on the floor, his back against one of the walls of the lab, staring at the floor between his knees. The officer looked uneasily into his eyes, unsure of what else to add.

"I know," Brian acknowledged and resumed his position. He was still in shock. What could have driven Neil so relentlessly over the edge that he'd not only been willing to kill, but to kill *him*?

"Brian ..." Melissa's familiar voice beckoned gently.

"Better not get too close," he mumbled a warning. "People who spend too much time around me tend to wind up dead."

"Don't talk like that."

"It's true," he sniffed. "Those who don't excuse themselves from my life voluntarily get removed somehow or another."

"I'm not going anywhere."

"Then you're not as bright as I thought you were."

"Enough!" she scolded him. "You're the one who told me that everything happens for a reason. The universe doesn't revolve around you any more than it does me."

Brian said nothing, stung more by her words than by his own thrown back at him. He couldn't tell her how unjust he felt this latest twist of fate was, either. He had only to recall her own experience to know she was right. It just didn't help.

"This is just really ... hard to take."

"I know," she comforted him, then sat down next to him and took hold of his arm. "I know what betrayal feels like."

"I guess I do feel some of that, but … somehow I don't feel like he looked at me any differently than usual. What could compel him to make that kind of decision—and what about what he said, that millions would die if you lived? It's just lunacy."

"I think you need to face up to the fact that Neil just cracked for some reason. You saw how agitated and distressed he was. Something inside just snapped."

"But why?"

"It doesn't make sense because there's no sense to it. He just reached the breaking point."

"How's Malcolm?" he asked, changing the subject.

"Fine. He just needed something to calm his nerves. They already took him back to his room."

"How are you?" he followed.

"A scratch or two from the glass, but fine thanks to you—again. How often do you think you're going to have to save my life?"

"I'd say until you learn not to bother with me."

"I wouldn't give you the satisfaction. Now enough of the whimpering. We'll get through this."

"You don't take any prisoners, do you?"

"Never have." Her smile somehow reassured him. "And I'm not going to start now. Speaking of prisoners," she noted, gazing across the room, "I overheard the Colonel muttering something about confining us. It looks like he's giving the marching orders to those two Marines."

Brian followed her glance and observed the grim-faced Colonel instructing two MPs and pointing to the two of them.

"I don't trust him, Brian."

"Why would you believe that part of what Neil said?"

"I don't need Neil's word on him. I haven't trusted him from the beginning."

"Better zip it," Brian advised, taking notice of the Colonel's deliberate strides in their direction. He was followed closely by the two sentries.

"These two Marines will escort you both back to Brian's room and will stand guard outside," the Colonel informed them. They exchanged a puzzled glance.

"It isn't permanent, obviously," he continued, "but this isn't over yet. I hope you recall that Neil had nothing to do with Kevin's death. Then there's Melissa's unexpected visitor. We've still got trouble, so I want the two of you together. At least I know I can trust you," he added, looking at Brian.

"Colonel," Melissa broke in, "how did you know we were in trouble with Neil?"

"We've been tracking him by means of his cardkey for most of the day," he answered. "We suspected he was the one who'd tried to kill you in the cafeteria, but we were waiting for proof. It took a bit longer than I'd expected, but we got it."

"What made you suspect him?" Brian asked.

"Lack of alternatives, initially. Only he and Deidre were with Melissa, and Deidre saved her life. What bothered me was the fact that anyone in the cafeteria could have wound up with the pie. Having nowhere else to look, we guessed that despite the randomness of it all, he was somehow connected to the incident."

"But the kitchen staff said no one had used their equipment," noted Melissa.

"He didn't have to. I gave him a day's leave while you two were still at Groom Lake. He lives less than thirty miles from Mount Weather. He also had access to the dossier we'd collected on you. We had his kitchen examined for evidence this morning and found a partially used bottle of peanut oil there. We got the results of the fingerprinting this afternoon. We still didn't know absolutely if the evidence was more than circumstantial," the Colonel added, "since it wouldn't have been strange to find his prints on any item in his own kitchen, but we kept watch on him anyway. We didn't think he'd try anything in Brian's room because he had no weapon. Once he left there and went back to his own room, we figured something was up. We followed him to the lab, and the rest you know."

"But how did he do it—the pie, I mean?"

"My best guess is, knowing the pie would be on the serving line at lunch, he was one of the first in line to make sure he'd get a piece. He took a calculated risk that no one else would have the same food allergy. He had nothing to lose by leaving the piece for you, hoping you'd take it. He couldn't very well offer it to you since that would amount to self-incrimination. He more or less engineered the circumstances where you would be vulnerable. If you didn't go for it, nothing would be lost, but if you did ..."

"Does everyone else know about this yet?"

"No. Once we trailed Neil to the lab, we confined Father Benedict and Dr. Harper to her room. They don't know why yet. You two are being put under the same protection as well. No one is allowed entrance. If anyone who's authorized by me wants in, they can use their own card. You're also not to leave under any circumstances until I say so. Is that understood?"

They both nodded.

"Good. *Marines!*" The two armed MPs snapped to readiness. "Get these people out of here."

The two guards accompanied Brian and Melissa to his room. Brian swiped his card silently and entered his access code.

"So where do we go from here?" she muttered as the door closed behind them.

"No idea," he answered, flicking the light switch. Nothing happened.

"Wonderful," she complained.

"Convenient is much more accurate." The familiar male voice resonated from the blackness in Melissa's ear. "Don't either of you move," the voice warned, accompanied by the double-click of his weapon.

59

The nations of the world will have to unite,
for the next war will be an interplanetary war.
The nations of the earth must some day make a common
front against attack by people from other planets.

—General Douglas MacArthur,
New York Times, October 9, 1955

"If you're going to kill us," Melissa said angrily, "at least have the courage to let us know who you are."

A nightlight on the wall in the adjacent kitchenette space allowed Brian and Melissa to distinguish the form of a man standing across the room next to Brian's desk.

"Just sit on the couch and listen, Miss Kelley. You of all people should know I have no intention of harming either of you, unless of course you give me no choice. Hello, Dr. Scott. I'm sorry we haven't been formally introduced."

"What do you want this time?" Melissa demanded.

"I'm here to try and get your butts off this base. It's the least I can do."

"Why do we need to get out of here so urgently?" Brian asked.

"Weren't you listening to your friend before they shot him? You've been used. The Colonel cannot be trusted."

"Since you were listening—and I'd like to know how you managed that," Melissa remarked, "you know my would-be assassin is dead. I'm no longer in danger."

"True, your would-be assassin *is* dead, and you aren't in any immediate danger. I never said the Colonel meant you harm, only that you can't trust him."

"That makes no sense," Brian insisted. "Okay, we won't trust him, but why do we have to leave?"

"Because," he hesitated, "... I owe it to both of you."

"I want to know who you are." Melissa stood up defiantly.

"No!" he shouted.

Their eyes adjusted; they could now see clearly enough to recognize that the man had pointed his gun at his own head. Melissa stopped, startled by the threat.

"Not until you hear what I have to say. Take one more step and you'll never know why you were brought here. I swear I'll shoot."

Melissa reluctantly sat down again. "Who are you?"

"I'll get to that. Right now, I need to tell you what I know—and quickly. You may find it useful in the future, assuming you have one. You were both brought here because the Group wanted a team of experts to be convinced that the disclosure of an extraterrestrial reality was imminent."

"We already know that," Brian noted.

"You know what they want you to know—their façade, their grand illusion to conceal their true intention. You don't have any idea what the real truth is. There is no extraterrestrial threat. They just need you to believe that."

"Then all the documentation about UFOs was phony?" Brian asked.

"No ... actually, that's all quite real."

"Then, how—"

"If you'll allow me to finish ..."

"Fine."

"Our government has indeed possessed technology for fantastic saucer craft since the mid-1940s. But, as you assumed early on, Dr. Scott, this technology was an outgrowth of Operation Paperclip."

"So it's entirely human."

"I'm no longer sure."

"I thought you said there was no extraterrestrial threat?" said Melissa.

"Pay better attention. The threat that you were told about is a fabrication. Whether there are real extraterrestrials is another matter."

"But—"

"Your questions will be answered if you don't interrupt. I won't give you another chance to do so. I don't have time for impertinent interruptions—and neither do you."

"Okay."

"I've been a member of the organization you know as the Group for the last six years. The Group is actually the current version of the organization responsible for the control of information about UFOs in this country—Majestic 12. Several of the documents you were shown refer to it. The documentation trail regarding UFOs is just as Major Lindsay described."

"No—he was lying."

"Yes, I know."

Brian and Melissa exchanged confused glances.

"As you discovered this morning, Dr. Scott, all the UFO documentation, though genuine, is subject to interpretation and does not necessarily yield the conclusions the Major steered you toward. There are contradictions because not everyone, even at high levels, knew what was going on. Not even Truman knew how Paperclip was being used by insiders to get the kind of criminals he didn't want recruited into the program.

"For what it's worth, Dr. Scott, your scenario of events is the truth. Paperclip scientists were nearly caught red handed in human experimentation that day and had to invent a cover story. The orchestrated myth that we had an alien craft on our hands not only deflected attention away from the truth, but it also served later on to disinform the Russians. The MJ-12 documents and other items you'll find in the archives are absolutely real, but some contain deliberate disinformation designed to convince the Russians that we could not actually be creating the exotic flying craft witnesses were seeing. By producing genuine documents and expertly making sure Russian spies got pieces of their contents, we led the Russians to believe that the saucer technology was as much of a mystery to us as it was to them."

"So are there any real aliens?" Melissa asked.

"It would seem so ..."

"So what does that mean?"

"Just what it sounds like, Dr. Kelley. A few weeks ago I would have said no. But things have changed. The thing that killed Dr. Garvey wasn't a Gray, and after listening to your presentation, Dr. Scott, I can't say for sure it was from another planet either."

"You *saw* Kevin killed?"

"Yes. I was the one who sent him to the Auroral Room and gave him access. What happened there was something I couldn't anticipate. I was hiding in the room when Garvey arrived. I had to make sure he understood that we had functioning HAARP technology at our disposal. This ... *creature* ... just materialized out of nowhere and squeezed the life out of him without even touching him. It was the most frightening thing I've ever seen."

"Are you sure it wasn't a Gray?"

"Don't insult me, Dr. Scott. Whatever it was, it was tall and powerful-looking. I know what a Gray is ... we make them."

"*What?*"

"We have the technology to manufacture the bodies—and they're actually alive. That's why the DNA in Marcus' lab was real. We not only can create such things, but we can materialize them at will through nanotechnology. We're a couple decades ahead of private industry in both genome manipulation and nanotech. Your colleague Dr. Bradley guessed that much."

"I don't believe you. How can you create life? We're not gods."

"Depends on how you define 'create,' Dr. Kelley. Tell me, what would you get if you cloned a human being?"

"A human being."

"Exactly. And you not only get something biologically human—which, of course, is determined by the DNA sequence—but you also get *sentience* and *intelligence*. Those properties are biologically transferable. Just as when a man and woman create a child the old fashioned way, the brain function and conscious life are contained in the genetics of what's been conceived.

"Nanotechnology just accelerates growth and development. We clone human cells, manipulate the genetic sequence, add a few interesting things, and *voila!* We get a sentient being that both looks like the standard Gray and is genetically related to humans. We take great care to retard their higher brain function and make them docile. We just need them for demonstrations now and again, or as eventual proof for convincing people of intelligent panspermia—that they created us, so we're really all just one big, happy family. Since we have the recipe for one Gray, we can now crank them out as we wish."

"Nice to know you aren't hindered by things like ethics," Brian said.

"The bodies—*our* bodies—in each other's rooms. You did that?"

"Yes, Dr. Kelley. That was your demonstration. If you had turned your respective 'partner' over, you would likely have noticed some imperfections. We can't duplicate things like hair styles and certain facial realities. You both need to realize that there's technology here to fake just about anything imaginable. The Group could produce real, irrefutable biological evidence of ET life or use ionospheric technology to visually fake an alien armada. It's easy. Haven't you ever read *Childhood's End?*"

They shook their heads.

"Wait a minute," Melissa said. "When Father Benedict asked for the logs to be checked, they indicated that no one had entered our rooms after we went in the night before. So how could you have done that?"

"The logs were never checked. He was lying to you."

His words stunned Brian and Melissa into silence.

"If you're wondering why he would lie to you, you'll have to ask him that, assuming you ever see him again. As for my little ruse, after you went to bed I had some knockout gas piped into your rooms to make sure you wouldn't awaken when I went into your rooms and planted the nanomaterial. Simple."

"What about the smell?" Melissa asked.

"The nano-assembly or 'body' had a timed deconstruction cycle programmed into the nano-replicating nanomachines. They essentially reversed the replication process. When the nanomaterial undergoes compositional breakdown, it gives off the slight odor you detected. If you had seen this happen it would merely look like the body was gradually disappearing before your eyes.

"The biggest risk in all this was that the body would break down into its molecular constituents before you woke up. I didn't care if you handled it or saw the body wasn't alive, just so long as you discovered it. The method I chose was sure to—pardon the pun—bring you together shortly afterward, so even if you thought you had a dead body in bed after you saw each other that day, you'd know that wasn't the case. Only Dr. Kelley would be able to process what had happened since I told her it was coming. The whole point was to give you and your colleagues a visual demonstration of what was possible."

"Mission accomplished."

"So you guys created Adam?" Brian asked, still shaken by Andrew's lie.

The mysterious visitor hesitated. "Probably ..."

Brian and Melissa couldn't miss the uncertainty in his voice. "But what?"

"I can't explain the mind scans. The Grays I know about couldn't do that, and we've used Adam before. They actually can't do much of anything, but they're so visually compelling that it doesn't matter. The plan was to keep you occupied in the conference room until the nanoprobes did their thing. We showed Adam your picture and told him to touch your arm at least once. Where the mind scans came from I don't know. I've been wondering if the thing that killed Garvey had something to do with it."

"What did it look like?"

"It was huge ... easily seven feet tall, maybe eight. I wasn't that close. The skin had a dark tan color. The head was sort of triangular, too, but it moved like a human."

Brian swallowed hard. "What was the Group's plan for all this—other than to make us believe their scenario?" he asked.

"The Group's ultimate plan is to militarize space. To justify that they need an enemy—and an enemy that will only cooperate or negotiate with them."

"What do you mean?"

"An alien threat justifies exotic weaponry in space, along with closed communications. An alien that the world thinks will only listen to a group of twelve men—men that supposedly have been standing in the gap protecting earth for fifty years—justifies global martial law and consolidation of power in those twelve men. All that you've seen here are elements that could make that possible.

"You can both imagine the impact of an ET reality and understand how 'reasonable' what I've just told you would be. This is about a power grab and the end of free society. Even in America—in our post-9/11 Homeland Security reality, the means of dictatorial control are in place. Banking, food supply, housing, travel, education, labor, the Internet, and so on—it could all be controlled and taken away through technology and centralized communications. If an alien invasion were projected on the sky worldwide and the 'aliens' said, 'Put these guys in charge or we're invading,' sooner or later there would be compliance. All that's missing is the catalyst. We could fake Armageddon if we wanted to."

"How did Dr. Bandstra's desire to kill me mesh with his goal of undermining the project?" Melissa inquired.

"I'm not sure what you mean."

"The mole on our team, you said his goal was undermining the project."

"Bandstra isn't the mole."

"What? Who is?"

"I'm not sure it even matters now since Bandstra went postal. He didn't know what the Group's true agenda was. I have no idea why he was so hell-bent on killing you."

"So why are you telling us all this? What's in it for you?"

Brian's question was met with eerie silence. He looked over at Melissa, whose stare was riveted on the shadowy figure.

"I have grown," the stranger finally spoke, "to despise the Group and what it stands for."

"But you could take them down without helping us?"

"Yes ... I could."

"So why didn't you?"

"Stand up, both of you," the man ordered from the darkness. "The time has come," he said cryptically, the gleam of his pistol catching their eyes.

Brian and Melissa complied apprehensively.

"Here's my personal passkey—the access code is 9663—and a rough floor plan of the entire base," he said, throwing the items on the floor at Brian's feet. "The way out is marked. It's a very convoluted route, since I've marked those doors that do not require a retina or palm scan. I can't guarantee you'll make it, but at least you have a chance. There's a jeep waiting topside at the final door. If you get out without alerting security, your own clearance badges will be good enough to get through the gate checks. It's the best I can do."

"Why don't you just walk us out?" Brian asked.

"Because I'll be dead."

"What's that supposed to mean?"

"It means I won't be alive—what do you think it means?"

"Are you going to shoot yourself?" Melissa asked.

"No ... one of you is."

"I don't think so," scoffed Melissa.

"You must be nuts," Brian added. "There's no way we're going to do anything like that."

"I think you'll fight for the job," he said, moving to the other side of Brian's desk. "You didn't ask me why I've come to despise the Group as I do. I hate them because of what they've had me do for them, how they've dehumanized me in return for their precious secrets. I guess the simplest way to explain why I'm doing this is ... guilt."

Brian and Melissa exchanged confused glances.

"I know it's impossible to make amends—it takes a despicable man to do despicable things. I'm sorry, Melissa ... for everything." He turned on the light on the desk, exposing his face.

Melissa gasped and stumbled backward. "This just isn't possible ... *oh my God!*"

60

In taking revenge, a man is but even with his enemy;
but in passing it over, he is superior.

—*Sir Francis Bacon*

"You bastard!" Melissa seethed, finally recovered from the jolt.

"You know this guy?" Brian asked in amazement.

"His name is Greg ... Greg Sheppard, my high school boyfriend turned rapist." Melissa turned away, her hand on her forehead, trying to process the turn of events.

Brian stared incredulously at the uniformed officer.

"After Penn State, I took my officer's commission," he informed them dispassionately. "I spent most of my time overseas, actually. I eventually wound up working in intelligence and Special Forces, serving under General Stanford Hartwig. He's now the leader of MJ-12. Six years ago he recruited me into the Group."

He watched Melissa closely. "When I saw your name on the list of targeted experts," he continued, "I couldn't believe it was actually you. If it sounds more consistent with my character, you should know I didn't decide then to help you. I knew you were going to be on the team for weeks and didn't care. It was only when I read the MJ-12 briefing on Dr. Scott that I began to think about the course of my life. You must understand, Dr. Scott," he turned his attention to Brian, "you've been watched from a distance for years, back to when you were in graduate school."

"That can't be right."

"It is. You went to the same church near D.C. as Dr. Bandstra. The Group had an early interest in him since he was viewed as an up-and-comer in defense policy. They planted several people in that church to get to know him, what he really thought outside the office. One happened to hear you give a lecture on your views of the divine image.

282

You mentioned its application to extraterrestrial life. That was enough to open a file on you."

"Why would that make any difference?" Brian could feel his own anger rising as he remembered the injustice of Melissa's story. His words about forgiveness echoed faintly in his mind, but he felt a loathing for the source of her suffering.

"It's simple, Dr. Scott. I see in you ... what I might have been—what I should have been but can now never be. I know you feel that you have little to show for your journey, but you have something I can never have again: integrity. You see," he said, straightening his uniform and standing erect, "what I did to Melissa wasn't the most heinous crime I've ever committed. When I read your file, the names of your parents leaped off the page."

"Why?" Brian asked, locking eyes with the officer. The odd feeling that he'd seen the face before troubled him.

"It's what pushed me to act against the Group. In my work with MJ-12 I was periodically assigned to eliminate obstacles to the Group's goals. Typically that meant intimidating UFO witnesses or researchers. Occasionally I was assigned to arrange the untimely demise of someone whose work threatened our technological monopoly or our secrecy. I never questioned the Group's decisions. I believed I was on the front lines of keeping the country secure by insuring our position of technological superiority. But the day I saw your file and read about you, I realized that I had been used to take innocent lives. Look at me closely, Dr. Scott. I'm the man who murdered your parents."

Brian gawked at the officer in utter disbelief, jaw wide open. Lieutenant Sheppard moved a step closer and removed his hat. Slowly his facial features visually harmonized with Brian's memories of the convenience store videotape. He *was* the gunman.

"I know it doesn't matter now, but you should know what I think is the real reason the Group wanted your parents eliminated. You had a strong relationship with Dr. Bandstra, whose position in the Department of Defense was deemed advantageous to the Group's long-term goals. Your unique skill set became ideal, even vital, to the plan for conditioning the populace to embrace an ET reality. I believe the Group found it favorable to emotionally isolate you, to make you more emotionally dependent on Dr. Bandstra. I'm sorry I didn't question their order."

"'Found it *favorable*'?" Brian said bitterly, his dumbfounded expression giving way to pent up rage. "The Group 'found it favorable' to just murder innocent people in cold blood so they could more effectively use me?" he shouted at the officer.

"Yes," the Lieutenant answered, holding up his firearm to make sure the safety was off. The weapon was the only thing keeping Brian where he stood.

Melissa moved silently to Brian's side, her mind suddenly captured by Brian's trauma.

"You're absolutely gutless!" Brian seethed through clenched teeth. "I could just—"

"Kill me?" the Lieutenant seized the opening. "I was hoping you would have as much contempt for my life as you do. I have no expectation that you would forgive me, and I don't deserve any compassion. Besides, there would be nothing to gain. I'm a dead man already. Coming here at this time sealed my fate."

"Why is that?" Melissa asked, staring at the gun.

"After your seduction fiasco with Dr. Scott, the Colonel gave orders that all master cardkeys, including those held by Group members, be taken off the security system. Consequently, I had to use my own ID card to get in here, the one you have now. It may be five minutes from now or five days, but sooner or later he'll discover that I came here and he'll put things together. Even if you don't succeed in escaping, I'll still be dead—eventually."

"My heart's breaking," Melissa taunted him.

"What did you mean by 'eventually'?" Brian asked resentfully, still seething with rage.

"They won't kill me right away. They'll do other things to me first. They don't do it to be vindictive. They just take the opportunity to utilize a human subject for one of their experiments. You do realize that the Nazi doctors had protégés, don't you? Antigravity is just a small slice of the Paperclip pie. They'll probably use me for their mind-programming work—Father Benedict will know all about that now since he figured out the Gottlieb connection. You have no idea how deep the well of MJ-12 goes, and who occupies space at the Group's boardroom table. Which is why ..."

The Lieutenant turned the gun around and extended the handle to Brian, "I don't want to die dishonorably by my own hand. I hope the information I've given you and the chance to get out of here without ending up as two more puppets in the hands of the Group are payment enough for this request. When you're finished, keep the weapon; you may need it. My only request is not to be shot in the back; I want to die like a soldier. I would be especially grateful if you would do it, Dr. Scott. I'd like to die at the hands of a better man than myself."

Brian stared at the shimmering, polished sidearm but didn't move. Melissa watched Brian closely, unsure of what his next move would be. She could see the temptation etched on his face, the building inner compulsion to lash out at the source of so much of his pain. She could identify with all of it only too well. Her mind raced back through her past, replaying the loss of her virtue in such an ignoble, repulsive way. She recalled Greg's smug expression in his father's office as her own father succumbed to the manipulative scheme that allowed her rapist and his fellow reprobates to go unpunished. Then there was the emotional torment of what had followed.

She followed the movement of his hand breathlessly as Brian took the gun. Her mind, stirred by the remembrances of the crimes committed against her, screamed for justice. She could tell by the cold, inflexible stare on Brian's face that he craved revenge as well. But inside her, another voice beckoned her to consider memories more recent— Brian's insistence that she forgive and move on, her own contemplation, lying awake at night, of taking his advice, those moments of emotional insight intuitively reassuring her this road less traveled was the right path. She looked once more into Brian's eyes and recognized the titanic struggle for what it would mean—a descent into moral ambivalence.

"Brian," she whispered, placing her hand on the arm that held the weapon, "put it down."

Brian closed his eyes, fighting the demons within that fueled his fury. Lieutenant Sheppard said nothing but remained at attention, awaiting the young scholar's decision.

"Put it down," she coaxed him again. "If you do this, your life will never be the same ... our lives will never be the same."

He turned and looked at her warm, lovely face, surprised at the calm he read upon it.

"It's the right thing to do," she said in a hushed voice, a faint, reassuring smile pursing her lips. She moved her hand to the gun and felt his grip relax.

"You're right." He handed her the gun.

She put her arm around his waist and hugged him, her cheek resting on his chest. She released him, observing the Lieutenant's troubled expression, and placed the gun on a nearby end table. Brian took a deep breath.

"I shouldn't get to decide who lives and dies, Mr. Sheppard. That's God's choice, not mine. I'd suggest you make the most of His patience."

The recognizable click of the door suddenly drew their attention from the tension around them. Father Benedict hastily entered the room and approached them. He looked disdainfully at the Lieutenant, but without surprise.

"What are your plans now, Lieutenant?" the priest demanded defiantly.

"How did you know—?" Brian asked immediately, before the uniformed officer, still at attention, could answer.

"There's a listening device in your backpack—in the lining of the smallest pocket."

Melissa spied the pack next to Brian's desk and wasted no time in checking. To her alarm, the priest's statement was true. There was a small hole in the interior stitching, and she plucked the device from it. "Looks like you forgot to tell us about this, Greg," she muttered angrily.

"He didn't put it there," the priest informed her. "I did."

Brian cast an uneasy glance at Andrew.

"It had nothing to do with trust," he tried to explain.

"How can he be sure?" the Lieutenant asked provocatively.

"Young man," Father Benedict addressed the Lieutenant curtly and approached him, "are you Catholic?"

"No, sir, I'm not," he answered, curious as to the relevance of the question.

"Would you agree that, like Dr. Scott, I'm a better man than yourself?"

"Yes," he answered, "that wouldn't take much."

Brian glanced curiously at Andrew, just in time to see him pull a pistol, fitted with a silencer, from his lapel and, in a single, fluid motion, fire a bullet into the Lieutenant's forehead. Melissa screamed, startled by the violent act.

"You die as you wished, then," Father Benedict droned, looking down at the body while replacing his weapon.

"Good God, Andrew!" Brian stammered, watching the blood and cranial fluid ooze from Greg's skull. "What have you done?"

"I think that's pretty obvious," he replied passively, acting as one who'd killed before. "What may not be as apparent is *why* I did it."

"I don't care why you did it! You just killed the man! How in God's name can you justify this?" Brian shouted.

"We're in the midst of a holy war!" he growled, his anger aroused. "The sooner you realize that, the better."

"So we're supposed to believe that you just murdered this guy in order to—"

"Save your lives? Yes, that's what you're supposed to believe." He glanced at the stunned woman.

"He was no threat; he was trying to help us," Brian protested. "I thought you were listening."

"We'd better get the Colonel," Melissa fretted. "I can't believe that guard didn't break down the door. Wait a minute, how did you get in here anyway?"

"The guard left soon after you entered. I sent him away when I dismissed the others. I got in because I have access to this room—to all the rooms, actually. I have from the beginning."

Father Benedict waited for a response, but Brian and Melissa were speechless.

"This man would have killed you both when he was done using you," Father Benedict asserted. "Although there's a remote possibility his guilt was genuine, he was most likely soliciting your trust for some future advantage."

"But he wanted us to kill him," Brian argued.

"I'll wager he was counting on your own goodness that you wouldn't go through with it," he countered.

"Sounds to me like a guess," Melissa charged.

"Really? Tell me, then, how did the good Lieutenant know you were going to be escorted to Brian's room?"

The two thought for a moment but couldn't produce an answer.

"How is it that the Lieutenant told you he was forced to use his ID card to enter your room, and not an override master," he interrogated Brian, "when I used my own override cardkey to enter just now?" he finished, holding up both cards.

Again, they were without a response.

"He lied, and I'll tell you why," he said confidently. "By having you use his ID card instead of the override, he gave you a chance to escape, but he also gave the Colonel a means to track you through the Facility. If you were caught, he could claim to have been overpowered or held at gun point—and to have made sure you got his ID card instead of the override so you wouldn't get far."

"That is possible," Brian conceded, looking at Melissa.

"How do you have a second card anyway?" Melissa questioned suspiciously.

"Even if I'm wrong about his motives," the priest went on, ignoring Melissa, "he would never have been able to avoid detection by the Group after today. Once he fell into their hands, he would have found some way to barter for his own life. He'd have delivered your heads on a platter somewhere down the road if the Group promised him his life. He'd have used you and then cast you aside. Your own refusal to kill him made my action necessary."

"I've heard of Jesuit ethics, Andrew," Brian said, shaking his head, still gazing at the Lieutenant's lifeless form on his floor, "but this—"

"But nothing. You made the moral decision since you lacked the knowledge of this man's propensities and intentions. You had no biblical right to take his life. I, on the other hand, killed him to save your lives. That's hardly Jesuit ethics."

"Give me a break!" ranted Melissa. "How would you know enough about him to defend killing him? And I'd still like an answer to my other question. Where did you get an override card?"

"He's a member of the Group, isn't he?"

"Yes, he told us," Brian noted.

"Yeah, you heard everything with your little spying device," Melissa sniped. "How do you know what the Group would have done anyway?"

"Because I'm a member as well."

61

"I don't even want to hear it, Andrew," Brian said with disgust.

"But what this man told the two of you is true!" he protested. "The Watchers are here!"

"So you killed the guy we're supposed to believe? Isn't this some choice, Melissa?"

"Yeah—believe the guy he just killed who told us the truth, since his intentions were false, or believe his killer."

"I tell you, they're here, and they've begun to prepare! You must believe me!" the priest pleaded.

"Frankly, Andrew—if that's your real name—I don't know which lie to believe."

"Or which liar," added Melissa, arms folded where she stood, glaring at Father Benedict.

"This whole escapade has been nothing but an elaborate façade," Brian growled angrily.

"You must get out of here," Father Benedict persisted firmly, "and I'm going to see that you do, regardless of whose side you think I'm on."

"How noble," retorted Melissa. "We're going to tell the Colonel just what happened here, either way."

"But you must know that the Colonel was part of all of this. He updated the Group regularly. The deceptions were deliberately planned."

"So why not tell us you were in the Group earlier?" Brian demanded.

"I had to maintain anonymity."

"To whom? The Group knew you were a mole."

"But the Group doesn't know I was working *against* them."

"Oh, this is rich," Melissa mocked. "Oh, wait a minute. Maybe the part about you lying about the security logs is better."

"I couldn't go to security and ask them to check the logs. It was too risky. It would surely have been reported to the Colonel."

"Whatever."

"Listen to me!" Father Benedict said, exasperation creeping into his voice. "I—"

His words were interrupted by a knock on the door. Brian and Melissa looked at each other nervously, wondering whether to answer.

"That would be Malcolm—God willing," Father Benedict told them.

"So now we're psychic?" Melissa jabbed. "Is that what the Group needed *you* for?"

"Malcolm is working for me. If it's him, plans for your escape are in place. If not, we're all in deep trouble."

"I guess there's only one way to find out." Brian strode for the door and opened it. It was Malcolm.

The wiry scientist entered the room without a word, un-characteristically serious. He looked first at the body on the floor, then at Father Benedict.

"Splendid work, as usual, Father."

"What?" Melissa exclaimed.

"Our Father Benedict," Malcolm began, "is a member of the Group, but you probably know that already, considering the circumstances."

"You knew that?" Brian asked incredulously.

"Yes."

"I suppose you are, too; it seems membership does have its privileges," Melissa taunted.

"Of course not," Father Benedict answered, "Malcolm works for me ... he's a fellow Jesuit."

Melissa could only stare, jaw agape, at the lanky, bespectacled black man. "But ... then ... you know, I don't even want to know." She threw up her hands. "I think I'm going to have a look in the mirror to see if I'm still me," she muttered, heading for the bedroom.

Father Benedict grabbed her arm. "You must stay and hear Malcolm. He can verify—"

"Go to hell." She shook herself free.

"It's true, Melissa," Malcolm acknowledged. "I met Andrew while I was in college at mass. We hit it off because of our common scientific interests." He glanced at Brian, who was just as shell-shocked as Melissa.

"I learned of Malcolm's interest in the priesthood shortly after we'd met," explained Father Benedict. "I encouraged him to consider my order because of its emphasis on scholarship. He earned his PhD first, then went to seminary. He took his vows less than a year ago."

"So how come the Group doesn't know this?" Brian asked.

"They aren't the only ones who practice secrecy as a profession," Andrew replied cryptically.

"I'm sorry for some of the suggestive comments I made to you Melissa," Malcolm said, turning his attention back to her, "but they were necessary for my cover."

"Stuff it. You're just another liar. God knows I attract them." Melissa stormed into the bedroom.

Andrew sighed and paced the room, gathering his thoughts.

"Surely you can believe Melissa's near death experience proves what the Lieutenant was saying. I was listening to your conversation, and you admitted as much."

"That's true," Brian agreed grudgingly, "the scenario he presented does have explanatory power. But with you coming in here like James Bond and blowing people away, I'm back to wondering who can be trusted."

"Man, you don't know how close that is to the truth," Malcolm said with his trademark grin. "Andrew here is the Jesuit version. He's been a Vatican insider and spy since World War II."

"What did you do then?" Melissa asked, emerging from the bedroom, still irritated. "Steal gold and art for the Nazis? Or maybe cover up the Vatican's piss-poor explanation for not helping the Jews?"

"Don't you dare speak to Father Benedict like that!" Malcolm objected, stiffening. The anger in his voice was genuine. "This man," he said, pointing to the elderly priest, "personally diverted thousands of Jews away from the death camps, even to the point of disobeying his vows of obedience to his Order when the Church vacillated on what to do about the Nazis! He lost dozens of colleagues in the effort, including a brother and a sister. Opposing this shame has been his life!"

Malcolm and Melissa stood face to face, the former staring down the latter, whose unflinching exterior relayed the skepticism she held inside her.

"I think we'd better hear it all, Andrew," Brian said, taking Melissa gently by the arm and guiding her to the couch. Malcolm moved to Andrew's side, but the old priest remained silent. Brian and Melissa waited.

"This is the great evil about which I spoke to you earlier, Brian," he said finally, a distant look in his eyes. "There was a time when those in power in the Church saw things clearly ... but this changed during the war."

He bowed his head, then continued. "The leadership of the Church shared Churchill's insight that the Nazis could not be stopped by anyone on the continent, but many of them lacked his moral resolve—he was a truly great man. I don't think Pious XII consciously chose to compromise with Hitler and the forces of darkness that drove him to his madness, but he didn't have the foresight to choose well. But all the time *they* were the real enemy, doing what they have always done ... trying to eliminate God's people, to destroy the chosen lineage when they could not infect it with their demonic spawn."

Brian felt a chill rise up his spine. He knew Andrew's prepared mind had already raced through dozens of intersections between the things the old man had seen in his past and what he had learned here in his role with the Group, things that Brian would never know, that he felt would compel him to believe the cleric. Yet, somehow, he had no need of proof. Andrew had seen the face of evil and set his will against it. The aged priest's enemies were his own.

"I officially retired from what you would call active duty several years ago when I turned seventy," he continued, hands folded behind his back, walking about the room, "but I never ceased working. I begged John Paul for the adjunct appointment I now hold at the university, and he graciously arranged it."

"John Paul and Andrew had been friends since the war," Malcolm informed them. "Like Andrew, His Holiness firmly believed in the old honor of the Jesuits, as do I."

"Our society was influenced by conciliarists," Andrew resumed his discussion, "those who believed in the myth of neutrality when it came to the Nazis. Even worse, it became infected by *them.*"

"You're saying there are Watchers inside your order, and the Vatican?"

"They may take any form they wish—you of all people know what the ancient texts say about them. This is why you were chosen."

"But I was brought here by the Group."

"You were brought here *by God!*" He stopped again, looking sadly at Brian. "I'm deeply sorry about what happened, Brian. I had no idea it was he who was trying to eliminate Melissa ... and neither did the Group, which is a very disturbing thought," he added, looking at Malcolm momentarily.

"Maybe Neil discovered some of what they really intended and he snapped," Malcolm speculated.

"That does seem to be the case, but it hardly seems possible. Or, perhaps he drew certain conclusions about what he knew in view of his discussions with Brian and myself."

"Go on, Andrew," Brian prodded.

"I tried to inform some of my superiors in the Church years ago of my suspicions," Andrew explained, returning to the subject, "but most of them laughed, enamored as they were by their anti-supernatural, modernistic theology. I had misunderstood Matthew 24, they said; I couldn't take Genesis 6 literally; I should disregard Enoch as contain-ing anything of value; Watchers were a myth, they argued; astral prophecy was a deception. 'This is the twentieth century, Benedict!' they declared. I knew they were wrong, though. Your dissertation brought all the ancient textual data together and confirmed all that I had ever suspected about these beings but never had time to study for myself."

"What's this about astral prophecy?" Melissa asked. "Do you believe that the second coming will be signaled by some kind of astronomical event?"

"Yes ... I believe that, but I don't know if it's coherent. That's why I enlisted Father Mantello at the Vatican Observatory. I have a theory—or rather, some ancient rabbis had ideas about astral prophecy and the appearing of the Messiah. I needed Father Mantello to check on some stellar convergences since I don't know much about astronomy."

"What rabbis?" Brian asked, his curiosity piqued.

"It's too complicated to get into now, Brian. All I can say now is that the Talmud contains the idea that the Pleiades and the two horns of Taurus are related to the revived house of Joseph and the appearance of the Messiah. What's especially alarming about the idea is that the Pleiades not only plays a role in the messianic appearing, but Jewish rabbis universally connect that constellation to the flood event, and we know what happened then with the Watchers. You know the Pleiades are an important part of UFO lore, too. There are important astro-nom-ical events related to all this coming soon, and the convergence of these things troubles me."

"How did you wind up in the Group?" Melissa asked, taking the discussion in another direction. Brian sat wide-eyed on the couch, the priest's words and their implications gelling in his mind.

"General Hartwig, the leader of the Group, and I were once best of friends ... in fact, he assumes we still are," Andrew continued. "When the occupation of Berlin began, Hartwig's father wound up stationed in Germany. After a few years he was transferred to Italy, where we met. His son, now the Group's General, had just turned thirteen. I was in my mid-twenties, in my first year of study at the Pontifical Institute in Rome.

"One day the elder Hartwig and I unwittingly found ourselves in a market that a small group of fascist terrorists had decided to bomb and spray with gunfire. The General's father was knocked unconscious by the blast, and I managed to drag him underneath one of the vegetable stands out of harm's way. He was grateful, and the son came to nearly worship me. Eventually the younger Hartwig went back to America, enlisted in the Air Force, and became seduced and twisted by the secrets to which his various assignments exposed him. He had no idea, of course, of my own activities."

"Are you sure he doesn't now?" Brian asked apprehensively.

"Yes."

"So why were you placed on the team?"

"When I learned of his involvement in continuing Paperclip projects, I was deeply disappointed. Nevertheless, I could see it was a providential blessing. I chose to present myself to him as someone who could keep him informed of Vatican activities, when I actually planned to use him. He still believes I identify with his causes. I knew from our own network of faithful Jesuits that Malcolm was working undercover somewhere in the southwest, but I had no idea where. I contacted General Hartwig, hoping to learn something about Malcolm, only to be solicited by the general to infiltrate this project team.

"I was shown the files of the three scientists already working at Area 51 who would be part of the team I was to observe, and I acted on the wonderful providence of being put together with Malcolm. As far as my specific duties, the General wanted me on this team for two reasons: to watch you, Brian, and Dr. Bandstra, since you were outsiders, and to help you in your own contribution to the project, if you needed it. I had read your dissertation, so when I learned you had been brought here, I was firmly convinced God was at work. Something very important was happening."

"You went well beyond observing me," Brian noted. "You said some pretty bold things about what you really believe—the Watchers and all that. That had to be quite risky."

"It was, but I needed to take any opportunity to show you the connections I see and believe to be the truth, and I also needed to discern if anyone on the Group knew anything or cared anything about the Watchers. As far as I can see, they don't. Their agenda is just as Lieutenant Sheppard outlined. They don't believe in ETs or Watchers; they're using a mythology they've concocted to accelerate globalism and guarantee themselves control. They are the masters of their own fate, or so they think. They're being used by an evil far more intelligent than them. There is an evil here ... lurking in the shadows of all that's done. Make no mistake about it."

62

Bravery is the capacity to perform properly
even when scared half to death.

—*General Omar Bradley*

"Father," Malcolm said, looking at his watch. "It's been nearly five minutes since I arrived here. We need to proceed."

"You're right. Has everything we discussed been arranged?"

"It has, but you have to get to the surface and past any guards to take the advantage."

"Then you had best be on your way," he said, and headed for the door, Malcolm following. "I hope to see you again, but if not ... I'm very proud of you, and be faithful to your calling."

"I will. We'll meet again, on this side or the other."

The two embraced, and Father Benedict ran his override key through the door. Access was denied. He tried once more with the same result.

"This is most unexpected," he remarked, anxiety creasing his face. "It worked when I came in."

"Are we trapped in here?" Brian asked, alarmed that anything could escape the priest's attention.

"No," he said calmly. "Someone wants to eliminate the use of override cards to force the use of the normal, issued pass cards ... probably to make sure everyone is tracked through the system," he deduced, rubbing his chin thoughtfully. A feeling of dread swept over him.

"Malcolm," he ordered, still meditating on the situation, "take my normal room card and leave; you know the code. No one knows you're in here since we admitted you, and it will appear—for the time being, anyway—that I've left the room if you're using my card on the outside. It'll take them a while to figure out who was using my card once we're discovered."

"What do you mean, discovered?" Melissa asked uneasily.

"Surely you don't expect to reach the surface undetected, Melissa."

"I don't know what to expect after today. I suppose you have a plan."

"Yes, and I'm quite confident we'll get off the base, and that I'll get back."

"Get back!" Brian exclaimed.

"My position in the Group is too valuable to lose. I can learn so much ... but surrendering my card necessitates some improvisation."

"Good. Think it through while I talk to Brian." Melissa took Brian by the hand into the bedroom.

"What is it?" he asked in a hushed voice.

"I don't trust him."

"Well ... I do."

"What he's saying just sounds ... crazy. Do you really believe this stuff?"

"Yes," he confessed, "but I have to admit, I don't want to."

"Then you'd better go. I just can't trust my life to people who traffic in lies."

"I'm not going ... without you," Brian said, surprised by the moment of boldness.

"What do I matter? You're the one he thinks he needs to get out of here. Besides, he's asking us to just leave. My whole library is here, and my clothes and my files. That stuff is my career," she lamented.

Brian looked about at his small quarters, pained by the thought as well. "I understand. Everything I own is here, but what good is all of it if you're not around to use it?"

"I don't know," she said in frustration. "It's just very hard ... to trust anyone."

"I know," he whispered, touching her shoulder, "but you can trust me. I won't just look out for myself, you know that."

She touched his hand where it lay on her shoulder and closed her eyes, clearing her mind. "Okay," she sighed.

The two of them rejoined Malcolm and Father Benedict, who was rifling through the pockets of the dead officer's clothing.

"Here it is," he said, handing Malcolm what Brian and Melissa guessed was the Lieutenant's own override card. It, too, failed to open the door.

"This confirms that all the override cards have been rendered inoperable," Father Benedict said, rising from the floor. "That means it's time for you to get going, Malcolm. There's still time to get Deidre out of here."

"Goodbye," he said shaking Brian's hand. "May God be with you."

He grinned playfully at Melissa, who hugged him in return. "Thanks, Malcolm."

"Figures," he said to Brian as he broke the embrace. "She hugs me now that I'm a priest."

"Be careful," Brian cautioned.

"I always am. Till next time," he added, then departed.

"Come here, both of you," Father Benedict insisted with a tone of urgency. "We'll have to use the Lieutenant's normal ID card. The Colonel doesn't know he's dead, so we should be able to buy some time with a Group member's ID. Unfortunately," he noted, removing a retractable knife from his pocket, "there's at least one entryway we can't negotiate without a required retina and palm scan."

"I hope you're not thinking what I think you are," Brian said, his stomach churning.

"What would that be?" the priest asked casually.

"You're not going to take his eye out and cut off his hand are you?"

"No, of course not. You are," he announced, handing Brian his knife.

"No way," Brian excused himself and backed away. "I'll never make it without throwing up, and why should I do it?"

"Assuming you get out of here, I'll be left alone. I can't have any of this traced to me. You need to do it for the same reason you need to carry my gun," he explained, handing that to Brian as well.

"We could take Greg's gun," Melissa interjected.

"No, it has to appear as though you disarmed me."

"But then my prints will be on a murder weapon!" Brian protested.

"Exactly. If they were mine, my cover would be blown. Now take my gun; there's no other way."

Brian reluctantly took the priest's pistol but refused the knife once more.

"I'm serious, Andrew. I don't have the stomach for it."

"Give me the knife," Melissa said in a resigned tone. The priest obliged. "Nothing I wouldn't have had to do in medical school," she deadpanned, kneeling beside the corpse.

"It's the right eye and right palm," Father Benedict instructed.

"Get me something to carry these in ... a towel maybe," she requested.

Brian complied hurriedly as Melissa grabbed the cadaver's forearm and began the ghoulish task. He returned just in time to see the point of the knife flick the eyeball out of its socket. He threw the towel at the priest's feet and turned away, fighting his gag reflex.

"Leave a little of the optic nerve so we'll have a way to hold it up to the scanner," Andrew said passively, watching Melissa's progress carefully. "Just pull the eyeball out another inch, and—"

"Father."

"Yes?"

"I can handle this."

"Is she done yet?" Brian asked queasily from where he stood a few feet away, watching Melissa insert the folded towel into Brian's backpack.

"Yes. Come here, I have some directions for you."

He took a deep breath and turned toward Andrew. Melissa went to wash her hands.

"Pay very close attention. You must do exactly as I say should the occasion arise. When we leave this room, behave as normally and calmly as possible. Get your backpack and put these in it," he directed, handing him two cassettes.

"What are these?" Brian asked, doing as he was told.

"I had Malcolm break into your computer yesterday and backup the hard drives. Your research is critical to what you'll be doing on the outside. I had him do the same to Melissa's. You can only take with you what will fit in your backpack."

"In that case, give me a second."

Brian went to his desk drawer without waiting for the priest's permission. He opened the drawer and glanced back briefly at Melissa and Andrew, both of whom, to his relief, had their backs turned toward him. He hastily retrieved the item from its resting place and put it in his backpack.

"There's one more thing, Brian," the old priest added upon his return.

"Yes?"

"If at any time we're confronted by base security or the Colonel, you must take me hostage—and it must be convincing. Walk directly behind me at all times so you can threaten me at a moment's notice. Put the gun in your belt and wear a light jacket over it for concealment."

"I don't know ... I'm not much of an actor."

"My life depends on it, so knock me around or put a choke hold on me—whatever it takes. They have to be convinced that I'm being taken from the base against my will. It's also designed for your protection. They won't shoot at you if you use me as a shield since I'm a Group member—but just to be safe, keep your head behind mine to guard against sniper fire. I'll help you by not putting up any struggle."

"Sounds like fun."

"Gee, I wonder who the alternate target might be," Melissa cracked nervously.

"They won't shoot at you either. The Colonel was absolutely beside himself after the attempts on your life. The ruse is for my and Brian's sake, as well as to keep us close in order to prevent them from separating and capturing us. Besides, I have something for you that will give them an incentive to leave us alone. Getting off the base will be relatively easy; it's afterward that worries me."

"I think I'll just take one crisis at a time, thank you."

"Speaking of which—fetch the briefcase from under your bed, Brian."

"I don't have a briefcase."

"Oh yes, you do."

Brian looked at Andrew uncertainly and disappeared into his bedroom. He emerged a moment later, the item in hand and a perplexed look on his face. He handed the case to Andrew.

"It's pretty heavy, Andrew," he said, setting the case down on the couch. "What's in it?"

"This is our insurance policy," the priest said seriously, but with a hint of mischief.

"Melissa," he said, kneeling by the couch, "surely in light of your field you recall the major concern the world had over at the breakup of the Soviet Union?"

"Of course. Everyone was afraid of what would happen to their nuclear arsenal. It was expected that their nuclear technology would be available to the highest bidder."

"Correct," he replied, fingering the case's combination lock. "Which groups were our greatest concern?"

"Terrorists, mostly Middle Eastern lunatics."

"Correct again."

"But would any of the former Soviet republics have sold any nuclear weapons to people like that?" Brian asked, wondering where Andrew was headed with his questioning.

"They may not have had to," Melissa responded, smirking. "The republics lost enough of their nuclear arsenal to destroy most of the human life on the planet. Hundreds of bombs and missiles were just 'missing' when they took inventory. Talk about incompetence."

"Wonderful."

"In fact," she continued, "they misplaced over one hundred nuclear bombs that could fit into something the size of ..." She caught herself. Brian read her thoughts instantly.

"A briefcase?" Andrew finished her sentence, popping open the lid. "You never know where one of those things might turn up, now do you?"

Brian and Melissa stood in entranced horror above the weapon of mass destruction. To their amazed chagrin, Andrew expertly flipped the switches, punched an extended code on the fixed keypad, and zeroed the timer.

"Not much more difficult than one of those confounded VCRs! Now how long do we think it should take to get off the base and to Las Vegas?" he asked.

"I don't like the way this is shaping up, Brian."

"I'm sure he's not going to blow us all up ... right?"

"Not unless the Colonel wants to die as well, or have his little antigravity squadron obliterated."

"What a relief," said Melissa.

"I'll give us, oh, say ... two hours. Synchronize your watches. Here." He handed Melissa a small device that resembled a handheld calculator, except it had only three buttons.

"What's this?"

"A remote detonator. It will stop the timer or detonate the device prematurely. The bomb stays here in your room, back under the bed; Melissa will carry the remote. To detonate the bomb you need to push the first two buttons in order and then release them simultaneously. The device routes the commands through a satellite and then to a beacon on this base, so we could detonate it from anywhere—that was Malcolm's idea. The third button will cancel this action—prior to release, of course.

"If we're engaged by anyone, especially the Colonel, you must tell him that the Lieutenant gave you the device and instructed you in its use. He is to let us go unfollowed to our destination. Once there, we'll phone him with the location of the bomb so he can defuse it. He'll believe you since the Group is in possession of several of these briefcase nukes. You're using me as a shield to avoid having to use the bomb. Understood?"

Melissa nodded nervously.

"Are we ready?" Andrew asked, looking them both in the eye. "Once you pass through this door with me, there's no turning back."

"I think we should pray first," Brian said, his pulse quickening.

"Absolutely."

Brian said a short prayer for safety and at his amen, Andrew swiped the Lieutenant's card through the locking mechanism.

63

Courage is fear that has said its prayers.

—*Dorothy Bernard*

The three figures moved down the familiar hallway of the Facility past the team members' living quarters. As Andrew had told them, the posted guards were nowhere to be seen. Andrew led them to an unmarked door roughly fifty yards from the conference room and carded into the unauthorized portion of the Facility.

The area was eerily quiet, as though a trap had been laid, but Andrew guided them without hesitation through a labyrinth of hallways, doors, and staircases. They walked casually, making little eye contact, and elicited no attention from the scant number of scientists or base personnel they encountered. Malcolm had been right. Look like you know you belong somewhere and you'll be amazed at the places you can get into. *Or out of,* Brian hoped.

"This has been too easy, Father," Melissa worried.

"If you're bored, things will get more interesting when we reach the elevator around the next corner," the priest warned, stopping near a water fountain to make their conversation seem normal. "That elevator is the only one on this side of the base that leads directly to the surface. They'll want to intercept us with a minimum of disruption for unengaged parties, and topside would be the logical place to do it. The door opens on the inside of the main hangar, where there would be plenty of room for the Colonel to position and maneuver his SWAT unit. Have your gun ready, Brian, as soon as the door opens. When we get into the hangar, we're looking for a black sedan with the license plate ALH-MJH. It should be near the gateway to the tarmac."

"So let's go," Brian insisted uneasily.

"We need the contents of the towel."

"Great," Brian griped.

"Listen to me closely now," he said ominously. "There's a large research room located directly across from the elevator; it's a distance of about fifteen yards. There will be a guard posted there, and he'll no doubt watch us closely. Brian, you need to take the hand and the eye out here before we reach the elevator."

"Why must I do it?" he complained, feeling his stomach heave at the mere thought.

"Because you are only a little taller than the Lieutenant. The scanners at this elevator are synchronized. Put the Lieutenant's palm inside yours and hide your hand in your jacket. Hold the eye in your left hand and make sure you're holding it by the nerve so that you can bring it up in front of your own eye quickly. The scan will take only a few seconds."

"Okay," Brian said, sighing, and closed his eyes, trying to displace his feeling of nausea. Melissa folded back the towel, revealing her grisly handiwork. Brian swallowed hard and matched his palm to the backside of the now cold, rubbery appendage. Melissa carefully wiped a bloodstain off the surface of the eye and handed it properly oriented to Brian, who had become appallingly pale.

"We'll stand behind you to obstruct the guard's view," Andrew noted as they assumed their positions in relation to one another.

"Don't worry about the guard," Melissa whispered to Brian as they moved. "He'll be no problem."

"Wha—"

"Trust me."

They finally arrived at an elevator adjacent to a large research room, and Brian took his place facing the elevator. Melissa turned and gazed through the large glass doors at the scientists and support personnel, who were busily engaged in their projects. She smiled seductively at the soldier stationed in front of the door as soon as their eyes met. He enjoyed the connection for a few seconds before varying his gaze to her companions. She heard the doors slide open and turned away.

Brian quickly returned the severed hand and eyeball to Melissa, who rewrapped them and placed the towel in the corner of the elevator. Brian watched the buttons light up successively as the elevator ascended rapidly toward their destination. He felt a tiny bead of perspiration trickle down his temple. He could hear himself breathing, and the pounding in his own chest seemed to reverberate audibly throughout the rising chamber.

"We're here," noted Andrew ominously.

Brian put his arm around the priest's neck and tightened his grip with a jerk. Father Benedict's fingers instinctively went up to clear his throat. His gasp for air as the door slid open conveyed a credible impression on the Colonel and his phalanx of guards, who were predictably waiting about twenty yards from the elevator, firearms pointed directly at them.

"Hello, Dr. Scott, Dr. Kelley ... I've been expecting you,"he greeted them cockily. "Are the accommodations really that inhospitable? Why ever would you want to leave us?"

"I have pizza waiting at the guard-post. You let us go, and I'll share."

"It will take more than sarcasm to escape from here, Dr. Scott."

"Will the life of one of your precious Group members do?" he threatened, tightening his chokehold on Andrew, who wheezed uncomfortably, and pointed the gun at his head.

"You're bluffing," the Colonel replied with a sly smirk. "This is no time for amateur hour."

"Am I? Perhaps you're wondering where Lieutenant Sheppard is."

The Colonel said nothing, his mood darkening.

"He's dead," Brian answered the unspoken question. "I put a bullet in his head. Have one of your lackeys check out my room."

"You don't have it in you."

"You're mistaken, Colonel. The Lieutenant came to my room to help Melissa and myself get off the base. He said he wanted to bring the Group down and that getting Melissa and me off the base was part of the plan. He was doing fine until he was dumb enough to hand me his gun and only then tell me he'd murdered my parents. It felt positively exhilarating to even the score."

"Isn't that a sin?" the Colonel taunted, buying time for some of his men to position themselves. Brian caught the movement out of the corner of his eye.

"Eye for an eye, Colonel. I'm just an Old Testament kind of guy. Now let us pass."

"But why kill Father Benedict? I thought he was your friend."

"I did too. The Lieutenant kindly informed me that he was a Group member, which means he stinks to high heaven like the rest of you. I don't like being betrayed."

"Neither do I," he growled, looking about the hangar.

"Well?" Brian shouted.

"Go ahead and kill him," the Colonel dared him. "He can be replaced. I'm giving you ten seconds to drop the gun or we start shooting."

He held up his hand to signal his forces, each of them taking careful aim. "Ten ... nine ..."

"You know, the Lieutenant thought you'd want to keep us here ..."

"Eight ... seven ..."

"... so he brought something else to the room and showed us how to use it."

"Four ... three ..."

"Melissa!"

Melissa held up the remote detonator for all to see, the first two buttons firmly depressed.

"Hold it! Stand down!" the Colonel shouted. His men relaxed but held their positions.

"Where did you get that?" he bellowed angrily.

"I told you," Brian replied, suddenly feeling more confident of the situation. "The Lieutenant was going to be at the controls, but unfortunately he's now unable to make the trip. The bomb is some-where beneath us, Colonel, and there are a lot of places to stash it."

"Why do you insist on dying today, Dr. Scott?"

"I don't plan to. I'd rather not have to use this, so I brought the good Father. Here's the deal, Colonel—"

"I don't make deals!"

"You're right; it *isn't* a deal. You have no choice. You let us pass and get off the base to where we're going, and when we get there, we'll call the base with the location of the bomb. What's the time, Melissa?"

"Just over an hour and forty-five minutes."

"And we'll use all of it, Colonel. If I so much as see a dust cloud come down the road after us or hear a helicopter, we'll detonate it remotely— and I'll be a lot more trigger-happy when we're off the base. Shoot either of us now, and you meet your Maker even faster. We get to our destination, you get the location. It's so simple even you can understand it."

"Vernon—" Father Benedict gasped.

"Shut up!" Brian yelled in his ear, jerking his head around.

"Do you really think the blast will kill us?" he jousted, a smug expression on his face. "We're half a mile above it."

"I guess you weren't listening, Colonel," Brian shot back. "I don't care if you survive. Just knowing that all your toys and God knows whatever else you've got on this base will be vaporized is satisfying. If I have to die, I'm going to do as much damage in the process as I can! Now get rid of the MPs," he demanded, aiming his weapon at the Colonel, "or it starts with you."

The Colonel stared at Brian, tight-lipped and agitated. The seasoned officer gritted his teeth, incensed at his adversary and his predicament. The Colonel deliberated a moment but knew he was out of options.

"Get out of here!" he snarled, then ordered the MPs to disperse.

The three headed slowly but deliberately toward the sedan Brian had spotted behind the Colonel on the far edge of the hangar. Melissa held the remote tightly, knowing what awaited if she dropped her cargo. Brian opened the door, still eyeing the Colonel. Melissa got into the back seat on the passenger side.

"In the back and down on the floor—face down!" Brian yelled at Father Benedict, loud enough for the Colonel to take note. "You so much as move and I'll reach back and put a bullet into your head!"

The priest complied, rubbing his throat and gulping for oxygen. Brian got into the driver's side. The keys were in the ignition.

"Head straight for the gate directly across the tarmac—none other," rasped Father Benedict as soon as the doors were closed. Brian sped out of the hangar, taking note in his rearview mirror of the Colonel's detail of men scattering in all directions.

"Can I deactivate this thing now before I pee in my pants?"

"Not until we're well away from here," he coughed, remaining where he was.

Brian sped across the airfield toward the gate as Melissa gripped the detonator tightly, her fingers turning white.

"We're almost to the gate," Brian informed Andrew. "It's already open."

"Are there any guards visible?" the prone priest asked.

"Just one."

"Is he armed?"

"Yes, but his rifle is lowered."

"The glass is bulletproof, so just keep going, no matter what he does," Andrew informed them. "If they're stupid enough to try anything, keep driving for another mile or so and then blow the place to hell."

Brian flew through the gate unmolested, to everyone's relief, and stayed on the dirt road leading to the interstate.

"How do I get to Las Vegas?" Brian asked after a few minutes, still tense.

"The directions should be in your visor," Andrew commented, finally rising from the floor, taking the seat next to Melissa.

She looked at him and then apprehensively at the device.

"I'm sorry, my dear, but you'll have to give it another half-hour. Try and relax; we're out of harm's way."

"Easy for you to say."

"You did quite well ... and have performed and behaved admirably in the last week or so. It appears I misjudged your constitution."

"Is that an apology?"

"Yes."

"Then I accept it. I'm glad I didn't provoke you any more than I did."

"You should be. I don't make idle threats—you can't when you do this sort of thing."

"I do think, though," she said, looking to the front seat, "that Brian was a little rough on you."

Brian peeked at the priest in the mirror. "You okay, Andrew?"

"I've been worse. I thought you were magnificent, Brian. I don't believe the Colonel suspects anything, which will make it possible for me to return. I still have one precaution to take, however."

"What's that?"

"You'll find out after we arrive in Las Vegas and make our call to the Colonel."

64

The world is a dangerous place to live,
not because of the people who are evil, but because
of the people who don't do anything about it.

—*Albert Einstein*

"Sir, we've located the device and disarmed it." The soldier saluted the Colonel.

"Any word on where the call originated from?"

"No, sir. TelCom thinks it was made on an untraceable cellular phone. They're confident they can track it eventually, but it will take more time."

"Let me know when they have something. And the ballistics report?"

"Another hour, sir."

"Good work, soldier. Dismissed."

"Yes, sir." He saluted once more. "Sir." A second officer acknowledged the gesture, and the soldier turned abruptly and left the Colonel's office.

"So what do you think, Vernon?" General Hartwig asked.

"It was brilliant," he said, smiling and shaking his head. "Vintage Benedict. He exceeds my expectations at every turn. And the Group?"

"They're convinced their plans have been compromised unless they eliminate Scott and Kelley."

"The Group certainly isn't abandoning the agenda, is it?"

"No, not at all. We can still use Scott's work for effective propaganda, and we'll take what we need from everyone's hard drive."

"So there will only be a short delay?" the Colonel asked.

"I expect so. I'd still like to know what made Sheppard betray us. I guess you can never have complete knowledge about a person, can you?"

"Unfortunately, no."

"How long before you can mop things up, Vernon? I told the Group that eliminating Scott and Kelley would be your redemption. After all, it was one of our own who sabotaged the project, not you."

"Tell the Group I know exactly how this whole affair will be resolved. Gather them tomorrow afternoon so I can brief them."

65

No love, no friendship can cross the path of our
destiny without leaving some mark on it forever.

—*Francois Muriac*

The dark green sedan pulled into a darkened corner of the dimly lit grocery store parking lot.

"Leave the car here," Andrew instructed the two of them, then got out. Brian and Melissa did the same. "We're four blocks from the city hospital. It's that way," he pointed. "Once you get there, go to the fourth floor of the parking garage. A car is waiting there for you. It's the green Taurus parked in the handicapped spot. Here are the keys." He handed them to Melissa.

"Where should we go?" she asked.

"There's an envelope in the glove compartment. It has all the instructions you'll need to make sure the Colonel and his men won't find you, plus a few other items."

"What are we supposed to do then?" Brian inquired nervously.

The old priest took Brian by the arms and looked squarely at him. "Expose them," he said sternly. "Tell the world what you've seen, but especially the Church. Give them the truth, no matter what the reaction. It's sad to say, but people of faith may be the hardest to persuade. They've become so acclimated to how they think the end will come—how they think events will unfold. But their theology is based on their own traditions and inbred 'theological correctness,' not on the ancient texts—they're too shocking. The Watchers count on this intellectual laziness and spiritual passivity. Have the boldness to believe the unbelievable so God's Church might be prepared."

"But ... how?"

"You have access to millions of people on the Internet. Study and then study more. You will uncover far more than you already know. You must publish anonymously for your own protection, and you'll receive no financial gain, but your reward will be great. God will illumine the hearts; you must expose the lie and unveil the truth."

"I'm never going to see you again, am I?" Brian murmured gloomily.

The priest released him without a word, his eyes darting to the concrete. "You mustn't let the loneliness you feel win the day," he said, evading the question's obvious answer. "The Evil One knows what you're about and will use this against you. God has been in the quiet frustration as much as these dramatic details of your life. He makes no poor choice, Brian. He will guide your path and meet your needs."

"I know," he said quietly, looking up at the stars, trying to contain his feelings.

"Melissa," he said, turning to her, "may God bless you on your journey and your new life. May I?" he asked, extending his arms.

She hugged him warmly, an unanticipated sadness sweeping over her, unsure of what to make of his words.

"Could I have my gun back, now?" he asked Brian.

"Good riddance," he replied and reached into the car for the weapon.

"I don't want either of you to worry about me," he requested, taking the pistol from his hand. "I know what I'm doing," he assured them with a smile, taking a handkerchief from his pocket. He quickly wiped the weapon clean and placed it in the palm of the hand protected by the cloth.

"Wh—"

Before Brian could even voice the question, Andrew raised the gun to his own left shoulder and fired a solitary shot. Andrew collapsed to the ground with a suppressed cry, the weapon falling from his hand.

"You ... must go ... now," he gasped to the two stunned onlookers, writhing on the ground in pain.

"What did you do that for?" Brian exclaimed incredulously, dropping to the stricken priest's side.

"The Colonel must believe," he said, wincing, catching his breath. "He must believe that I had no part in this. He'll kill me otherwise."

"We're taking you to the hospital," Melissa insisted.

"No ... I'm going inside the store." He struggled to his knees.

"It's almost midnight!" she argued. "They're probably closed!"

"No," he protested, blinking, touching the bloody wound. "Nothing closes in Las Vegas. There are still a few people inside ... I'll be all right. Help will be here soon; they're only blocks away. Now go!" he demanded with another gasp and headed for the store.

Brian and Melissa looked at each other, jolted again by the twist of circumstances. Reluctantly, Brian retrieved his backpack from the car and took Melissa by the hand.

"You can't be serious!" she protested, looking back at the staggering silhouette, resisting Brian's pull.

"I am. He knows what he's doing. We have to trust him. Come on." He tugged at her arm.

Melissa wavered for another moment, but then, with a disgusted sigh, resigned herself to what was unfolding.

66

"It's good to see you again, Vernon."

Father Benedict opened his eyes at the sound of the door opening. "I thought more than a few times that it wouldn't happen again," the priest responded, smiling weakly.

"I thought so as well when the hospital called us."

"I don't remember much about the transport," the priest acknowledged. "I remember hearing the military was taking charge of me, but the medication got to me in the elevator."

"You got the royal treatment—an all-expenses-paid helicopter flight back home," the Colonel informed him, taking a seat on the edge of his bed.

"Have you caught them yet?"

"No, we haven't. I don't have any idea where they are. Of course, I'm not looking, either."

"What?" the priest asked in alarm. "But the General came by this morning, and—"

"The General is an obese buffoon."

"You had best watch your tongue, Vernon," Father Benedict scolded, scarcely containing his shock at the Colonel's insubordination.

"You do realize that I wanted them to escape—oh, no, I guess you don't," the Colonel said with a confident wink.

"The Group will kill you if they heard that. What are you doing?"

"I needn't worry about the General any longer, or the Group for that matter."

The priest cast a wary glance at the officer. "What are you saying?"

"They're dead," he said passively. "I killed them myself on my way over to see you."

"Wha—have you lost your mind?" Andrew cried. "Someone will find them, and—"

"No one will find them; it's already taken care of."

"But someone will miss them!"

"Who?"

"Someone, anyone!" Father Benedict insisted, endeavoring to remain calm. "Most everyone on the base knows what happened here!"

"I've already circulated a memo that the 'escape' was only a readiness exercise. Handed out a few reprimands, a few commendations ... no problem, actually. After all, there's no more secure facility in the world than Area 51."

"But why kill them?"

"They'd outlived their usefulness. It isn't complicated."

"But ..." Andrew sputtered, at a loss for words, "... how did you kill all of them?"

"The same way I'm going to kill you."

"Vernon ..." Father Benedict's face hardened. "I know there were many in the Group who despised you, but it makes no sense to kill your supporters."

"Bravo, Andrew!" the Colonel praised, rising from the bed with mocking applause. "Take a bow, old man!" he taunted, looking into the priest's perplexed eyes.

The Colonel approached the head of the bed, exuding a satisfied air of conquest.

"You think you understand what went on here?" he asked the prone figure with contempt. "You understand *nothing!*"

"How did you find out?" Father Benedict asked, resigned to his fate.

"Don't be so hard on yourself, Andrew," he said condescendingly. "I could cite Dr. Scott's slipup about the gun—while he was threatening me, he inadvertently said that he'd taken Major Sheppard's gun and killed him with it. A ballistics test proved that to be false, of course.

"I also checked the logs into the room where we keep our nukes. Naturally, there was an override code in the system, but what was more important was the time. You see, Andrew," the Colonel fixed his gaze on the elderly man, "Lieutenant Sheppard was with me at the time the override was recorded. I knew you were the culprit, since no one else in the Group would be smart enough or resourceful enough to come up with such a foolproof way of getting off the base. It was a wonderful idea. And the self-inflicted gunshot—a simply marvelous detail!"

The priest closed his eyes in chagrin.

"This blunder notwithstanding, I've known from the beginning who you were and whose side you were on. Certainly the Lieutenant was an unexpected traitor, but I wanted all of you together to see how it would play out. I sent a message to the General for the whole Group detailing the Bandstra incident in which I 'accidentally' let it slip that I'd be holding Dr. Kelley and Dr. Scott in his room. Once you entered as well, I had the security system disallow the overrides so I could track you.

"In yet another stroke of genius, you dismembered the Major, a scheme that bought you some time while we looked for Dr. Bradley and Dr. Harper—and we will find them, I can promise you," he said, not attempting to conceal his amusement. "What a creative mind! I am sincerely going to miss these jousts, Father. It isn't often that one of your kind can keep me thinking."

Andrew felt a chill.

"You believe that the General brought you on board to watch Dr. Scott and encourage him in his contribution to the project. Who do you think planted the idea in his mind after you got in touch with him last year?"

Father Benedict remained mute.

"Let me see, now. You believe that the ultimate goal of the Group was to position themselves as the only hope for a peaceful resolution to a perceived extraterrestrial threat. Through technological means, the Group could engineer a variety of extraterrestrial events and put forth undeniable biological proof of extraterrestrial life that would convince leaders of nations around the world that they must surrender their authority to them. Scholars in theology, psychology, and fringe religious beliefs were brought in to lay the foundation for quieting the most troublesome groups from the start. The Group would reluctantly take control of earthly government, and then only because a new humanity—one now united as a species, illumined by the knowledge they were not alone in the universe—pleaded with them to do so. How does that sound?" he asked, smiling scornfully.

Andrew turned his head.

"Let me assure you, Andrew, you were correct in all this, but you couldn't possibly know that it didn't matter. The Group had their agenda, *but I have a different plan.* Their blind ambition made it easy to manipulate them, and some of their ideas will be useful. Your predisposition to believing the entire alien phenomenon was evil allowed me to manipulate you. They're dead now because I no longer need them. You'll die for the same reason. I got what I wanted from you."

"And what was *that?*" he asked, his anger rising.

"Dr. Scott, of course."

The Colonel enjoyed the priest's desperate look of bewilderment. "Oh, I'll explain in a moment." A thin smile creased his face. "Yes ... in a moment. First, let's discuss some things that you don't know—some things that have been gnawing at you for weeks, that you can't piece together. For instance, what made Dr. Bandstra behave the way he did? And why would he ever want Dr. Kelley dead? Curious?"

"Yes," the priest admitted grudgingly.

"Dr. Bandstra did what he did because he *understood*. He was able to correctly pinpoint the true agenda—at least part of it."

"You're working for *them!*" Father Benedict snarled.

"My, my, it's good to see you can still become so incensed!" The Colonel chuckled. "But you've missed the mark again. I know what you and your ilk have been looking for all these years," the Colonel seethed, suddenly overtaken by a torrent of bitter emotion, "squirreled away in your monasteries, libraries, and observatories, searching for clues to our plan and peering at the heavens for a sign of the Nazarene's coming. Your bumbling efforts are only portents of your own doom. Oh, yes, the modern world will define divinity in extraterrestrial terms, and when the hybrid appears, he'll be hailed as the once and future god-man. We don't need to prove any religion wrong; we need only redefine the terms of the debate so everyone wins ... until we claim what is rightfully ours."

"Wh ... wh ... why are you telling me all this?" Father Benedict stuttered, terrified by the words as well as the wicked glint in the Colonel's eye.

"Because I want you to die in despair," he hissed, pressing his face to Father Benedict's. "Look upon me!" he commanded, abruptly stepping back from the bed.

A voice suddenly burst into the priest's head. *Look upon me and know your failure is complete!*

Father Benedict watched in unsuppressed horror as the Colonel's body transformed before his eyes, replaced by a towering, mesmerizing, reptilian form, it's thick, powerful chest heaving in anticipation of the kill. The Watcher lowered its narrow, serpentine face toward the helpless priest, its black, slanted, unblinking eyes locking onto its victim.

Your puny, pathetic mind cannot grasp the coming reality, its voice exploded in his mind. *For millennia we have cultivated the belief in humanity that their gods come from the stars—Sirius, Orion's belt, a twelfth planet—and*

that we are the ones who seeded life here, that we are even now taking your wom-
en to help prepare humanity for their own approaching evolutionary ascension,
all for this moment, the moment of revelation, the time of humankind's duping.

We have dangled our knowledge before all who have coveted power. Stories
of our wonders punctuate your ancient texts. Tales of the spiritual masters we
fathered are the basis for your religions. When we unveil ourselves as antiqui-
ty's benevolent alien creators, the world will believe and worship! Yahweh took
our fathers; we will take His children!

"No!" Andrew objected boldly, suddenly energized by the creature's rant.

Yesss, it hissed again in his mind. *And you have helped us!*

Andrew cowered in his bed as the Watcher approached his bed-side.
He could smell the stench of its breath, feel the warmth of its shining body.

You were brought here for one reason and one reason only, fool: to convince
your beloved Dr. Scott of our presence, and that we are the truth behind the
imaginary extraterrestrials upon whom humanity is so fixated—to convince
him of the truth!

The Watcher beheld the bewilderment in the priest's expression.
Mocking laughter filled Andrew's mind.

You see but do not perceive, listen but do not hear. He and the woman are
both indispensable to our plans, and now you have ensured our success!

"Brian will never help you. He'll expose you!" Andrew said, enraged,
still unable to comprehend the creature's narration.

We're counting on it. We know he'll be faithful to your feckless Christ. This
is why he was chosen.

Andrew's face flushed with rage at the Watcher's blasphemy.

You still do not understand. The great, viperous being stood erect, his
head nearly touching the ceiling. *Your feeble-mindedness testifies to Yah-*
weh's ineptitude at granting dominion to your kind. Can you not conceive of
our goal? Dr. Scott will blaze abroad the truth of the extraterrestrial façade, but
who will listen to him? Only those who follow Yahweh. They will be the lone dis-
senters when the new age of human evolution is ushered in by an apparent alien
truth; they alone will resist our presence; they alone will withdraw from the new
global society; they alone will act to destabilize the new civilization that has
dawned. Why? Precisely because what you have sought will be accomplished—
they will have been warned of our true identity and strategy.

And when the followers of Yahweh are perceived as a cancer by the global
throngs who call us blessed, humanity won't just condone their annihilation,
they will cry for it—and we will eagerly oblige! You and your believing rem-

nant will be a glorious holocaust to the mighty Helel, he gloated triumphantly. *You—have—played—the—fool!*

"You can slay us on your altars," Andrew declared, glowering defiantly, "you can rob us of our children, you can throw us to your crazed mobs, you can choke your ovens with our bodies, but each murder will only yield one more set of feet—*human* feet—at which you will grovel on the day of His coming. May God grant me the privilege of personally pronouncing your sentence!"

Enough! the malevolent entity screamed in fury.

Father Benedict's body suddenly became taut, his limbs frozen by an unseen force.

Look at the great Benedict, the creature mocked, looming over the priest's thin frame, *the storied defender of the faith. Where is Yahweh now? Where is your Jesus, your hero? They are nothing! How long I have waited for this day! You have opposed us for the last time.*

The Watcher stood motionlessly above Father Benedict's twitching, convulsing body, relishing his suffering. Blood streamed from the old man's eyes, nose, and ears, but this was not enough. Andrew's limbs began to flail wildly, forcibly contorted into unnatural movements. The popping of limbs from their sockets punctuated the air, but the sadistic being's lust for his enemy's misery was still not gratified.

Even as he saw the life expire from the priest's eyes, its hatred for the faithful priest would not be quenched. By sheer thought, the Watcher effortlessly lifted the broken corpse above the bed and began to pummel it into the mattress. The frenzied pounding drove the bed, inch by inch, across the floor. Finally the battery ceased, Andrew's lifeless body coming to rest on its stomach, yet his face right side up, his neck having been crushed in the onslaught.

Without a word the Watcher morphed into the familiar figure of the Colonel and left the room.

67

*There will come a time when you think
everything is finished. That will be the beginning.*

—Louis L'Amour

"Thank God Andrew finally discovered flight," Melissa moaned as she and Brian left the airport car rental agency. "We must have driven three thousand miles over this last week."

"Twenty-eight hundred, actually," Brian noted as they walked into the terminal. "You're right—even I'm looking forward to a flight. At least the accommodations were relatively comfortable."

"Yeah, but you can have the 'drive all night, sleep during the day' routine—and then there's the crisscrossing all over the country. I think I've been in more states in the last week than I'd been in my whole life."

"It's all about misdirection."

"Well, I'm vowing right here and now to never again take a trip that can't be completed in half a day."

"Want to get a bite to eat? Andrew's instructions just said to be here by noon. We're a couple hours ahead of schedule."

"No," she answered. "I just can't eat anything right now—especially any more fast food."

"Still sick?"

"Comes and goes."

"I thought you got something for that yesterday. Did you take it?"

"Yeah ... I used it."

"You look a little pale," Brian noted, bending slightly to get a good look at her face. "Let's sit a while."

Brian took her by the arm and found a seat. "Let's see what's in Andrew's last instruction envelope while you rest," he suggested, retrieving it from his backpack and handing it to her.

"Do you have any change?" she asked as she read through Andrew's final installment. "Maybe a soda will help take away nausea."

"I think so," he said, unzipping a smaller compartment inside the pack. "Yep, here's some—"

Melissa turned as Brian stopped mid-sentence. He was staring into his backpack.

"What did you do, leave something half-eaten in there?"

"No," he said, extracting another folded envelope from the pocket. "I completely forgot this was here," he said somberly. "I put it here while we were still in the lab after Neil was shot."

Melissa recognized it on sight as the envelope Neil had insisted Brian take during the standoff in the lab.

"Open it," Melissa prodded.

Memories of the lost friendship flooded Brian's mind as he sat unresponsively next to her.

"Would you like me to do it?" she asked sympathetically.

"No ... I can handle it," he sighed, tearing open the top. He pulled out two pieces of paper, each filled with an unbroken running string of Hebrew letters. Three portions of the printout were circled. A third piece of paper was a letter.

"What is that?"

"I don't know."

"Can you translate it?"

"Not at sight without word breaks ... it looks like meaningless gibberish. Weird, the same few letters keep repeating in different combinations."

"What do you make of it?"

"No idea."

"Maybe the letter will help."

Brian folded up the lettered pages and placed them into his backpack. He turned his attention to the third page. He began reading silently and was soon shaking his head.

"Come on, let's hear it."

"I can't believe it," Brian said, his countenance lifting. "Apparently Neil was working out a way to get me off the base."

"Before or after he killed me?" Melissa asked wryly.

"Sorry," Brian reigned in his enthusiasm, reminded of the context for the material. "This is an explanation of his arrangements for me. I have ticketless reservations waiting for me to go to California. He got me a job at the Claremont Graduate School of Theology as a Semitics librarian. A real job in my field—and in California! He says here," Brian kept reading, his excitement building again, "that the president there used to be a friend of his at Hopkins. This is amazing—I have a new name, social security number, and bank account with $100,000 in it. Looks like Neil gave me his salary for his work on the team. Can you believe it?"

"That's ... wonderful," she said quietly, returning her attention to Andrew's letter still in her hand.

"So what does Andrew command now?" Brian asked, turning his attention to the pages in Melissa's hand.

"It's sort of like Neil's ... at least the intent. I don't know if you want to hear this."

"Why not?"

"Want to live in North Dakota?"

"North Dakota?"

"Yeah—it's the state above South Dakota. Not the end of the world, but you can see it from there."

"What's in North Dakota?"

"Farms, a few trees ... an occasional biped."

"Come on, Melissa."

"Well," she paged through Andrew's correspondence, "Andrew made arrangements for both of us. I'm now a visiting professor of American Church History at St. Ignatius College near Fargo, North Dakota."

"Sounds nice."

"Not really," she said, amused at the priest's explanation. "It seems that the position was created specifically for me. Andrew and the president are fellow travelers, ecclesiastically speaking. His letter says he's been soliciting donations for the college for almost twenty years ... it's devoted to what he calls 'the original principles of the Society of Jesus.'"

"Sounds like it would be a pretty conservative school."

"No doubt. The president there has agreed to use part of the donated funding to establish the position with the intention of making it permanent. Salary's about two-thirds of what I was making at Georgetown."

"Things have to cost much less in North Dakota. You'd probably be about the same."

"Yeah, think of all I'll save not having to buy summer clothing."

"Okay, okay. What else does he say?"

"I'm now Melissa Carter. Here's my new credit card to prove it." She flashed the plastic at him. "Probably the last name of the local dairy princess. The rest is pretty much what Neil did—new ID, social security number, bank account ... with $30,000 in it. Andrew says it's to get me started."

"Doesn't sound too bad."

"Want to know what your new name is?"

"As long as it isn't Elvis."

"I wonder what Andrew was thinking?"

"Let's hear it," Brian prodded with some urgency.

"You're Brian Carter."

"The same last name?"

"Now what do we make of that?"

"Brother and sister," he said quickly. "You don't have to worry."

"Who said I'm worrying? Besides," she continued in a more subdued tone, "this arrangement is nothing like what Neil has for you ... and mine just isn't what I had, either."

"I'm sorry about your job," Brian empathized, trying to spin the opportunity the best way he knew how, "but what Andrew has arranged is still quite an opportunity. You'd get to mold your own department, your own major ... you probably couldn't write much the first couple of years, but you'd be set. You could get into a house, too."

"You're right," she sighed, "I should be more grateful. Want to hear your setup now?"

"Sure," he agreed, somewhat warily in view of her comments.

"First the bad news: The short version is that Andrew didn't find a job for you. In fact, he says he didn't even try, since, and I quote, 'You have a job to do already to which you need to devote all your energy'."

"So I'm an unemployed North Dakotan. Not much of a transi-tion, really. Do I have a credit card? It'll be handy for groceries and toilet pa-per."

"Yes, and you also have some cash—this is the good news. Andrew says that during the last four years of his employ at the University of Arizona he managed to live on just under half his salary each year. You now have the remainder. I'm sure it must have been his life savings, since he'd been under a vow of poverty prior to his university post. It's around $50,000."

"Wow," he said, awed more at the generosity than the amount. "I've never had money like this."

"It's half of what Neil's offer has, but you know," Melissa suggested, "the way he has this set up, even with the names, you have no actual ties to North Dakota. You could wire the money under one name and one account to the other account Neil has set up for you in California. You could close the North Dakota account and basically disappear. You'd have a six-figure bank account, your job, and sunshine. Looks like you're set."

Brian sat back in his chair, overwhelmed at the hand of grace he'd been shown. Melissa sat quietly as possibilities ran through his mind.

"How would I wire the money? Could I just call the bank and have them do it?"

"Sure, but if you closed the account entirely they'd most likely want a written letter of permission."

"Boy ... it's like a dream come true."

"I'm going to get a soda and a paper," Melissa informed him unenthusiastically, handing the paperwork to him.

"Okay, I'll get our seats taken care of while you do that."

Brian got in line at the ticket counter and shuffled through the papers for what he'd need. His thoughts drifted back over the events of the past few months—the upheaval, the extraordinary circumstances, the deceptions, his personal losses, his new, bizarre commissioning by Andrew, and ... Melissa. The thought of her prompted him to look back at the small stand where she stood.

The war between his head and his heart had begun before she'd even excused herself. He knew from experience that a job in academia—particularly one this suitable—was a rare commodity. He'd convinced himself that he'd never be employable in his field again. Yet here he was, on the threshold of a career that would keep him close to the life of study he wanted so badly. He coveted the job, but ...

He watched Melissa move back to her seat in silence. She looked the same to him as the first time he'd seen her, but there was something different now; she had changed. His heart sank as he got closer to the counter. Now that the future path was emerging, he could clearly see that he had gained so much through the ordeal, despite the tragedy with Neil. But what had Melissa accrued? To be sure, he'd had an impact on her life for the better, but she'd lost the thing that defined her identity in her own mind, her teaching post—and one at a prestigious university at that. Andrew's efforts had indeed been generous, but Brian knew what a step down it would be for her. He also knew that it would be terribly difficult for her to adjust to the new location—no family, no friends, no colleagues.

Melissa sipped her soda and flipped through the paper with disinterest, trying in vain to divert her thoughts from what awaited her. The nearly twenty-four hours that had elapsed since yesterday had not managed to alleviate her fear, but she'd managed to conceal her emotions from Brian.

Nothing could be worse than what you've already endured, she tried to convince herself, but deep down, she knew this was different. This really was much more than she could handle. Nevertheless, she steeled herself against involving Brian in her state of affairs. He'd been through enough, and now his moment of opportunity had come. She sensed tears surfacing in her eyes and fought to maintain control. She glanced up at the ticket counter. Brian was nowhere to be seen.

In a panic, she stood up, the newspaper scattering on the floor, and scanned the rows of waiting passengers, praying that they hadn't walked into another twist of fate. She hurried down the line of ticket booths hoping he had just changed lines. Nothing. She turned around and scanned the faces of people coming and going. There were so many. She wanted to call out his name, but the fear that whoever had grabbed him would find her as well paralyzed her. She started to cry, then felt a hand on her shoulder. It was Brian.

"I'm sorry, Melissa," he apologized, catching up to her.

"Don't *ever* do that to me again!" she blurted out at him, shaking. "How could you do that after all that's happened?"

"It won't happen again," he assured her, steadying her. "I had to make a phone call."

"The money?"

"Yeah."

"Well ... I guess it won't happen again, then," she remarked, recalling her earlier advice to him. "Why didn't you just tell me you were going to use the phone?"

"Because ... I didn't want you to know what I was doing," he confessed, handing her ticket to her. "You would have just tried to stop me."

"What are you talking about?"

"I'll tell you on the way." He evaded her question, removing Neil's letter from his backpack.

"No, tell me now," she demanded, becoming suspicious.

Brian looked at her and then took a few steps to a nearby trashcan. Without a word he tore Neil's job offer into pieces.

"What are you doing?" Melissa exclaimed, trying not to raise her voice too loudly, grabbing his hand before he could drop the fragments into the trash. "Are you crazy?"

"I don't need it," he replied calmly.

"But you can't just throw away a career ... what are you up to?"

He looked down at his feet, avoiding her gaze.

"What did you do on the phone?" she persisted, placing her hand lightly on his chest.

"I transferred the money Neil gave me ... to your account—all but ten thousand of it anyway."

"*What?*"

"I thought you should have it," he tried to explain. "I could become a target in the future, and anything can happen. I figured if I died, I'd want you to have it. It's better to take care of things now. I left the account open, though; it might be useful someday. Don't bother arguing with me about it, either. I won't give you my account number to change it."

A blush filled his face. He pulled back his hand, still holding the shredded letter. Melissa refused to let go.

"What about the job? You're certainly going to need it—more now than ever."

"I'm not taking it. I'd like to go with you ... if that's okay."

"But isn't it what you always wanted?" she questioned, scarcely able to believe what she was hearing.

Brian looked down at her and into her eyes. "Not anymore."

Melissa stared at him, wide-eyed, stunned by the gesture, but only for a few brief moments. Without warning, she began weeping, the pent up emotions inside her overflowing. She put her arms around him and embraced him tightly.

Brian threw the pieces away and put his arms around her trembl-ing figure. He let her cry, unsure of what to make of her reaction. "Let's sit down again," he said gently after a few seconds. "We don't want to draw too much attention," he reminded her, noting the curious glances of several onlookers.

"Right," she said, sniffing, "I'm sorry."

"There's no need to apologize. This just isn't the argument I was ex-pecting."

"You'll get no argument," she said, drying her eyes with a tissue. "I'm so relieved. I was hoping you'd come with me ... I just wouldn't know what to do."

"I know it would be lonely at first, Melissa, but surely you've moved before."

"That isn't it." She caught herself lapsing into tears once more. "Oh Brian ... *what did they do to me?* I just don't know how ..."

"What is it?" he asked, alarmed by the confused, terrified expression on her face. "What's wrong? *Tell me!*" he urged.

"I'm pregnant."

Acknowledgments

As many writers have testified, writing a book is never a completely single-handed undertaking. There are many people along the way who played important roles in the creation and publication of *The Façade* and its rewrites.

I would like to first thank the one person who was truly indispensable: my wife Drenna, in whose honor the dedication is written. Without her sacrifices of time and energy in caring for me and our children, I never would have been able to write *The Façade*.

Naturally, I want to thank all those who purchased, read, and enthusiastically reviewed *The Façade* on Amazon.com and other sites during its initial release. I would also like to thank by name my preliminary readers, those individuals who donated their time to reading the very first draft of *The Façade* prior to its birth as a self-published novel, and who whose comments or expertise in certain areas made it a better read. Their comments and suggestions along the way were critical, encouraging, and stimulating: Roger Black; Linda Melin; Janet Sommers; Mike and Gail Olesen; Tom (Dean) Walsh; Jon Terrill; and Lucy Burggraff. I also wish to thank several people whose comments specifically led to improvements in subsequent versions: Randy Ingermanson; Lynn Marzulli; Stan and Holly Deyo; my parents, Ed and Jan Speraw; Rob Holmstedt; Don and Evelyn Loewen; Bill and Sharon Redinger; Bob Boomsma; Lori Heiser; Joe Hermanny; David Sielaff; Craig Hines; David Mitchell; Derrel Sims; and David Finton. Others who read portions of the manuscript or offered other forms of support are Ashley Green, Jim Sheard, Jim Wilhelmsen, and Jeff Gerke.

Several people deserve special recognition. Gratitude must be showered upon my friend, Doug Vardell. Doug not only read the manuscript or book over a dozen times, but also provided crucial help in editing and was a source of constant encouragement. Doug, your input was vital. Kira Mitchell deserves recognition for proofing and formatting the Acid Test Press version of the book, and Elizabeth Vince for copy editing the Kirkdale editions. Guy Malone has been the book's most persistent supporter. His "Alien Resistance" website has been a great help in the promotion of *The Façade*. Guy, wherever this book finds you and the Resistance Kitty, thanks. Free and Amy, you both deserve accolades for your consistent spirit of service toward me during my time at Roswell over the years and for promoting *The Façade* through the ARHQ. Curtis Lundgren's special kindness in his concerted, though unsuccessful, attempt to get the book into the mainstream will forever be appreciated. Thanks for "getting it" Curtis, even though others around you couldn't think outside the box. Dick Purdue was the prime mover behind keeping the book alive after my initial self-publishing "success-debacle." It was wonderful to have Dick sell the book while I finished my dissertation. I'd also like to express gratitude to all the folks at *Coast to Coast AM* for giving me a platform: Art Bell, George Noory, Ian Punnett, Barbara Simpson, Tom Danheiser, and Lisa Lyon. Bob and Dale Pritchett of Logos Bible Software deserve thanks for their enthusiastic response to the bookand a work environment that embraced me and my "hobby." Dan Pritchett deserves the applause of everyone reading this, as he brought his internet marketing genius forward to revive *The Façade* in its print form in 2007. Finally, thanks to all the individuals at Kirkdale Press for introducing *The Façade* in its current form.

—Michael S. Heiser, Bellingham, Washington

Publisher's Note

We hope you enjoyed *The Façade*. If this book left you on the edge of your seat, challenged you in what you believe, or impacted you in any way, we'd love to hear your feedback. Visit Kirkdale Press on Facebook, leave a review on Amazon or Goodreads, and join the conversation at ReadTheFacade.com or Michael S. Heiser's homepage, DrMSH.com.

And be sure to check out *The Portent*, the second volume in *The Façade* Saga. Learn more at ReadThePortent.com.

About the Author

Michael S. Heiser earned an MA and PhD in Hebrew Bible and Semitic Languages at the University of Wisconsin-Madison in 2004. He has also earned an MA in Ancient History from the University of Pennsylvania (major fields: Ancient Israel and Egyptology). His main research interests are Israelite religion (especially Israel's divine council), biblical theology, ancient Near Eastern religion, biblical & ancient Semitic languages, and ancient Jewish binitarian monotheism. Mike's full academic CV can be found on his homepage, http://www.michaelsheiser.com.

Mike is currently the Academic Editor at Logos Bible Software in Bellingham, WA. Before joining Logos, he taught biblical studies and history on the undergraduate level for twelve years. He currently teaches biblical Hebrew and Greek online through his MEMRA Institute.

Mike maintains three blogs that focus on his interests: *The Naked Bible* (biblical studies and biblical theology); *PaleoBabble* (fringe beliefs about archaeology and antiquity); and *UFO Religions* (how popular beliefs about UFOs and extraterrestrials shape religious beliefs and worldview). He podcasts on biblical studies at the *Naked Bible Podcast*.

Mike has been interviewed on a number of radio programs such as *Coast to Coast AM*, where he has been a frequent guest. He is best known for his critique of the ancient astronaut theories of Zecharia Sitchin, modern Jesus bloodline myths, and the belief in Bible codes.

If you're interested in having Mike speak at your conference or on your radio or TV program, podcast, or blog, please contact Kirkdale Press.

Brian and Melissa
thought they were safe . . .

They were wrong.

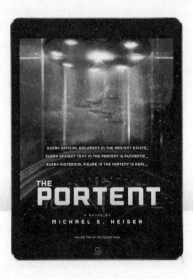

Living under false identities, Brian and Melissa have done everything in their power to hide their past. Heart-pounding and terrifying revelations await in *The Portent*, volume two of *The Façade* saga.

Download the free Vyrso app and get *The Portent* today.

Visit Vyrso.com/Portent to learn more.

Vyrso.com/Portent • 888-875-9491 • +1 360-685-4437 (Int'l)

 Vyrso